SANGUINE MOON

Book Two
Camazotz Trilogy

By Jennifer Foxcroft

Sanguine Moon
Jennifer Foxcroft
Copyright © 2016 by Jennifer Foxcroft

First Edition. December 2016.
Published in United States of America

Written and published by Jennifer Foxcroft
Cover design by Cate Pepper 2016

Print ISBN: 978-0-9909895-2-3

Acknowledgments

To my family and husband. Thank you all so much for helping me get Sanguine Moon out into the world. It was a tough slog at times, but your support and encouragement got me to the finish line. I love you so much and can't wait to do this all over again for the final installment.

To my beta readers: Jen, Betsy, Stacey C, Stacey B, Irene, Leanne, Sandii, Marian, and Erin. Thank you all for saving my sanity and getting this book back on track when my crazy imagination went off course. Your feedback was pure gold. Thank you for your honesty and for making me think about where I really wanted my characters to go. You are the best support crew a girl could ever have.

To the world's best line editor. Betsy, you are a legend. Some days when I read your comments I think you share my brain. You always manage to find the areas that concern me, and that's fascinating and brilliant at the same time. Thank you for the long hours you put into reading and rereading and checking again to help me make this the best book it can be.

To my proofreader, Ellie. Thank you, gorgeous girl, for giving my manuscript the once over with your keen eye for errors and typos and things that just shouldn't be there. I really appreciate it.

To my mates who helped me research the tiniest details without telling me to bugger off. You know who you are. Your patience with me is priceless, especially when I was being a goof. It might be a minor detail mentioned briefly in only one paragraph, but you helped me find the facts and get it right. Thank you.

Dear Readers,

Welcome back. Lots of new Camazotz appear in Sanguine Moon. If you are getting confused as to who is who in the Camazotz zoo, then please refer to the character list.

Happy reading,
Jennifer.

1

Painkillers

ROCKS cannot die.
He just can't.
I will not let that happen.

He's not going to survive this. Decker's words ring in my ears. But his injury is only a broken arm. Why are the Camazotz acting as though the sky is falling? I chew on my bottom lip. Decker's not the type of bat that says stuff to scare me. His heart is bigger and warmer than half the Camazotz put together, and he respects his brother too much to want to mess with my head. But return Rocks to Blood Mountain? Their roost? Seriously? That can't be a real place. If it is, then no wonder people believe they're a bunch of vampires.

Google is my lifesaver.

Rocks is resting on the couch with fresh ice on his broken arm. I'm in Dad's study staring at the computer screen. Blood Mountain—it's a very real place north of Atlanta in the Chattahoochee National Forest. The name sends a shiver down my spine, but I guess it's because I understand the significance of it more than most. The clock on Dad's desk reads five a.m., but I'm not the least bit tired. My brain is having a hard time processing everything that has happened in the last twenty-four hours, and that's probably a good thing. Just thinking about the mess I'm caught up in causes the lump of terror in my throat to expand, and my lungs to tighten with a need for more oxygen.

Stay calm.

Too much depends on *me*. The vision of staring down the barrel of the gun that thug Mullins held in my face keeps flickering behind my eyelids. The logical part of my brain wants me to stop thinking about it as it's only adding to my stress levels, but I can't seem to shake it. What if he'd pulled the trigger? Where's my inhaler? I close my eyes and take a deep breath, letting my lungs expand as much as they can.

If I don't get my shit together, my boyfriend might die—according to all the Camazotz that know about his injury.

I will myself to stop fretting about the Vipers' gang members that were ordered to dispose of me. Less than eight hours ago, Decker and Jeremiah locked my kidnappers in a rusted-out chicken shed on the property where they'd taken me. I need to have faith those two thugs are still imprisoned and haven't raised the alarm yet. The last thing I need is that pair showing up at my house—again. The fact that the Vipers know where I live causes my windpipe to constrict. But I can't let that worry me on top of everything else. I have a bigger problem. Rocks. He needs medical treatment immediately.

They won't be able to charge me with murder this way, even though it's a death sentence …

Joey's words haunt me. They add weight to Decker's comments. I'm so confused. I picture his heavy boot crushing Rocks' outstretched wing. I hear Rocks' cries of agony when he woke in that metal cage. Why is a Camazotz connected to those drug-dealing Vipers? And why does he want Rocks dead?

My temples ache. I'm overloaded with too many fleeting, horrible images. *Focus. Calm the fudge down. You can do this.* With the number of thoughts bouncing around inside my head, I'd swear the Camazotz were nearby.

Returning to Google, I search for directions to get Rocks back to the colony. Their secret mountain roost is a twenty-five mile drive from the market, but probably less than fifteen miles as the bat flies.

I need a plan. My parents will be home from their reunion weekend tomorrow night. Between now and then, I need to get Rocks to a doctor to set his broken arm, return him to his colony at Blood Mountain, avoid being kidnapped by the Vipers for a second time, stay alive, and get some sleep so my folks don't take one look at me and wonder why I'm channeling a zombie.

For a millisecond, I contemplate visiting the police station and reporting the location of those thugs. The aftermath of that action hits me in the stomach. Questions—too many questions. I'd have to explain what I've been up to for the last six months to my parents. They'd know I was a little liar and the biological daughter of the devil. They'd never look at me the same again. And since I'm not the daughter those idiots were looking for, I have to believe they'll leave me alone and focus on finding Sophia instead.

My other sister.

Sugarplums.

The sunlight peeping through the blinds stirs me from my mental chaos. Time is ticking, and I can't waste any of it thinking about Sophia Ascari. That's a Google search for another time. Creeping silently back through the house, I check on Rocks. His long legs hang off the end of our couch. The darkness of his clothes is a stark contrast against my parent's beige and cream living room. His face looks pained, and a sheen of sweat is making his jet-black hair stick to his forehead. I watch his chest rise and fall wondering if every breath causes more pain. The ice resting over his arm has melted, but before I can move to replace it, one of his eyes cracks open for a moment. He attempts a smile, but it's replaced by a frown as he tries to adjust his arm.

"Don't move." Kneeling next to the couch, I rest a cool cloth over his forehead and he sighs. "How are you feeling?"

His voice is raspy and he doesn't open his eyes. "Been better."

"I have a plan."

That gets his attention. He looks at me, and the pain in his eyes slices open my heart. "The only plan you need is one to get me off this couch. I can't stay here to d—"

"You are not going to die," I cut him off. "I'm serious. That's not happening. Let me take care of you. You have no idea what modern medicine is capable of. A broken arm is easily fixed."

"Connie, you have to face facts." He closes his eyes again and tries to get more comfortable on the couch. He grunts with pain and grits his teeth together. I know he's trying to be brave for me, but he doesn't need to be …

I race up the stairs, down the hall and into my parent's bathroom. Rummaging through their medicine cabinet, I strike gold. Dad was on heavy-duty painkillers early this year when he hurt his back rappelling. They made him say the funniest stuff, but he wasn't in any pain. Grabbing the small orange bottle, I'm back next to Rocks with some water faster than he can flip.

"Take two of these." I put the pills to his lips, but he shakes his head.

"Stop trying," he wheezes.

"Rocks, this will take away the pain so we can move you." He frowns, eyeing the bottle I'm holding up. I know he's thinking the 'move' means taking him to a place where he can die quietly, but my plan is getting him into my car and to the hospital. After he swallows the pills, I refill the ice bags and soak the cloth on his forehead in cold water. He's burning up. I don't like the fact that his body is displaying signs of fever. A broken arm shouldn't cause that—well, not in an aeronaught anyway.

Crouching on the floor beside Rocks, I stare at his gentle features— my amazing Camazotz boyfriend. My head shakes in disbelief before I can stop myself. I sigh and my mind skims over the last six months.

My boyfriend has abilities I didn't know existed until the end of last summer. Abilities I would never have believed possible until I saw them with my own eyes. He can fly—like for real—because he's a shape-shifting vampire bat. As everybody knows, vampires aren't real. Last July, I thought they were when I first met Rocks, and my reaction to him still makes me cringe. I armed myself with garlic and sprinkled him with holy water. I suspect the real reason the legend of vampires has come about is because humans—or aeronaughts as he calls us—have witnessed the Camazotz flip from human to bat form, and our fear makes us assume the rest of the gory tale.

The truth is five hundred years ago, a shaman cursed—or blessed, depending on who you talk to—a village. The Spanish were trying to conquer the Zapotec people. Rocks explained that the plan was to ambush the Spanish invaders from behind by turning the village into bats, having them fly in behind the army, flip back to human form and catch their opponents off guard. The plan failed, and the shaman responsible for the magic was killed before he could reverse the powerful spell he had used. Rocks and his ancestors have been shape-shifting Camazotz, living in secret, ever since.

Secrets. I used to think secrets were exciting, like I was the member of some private, exclusive club. Now I know the truth. Secrets equal trouble when you least expect it, and I'm carrying around way too many tiny, ticking time bombs for my liking. They mean lying to my friends and family, and the more lies you collect, the more difficult your life becomes. I've learned that the hard way.

Last night, I experienced things I never wish to experience again—like being kidnapped by enemies of my real father—Enzo Ascari. That's another secret to add to my growing stash because I don't want to risk Chad and Kelly's lives anymore than I risked my boyfriend's. If my folks find out about Enzo… Stop—I can't go there right now.

Rocks.

Rocks is my focus. I hope Jeremiah and Decker made it safely back to the roost. I try to imagine them telling their leader, Strickland. I should've given them Rocks' phone. But with the Sire's irrational hate of technology that would only put me in deeper crabapples with the colony members. If Rocks dies, I've been warned that I'll have to pay for his death—with my blood.

Rocks is deathly still, so I tiptoe back to the kitchen and rinse the cloth from his forehead till my fingers freeze from the cold. Once the painkillers kick in, my plan is to get him to the hospital …

Sugarplums!

How on earth am I going to pay for his broken arm when Rocks doesn't have insurance?

An earsplitting cry of agony fills the house. I'm back in the living room a second later. Rocks has flipped. He's suddenly a bat, and with his wing broken, he falls straight onto the couch unable to keep himself airborne. He screeches and wails, flailing around trying to get his body off his crushed wing.

"Holy fudge. Stay still. Let me help."

I hook my finger under the large claw on the top of his good wing, lifting him slowly off the couch until his body weight is off his injured wing. He screeches again and I watch as his little bat eyes scrunch closed. The pain must be unbearable. I can't even imagine. As gently as I can, I lay him flat on the couch with his broken wing outstretched beside him. He's panting; I know it's to work through the pain so that he doesn't scream out and upset me. Rocks would do anything for me—at any price—so hiding the pain that I'm sure is pulsing through his system is so his style.

"I don't mind if you cry out. Must be excruciating." His eyes meet mine and I see the human intelligence behind them. "We might as well use this chance to get you upstairs in bed."

Eeek! Eeek!

"No? Where then?"

Outside.

Rocks' voice echoes inside my head. Each time he speaks to me telepathically, it seems to get easier. I'm not gonna lie and say that a male voice rattling around in my head doesn't freak me out a bit. It's crazy weird, but convenient when your boyfriend's a Camazotz.

"No way! It's going to drop below freezing today. You'll—"

Inevitable.
Please.

I don't like Rocks being so insistent that he's about to die. Not if I can help it. Reaching over, I slid my hands under his body. He hooks his claw over my forearm to steady himself as I lift. His heart-breaking screech makes me flinch. I walk as evenly as I can, trying not to jostle him.

Open door first.

"No need. I'm not putting you in the garden like some unwanted pet. Forget it." I give him my best don't-mess-with-me evil eye as I take one step at a time. "If you were just a bat, I wouldn't even put you out there, so since you're not, no chance." He closes his eyes and doesn't argue further—a sure sign that those painkillers haven't kicked in.

Secret five hundred and forty one—Rocks has been staying in our guest bedroom while my parents are away. Only a teenage boy raised in the old-fashioned 1865 manner of the colony would have found the time to be this tidy. A smile graces my lips when I see how neat and organized his room is.

"Trust you to make your bed."

Always.

His little body stiffens as I lay him across the quilt. He doesn't make a sound, but starts panting again. Before I can finish laying out his broken wing, he flips.

"Shit!" I jump, caught off guard by his sudden appearance.

Rocks is sitting half on the bed, half off and groaning loudly. He grabs my shoulder with his good hand as his swollen hand lands in his lap.

"Oh, God." He closes his eyes, looking toward the ceiling, holding his breath. I gently push the long hair hanging over his eyes to the side. "I feel ..." He sways to the left, completely off balance so I steady him by the shoulders. "Aaaggghhh, shit."

"Sorry." I loosen my hold, but I'm worried he's about to fall off the bed. "Are you okay?" Stupid question. "Sorry. I know you're not."

"S'okay." He gives me a half smile.

Flip!

This time his batty alter ego has landed on his back. His squawk of pain isn't quite as loud. I'm guessing the painkillers are starting to work. His good wing thumps up and down against the mattress.

"Shhh, stay still." I don't know whether to turn him over or not. But before I can decide, he's human again. He's landed really badly, face planting it on the mattress, and despite the painkillers, cries out in agony.

"Connie," he pants, trying to roll over off his arm, but his hand is wedged under his hip. "Help me. God. What's happening to me?" The look in his eyes screams panic.

I'm so not the nursing type. Watching his torment is killing me. It's almost like my body feels every flinch and jolt of pain that tortures him.

There's a real physical ache in my chest thinking about his broken bones grinding together. I don't know what to do and being helpless drives me insane. Rocks loops his left arm around my shoulders, and I try to lift the giant boy off the bed enough for him to pull his hand free.

He grits his teeth and grunts but doesn't cry out again, and for that, I'm thankful. Once he's on the bed again, I collapse on the floor on my knees and wipe the tears from my cheeks. What have I done?

Flip!

Crushed wing …

Flip!

Sideways boy …

Flip!

Bat screeches …

Flip!

Apologizing boy …

Flip! Flip! Flip!

Watching this excruciating cycle is tearing my chest open. I want to run and hide under my covers, but he needs me. I got him into this mess, so it's my job to fix his bad wing when he lands on it, even though we both know he's going to flip again.

The painkillers have taken away his control.

This new predicament is my fault entirely—first, his wing, and now, this unnecessary torture. When am I going to learn that what's normal for me, might not be normal for him?

It's close to midday before Rocks is finally human for more than five minutes. He's burning up, and his shirt is wet with perspiration. The constant changes have exhausted him even further. I run to the kitchen for iced water, but he refuses to drink.

"Not yet," he pants. "Sorry, Beans."

My nickname makes my chest feel as though it's been split open with a pickaxe. God, this boy never ceases to amaze me. The thought of him bothering to use my nickname when he's suffering pain beyond what I can imagine, brings fresh tears to my eyes. I love him so much.

"I'm sorry. I think the painkillers were too much." I wipe his forehead, and then the tears on my cheeks. He nods. The colony don't use any form of modern medicine. Rocks resents the Fold members that deny the colony access to treatment that could have possibly saved many of the Camazotz that died recently in the owl attacks. But maybe his leaders are right …

Watching Rocks out of control on a simple painkiller makes me wonder if the Sire really does know what he's doing after all. There is no way I can take him to the hospital in this state. His secret would be out in the blink of an eye—literally. There's so much I still don't understand about how the curse works, but there has to be a middle ground between shunning technology and keeping their secret.

"Can't control myself," he rasps. The sinking feeling inside tells me ominous dark clouds of doom have parked themselves permanently over my house. These days I stumble from one disaster to the next.

Holding Rocks' left hand, I revise my plan. I wish my mom were here—although she'd probably collapse if Rocks flipped. When Mini, my twenty-three-month-old sister, had the flu, Mom stayed awake around the clock for days on end till the worst of it left her little system. For the first time in my life, I resemble my adoptive mother with my bedside vigil—only I'm not so calm and collected.

"Get some sleep," he croaks. I look up to see he's watching me. "Must be tired."

Oh Rocks. I shake my head. I'm exhausted but I won't leave him while he needs me.

"I'll stay until you're stable." We gaze at each other for several minutes. The way he's looking at me is … unfamiliar. I can't pinpoint the look in his eyes as they slowly roam my face, doing a lazy circle over and over.

"So beautiful," he whispers. His words set my ears to instant inferno level. "Thank you," he adds before a coughing fit racks through his body causing him to cry out. I offer him water, but he shakes his head.

"For what?" I ask. Tears well in my eyes, and I try to blink them into oblivion. Why would this boy thank me when I'm the one responsible for his situation?

"For being my girl." My tears break free and I don't care. This isn't how I imagined my first week of having a boyfriend would turn out.

"Don't cry. Won't be long now." He closes his eyes.

I want to argue with him that his death will be decades from now, but I don't want to exhaust him any more than I already have. I also hate to admit to myself that I really don't know enough about him to be sure anymore. His normally pale skin has a nasty, grayish tinge.

"Now I know why" —he takes a deep breath and moves his right arm across his chest with a grunt— "why the Batman never had a girlfriend."

A frown creases my forehead before I can stop it. "What are you talking about? And how do you know about Batman and Superman?"

It's something I've wondered since I first visited the market and saw exactly how isolated from the real world he really is. When we first met, he told me he wasn't a vampire but more like Batman. Rocks has very little experience with modern pop culture since he doesn't have a TV at the colony and has never even been to the movies. I pull the chair I'm sitting on closer to the bed and lean my arms on the mattress, barely touching him.

He opens his eyes, and I brush his long hair out of the way so he can see better. "Alex Green gave me two comics. Highly contraband stuff," he says quietly, between labored breaths. "Strickland would've had a fit if he'd known."

I'm confused. He's not making sense, and I wonder if the painkillers are still affecting him.

"He sounds like an aeronaught."

His lip curls up on one side a little. "He is. Celand's boyfriend."

Holy fudge sundae!

For months, I've wanted information on Rocks' mysterious missing sister, Celand, and now he tells me. If he weren't already in pain, I'd thump him one. Before I can ask the dozens of question zipping through my mind, he continues.

"Gave me Batman and Superman. I read them over and over until they fell apart. It fed my fascination with your world, but it wasn't enough. I needed more."

"Why didn't you ask him for more?"

"Never saw them again. Didn't realize that Alex was coming to get Celand. She was leaving the colony." He winces. "Nobody realized until it was too late." He closes his eyes again and I wait. "She's dead."

"Oh my God, I'm so sorry." I squeeze his fingers gently. "Why are you telling me this now?" I really don't understand. Previously, he's always shut down any conversations involving Celand, and his stubborn refusal to discuss her has caused more than one argument between us.

"You need to know why they'll come for you."

Rocks opens his eyes once more. I slowly close my mouth. It was hanging open imitating a Venus flytrap.

"It's not only me that you're going to pay for. I'm not the first death the colony has blamed on an aeronaught."

2
Vultures

CELAND had an aeronaught boyfriend.

She left the colony with Alex Green—and now she's dead. This changes everything.

The hate the colony has for me isn't really for *me* personally. It's for being an aeronaught and opening a door to freedom they're desperately trying to keep closed. Before I stumbled—literally—into their lives that night in the forest, another aeronaught had already given them a reason to hate me. Their hate is about protecting their blood, but mine is now in danger of being spilt.

"She ran away with Alex? What happened? How did she die?" I know he's not in the best state to be bombarded with questions, but this information could be vital.

Rocks is lying perfectly still with his eyes shut. His chest slowly moves up and down. He's damp with sweat, but his temperature has come down a little. Eventually he answers.

"I wish I could tell you. Been trying to piece it together for years."

"But—"

"She never spoke to me about leaving. I told you they think I'm the human misfit. My whole life" —he coughs and winces— "I was seen as a traitor to Camazotz blood. A few months before she disappeared, Celand started to visit more and hang around with me in human form for days on end. She was full of questions on what I thought life as a human was all about. I was so happy. I thought she was going to stand by my side in wanting to integrate and modernize us."

He opens his eyes and the suffering I see swirling around in their dark blue depths I don't think is from his arm. "But she left. She didn't even offer to take me with her. I would've gone if she'd only told me what she was doing. And now, she's dead."

My mind races over this information. The betrayal he must have felt at her leaving, when she escaped to the world he'd always craved must have been enormous. And to make matters worse, the Fold would have pointed a finger at him for sure. I imagine him stunned and desperate, trying to convince them he didn't know she was leaving, or where she had gone.

"How?"

His eyes close again, and he shakes his head. The conversation's over. It's more than I've ever gotten on Celand before, and I should be grateful, but I get the impression it's the tip of the iceberg. Maybe he doesn't know how she died? I wonder about Alex Green. Who is he? How did they meet? My discovery of their secret world was purely by accident. How did he find out Celand was a Camazotz?

Rocks' breathing evens out, and I don't dare move. He's fallen asleep. My mind recounts all the times Celand has been mentioned. At the blood ceremony, Macallister and Cypress—two of the Fold members—spoke of paying Celand's aeronaught a visit. I realize they were talking about Alex Green, and think he's responsible for releasing the Great Horned Owls into the forest surrounding the market.

Rocks described Alex as Celand's boyfriend. Surely that means Alex wouldn't want any harm to come to her family or the rest of the colony? If Rocks decided to walk away from his wing to be with me, I would never wish them harm—let alone a violent, ugly death. And if Alex Green had met some of those not so friendly Camazotz, he'd be nuts to pick a fight with them on purpose. I mean, let's be honest, enemies that can fly and see in the dark have a slight advantage over a run-of-the-mill human.

The home phone ringing pulls me back to the present. I avoid the squeaky floorboards as I race down the hall to my parent's bedroom to pick up their line before the noise wakes Rocks.

"Hello?" I try to steady my breathing.

"Sweetheart, how are you?"

It's Mom. Her cheerful voice causes a sharp ache in my chest. My mom. The woman I have given so much attitude to for the past six months, none of which she deserved. In fact, she deserves a medal of honor for raising the daughter of a drug lord and loving me regardless of whom my real relatives are.

"Good," I whisper, squeezing my eyes shut. "You?"

There's a pause that makes me hold my breath. Dad recognized something was wrong when he spoke to me while I had a gun pointed to my head yesterday. How can that only be yesterday? I rub my temples with my free hand. Will Mom know I need her now too?

"Con, is everything all right?" Two words have left my mouth, and she's onto me. I exhale, not bothering to hide the sound of my misery.

"I miss you. I really do."

"Oh, sweetheart, I thought" —she lowers her voice— "you'd be hanging out with Rocks while we were away."

Mom doesn't know Rocks and I are dating. We only got together six days ago on Christmas Eve. I know she approves of him because she thinks he's the most sweet-mannered boy she's ever met, and his love of my baby sister, Mini, catapulted him to 'perfect boyfriend material' status.

"He's had an accident. Broken his arm."

"Oh my God, is he all right? Whatever happened?" Her voice fills with genuine concern, and I have to fight the tears that are about to erupt.

No, don't ask. Please.

Her questions will lead to more lies, and I'm sick to death of lying to her and dad, but the lies are for their protection now. They can't know about Enzo Ascari, and they definitely can't find out about the Camazotz.

"He's in a lot of pain. You coming home tomorrow?"

"Um, no, honey. Your father decided to drive home via Richmond. He's always wanted to stop off in Virginia instead of driving right through. Listen, I'll talk to him, and we can come home instead."

"No, it's fine. There isn't really anything you can do. I'll see you on New Year's Eve then? Okay?"

This is actually good news. It gives me another day to sort out what to do with Rocks, his arm, and the Camazotz that will come for me if anything happens to him—without my parents and Mini becoming targets too. Dad gets put on the phone, and I'm forced to add two more lies to my tally, but in the end, they decide to stick with their plan to visit Richmond.

The call ends right before I burst into tears.

"You cannot tell them," I chant, collapsing onto their bed.

I want to tell them the truth. It's taken me months, but I finally want to tell them everything that's happened. I want to let the story of my birthday letter and my subsequent search for my birth parents pour out of the hole inside me where I've hidden it.

I want to share the terror of yesterday at that farm with those awful men. If only I could crawl into the protection of my father's arms. I cover my face with my hands and pray they never find out. Chad can't keep me safe from the Vipers. For the hundredth time, I wish I'd never gotten that stupid letter.

The biggest secret I'm keeping is that my birth mother, Josie Hendersen, offered me up for adoption to prevent my biological father from discovering my existence. She did this because Enzo Ascari is not a nice man. In fact, he's the alleged leader of the biggest drug ring on the East Coast. According to the Internet, the Vipers are his biggest competitors, and two of their thugs kidnapped me to use me as leverage against Enzo—only Enzo doesn't know I exist. *How fudged up is that?*

I can never share this secret.

I must keep it, or otherwise I will be responsible for more than just Rocks' blood on my hands. If anything happened to Chad and Kelly, or gorgeous little Mini because of me, I'd never forgive myself. I'd never be able to live with knowing I had put the most loving parents in the world in danger. It's a risk I simply cannot take.

My only hope is that now the members of the Vipers' gang know that I'm not Sophia Ascari, and I'm not about to take the witness stand and give evidence sending their boss to prison, they'll leave me alone and go back to finding her instead. I'm worthless in their game. Taking a deep breath, I push my fear of men in vans and drug deals into my emotional elevator pit and jam the doors closed. Rocks. I have to focus on my boyfriend and getting him medical treatment.

I JOLT AWAKE to the sound of Rocks groaning. My phone shows it's after four in the afternoon. The pain in my neck confirms I fell asleep in the chair by his side. From the messages on my phone screen, Tiff has been spamming me. Thank God I put it on silent. My best friend is probably wondering why I haven't kept her updated on my alone time with Rocks. If only she knew …

I love Tiff, but I can't deal with lying to her on top of everything else. I thank the universe that the Bun Lovin' Barn, where I work, is closed for three weeks.

"You okay?" I rub my face to wake up. It's too little sleep, and I feel as though I'm coated in wet concrete. The adrenaline from the rescue has long left my system. "You need to eat. I'll fix you something."

Rocks reaches for me with his left hand. "Sit with me. Not hungry."

"You haven't eaten since" —I blink trying to figure out what day it is— "yesterday morning. I'm making you something." I stand, stretching my spine. "When did you last flip?"

"Around midday—maybe. I feel in control again." He sighs. I know he's remembering the agony from this morning.

Despite his protests, I heat a can of chicken noodle soup and sit on the edge of the bed to spoon-feed him. He frowns after his first mouthful and sniffs the air, wrinkling his nose. I can't stop my smile.

"It's from a can. Mom has spoiled you with her home-cooked meals and baking. Loads of people call this dinner."

Feeding him is a slow process. I've never seen Rocks this physically drained before. He's so strong and fit from all his flying and seeing his weakness worries me. He accepts a few bites of buttered toast and licks his lips. I want him to eat the whole can and hold another spoonful to his mouth.

"Wait," he says, rubbing his stomach. "I don't feel so good."

"You're nearly done. Just a couple more." I try again, and he takes another mouthful.

I load the last fat noodle onto the spoon, but before I can offer it to him, Rocks' eyes open wide. His whole body stiffens.

"What's wrong?"

"I don't—"

Rocks jerks off the pillows supporting him, leans over with a strangled moan of pain, and vomits all over the carpet. He empties his belly of the chicken, the noodles, and the soup as I try to prevent him from falling off the bed—his broken arm not helping one little bit. When he's done, I roll him over, and as delicately as possible rest his arm across his torso.

"What's happening to me?" He looks more scared than Mini the day she watched Toy Story. That bald doll head on the spider's legs still makes her cry.

"You're sick, like, you know, you vomited. I don't understand why though."

He swallows and I grab some water knowing what he's tasting isn't pleasant. "I've never done that—vomit—before."

How can this be? I must be stressed beyond ridiculousness because I'm finding it hard to cope with this new information about his Camazotz self.

"Weren't you ever sick as a kid?"

"I've been sick, but never vomited human food. I only ever fed as a Camazotz until I met you."

I hold his cool hand between mine. "It's no fun, huh?"

"Not my favorite," he replies, trying to smile. Suddenly, he tries to sit up, bumping his leg against me as though he going to get out of bed.

"What are you doing? Lie down."

"I made a mess." He wrinkles his nose reminding me of the smell that I'm trying hard to ignore. Breathing in through my mouth isn't helping.

Silly Camazotz.

His sense of responsibility—no matter what it costs him—is one of the reasons I fell for this flawless, magical boy. Then again, a flawless boyfriend wouldn't stain my mother's new rug—maybe I can blame Mini.

"Stay in bed! I've got this. Mini's an expert at projectile vomiting. Trust me, that was nothing."

His room smells slightly better, like he vomited a bunch of lavender instead. I sit on the bed scanning his body for hints as to what it's going to do next. The twitch of his nose makes me crack open the window despite the cold air it lets in. Unfortunately, the olive-green, plastic laundry bucket sitting next to him almost matches the pallor of Rocks' complexion. He's gone from gray to green, and I'm not sure which is worse. We've tried a cupcake minus the frosting, dry crackers, ice cream, and lemonade. All of which have been ejected from his system.

I wipe his sweaty forehead, not liking his still higher-than-normal temperature. "You don't know how lucky you are surviving your childhood without puking."

He pulls a face for reminding him, and I don't blame him. Not exactly the romantic conversations I thought I'd be having this soon in our relationship. "Before I met you, I'd only tasted Bavarian crème-filled doughnuts."

I wonder if there'll ever be a day when Rocks doesn't surprise me. It certainly won't be any time soon, I'm betting.

"I don't think I've had a Bavarian crème-filled doughnut. Explain, mister." I smile at him and wipe his forehead. "Where on earth did you get one?"

"There's a German cake shop in Helen. I used to beg Judge to take me with him when he'd go into town to collect our mail orders. He would rarely agree to it because of the pressure the Sire put on him, but on the occasions he would let me accompany him, I'd head straight to the bakery and stare at all the cakes."

I picture a younger version of Rocks, hands against the glass cabinet inside the bakery, that smile of awe spread wide across his features. His nose analyzing the delicious aromas filling the store, trying to choose one tasty treat on which to spend his few hard-earned dollars.

"First time, the lady in front of me bought six of them and told the baker she'd driven all the way from Atlanta. Figured they had to be good and got one. Every other time I visited, I couldn't imagine anything else tasting better."

"That good, huh?"

He nods slowly, not wanting to cause his stomach to react, or his arm to protest with the movement. "Judge never once said anything to me about it. He never told Strickland either. I was so grateful. He's never said it, but I think he accepts this side of me."

I recall the Fold member with the jagged scar running down the length of his face, and the kindness he showed me when he bandaged my hand and kept me on my feet during that blood ceremony. I wonder how many other Camazotz would accept Rocks for who he wants to be if a few influential members didn't ostracize him.

There's no doubt that Rocks is getting worse. His sweat-drenched shirt clings to his lean body, and he hardly opens his eyes. It's as though the weight of his eyelids are too much. I can't risk taking him to the hospital until I'm sure he won't flip.

He rests his cool hand in my lap. I stroke the length of his fingers between mine, hoping with each pass to give him comfort. I would do anything to take away the pain that I've caused him. I stare at his gorgeous hands. His nails are short and impeccably clean for a teenage boy. I trace the outlines of his nails before I stroke the length of his fingers from knuckle to tip.

This is a rare opportunity to study him up close. The red metal bar that pierces his eyebrow makes me smile. Remembering he got it so that I would recognize him in the dark when he's a bat ignites a fuzzy feeling in my stomach. I study his face. His perfect lips that rarely break into a full-blown grin, but will always bless me with a shy smile. My fingers itch to touch his jet-black hair—hair I love watching get flicked out of his eyes when it hangs too low over them.

Why is a broken arm—or wing—causing a fever and the vomits?

Why did Decker cry like he'd never see him again?

Rocks' face is as calm as the ocean on a still day. It's peaceful, but I know the pain he's suffering with each and every movement. This gorgeous, gentle boy is being brave for me. The sheen of perspiration is the only giveaway. Dread creeps up my spine. I'm tired, exhausted actually, and I sense my brain isn't connecting the dots. If anything happens to him, I'll never forgive myself. Tears silently wet my cheeks. Never in a million years did I think finding my biological parents would bring this kind of violence down upon us.

The lies I've nailed to the cross of my conscience are piling up, and what were they for? Answers? Do I really have any more answers about who I am? I don't have a freaking clue. All I know is that I don't want anything to damage my relationship with my adoptive parents—my real parents. I would be lost without their love and support. I try to imagine Rocks' life at the colony without the support of his parents. The snide remarks and judgmental stares that follow him. I've never seen disappointment of that magnitude in Mom or Dad's eyes, but if they found out I know about Josie and Enzo, then Rocks and I might have something else in common.

The tears fall off my chin, but I won't risk disrupting Rocks. My fingers continue their circuit of his beautiful hands. Without opening his eyes, he speaks. "No tears, Beans." He manages half a smile.

"How did you know? I was trying to be so quiet."

One eye opens and then closes again. "I can smell the hint of the ocean on the breeze."

What breeze? Oh God, is he hallucinating?

He looks at me for a brief second. "I'm imagining I'm good as new and flying high on a moonlit night. Whole. Unbroken. Alive. But the smell of your tears brought me back to earth," he explains.

I sob. I can't hold it in. "I'm sorry." My fingers halt.

"Don't be. I wouldn't change a thing."

I want to ask him how it's ever going to be okay, but he needs rest. If he's saying that to give comfort—as I know Rock would—I don't want to argue. His fingers flex out straight in mine.

"Don't stop." He wiggles them. "Feels nice."

I resume my circuit, tracing the length of his middle finger. "I can't believe you fly with these. It's … it's so hard to believe even though I've seen it."

Silence settles over us. I continue to comfort him and include tracing the tattooed patterns on his forearm while his breathing evens out at last. The painkillers have finally left his system, but he's beyond exhausted from his repeated flipping. While Rocks dozes, I take a much-needed shower and scour my body of the filthy touch those two thugs left on my skin. The hot water burns, but I don't care. Enzo Ascari has tainted me even though we've never met. Dressing in my room, I keep one ear alert for noise from the guest room.

Rockland?

"Holy shit!" An angry, deep, male voice was just inside my head. Not caring that my jeans are laying on the bed instead of on me, I tear down the hall to check Rocks.

"I'm alive," he whispers, facing the window on the far wall. "Leave her out of this. It's not on her hands."

He's talking about his blood—his blood *not* being on my hands. But he's wrong—it is. I might not have crushed his wing under my boot, but I was the reason he was there. The reason he was vulnerable and unconscious in the first place. Nothing has ever been more my fault.

It will be.

"Who is it?" I ask, wondering who'll be knocking on my door if …

"Ash, his brother Cedar, and Mackie. Not exactly friends of mine."

We can wait.

That does it! I understand that I'm responsible, but I'm not hanging around upside down in a tree simply waiting for him to die. I'm trying to come up with a plan to save his life. How dare they sit like vultures on a carcass! I storm across the room, swiping the curtains out of the way and pulling the window wide open. Night has fallen and the crisp winter air hits my bare skin.

"You listen here, you—you, ugh!" I yell. Neighbors be damned. "You're going to be waiting a long time because he isn't going to die. I'm going to prove to you that my ways can save lives. Just you wait and see." I barely refrain from calling Ash 'fang features' before slamming the window with such force the frame creaks.

"Connie—"

"Don't. I have a plan, and I'm not letting anything happen to you."

Rocks' eyes dart to my bare thighs and away. His cheeks get the first hint of color all day, and I feel my ears flame. I pull the end of my tee over my butt and crabwalk to the door to finish getting dressed.

Close to midnight when I hope the hospital won't be a mad house, I'm taking him to the ER to get his arm set. My plan has flaws, the first of which is how the hell I'm going to get a six-foot-four, very sick boy to my car. But where there's a will, there's a way.

The microwave chimes telling me my canned soup is ready. I know I'm in for a long night, and despite the fact that I'm not the slightest bit hungry, I'm forcing myself to eat. I'm going to need all the strength I have to pull this off. A knock at the door sends hot soup down my clean sweater. The clock on the microwave shows it's after eleven. The only folks I know who would call at this hour are either of the aerial variety, or are in the narcotics business. I tip toe to the front door and look through the peephole, letting out the breath I was holding when there's a friendly face in sight.

The boys—Decker, Ezra and Jeremiah—are all fidgeting on the porch.

"Oh, thank goodness it's you guys," I say, holding the door wide. My eyes dart to the trees lining our fence.

"Who else were you expecting?" Decker asks.

"Are Ash and the death squad still out there?"

A cacophony of voices rings out in our small foyer as they all speak at once. That got their attention. The three of them—including the most silent Jeremiah—bombard me with questions.

"Wait. Wait. One at a time." I answer as many of the questions my brain was able to process. "Rocks is alive. He's not great, but okay. I heard Ash in here." I point to my temple. "They were here around six. Waiting to witness him die. I have no idea."

The boys look as stunned as I feel. Ezra swears and paces back and forth.

"What's going on? Does the Sire know?" I need answers of my own.

Jeremiah nods, but Decker answers. "I had to tell him, Connie. I'm sorry. Rockland is his first-born son. I wanted to give him the chance to say goodbye, but—"

"Oh, sugarplums, is he out there?" I look toward the door, my heart hammering in my chest. I can't stop my hands from covering the soup stain on my sweater. Yelling at Ash is one thing, but I'll need clean underwear if I have to face Strickland.

"No." Decker's face drops. "He didn't come."

Knowing Rocks' half-brother as I do, he's no doubt feeling the sting of disappointment too. If Chad was informed that I had a life threatening injury, I know for a fact nothing would keep him from my side. He would want to be with me for the last moments of my life. Poor Rocks. I really have pushed a bigger wedge between him and his family.

"Those Camazotz shouldn't have come here," Ezra informs me. He explains that a Fold meeting was held once the news of Rocklands' injury spread. The Sire ordered all Camazotz to remain at the roost after the wings lead by Cypress and Macallister started calling for a witch-hunt.

"A witch-hunt?" I repeat, aghast. "Me? A witch? What the hell is that crazy goat killer at the colony if *I'm* the witch?" I recall the strong scent of herbs and the long flowing robes that trailed behind the twirling medicine woman that performed the blood protection ceremony. If that isn't a bunch of hocus-pocus I witnessed, then I don't know what is.

My outburst actually makes Jeremiah—Mr. Super Serious—crack a smile. He shakes his head and looks away when he notices I see it, but doesn't say anything.

"Be cool. We know you're not. It's just, um, there's more to this than just you," Ezra says.

"I know. Rocks told me about Alex Green."

Three sets of eyes widen simultaneously. "He did?"

I nod. "But if Strickland ordered everyone to stay at the roost, then what are you guys doing here?" I channel Kelly and give them the evil eye. I'm sick to death of being the last to know what's going on. They fidget. I glare at Decker figuring he's my best chance since he told me about Blood Mountain, and in doing so broke their most steadfast rule. I know the moment he cracks since he looks away and sighs. He reminds me so much of Rocks, it hurts.

"I wanted to see my brother," he says, looking me in the eye. "And, well … Jeremiah and I sorta did something last night."

That dark storm cloud of doom that I swear has parked itself over my house obviously hasn't moved. My skin prickles from watching how uneasy the most relaxed and laid back Camazotz I know is, as he tells me this.

"What—did—you—do?" I give Jeremiah a look, but I could learn a thing or two from him on nasty glares. He seems completely immune to my most lethal stink-eye.

"You know how you asked us to get rid of the van?" I nod and swallow hard. "Well, we did." Decker looks at Jeremiah who shrugs.

"Decker!"

"Okay, okay. Well, there was a bag of money in the back of it, and we hid it in your shed."

My vision falters; my chest tightens; my lungs don't seem to be processing oxygen at all. Strong fingers lock around my biceps and hold me upright.

"Move her to the couch, you idiot." Jeremiah's voice helps me surface through the heavy fog that has swallowed me whole. I feel my knees bend and the softness of the couch beneath me.

These completely clueless imbeciles stole drug money from the Vipers' gang—who tried to murder Rocks and me less than twenty-four hours ago—and have hidden it in Chad's garden shed.

Decker is kneeling in front of me—the worry evident in his dark blue eyes. "Connie?"

How do I explain the magnitude of their actions to three young men that have been raised in a community stuck in the 1860s? How do I explain illegal drugs when I know none of them have ever taken a headache tablet? I want to cry. I want to scream. I want to smack their thick skulls together. I sigh, accepting what's done is done.

"How much money?"

"More than Jeremiah and I could carry. That's why we brought Ezra too. But we didn't take it all. We left some in the van."

More than two Camazotz could carry! Maybe I will cry. That's too much money to go unnoticed regardless of the fact they left some behind. "Let me think. Go sit with Rocks and just let me think." I rub circles on my pounding temples as they trudge up the stairs.

It turns out their impetuous stupidity might be the answer to one of my problems. Rocks doesn't have medical insurance, and even with all the practice I've had I didn't know how to lie my way around that.

Just before midnight, I fire up the coffee machine. Caffeine is all that will get me through what I'm about to do. A moment later, Decker is at my side, his Camazotz nose unable to resist the fresh brew and the lure of a technological gadget.

"You aeronaughts are addicted to this stuff," he says, watching my every move and eyeing the coffee machine like he wants to tuck it under his wing and abscond with it. "We get so many people asking where to buy it at the market. You should see the looks they give us when we tell them we don't sell coffee."

"Aeronaughts are like totally addicted. Coffee shops are gold mines. You so need to open one. Wanna try some?" I don't know whether giving him caffeine is wise after witnessing Rocks on pain meds. He nods and it's the first sign of happiness I've seen on his face. "Can you guys get Rocks into my car? It's time."

"You know it's not going to work, right?"

"Do you think he'll flip? In front of the doctor?" That's my main concern if they try to sedate him.

"Nah, it's just not going to save him." The anguish I witnessed last night when Decker said what he thought was his final goodbye isn't present in his eyes, but I can tell he's using everything he's got to hide it.

I sigh. "If I don't do anything and sit back and watch Rocks fade away, I'll gladly hand myself over to whomever comes after my blood. But I can't do that. None of you understand. I *know* what modern medicine is capable of. You have to trust me." I load up his cup with cream and sugar and slide it over.

"But modern medicine can't turn you into a Camazotz, can it? So why on earth do you think it would work on us?"

3
Blood Donor

JEREMIAH and Ezra are standing in the far corner of the room holding their noses when Decker and I join them. I roll my eyes and shove the steaming cups under their delicate noses. My nose had forgotten about that lingering smell. Good thing the coffee will drown out all evidence of Rocks' rough afternoon.

"You have to tell her," Decker says, taking the seat by his side.

"No. Don't upset her," Rocks whispers.

I crawl across the bed as gently as I can to be close to him. "Tell me what?" I look at the boys, but in unison they start gulping their coffee, braving its scalding temperature. "Rocks? If you know why the hospital won't work, tell me! What am I missing?"

I'm pretty sure less than half my brain cells are currently functioning on the tiny amount of sleep I've had. The caffeine is firing up a few more neurons, but I sense there's a Camazotz problem I haven't accounted for in my put-a-cast-on-his-arm-and-let-it-mend plan.

I explain to the boys about casts and hospitals and that his arm will be healed before Spring. Decker and Rocks exchange a knowing glance—only I don't know what it means. Jeremiah shrugs when they look at him, and Ezra asks for more coffee. What the hell are they so worried about?

Ezra clicks open his pocket watch, before jerking his head toward the door. I catch a brief flash of agony crossing Decker's face before he rests his hand on his brother's leg.

"Uh-uh, you aren't going anywhere. If you three don't spill, I'm gonna … gonna … scream if you flippin' flip." My threat causes Rocks' eyes to fly open, and the looks I get from the silent trio would be priceless if the circumstances were better. I rack my brain for all the facts I know about the Camazotz … and then it dawns on me. He can't stay human for six weeks while his bones mend. "Hang on, you guys are worried about the flip?"

Decker's eyebrows almost disappear into this hair, before he nods.

"Duh, put blood on the cast," I suggest.

When Decker's shoulder sag once more, I know I'm still not connecting all the dots.

"That won't work, Connie. We keep trying to tell you."

"No, you aren't telling me jack!" I rub my temples and suddenly the light bulb clicks on. "Oh, fudge me. Your bones." I take hold of Rocks' good hand and cradle it in mine, tracing the long, still intact bones. "When you flip, your bones will move. They won't be where the doctor set them." *Ouch.* The thought alone makes me wince.

I don't understand why the boys are being so tightlipped all of a sudden. I know way too many Camazotz secrets for them to get shy on me at this point.

"I'm right, aren't I?"

Decker nods slowly, and the others join him. Silly Camazotz. My subsequent smile must be dazzling because Jeremiah's frown deepens to a scowl. "Well, that's easily solved. You don't need a doctor, Rocks— you need a vet!"

THE FACT THAT the Camazotz had no idea of the existence of veterinary medicine turns me as mute as Jeremiah on a bad day. Vets have been around since the ancient Egyptians so their Victorian-era head-in-the-sand ways are no excuse.

"You lot have had hundreds of years to experiment with bat medicine!"

"Of course. Our shamans heal what they can, but broken wings are a curse," Ezra answers. He looks at his fob watch again, frowning.

Curse my butt. That loopy medicine woman Sylvana needs to go. Her and her stinky herbs would have no chance healing broken limbs, but that doesn't mean it's not possible.

"Is there a curfew?" Rocks croaks. Even sick, he doesn't miss a beat.

"Colony lockdown. Strickland's orders," replies Jeremiah.

"Get out of here," he groans. "Now. You shouldn't have come."

"We volunteered for a patrol, but Ezra's right. We'll be missed if we don't hit the sky soon," Decker explains.

They can't leave me now. I'm not even sure if putting a cast on a bat's wing is possible, but that part can wait. What I don't have is goat access to feed a recovering vampire bat. I'm gonna need some serious Camazotz help. Right now, I need to assume I can convince Feathers' vet to save Rocks, but that kinda feels like the easy part of my predicament. Jeremiah and Ezra move toward the doorway, clearly unconvinced by my vet suggestion.

"Wait, how am I going to feed him?"

More silence. These bats are gonna wish I hadn't drunk that third cup of coffee in a second.

"We can feed him, but … well, not here," Decker admits, looking at Jeremiah and Ezra, but noticeably not in his brother's direction.

"You mean I have to get him back to Blood Mountain?"

The intake of air into Rocks' lungs reminds me that he didn't know I know about their secret batty headquarters.

"Who told her?" He tries to sit up, and the sudden movement causes him to grunt loudly. "Who?" he half yells.

My eyes automatically flick to Decker and Rocks swears softly.

"Brother, why? No! Why?" He covers his eyes with crook of his elbow, the noises still coming out of him are closer to a growl than a groan. "They'll sentence you to death, and God only knows what they'll do to Connie!"

"I couldn't—" Decker's words fade as he stares at his feet.

"You couldn't what?" he snaps. His eyes are the most focused I've seen them since the pain meds wore off. Rocks is absolutely livid. "What have you done?"

"I didn't want to lose you, okay? I freaked out. Seeing you broken last night, man, I couldn't give up on you! I knew if anyone could help, it would be Connie."

"Hey," I intervene. "Yelling won't change anything. I know now. The end. Let's make a plan to get you back there."

"No!"

"Rocks, what do you mean, 'no?'" How can he be this stubborn? He's blocked every idea I've had to fix him. "Do you actually want to die?" I ask, the words tasting bitter on my tongue.

"No, I never want to leave you," he states, still trying to sit up higher but failing. I grab the spare pillow and help wedge it behind his back.

"But I don't want my brother to die either. Or dare risk what the Fold will do to you. This is our most sacred promise, Connie. We swear on our lives to take that location to the grave. Decker should not have told you."

Now I understand why Jeremiah wanted nothing to do with it last night. This also might be why they aren't eager to divulge any new Camazotz information.

"Can you come back for him tomorrow night?" I send up a silent prayer the vet can get his wing set immediately, but nobody'll meet my eye. "For fudge's sake, talk to me!"

Rocks jerks at my tone, but then seems to deflate before my eyes. He sighs. "If the boys have patrol tonight, they won't be allowed back on rotation until all the other males of age have done their turn. Depends how long the lockdown is for."

When the boys confirm it could be over a month before the three of them will get the chance to return, my heart sinks. With the market closed for winter, the Camazotz stay close to the roost even to feed, and feeding takes far less time than flying to Atlanta and back. With Rocks' large size as a bat, it will take the three of them to airlift him home over that distance, and Strickland will be watching them closely.

The only way he's going back to Blood Mountain to be fed is if I deliver him. Another heated discussion follows my suggestion, and I'm ready to argue all night in order to win, until Ezra points out that regardless of whether Rocks heals, the Fold will sentence Decker to death.

Rocks will never let that happen—even if it means dying to save his brother.

Thankfully Decker is on my side. It's almost ugly witnessing him resort to begging Rocks to try to live. Jeremiah inches closer to the door. He's clearly as upset by the scene as I am. I have to help.

"Rocks, if you die, a part of me will die too."

That stops all conversation, and Rocks looks at me for a long moment with the saddest eyes I've ever witnessed.

"No, Connie."

"Yes. You'll take part of me with you. Please don't do that. Help me. Don't give up."

My admission and his exhaustion are what finally make Rocks cave, but on one condition. Rocks vows that he'll claim responsibility for disclosing the roost location to save Decker's neck; however, he's not happy about the unknown risk to me.

By the end of it, I'm not happy with the thought of saving him only to have his fudged up bat family put an end to him. My head is spinning, and the coffee sours in my gut.

"Maybe you can risk it," Jeremiah adds with his signature shrug. "You're Strickland's son. Zander and Judge won't vote against you."

Wait a minute; two out of seven leaders voting for him are not the kind of odds I'd stake my life on.

"No way. What if all the others vote differently? No!" I fold my arms, still slightly confused as to what I'm now asking. A second ago, I was in favor of taking him to the roost, and now I'm arguing the opposite. These Camazotz and their freaky laws are doing my head in. The bottom line is I'll do whatever it takes to save my boyfriend. "Forget it. You're staying here. You can feed from me."

I might as well have released an owl in the room. All the boys start talking over the top of each other, including Jeremiah.

"Strickland would *definitely* end you if—"

"—no blood bonds."

"—but she offered?"

"How will the Fold know?"

My head is spinning as I try to follow what the hell they're all talking about. Rocks looks positively horrified by my suggestion, and I have to admit I'm a little hurt.

"Enough!" Rocks shouts. I feel bad when he closes his eyes and his chest rises and falls with labored breaths. We're only adding to his already weak state. "You need to go. There'll be more blood spilt if the Sire works out you were here."

Rocks is right. It's after one a.m. and the boys have a long flight back to the roost. Considering they aren't even supposed to be here, I don't want them in any more danger. This is another strike I know will go against my name if they're discovered missing. Heading downstairs, I give them time to say goodbye. I know they believe deep down it'll be the last time they see their friend alive.

When I return to the bedroom, Rocks reaches for my hand. His fingers are chilled to the bone. "How do you feel?" He won't open his eyes. "I can get you another blanket."

"Please. Very cold."

He needs food, or at least some water. He hasn't eaten anything for over thirty-six hours, and Mr. Hollow Legs must be starving.

"I'm going to heat up some dinner. You feel like anything in particular?"

Nothing.

"Rocks, look at me." He slowly opens his eyes and what I see scares me. His pupils are huge, and I can tell he's having difficulty focusing. Those arguments have left him drained. "Shit, how do you feel?" I place the back of my hand on his forehead.

"Tired. Not hungry. Sit with me."

"No, you *have* to eat. I'm getting you some dinner, and you're going to eat it."

"Please, Connie," he begs. "Come here." He holds up his good arm, indicating for me to join him on the bed. I slip in under the extra blanket and snuggle close, glad for the physical contact after he turned down my blood offer.

Before long, he whispers against the top of my head. "I want you to know it's all right. You tried. And I wanted you to try so that you won't feel guilty … later." I look up and he's watching me, sadness filling his ocean-blue eyes. "I don't want to you blame yourself for this."

"Rocks—"

"No!" I try to move away, but he grunts, holding me to his chest. "I love you. I had no choice but to try to rescue you from those men. I couldn't fly away and leave you there. That's not what you do for the ones you love." His words melt my resolve and quiet sobs fill the room. "If anyone is to blame, it's that bat. If only we knew who he was, the colony could go after him instead," he adds.

"I'm still sorry this happened," I whisper. "But just so we're clear, I'm not giving up yet."

His hand plays with my messy hair, and the repetitive action calms me. Rocks has always loved my golden blonde strands. It's such a contrast to his jet-black locks, and the most obvious sign that I'm not a Camazotz—and never will be.

"I once told you that you were worth it, and I meant it—I still do. I wouldn't change a thing."

I take his hand and press it against my lips. "What can I get you?" I sniff.

He shakes his head. "Just talk to me."

"But you must be hungr—"

"No, just talk."

To avoid another argument, I agree to talk if I can get the laptop first.

By three a.m., with the help of trusty Google, I've got a new plan. Rocks is curious about what vets can do, but extremely dubious. I've been watching a video about a vet in California who has successfully saved bats with broken wings. I'm studying the x-rays of the broken wings she's successfully fixed and reading about each bat's recovery.

"Oh, shit!" I exclaim. Rocks knows I rarely swear. If my baby sister ever utters a cuss word, my parents won't give me another cent of allowance money, but at a time like this, it's warranted. I look at Rocks. "Oh my God, you need blood, like right now, don't you?"

If only I'd had coffee earlier today and worked out what was wrong with him sooner. I glare at him over the top of the monitor.

"That's why you're turning this creepy gray color." He closes his eyes and turns his face toward the window. "Do not avoid me. You might not tell me everything, but I'm not stupid. You once said that vampire bats need to feed regularly. Right?"

Opening a new Google tab, I type in my search. I know that being a Camazotz isn't exactly the same as being a wild vampire bat, but quite a lot about their physiology is similar. I start scanning the information before me.

"'Vampire bats can only survive two days without feeding.'" I read out loud. "God damn it, Rocks! You're thirsty, aren't you?" I harden my glare.

"Yes."

"What the hell? Do you actually want to die?"

"I wanted to see what would happen," he whispers.

"What would *happen*?" I screech. When he winces, I take a slow breath. This is not the time to test out the effects of being human. "You mean by staying human when injured?" I growl.

He nods.

I fist my hands as my temper bubbles up inside, but I have to calm down. He's sick enough. I'm slowly but surely learning how his brain works. Rocks hates his dependence on his Camazotz side. The only reason I even discovered he's a Camazotz was because the night he helped me in the forest, he ran out of time and couldn't prevent his flip. Rocks has been trying not to drink blood since we've become friends, and because my mom's happy to feed him, he's been surviving on mostly aeronaught meals. Now he needs to release the animal inside in order to survive.

"You can't help that your body needs blood."

I wait for a response. Whenever Rocks has Camazotz news that he knows I'm not going to like, he stalls—like he's stalling right now. He won't look at me, and it's not because of the pain in his arm.

"Maybe I can. Maybe this is what it feels like. Maybe I just need to tough it out."

My gut is screaming at me to trust my theory. He's a Camazotz, and he's not reacting the way a human does to a broken arm.

"No, you need blood now. You can drink from me?"

The idea of Rocks feeding from a human has always been an issue. It completely and utterly freaks me out. He's always assured me that he only ever feeds from the animals he keeps at the market. But this is different—a life or death matter. The blood in my veins can solve our problem. I just need to not think about it too much, and I'll be fine. I swallow.

"No." He closes his eyes and pulls his hand from mine.

I can't believe I'm this calm talking to him about drinking blood—my blood. Last Halloween when he warned Mini and I not to go trick-or-treating because some of the not-so-aeronaught-friendly Camazotz might try to eat us, I was a mess. I imagine holding my wrist out for Rocks to feed from as a bat. I can't stop the shiver that runs up my spine. Gross, but then I think of the alternative—he dies before I ever get him to the vet. His family will blame me and come after my blood anyway, so I know whom I'd rather give it to.

"Come on. Flip." I hold out my wrist. "Don't you want to drink my blood?"

I watch his Adam's apple bob as he swallows. His need for blood is barely contained by his cool control. Sometimes I'm so out of touch with what's going on around me it's ridiculous. Rocks is so in tune with me and my needs it freaks me out. He says it's because he trusts his instincts. For the past six months, I've been trying to listen to my intuition, and right now it's telling me to feed him blood or else.

"Rocks?"

"I need to feed, but you are not on the menu. Never."

"But my blood can sustain you better than anything else. You said it's powerful. If it means the difference between you living or dying, Rocks, then just flip and … sip." I need to lighten the mood.

Rocks opens his eyes and his shy smile appears. I've missed seeing him smile.

"Flip and sip, huh?" His smile grows. My lips curl up mirroring his. "Hmm … tempting, but no chance. There's no doubt that you'd be delicious." His eyes roam my face, and I know he's looking to see if he's freaked me out. "Sweet from all that sugar in your Mom's baking."

"I'm serious."

He swallows again and tries to hide the grimace of pain that hits him as he moves slightly. "I know, but I never ever want to look at you like you're an easy meal. It's never going to happen, Connie. And you're human. I just want the chance to be a human boyfriend. If I feed from you, you'll never look at me the same. I know it. Things will change between us, and then I would rather die."

I can't hide the tears that spring up the instant his words hit me. I know it upsets him to see me cry, but his words have upset me more. The fact that he's placing my comfort above his life isn't right, but then again, it's so Rocks. I get up and leave the room. I cannot sit and watch his slow and painful death—I can't, and I won't.

AS I GENTLY push the cold metal, the neighbor's gate squeals louder than Mini on a swing set. My sneakers manage to locate every twig and crunchy leaf covering both front lawns. I'm making more noise than a busload of eight-year-olds amped up on a sugar high. By the time I make it to Rusty's doghouse, he's sitting in the dark wagging his massive tail. He lurches to the end of his chain, adding clinking metal to the melee, when he sees I'm coming toward him and not heading to the Gill's back door. If Rocks won't drink from me, then Golden Retriever it is.

I push aside the guilt at the thought of pimping out Mrs. Gill's beloved pup. Rusty's exuberant excitement at four a.m. is because he's convinced I'm taking him on a walkies. *Yeah, no, it's chow time for my boyfriend, pup.* He eagerly follows me up the porch, into the house and to Rocks' side.

"Okay, then, how about a real hot dog?"

Rocks doesn't open his eyes, but his smile makes my petnapping justified. Rusty's wet nose nudges his hand as his tails beats a rhythm on the floor.

"You'll need to calm him. My goats are used to us, but other animals need to be asleep to make it safe."

Knowing Mom would freak doesn't deter me. Rusty accepts the invitation to join Rocks on the soft, warm double bed. He curls up beside my patient, happy to be settled inside out of the cold. I move the chair to be closer to Rusty's potentially snapping jaws, grab the laptop, and wait.

Google maps and I are new best friends. My research keeps me awake as our four-legged blood donor enters dreamland. Without a word, Rocks is human one second and a bat the next. I admire his courage for not screeching when he lands on the bed with a soft thump, thankfully not on top of his wing. Rusty doesn't flinch. I pull my best "do you need help" face, not wanting to risk the noise of moving or speaking.

> *Stay there.*
> *Hands near jaws.*

I watch as Rocks uses what little strength I'm sure he's got to jump once, putting him closer to the retriever's shoulder. He's behind Rusty's head, which I'm guessing is the safest place to snack. But my heart almost breaks at the sight of his mutilated wing twisted beside him. The pain must be intense, but I'm pleased to see his will to live return.

> *Close eyes.*
> *Please.*

I roll mine, but do as he requests. I'd probably be embarrassed too if our places were reversed. My open hands hover close to Rusty's snoring head, and I hope I can catch him in time if he wakes without my eyes to help. Rusty seems far more co-operative than my first victim.

My initial idea was my three-legged chinchilla, Feathers. Only Feathers had a differing opinion on being dinner. Since she's mostly nocturnal, there wasn't any chance of her falling asleep. Standing next to the bed, I held her fluff ball body flat against the mattress while Rocks flipped. The mere sight of him gave her super-chinchilla strength, and despite my firm grip on her, she clawed her way up my body till she was precariously balanced on my head—as far from the scary blood-sucker as she could get—screeching her little lungs out. The irony of my pet mirroring her owner's first Camazotz encounter wasn't lost on me.

The minutes drag by, and it's hard to tell how long it takes before I hear Rocks' human groan of pain. He lifts his red, swollen wrist across his chest and lies back. His face is noticeably less grey as a tinge of pink returns to his cheeks.

"You just saved my life."

I bite the inside of my lip so that I won't cry.

"Thank you, Beans."

"You're welcome. Get some rest."

I HAVE A very solid plan, and it's going to work because failure this time is not an option. The sun is rising on my second dawn without a full night's sleep. I grab the printouts and tiptoe back to the guest room. Rocks is resting, but awake. I can't believe the difference a pint of blood and a few hours sleep has made.

"I need your help. In an hour, we're going to the vet. I'm going to get your wing set, and then when my parents get home, I'm taking you to Blood Mountain. I need details of how to find the roost entrance. Can you tell me while you're still human?" I hold up the maps of Blood Mountain.

Rocks' look speaks volumes.

"Don't start with me," I threaten. "I'm serious. I know that vampire bats can feed each other when food is scarce. So that means the Camazotz can keep you alive. I just need to get you back to them. Right?"

He nods. "Yes. They can keep me alive, but it will cost—"

"Let me worry about the vet bill. You worry about giving me clear instructions to find your front door."

"It's not the vet bill I was thinking about, but I will repay you for that."

The printouts are suddenly forgotten. "What now?" I sigh, trying not to curse the Camazotz to hell and back.

"I'm serious about taking the blame for telling you about Blood Mountain. My life could be forfeit whether I survive this or not."

My relief at seeing him better is so short-lived. I guess I'd already clung to Jeremiah's thought that they won't really go there with the Sire's son.

"Well, stay here then. I can start up a dog-walking business."

"Your parents are not going to let you keep a bat. You'll have to return me. It's our best chance."

"But—" The sick feeling at the thought of losing Rocks returns with a vengeance. But he's right. Mom will never ever agree to let me keep a sick bat.

"Connie, trust me."

In the end, I agree to return him to the roost even though the Fold will decide his fate. He explains the Fold vote when a blood oath is broken, and circumstances do affect the results. He says he can't risk Decker coming clean and telling the Fold the truth, and since Decker is the world's worst liar, that's a high possibility. If Rocks can save his brother, then he must. I have to trust his father won't let him die after I prove a broken wing isn't a death sentence.

"Plus with all the deaths recently, the Fold is already worried about our numbers."

Rocks spends the next half an hour describing exactly how to find the entrance to his colony's secret roost on foot. It will be a rough hike since their underground cave entrance is off the beaten path, but he'll be able to guide me when we're close using his telepathy. He describes the entrance and tells me I'm going to need Chad's help. Finally, the black clouds of doom seem to be lifting—sort of—if Strickland can be trusted to save his son.

"If this works, I'm going to miss you," he says.

"Me too, but at least you'll be alive. When does Sanguine Mountain Market open?"

"Depends on how long winter lasts."

Rocks tells me that even though the Camazotz don't have to hibernate, it just makes life easier since most other bat species do hibernate during winter. If too many people saw them as bats during the snowy winter months, questions would be asked. So ever since they settled in Georgia, they hide away in their roost all winter.

Rocks takes my hand and places a soft kiss over my fingers. "Will you, um …"

"What?"

"Wait for me?"

Oh Rocks, you silly boy. "Of course, I'll wait for you. You're not going to be out of action for that long. Two months maybe?"

He smiles and opens his arm for me to snuggle up beside him. His body temperature is closer to normal again. The fever has passed.

We've still got some time before we need to leave for the vet, so I make the most of his openness about the Camazotz. Maybe the pain has lowered his guard. I'm trying to imagine hiking in the mountains and coming across a group of Camazotz if I didn't know about them— all that black leather, blood-red velvet and lace. They must get some serious stares.

I guess people aren't exactly surprised to be attacked by vampire bats in a place called Blood Mountain. Not that attacking humans is allowed by the Sire—except at Halloween—but still, it's a wonder the locals haven't discovered them. I fire off as many questions as he has the energy to answer.

"But the place must be teaming with hikers, tourists, and hunters? Isn't it … like … risky? Don't people notice you suddenly appearing?" I roll onto my stomach so I can see his face better.

"Not at all. There are hundreds of us. We need to have some humans around so that it won't be odd seeing people appearing in the middle of nowhere. If the area was isolated and mostly deserted, and an odd hiker came through, then they would take notice of us appearing. Since it's a popular place, people just mind their own business. If any of us are in human form and come across hikers and the like, we act like hikers too and talk about the area. We know the mountain better than anyone and can usually stay well below the radar."

"But your clothes, well, not your clothes—you always look—" I can feel my ears warming, and the look in his eyes tells me he really wants to know how I honestly see him. "You always look so mysterious and sexy in those vests." He grins. Talking seems to have distracted him from the pain.

"Sexy, huh?"

My ears have ignited and I imagine they're glowing red. I nod and smile not caring that he knows I'm embarrassed. "But the girls, I mean, they don't look as though they're interested in hiking or nature. They look as though they're heading to a burlesque dinner show."

"A what?"

"Never mind." I let my eyes roam over his face slowly—his straight nose, his high cheekbones. He's so good-looking I want to pinch myself. I stare at the red metal bar piercing his brow. "That's gonna have to go."

"What?"

"Wild animals don't normally have piercings." He smiles and nods. "Oh shit, the vet's gonna see your wing tattoos!"

4

Intruder

ROCKS is in the passenger seat in Feathers' carry cage. Guilty doesn't even come close to describing how I felt putting him in there. He's not an animal, but then again, he is. My handbag rests on the floor, jammed with large bills. To say I feel dirty again is an understatement, but this is for Rocks. I'm only touching drug money to save a life. I don't even want to think about the look I'm going to get when I hand that over, but under no circumstances are Chad and Kelly paying for this.

The boys divided up their acquired funds evenly between the three wings. When I asked why they weren't splitting it into four stacks—one for each of them—they said at the colony everything is split according to wing regardless of member numbers. So Jeremiah and Ezra, being from the same wing, only count as one share. I think of lonely little Moonshiner—Rocks' nine-year-old half-brother—and am happy that he would get his share of colony resources regardless of the fact he's the sole member of his wing.

The looks the boys gave me when I told them I didn't want my cut, confirmed how crazy they think aeronaughts really are. They kindly set aside enough money to cover the vet bill. But when they tried to tell me the total tally of the drug money, I blocked my ears and sang Jingle Bells at the top of my lungs. One thing I've learned since last July and that stupid letter is that some information is best *not* known.

I pull into the vacant parking lot. "I'll stay with you. Don't worry."

No drugs.

Will flip out.

"Yeah, you don't have to tell me that twice."

Rocks told me earlier that, from what he's learned about aeronaught eyesight, his tats will be safe. I only noticed them holding him up with direct sunlight behind his wings. So somehow I need to prevent the vet from holding his wing up to a light and make sure he's not sedated in any way.

"Feathers isn't sick I hope," Dr. Gandy asks when I lift the carrier onto the stainless steel counter.

"No, I've got a far more interesting case for you, Dr. Gandy. A bat with a broken wing."

He frowns, pushing his dark rimmed glasses up his nose. "There isn't much I can do, and besides, you shouldn't be touching a sick bat. You should know better."

"I had rabies shots recently. Plus, I know this bat doesn't have it—none of the usual signs present. I've been monitoring him for a couple of days while I did some research."

"Connie." He frowns, but the look in his eyes shows he's secretly proud.

"What? You taught me what to look for. I learned from the best." I smile and hope I look suitably innocent.

I need to ignite Dr. Gandy's curiosity. His job is to save animals, but he never wants them to suffer. A little inter-veterinary competition is required. If that woman in California can fix bats, then why can't he?

Dr. Gandy peers into the carry cage while I start spreading out the pictures from the procedures the other vet successfully performed. Wing x-rays, surgery shots, bandage technique, it all gets shoved under his nose.

"'There isn't much I can do,'" I imitate in my deepest voice. "Look at this. These bats can even fly afterward. I thought you'd like the chance to add a new species to your patient list." I cross my fingers.

Dr. Gandy leans over and starts flicking through the step-by-step pictures. Rockland's bones are so tiny, they shouldn't need surgery, just bone alignment. A simple little splint, followed by bandaging his folded wing against his body, and the bones should mend. I freaking love the

Internet. Actually, I love people's need to display their success in step-by-step diary entries like that Californian vet did.

"Hmmm … have to admit I wouldn't have thought this possible, but … very interesting. Let me sedate the fellow and do an x-ray."

"Actually, you won't need to. He's very calm. Must be in shock or something. I'll show you." I lift Rocks out of the carry case and place him on the cool metal. He doesn't make a sound, but I know I've hurt him. "I find saying out loud what you're going to do to him works really well." Dr. Gandy raises an eyebrow at me and hands me a pair of gloves. He watches as I spread out the injured wing and explain what I think needs to be done.

"He's certainly large and healthy. Would be a shame not to try to save him."

Rocks had told me the Camazotz were unnaturally large in comparison to plain old garden-variety vampire bats. I pray Dr. Gandy doesn't ask why a vampire bat is even in this neighborhood since they aren't native to this part of the planet.

I THANK MY animal-loving guardian angels for all the times I've been to Dr. Gandy over the years with wounded animals. He knows saving animals is my number one favorite obsession—even above my nail art—so the knowledge I had about this bat, and what was wrong with it, didn't raise too much suspicion. He even allowed me to assist with the x-ray and said I should consider veterinary science as a career.

Rocks is resting on my bed. His wing is secured to his body with a gauze bandage, and he's had German shepherd for lunch. Never in a million years did I think I'd be absconding with peoples' pets so my boyfriend could munch on them. Aztec, the fifteen year-old deaf shepherd from down the street is lying on my rug. He hasn't moved a muscle even when Rocks chomped on his neck.

"He's not dead is he?" I lean over the bed to see if I can spy chest movement.

No!

Not knowing how long it takes for dogs to replenish their blood supply, I couldn't risk poor Rusty again. Since old Aztec spends 90 percent of his time napping, he was the perfect choice, except now I'm worried I'll have a dead dog to deal with. I eye Rocks.

Can sense heart beat.
Trust me.

"Sorry. It's just that he looks dead." I lean over and nudge his rump. His little snore settles my frayed nerves.

You okay?

"Yeah, it's just not what I thought it would be." I have to be honest. Rocks let me watch him feed this time. Since I met Rocks, he's been trying to work out where he belongs in the world. His colony scorns the fact that he feels more comfortable in his human form than as a Camazotz. As a result, he's on the verge of being kicked out altogether, particularly since his friendship with me has become common knowledge.

Gross?
To watch?

Oh boy. I promised myself I would never lie to Rocks. He only ever tells the truth, and I have lied to enough people in the search for my birth parents. "Not exactly. You want to know honestly?"

EEEKKK!

"If I think about you drinking blood, then that's a bit gross. But watching the bat do it, well, it kinda made me curious. You know my animal love. So as a bat it's okay, but at the same time I know it's you in there—both parts of you—so, yes and no, but mostly no. It's fine." I smile and hope I haven't said the wrong thing, if he even understands what I just said. I never want him to doubt himself because he does that enough without my help. "Wow, no wonder you're confused about who you're supposed to be."

> *Thank you.*
> *It is.*
> *Confusing.*
> *They're here.*

"Who?" I listen, scanning for bat tones, but it's close to midday. Then I hear the engine shut off, signaling my folks have arrived home a day earlier than expected.

My feet have carried me down the stairs and onto the porch before I can stop myself. Ever since my birth mother sent a letter on my eighteenth birthday explaining that I was adopted, the words Mom and Dad have caught in my throat. I've had trouble saying them out loud. I was so heartbroken and then consumed with anger that they didn't tell me. Now that I know who my biological parents are, I'm so grateful the universe gave me to Kelly and Chad. They're my mom and dad— regardless of whether our blood types match or not. *Those people who I do not deserve* are thankfully home at last.

The tension in my shoulders eases a smidgeon at the thought of adult help. I'm exhausted, and even though part one of this plan has worked, there's still a long way to go before Rocks is out of danger. I can't shake the fear that if I mess up, I might prove Decker right.

My parent's annual college reunion has revived their spirits. Dad gives Mom a kiss as he passes her to get Mini out of her car seat. Just watching them—being alive and able to watch my family—brings more tears to my eyes. Two days ago, I thought I'd never see them again, but with all the stress over Rocks, I'd pushed those feelings to the bottom of my emotional pit. I launch myself off the porch and engulf Mom in the tightest bear hug she's had from me in years.

"Connie, sweetheart." She tries to pull away, but I cling to her. "Are you all right?"

I swipe at my eyes. "I missed everyone so much. It's good to see you." I can't tell her that I thought I might never lay eyes on them again when I was kidnapped.

"How's Rocks? Tell me what happened." Her genuine concern for my secret boyfriend hurts my heart. I've been such a thorn in their side, and she's not punishing me for it.

"He's at home," I lie. "His arm got crushed." The truth. "His folks were felling a tree and it went wrong." What's one more lie? Dad is unpacking the car with gusto. Even after a long drive, you can't keep that man down.

"But he's fine?" I shrug and figure that's not a lie. Maybe I just need to answer with non-committal gestures from now on. "I was kind of hoping to find him here with you when we got back." Mom smiles that knowing smile. She would love to hear that Rocks and I are an item. But it's too new, and with everything that comes along with Rocks being a bat boy, I kinda want to keep it to myself for a while.

"Mo-om."

"Oh I know, but he's so lovely. I'm sorry he got hurt. Tell him, won't you? I'll bake him some of his favorites, and you can take them up to the market?"

Oh fudge me! Lies get you nowhere. This gets proven to me time and time again. Thinking of what whopper to spin her next pains me. I've lied to them enough, and I want it to stop. Up until now, it's been so easy to let them slip from my lips without leaving a bitter aftertaste. Letting her bake dozens of treats for Rocks that I'll end up dumping in the trash seems wrong.

I understand why Mom and Dad lied to protect me for the past eighteen years. I didn't need to know that my real flesh and blood father runs the biggest drug operation on the East coast. The lies they told me had a purpose. They were actually a safety net that I wish was still tight around me. The lies that I've been telling my parents cut a hole in that net. And nothing I can do now will change that.

"Ah, the market is closed for winter, so his family all, um, go north." God, I'm crap at this. North? Really? They aren't migrating ducks for crying out loud, even then that would be south. *Idiot.* Who would actually volunteer to spend the winter in worse weather?

"Oh, you won't be seeing him?"

"No." Finally the truth, and I let the real emotions that accompany that thought show on my face.

Mini runs up and tackles my knees. She has a giant, purple, egg-shaped bump on her forehead.

"If only I'd listened to your warnings about those McNamara twins. Totally out of control. I didn't have the heart to tell Penny." Mom brushes her fingers gently over Mini's head. I pick her up and hug her tight.

"What happened?" I ask.

"They used Mini as a shuttlecock! A shuttlecock? For a game of badminton! I'm so glad we were blessed with girls." Her smile lights up her eyes.

Blessed with girls. Her words rattle the cage that holds that secret. It really doesn't matter that I'm adopted, but I want to tell her I know. The only problem is all the crazy complications that come along with my admission. I don't want to cause them any stress or worry. I bite my tongue and sigh, burying the urge to come clean. I need to let life return to how it was before the letter arrived—simple, stress-free, and happy.

"When you have a minute, I've got something in my room to show you both."

WHILE I WAIT for my parents to finish unpacking, I use the time to research everything and anything on Sophia Ascari, the Vipers' murder trial, and Enzo. Now that Rocks is stable, I can slowly piece together what the Internet knows about the family I've never met, and hope to goodness I never will.

I angle the laptop so Rocks can see from my bed. "Yep, that's her all right."

A recent photo of my sister is filling the screen. Finding my parents was nothing short of devastating, but suddenly being told I have a sister has left a weird feeling wriggling around inside me. A sibling. I stare at her features the same way I did Josie and Enzo. We are so similar it's freaky, and that fact lessens the wriggling a little. There's someone else in the world just like me. But is she?

She works for Enzo, something I would never do, but I can't shake the curiosity about what she's like as a person. Would I recognize parts of me if I spoke to her, or am I more like Chad and Kelly than I realize? In the photo, she's surrounded by police officers—not exactly something I'm familiar with—so maybe the only thing we share is DNA and a family resemblance. The article states that they have set a date for the trial at last.

Read it.

Glancing over my shoulder, I check for signs that we're alone.

Still downstairs.
Can hear them.

"Thanks. Let me know if they come up." I half whisper. Who knew having his Camazotz hearing would be this handy. "So it says she's giving evidence at the trial in March. She apparently witnessed Mitchell Jones—he's the gang leader—and his second in charge, Raymond Ramirez shoot two plainclothes cops." I scan the rest of the article. "According to this, nobody really knows if she did see it, but the facts all point to the Vipers being responsible regardless. I guess they don't care so long as those guys do time."

Time?

"Go to prison."

Worried.
About you.

I turn and face Rocks. It's kinda weird having a conversation with a bat. Then again, I talk to Feathers all the time; I just don't expect her to answer. "I'll be okay. I mean, they're not after me now anyway. And Enzo doesn't know I exist." I shrug.

I have to admit the reality of my situation is only beginning to dawn on me. My bat protector is going to be out of action for six to eight weeks. I'm on my own again, and after what happened two days ago, it is starting to freak me out. Not to mention the fact that the boys stole a lot of money from my abductors. If the Camazotz don't come for my blood, the Vipers might.

What?

"Nothing."

Tell me.

Even when he's a bat, I can't hide from Rocks. "I was thinking about the money." I bite my lip. "I just hope they're too busy trying to keep their boss out of prison to worry about me."

Me
Stay.

"Pfft, and do what exactly? You're grounded you know." I stare into his alarmingly intelligent eyes. "Thank you for the offer. I'll keep my head down. Don't worry."

Should have.
Kissed you.
More.

Oh Rocks. Don't make me cry. My poor emotions have been through the wringer. I take a deep breath, trying to stay calm. Rocks is thinking he's not going to get the chance to kiss me again because a) the Vipers will get me first or b) he's not going to make it. Either option is unacceptable.

"Well, you'll just have to get better and come visit."

Parents coming.

Listening, I hear mom and dad on the stairs. I cross myself, praying this will go smoothly.

"How about we order take-out?" Mom's voice drifts down the hallway. Next moment, she steps into my room—and screams.

"Shhh … no!" Too late. I so didn't think this plan through. I seriously must have some kind of brain defect for not predicting this exact scenario. A quick glance at poor Rocks confirms he's unconscious. "Mom, be quiet. You'll scare him," I say, walking around my bed to get between her and Rocks before she throws him out the window. Dad is frowning and holding Mom upright.

"What on earth is that … *creature* doing on your bed? Heavens above. Where's Mini?"

"She's asleep. Well, she was," Dad answers. "Connie, what are you doing? One of those things attacked you."

I hold out my hands to prevent either of them from getting any closer. "Listen. There's absolutely zero rabies threat. He's been to see Dr. Gandy. So both of you take a deep breath and calm down." I eye them. "I found it, rescued it, and Dr. Gandy has shown me where to release it. But I need your help, Dad."

If this weren't Rocks' life we were discussing, the looks that flit across Mom's face would be hysterical. Her emotions wash over it, changing by the second, nothing is hidden, and it makes me wonder if that's why Rocks can read me so easily. I've picked up her habit of wearing my thoughts on my face. Blood and genes don't have a thing to do with it.

"Is it dead?" Dad's peering over my shoulder, studying Rocks.

"Um, sedated. He'll wake up in about ninety minutes." I give Mom the evil eye, but she's oblivious.

"Aren't you scared?" she asks, her face now showing complete and utter disgust.

"If one dog bit me, does that mean I'd never help another dog ever again?" Dad's face shows he can't argue with that logic. I focus everything I have on him because he's my ticket to saving Rocks. I explain about the underground cavern located on Blood Mountain, and that we'll need his rappelling gear to return this bat to his colony that is hibernating for the winter. My heart sinks a little when Dad doesn't look convinced.

"It won't work. It's probably going to die."

"Daddy, please. If I don't try, it will die. I can't let that happen." Everyone telling me Rocks is going to die is wearing thin. I swallow the sob that is itching to escape because Dad thinks this is just some stupid, filthy bat. "You said you wanted to take me rappelling, remember? Well, now we can do something you love, and something I love at the same time. Please," I whine.

Mini starts wailing from her room, and Mom takes that as the perfect reason to get as far away from the bat on my bed as possible. I stare at Dad. He's watching me closely. I can feel my eyes filling with tears but don't want to risk blinking. "Over the past six months, I've been ... well, I haven't been me really. I'm sorry—so sorry—because I know you both love me."

His face shows shock as he reacts to my words. "Sweetheart, of course, we love you. Why on earth would you think otherwise?"

I shrug. "If you do this, I'll be old Connie again. I promise." A frown creases his brow, and he eyes the bat for a moment. I have to get him to agree. "Aren't you at least curious about the underground cave? It will be the most exciting abseil you've ever had. Trust me."

Knowing Dad, the allure of an exciting adventure that his fellow rappelling buddies haven't experienced might be my ticket to getting him to agree to this madness. It's worth a try.

"Okay, I'll help you, but on one condition."

"Anything."

"You paint your mother's nails. If I have to hear once more how you don't have time for her any more..." He grimaces and shakes his head.

I smile because not only is that a super-easy bargain, but the fact that mom missed me as much as I've missed her sends a warm glow through my chest I hope never fades.

THE ROAD HUGS the mountainside like a snake twisting around a tree branch. We drive up and down, and up again as we pass over the surrounding smaller hills that all lead up, up, up to the king—Blood Mountain.

Rocks informed me that Blood Mountain is the highest peak on the Georgian section of the famous Appalachian Trail. It starts in Georgia and ends all the way up in Maine over two thousand miles away. He said that's why it's the perfect place for them because there's just enough traffic for the Camazotz to go unnoticed.

Giant trees hang over the road in places casting long winter shadows across the asphalt. Rounding one blind corner, Dad swears and quickly moves over to avoid an exhausted cyclist who was obviously suffering from delusions this morning when he thought it was a good idea to ride up this bad boy. I'm impressed he's made it this far.

Two more hard corners.

"I think we're really close," I say, hoping Dad won't call me out on how the hell I know where we are; all the corners we're twisting around are lined with ancient behemoth trees and look identical. Our plan is to stop off at the Mountain Crossings store—Dad has always wanted to visit and get a t-shirt—before starting our hike. It seems the store is just as famous as the mountain, and Rocks had said it's up the road from the parking lot we need.

Pulling off the road in front of the large stone building, I ask Dad not to mention the secret cave and explain that Dr. Gandy didn't want hikers upsetting the local bat population. Another lie, but who's counting now? He grunts, and I pray I'm not bringing more unwanted attention down upon the Camazotz. I'm in enough trouble as it is.

I watch while Dad goes and speaks 'hiker' with a bearded dude hugging a steaming mug outside the store.

"You doing okay?"

Yes.
You're warm.

Rocks' admission makes my ears flame. He's been snuggled on my boobs inside my hoodie for the whole trip, and I don't even care. Well, I might care a little bit, but I'm trying to be mature about it. I couldn't bear the idea of putting him in the plastic carry cage again, and he needs to be kept warm and comfortable. He can hop in my bra if it eases his pain. If I were going to get all self-conscious about it, then the fact that he looks way too comfortable would make me dig a hole to bury myself—but I'm not. Besides, this is last time I'm going to see him for a while, and since he's my boyfriend, I figure he's allowed to "rest" there for now. Although if Dad knew who was really down my top, I'm sure Rocks would be riding in the trunk. I blush at the thought of telling my dad I have a boyfriend.

Look up.

"What?"

Out window.

Lowering the window, I lean out, trying not to disturb Rocks.

"Huh? No way."

Aeronaughts are odd.
Perfectly good condition.

To the left of the store is a massive, old tree. It's easily forty or fifty-feet high, but it doesn't appear that big because of its giant siblings covering the rolling mountain ridges surrounding us. Hanging from the lower branches are dozens and dozens of hiking boots. It's not at all what I was expecting when Rocks told me to look up. Even with that many pairs of boots hanging in the tree like weird Christmas baubles, the tree is in no way diminished by them. It gives it an odd beauty.

Pairs of boots only hang from the lower section, but some of the hikers must have a pretty mean throwing arm. Climbers or hikers must tie their old boots together and launch them into the tree after they summit Blood Mountain. Or maybe after they buy a new pair at the store? Who would buy boots in the middle of nowhere on a mountainside? Wouldn't that be the sign of an unprepared hiker to wait until now for boots? I stare at the different pairs in awe. Who started it? How long have they been there? I guess if I was fluent in 'hiker' I could find out from Mr. Man-Vs-Wild still chatting to Chad.

"Yeah, that is pretty odd. Are any of them your size?" I smile at him.

Check Decker's feet.

"Decker stole a pair of these?" I don't know whether to imagine a bat wrestling with the boots, the laces all twisted up around the branch, or whether he flips high up on a sturdy limb and picks his way through the dozens of sizes and designs.

Not stealing.
Recycling.

I laugh. "You told me you didn't know about recycling at Christmas?"

Fast learner.

Dad returns with water, a t-shirt for me and him, a small map, and a radiant smile. He's obviously been told we're in for a treat and is excited at the prospect. "The parking lot's just down the road. Two minutes."

The first thing I notice getting out of the car is the sound of running water. But looking around the parking area carved out of the forest, I can't see any sign of a stream. Rocks must sense my confusion. I sniff the clean, forest air and it chills my nose.

Left.
Down below.
Under road.

Before I can investigate, I need to keep us both warm. I pull on my down jacket and slowly zip it up so that Rocks is peeking out over the zipper. He's secure and warm for our hike.

When Dad re-checks our gear, I walk under a massive fur tree that hangs over where we parked. Rocks is correct. A little stream bubbles over the uneven stones below the parking area. The water is crystal clear, and I'm betting would taste wonderful on a hot summer's day.

Dad is over by the information sign checking for alerts, or whatever kinds of things dads check for. Heading up this trail in winter isn't the smartest move, but we can't exactly wait. Luckily, there hasn't been much snow over Christmas so the trail should be clear.

Dad is in his element. This is his world—hiking and rock climbing—so I'm not going to give him a hard time for taking our safety seriously. I've fallen into a habit of little snide remarks and eye rolls when it comes to my parents over the last six months. It's a habit I'll gladly break because I'm so grateful he's helping me return Rocks to his roost.

"You ready?" He smiles. I nod and follow him off the asphalt.

Ferns grow on the ground where the light pierces the thick canopy of forest branches. The canopy isn't very impressive as the bare branches showcase winter's hold on the landscape. Birds sing from above, but I can't find them. The path is quiet due to the time of year, and with each step we take trekking higher and higher, my lungs begin to wheeze, and my thigh muscles burn. *Crabapples, this is hard work.* Dad gives me his hand to help me over a couple of icy sections and looks as though he's barely even raised a sweat. My fitness is embarrassing.

The summit of Blood Mountain has a little stone cabin on the top. The view is amazing in a desolate kind of way. In summer, when a kaleidoscope of different greens cover the landscape, I imagine it's spectacular, but now it looks barren and remote—the perfect place to hide a colony of Camazotz for the winter.

Behind cabin.
No path.
Walk down.

Dad looks at me like I've announced the world is flat when I tell him we need to take the path—that isn't really a path—off the side of the summit. To his credit, he doesn't say anything, but I have a feeling he's making mental calculations of our exact location for later when he's sure I'll have us both completely lost. I'm convinced the only reason he's trusting me is because he *thinks* Dr. Gandy gave me these super secret, special instructions on how to find the bat colony.

I follow Rocks' mental directions. Taking a left at this tree, climbing over a moss-covered fallen log, past this boulder or that. Dad follows carrying the ropes we'll need to get into the cave, and I'm praying he really is remembering how the hell we get back because I certainly won't have Rocks' voice in my head as my personal GPS.

We pass dozens of large boulders overgrown with red lichen. Rocks tells me that some people believe that's how Blood Mountain got its name. I have to bite my lip from answering him and try to convey my interest with my eyes only. I want to say that the colony is practically advertising their roost location with the design on their paper shopping bag at Sanguine Mountain market.

Gnarled tree.
Entrance below.

I spy the ancient pine. It stands out being one of the only trees in the area that isn't deciduous. The wind must have battered it in its youth because its wide branches are spread across the mountainside, twisted and irregular. It gives it a stunted appearance rather than the normal straight-as-a-ruler pine that aims to touch the sky. The trunk would take at least four people to circle its circumference with their outstretched arms—it's enormous.

When we get closer, I see it's growing close to a rocky outcrop of grey boulders that it partially shields. One large moss-covered rock stands like a lonely sentinel next to the base. It's trying to cover the dark, black gash in the mountain behind it.

"This is the entrance," I call to Dad, standing next to the tree, a few feet from the gaping hole to the underground cavern. Dad catches up, a slow smile spreading across his features.

"This'll be fun. Can't believe I've never heard about it before." He starts examining the boulder and trunk for a place to secure our lines. Dad is anxious about lowering me—the rappelling beginner—into an unknown cavern. I insist that I need to return the bat before he disturbs them with his sightseeing. He agrees that I can go first so long as he can test the depth of the drop first. A massive coil of rope disappears into the pit. Dad and I both listen to see if it hits the bottom. Nothing.

Aeronaughts! Aeronaughts! Aeronaughts!
Aeronaughts! Aeronaughts! Aeronaughts!

A chorus of alarmed voices rings between my ears. I jump, grabbing my head between both my hands, and Rocks squawks in surprise. Dad turns around and frowns, the silence of the forest making my display even weirder.

"You okay?"

I'll never get used to other peoples' voices rattling around in my head. I imagine the horror that's showing across my face. My smile feels plastic so I try to smooth my features and act nonchalant—who am I kidding? I'm standing on the side of a mountain with a bat clinging to my boobs feeling like I'm going to be hung, drawn and quartered by the angry mob dwelling below ground. Yeah, I must look super calm. Dad turns and starts pulling the rope back out of the chasm, grinning widely.

"Don't be nervous, sweetheart." He thinks I'm nervous? Yeah, I'm not so much focused on the 'dangling off the end of a rope in the dark' as I would have been. More worried about being let back out of that hole—alive and not bleeding.

Rockland home.
Stay calm.
Everyone flip.
Now.

Rocks is communicating with his fellow Camazotz. Feigning nonchalance is hard when there's a yelling match between your temples about the ethics and consequences of bringing an aeronaught to their highly classified home. Sweat runs down my forehead. I don't like the fact that more than one voice is mentioning the broken blood oath. Am I handing Rocks over to be sentenced to death at a later date?

Fudge me!

"What's the welcoming committee going to do to me when I get down there?" I ask under my breath, as Dad starts whistling some old Western movie theme.

You're safe.

Can't say that I feel it after hearing the aggression in their tone, but deep down I know Rocks would never willingly put me in any danger. Then I remind myself that I'm the one that insisted on this harebrained scheme. I take a deep breath and go to my father. He helps me with the harness, careful not to disturb Rocks, and places the ugliest helmet on my head. *Awesome.* I'm going to trespass on sacred Camazotz soil looking like the world's biggest loser.

Dad's safety lecture ensues. I thought the one in the car was bad, but that was before he saw the chasm. The worst part is the start. That involves me stepping backward off the entrance boulder into thin freaking air and trusting the ropes to hold. My hands shake, and if it weren't for the fact that I can see my legs, I'd be convinced I left them in the car—they've gone completely numb from fear. The last thing Dad does is click the helmet lamp on and rap his knuckle twice on my helmet.

"It's about 150 feet from what I can measure. You're going to be blown away." He grins. I swallow, staring at the red coils of rope by his feet. "Have fun."

"You're kidding, right?" His laughter doesn't help as I step back onto nothing.

I'm doing this for Rocks.

I'm doing this for Rocks.

It takes a moment for my eyes to adjust to the instant darkness. The entrance is barely five feet wide and maybe six foot across at its deepest part. Not much light follows me below the surface. My harnessed body slowly spins in the void and what I see takes my breath away.

"Holy sugarplums will you look at that."

5
Suits

THE silence is overwhelming.

After the yelling match that just took place in my head, the Camazotz are suddenly dumbstruck. It's undoubtedly the helmet. Then again, they're all probably soaking up the details of the device that's allowing me to breach their sanctuary. The cave entrance is perfect to protect the colony from nature's enemies, but not from pesky, rappelling aeronaughts.

The warmer air in the cave caresses my chilled cheeks. Dad had explained that cave temperatures rarely fluctuate all year since they aren't affected by surface temperatures. Now that it's winter, the cave is warm. Making it the perfect winter hideaway for the colony.

Now that I trust the ropes and Dad up above, I'm stunned by the vast nothingness that surrounds me. My helmet lamp illuminates a mere fraction of the cave. I can sense their eyes tracking my descent, and the beam of light catches the odd Camazotz winging itself to safety.

I use my senses like Rocks has taught me. Taking a deep breath, I get a whiff of strange scents. "Is that smoke?"

I look around behind me, which causes my whole body to slowly rotate on the dangling ropes. In the far corner of the cave is a glowing brazier. It's abandoned, but the ground is littered with small objects, proving it wasn't deserted a moment ago.

The section of ceiling I can see above is completely covered in bats—Camazotz—Rocks' colony and family. Distinct groups can be seen huddling together, no doubt each wing. The sheer number of them amazes me. I wonder where the Land wing is and what they're thinking now. Suddenly my feet touch loose gravel—my ride is over. I stare up at the crack of light filtering through the entrance and feel tiny in the vastness of the chasm. Dad instructed that I had fifteen minutes to find a spot for Rocks and then signal to be pulled to the surface.

"This is amazing," I say to Rocks as I unlock the blue carabiner and detach from the lines. "Shit!" My hand flies up to protect Rocks on instinct.

Three men have flipped almost on top of me in the darkness. My heart is beating double-time, which Rocks can probably feel. Strickland, Cypress, and Ash are my not-so-welcoming committee. Ash and his fang tattoos are mere inches from my face.

"You're dead, naught!" he growls.

Rocks starts squawking and wriggling around inside my jacket. The sound echoes off the hard, limestone walls.

"Silence," Strickland commands, gripping Ash's elbow. I angle my headlamp straight up so I don't blind them all, as I look from face-to-face in quick succession.

"Who the hell is on sentinel duty?" Strickland sneers, looking at Cypress. I swallow the lump of dread, praying it wasn't an aeronaught-friendly bat that's now in trouble.

A second later, a kind face appears out of the gloom—Decker. Rocks' half brother and his sire, Judge—with the puckered scar that runs the length of his face—have flipped and joined the group. Decker muscles his way between me and Ash, standing his ground. The boys are chest-to-chest and stare each other down in a way that makes my blood run cold.

"Leave her alone," he snarls. Looking across to Strickland, he adds, "She has saved your son."

Even I can sense the venom in his words. Decker should not be challenging the colony Sire on my account, considering I just crashed their slumber party.

"I know I'm not supposed to be here, but what else was I going to do? I couldn't let him die." I unzip my jacket and gently lift Rocks from my torso, holding him toward Strickland. "His wing will heal. Trust me. You can feed him, right?"

I look around the circle of faces—three murderous and two grateful. All of them are focused on his bandaged wing and the two small wooden splints sticking out the top of the bandage. I'd give up my cell phone for a whole month to know what's going through their minds.

Decker steps in and takes Rocks from me. "Yes, we can feed him. Will it really heal?"

I nod. "Will take time though. Since this is a first, I think he should wait the human healing time rather than the bat."

"I owe you," he replies softly. I wonder if he's thinking about the blood oath he broke, and the fact that all present think it was Rocks.

She saved me.
Thank her.
Father.

Strickland's eyes go wide. Even in the darkness of the cave, I can clearly see he's livid.

"Do *not* tell me what to do when you have broken our highest law. You brought an aeronaught to our place of refuge," he spits between gritted teeth. "Do our blood oaths mean nothing to you now?"

I need to do something. Rocks was in no condition to argue with me when I thought of this plan. Strickland will never believe how much of a fight he put up. Or that he was willing to risk dying.

"Rocks told me his life would be forfeited if he disclosed this location to an aeronaught. Well, the way I saw it, his life would be lost if he didn't tell me. I pressured him to do it. I believe, and so does the veterinarian—the special doctor—that he can survive this. His life is in your hands. And I swear to you on the lives of my family, I will not tell a soul."

Cypress—the Fold member with the violent tattoos inked over his bare torso that depict humans gushing blood from puncture wounds—bares his teeth in an angry grimace. I look to Judge, hoping for support.

"She's trying to save your son's life, Strickland," Judge says in a voice that calms me.

"I know you blame me for what happened, and believe me I feel responsible, but just so you know, it was a bat that crushed his wing."

Five sets of eyes are suddenly on me. "Explain," Strickland commands. Strickland's personality reminds me of cold steel, such a contrast to his warm-hearted son.

"When Rocks came to rescue me, there was a Camazotz involved. A Camazotz did this to him. Find that bat!"

"She's lying. How on earth would one of us be involved in aeronaught business?" Cypress sneers.

It's true.

"It's irrelevant. What matters is—" Strickland says.

"Irrelevant?" I gasp. "It's irrelevant who tried to murder your son?" Judge takes a step closer. I sense I should not be taunting the Sire on his turf. Strickland's eyes narrow, and I instinctively add to the distance between us. "I'm sorry. I should go."

"Do not return to this place or you will pay," Ash growls. The three of them turn their backs on me as though they're about to flip.

"Um ... ah ... you see ..." *Oh crabapples.* They're going to kill me when they hear this. "Strickland, sir?"

The Sire half turns, not even bothering to look at me over his shoulder. I swallow the lump of lead that's lodged in my throat. "My dad is about to come down here for a ... quick look ... um, everybody better flip."

Curse words that I won't repeat are uttered from the three not-so-aeronaught-friendly members. I stammer and stutter, trying to explain that the only way my dad would agree to this trip was if he got to explore the cave for a few minutes. If looks could kill ...

Strickland starts issuing orders resulting in Cypress and Ash flipping instantly and disappearing into the gloom. I'm trying to process what he's talking about. Rocks' good wing is hanging over Decker's shoulder, so he's resting sideways on his chest. His eyes never leave mine.

Turning in a circle, I look to the brazier and that's when I notice a hay bail. An instant later, four Camazotz flip and start clearing away their little campfire set up.

Decker says narrow passageways and tunnels run deep into the mountain off the main cavern. They keep a couple of animals for feeding if extreme winter weather descends on their mountain, making it too cold to venture out to feed. I watch two of the men slide a wooden beam between the bars of the brazier and carry it away.

Now that Ash and Cypress have left, my heart rate slows. Since I'm not in fight-or-flight mode, I take a few steps into the darkness, exploring another part of Rocks' life. The cavern is enormous. The beam from my headlamp runs out before it reaches the far wall. To my right, I notice a reflection. There's an underground stream running along the sidewall. The gentle trickle of water adding to the ambience of the cave.

Show her.

Decker immediately steps closer and takes my hand. He leads me a short distance toward the running water that suddenly disappears underground. We round a massive chunk of rock, but as I look up I see it's a giant stalagmite. It stretches up toward the roof of the cave and must have taken centuries to form.

"Crouch down and shine your light in there," Decker says in my ear, as he angles my headlamp at a black hole at ankle level.

Kneeling down, the beam of light illuminates a magical scene. "Oh my God."

Decker chuckles. "Impressive, huh?"

Near ground level, there's an open fissure in the cave wall, and when I peer inside, it takes my breath away. There's a round, glowing pool of deep, blue water, but that's not the impressive part. The low ceiling of this little alcove is covered in hundreds of shiny, stalactites. Hanging down, they remind me of some creepy dinosaur's mouth—one that has rows and rows of razor sharp teeth one behind the other. The occasional drips from the tips of the tiny mounds sends a ripple over the still water.

When Decker leads me back to Strickland, the hay is gone—all evidence erased. "If your father returns here *ever* again, he will pay a blood price." The Sire has spoken. I nod and return to the ropes hanging from the ceiling.

"Wait." Decker says, and the Sire stops. "We need to get Rocks up on one of the ledges. Maybe Connie should do it so we don't mess this up." He points to the small wooden splints poking out the top of the bandage on Rocks' wing.

A discussion between Strickland and Decker takes place. He's more respectful than he was earlier and that allows my heart rate to stay low. Decker explains it would be best to place Rocks on one of the small ledges high off the ground. If he's going to be in the cast for two months, it will get tiresome handing him off from person to person down here. If he's on a ledge, he'll be safe and more independent.

I hook into the harness once more as Decker places Rocks inside my jacket. Giving the signal to Dad, I'm slowly pulled off the ground. When I'm half way up, a dozen Camazotz appear, take hold of the rope and pull me into the darkness on my right. I must weigh more than they expected because Decker's voice sounds inside my head asking for twice that many bats to help. I lose count of how many respond to tug me toward the side of the cavern. Dad's probably wondering what the hell I'm doing as the rope becomes taut.

A second later, Decker flips on a ledge that's barely wide enough for him to sit on. He digs his heels into the rock and leans over to grab my hand, anchoring me to the wall. The Camazotz holding the rope fly off, and with my free hand, I unzip my jacket.

Handing Rocks over leaves me with a sense of foreboding. I have to have faith that the fascination of whether he really can survive a broken wing will prevent the Fold from doing anything drastic.

Be careful.

"Get better," I say, looking at Rocks. Decker has placed him on the tiny ledge. I want to touch him one last time, but I can feel Dad yanking on the ropes above. Decker lets go of my hand and I swing freely across the open cavern.

Back in the parking lot, Dad is on a rappelling high. He's always super agreeable whenever he returns from his adventures, and finally I understand why. It's usually a great time to ask for extra nail polish money because he often says yes without thinking.

"That cavern is one of the most amazing places I've seen," he says, stowing the gear in the trunk.

Fudge. He cannot under any circumstances bring his buddies here. "You promised me you wouldn't come back here, remember?"

Dad huffs. "Yeah, I won't tell anyone. Damn conservationists," he mutters. "Actually, all those bats … kinda creepy, don't you think?"

I freeze. "Huh?"

"I don't know." He pulls a face. "Felt like I was being watched."

"Well, they were. Probably getting ready to escape from the big, noisy human intruders."

"No, not like that. More like they were *aware*. Silly, huh?" He shrugs.

"Totally." Oh, good grief!

THE LAST FEW days of my Christmas vacation suck without Rocks. Knowing he's not going to visit for at least eight weeks brings the dark clouds of doom back with a vengeance. Neither of us knows how long his wing will take to heal. This is new territory, and since he can't flip, texting him is useless.

I dump my backpack on the floor and take a seat at our kitchen island. The house smells of my favorite—beans—but it's a cruel reminder of the boy that nicknamed me after them.

"Here you go," Mom says, placing a small bowl on the counter. "How was school?"

I shrug one shoulder as my hunger evaporates. I miss my boyfriend, but it's more than that. Rocks wasn't just my boyfriend; he was my best friend and secret keeper. Since I met him last July, he had become part of the family. I shove the barely touched bowl away, apologize, and retreat to my room.

Firing up the laptop doesn't help. I've been so obsessed with discovering the identity of my birth parents that now that the search is over, I don't know what to do with myself. I read more about vampire bats, but that doesn't ease the churning in my gut either. I hope he's doing okay. What if he can't fly again? I wonder. That line of thinking twists my intestines into a knot. I close the laptop and pull out my suitcase full of nail polish.

By my tenth Rocks-less day, I'm ready to jump out my window. It's Saturday, and last night's Bun Lovin' Barn shift not only sucked, but dragged on for all eternity. No super cute, Victorian-mannered gentleman was waiting to escort me home. Rocks never got the chance to walk me home since we'd started dating. I know we would have stopped off in the park to make-out, and I was looking forward to that more than anything. Getting a lift from Tiff was a poor substitute.

I spend way too many hours sitting by my window staring at the trees. Hoping. Then a moment of reality hits, forcing me to accept that Rocks isn't going to come flying in anytime soon. He's at the roost, and I bet those Camazotz girls are showering him in love and affection.

Fudge sundae.

I drag my nail polish supplies down to the living room and set up on the coffee table. It's time to come good on my deal with Dad and give Mom's nails some long overdue attention. She's sitting on the couch cutting out recipes from a stack of magazines. When *the mother I've been ignoring* notices I'm setting up my supplies, my guilt skyrockets. Her face lights up the whole room, and she immediately sits on the floor and places her fingers out wide on the coffee table. I'm the worst daughter ever.

"Got a design in mind?" she asks.

"No. You?" I sit opposite and let the quiet calm that my nail art brings wash over me. The smells of polish and acetone fill the air. I have to get out of this funk I'm slowly drowning in without Rocks. Mom starts flicking through the nail designs I've downloaded to my phone.

"You heard from Rocks?"

I flinch. When I look up, she's focused on me and not the phone. I glance over at Dad in the armchair, newspaper blocking us from view and shake my head.

"Did you two hang out here before he hurt himself?" she says quietly, fishing for clues.

I want to tell her, I really do, but it's ... complicated—my least favorite saying in the entire universe. But when it comes to Rocks and I, it's actually true. My mood darkens as I think about all the secrets I'm still holding and wish I could share with her. My brain floods with questions about my adoption, but after I take a deep breath, I know that subject is best left buried. Part of me is convinced the reason they didn't tell me I'm adopted is because they know about Enzo Ascari. But, if that's true, I can't work out why Dad reports Enzo's evil-doings like clockwork to Mom during their daily husband-reads-the-news hour. If he's such a secret, why mention Enzo's name? Or is he closely monitoring Enzo to keep track? Or do they have no clue whom I'm related to?

Fudge me. My brain hurts, but my heart hurts more. What I do know is that the pain in my heart lessens each time I call them Mom and Dad again.

Mom is staring at me. I try to clear my mind of the endless loop of questions and take another deep breath. "He popped in the day you left, but …" I shrug.

"You miss him, don't you?" she whispers.

"So much."

My admission causes tears to well in my eyes. Rocks has not abandoned me, but I feel so upside down. I never knew my feelings for a boy could be this powerful. Six months ago, I didn't need him to start my search for my parents, but now I miss him so much it aches. I rub my stomach wishing it were that simple. There's more to it than simply missing my boyfriend.

With every day he's not here, and with all that happened, the feeling of vulnerability is growing. But that's not all, I'm starting to feel scared—scared for him mostly, but scared also about what will happen if the Vipers decide they want their money back. My intuition has never been great, but it won't let me forget that the Vipers think I stole their cash. I bite my lip hard to prevent myself from spilling everything to Mom. The cops would be called, and it would be nothing short of a disaster. No media or police attention needs to be given to my family. They need to stay off the radar—safe and anonymous. Mom squeezes my hand.

"Ooh, how about this design?" she says, holding up my phone.

The screen shows tiny purple—oh, crap—owls.

"You haven't done them before, have you?"

I try not to look disgusted. "No."

"Perfect." Yeah, the perfect reminder of Rocks' enemy number one, or are they? That Camazotz Joey is a total mystery. A mystery I'm not going to solve without access to that bitchy bat, Zabreena. How does she know him? I rub my temples before adjusting Mom's left hand on the table.

My kidnapping and Rocks' wing drama forced his biggest problem—the owl attacks on the colony—from my mind. Questions. Questions. Questions. It's all I've got. When am I going to get some fudging answers? I start with the base coat and let the fumes bring order to the chaos in my brain.

Who released the Great Horned owls that are attacking and killing colony members?

Who the hell is Joey?

Why is he working for the Vipers?

Why does he loathe Rocks and want him dead?

Does he share the same ideals as the Mac and Plant wings that want my blood?

Is this a wing conspiracy?

"Listen to this," Dad says. He's pointing the remote at the digital box below our flat screen rewinding a news story.

A pretty, red-haired news anchor fills the screen. "Residents of Floyd County have reported five bat attacks since the New Year. First, three teenage girls were attacked at dusk, and now an elderly husband and wife while out walking. Witnesses are yet to identify what species is responsible. Local wildlife officials are looking into the matter amid fears that rabies may be the reason behind this unusual aggression. Hikers are urged to take care and be on the lookout."

When Dad's eyes move to my forehead, I realize I'm rubbing my scar. Given all I know about bats, this can't be a coincidence. It's winter. Real bats hibernate according to Rocks. What the hell is going on?

My enthusiasm for life at present means the parking lot is full by the time I drag myself to school on Monday. Finding a spot down the street, I half jog to make it to class before the bell. Near the school gate, I catch my reflection in the heavily tinted windows of a shiny Lincoln Town Car. Not wanting to have Tiff on my case about what's going on from my ragged appearance, I stop and use my fingers to comb my hair into a high ponytail. My blonde hair stands out in the dark reflection and stirs the image in my memory of the golden girl standing with the midnight boy in the forest.

My window mirror begins to slowly vanish, and I gasp, stumbling backward realizing the car is occupied. The tinted glass lowers to reveal a man in his early thirties with greased down, sandy-blond hair sitting in the passenger seat. His cologne hits me as I turn and run to class.

English with Tiff starts my week. I used to love English, but that's the one class I share with Parker Reed—the wrestling jock I dated for a nanosecond. I was trying to take my mind of Rocks back when I believed a Camazotz would never be interested in a boring aeronaught.

"You spoken to him yet?" Tiff whispers as Mrs. Yamaguchi turns to write on the board.

"Nope." She rolls her eyes. "What? Why should I?"

Parker ran off and left me behind the gym when we—actually he—got attacked by Rocks and his friends. Parker doesn't know that I *know* I wasn't in any danger—that's not the point. The point is he left me. He was more than happy to hang around going for the boob grab, but the second there's trouble, he takes off faster than Mini in a toy store.

"He was scared. What are the odds of you being attacked twice by bats?" She frowns. "For your sake, I hope that doesn't happen in threes."

So do I. The last thing I need is another Camazotz attack.

After school, we decide to head to the mall. Mini's second birthday is next week, and I haven't really felt like shopping. Brandy and Mary Lou are going to meet Tiff and I outside the toy store.

"Where the heck are you parked?" Tiff asks. I point down the street to the last car in sight. "Well, that explains why I couldn't find you before class, sleepy head."

A chill runs up my spine the instant I spot the black Town Car and that same man wearing a suit leaning against the door. He has a younger friend, who's built like he's related to Rambo, standing at attention next to him. I study my scuffed boots as we walk past. My lungs constrict telling me my gut does not think this is a coincidence.

They're not here for me. They're not here for me. They're not here for me.

The urge to look over my shoulder is too much. As suspected, their eyes are on me, and I quickly look away. Why are two men in suits standing on the curb outside my school?

"Let's get out of here."

Tiff looks at me funny, before glancing over her shoulder. "You okay? You're a bit pale."

I dig through my backpack for my inhaler as we stop by my Honda. I can't help but glance again. If they're watching the school, then they're simply waiting for some rich kid …

Rambo and Co. are not leaning on the car. Instead, they're standing in the middle of the sidewalk, both with their arms folded, facing Tiff and I. She looks from me to them as I fumble with my keys.

"I know that look."

"What look?" I lock the doors once we're both inside.

"It's the same look you had the night with that van."

6
Seahorse

Bat POV

THE cave erupts into chaos the second the large aeronaught male disappears from view through the high entrance. Camazotz take flight, filling the gaping cavern with a cacophony of screeching as they flit from one perch to the next. Their sonic senses prevent collision as they narrowly miss one another in the harrowing aerobatics display. The Sire's voice is heard loud and clear in every Camazotz mind. He lists the males he wants to secure their perimeter when that ghastly girl and her father depart.

Zander.

Harland.

Ash.

Jeremiah.

Jet.

Foxhunt.

The six bats leave their wings, darting through the squall of bodies, to quickly pass under the yawning cave entrance. They don't linger in the beam of light that peters out a dozen feet down as the aeronaughts are still above ground. Strickland is occupying the Sire's den to the left of the entrance. It's a large, hidden alcove dug high up into the mountainside. It allows him to keep a watchful eye over his domain and monitor all comings and goings from the roost, yet is safe from enemy breaches.

All the bats, including the Fold, roost lower to the right in the large, open cavity to give the Sire the space and respect he commands. Life at the roost has been this way since the Camazotz first discovered the hidden caves when they claimed Blood Mountain.

His young mate, ScarletFall, is hanging by the entrance to the alcove. Her slender body quivers from witnessing the horror of aeronaughts breaching their aerial sanctuary with apparent ease. She had seen climbers once—with similar harnesses—on a sheer, rocky, outcrop four peaks over, but never dreamed they could use that equipment to enter her home. Strickland waits on the ledge of the opening, his wings spread wide in a dominant stance, waiting for the summoned males. They assemble in order of rank with Zander front and center, and the others steadily beating their wings to hover close behind.

> *Follow them.*
> *Guard duty till nightfall.*
> *Check forest.*
> *Be vigilant.*

The bats move to the entrance to wait until nothing but birdcalls and the gentle sway of pine needles can be heard from above.

Decker has recruited Baxter, Bailey, and Moonshiner to bring enough straw from the far cavern to build Rockland a soft nest for this two-month recuperation. He clings to the cave wall above his brother watching the little bats flying toward them, their claws full.

> *Gentle.*
> *Slow down.*

He commands the eager bats as they approach in a line. Baxter lands with the grace of a fledger and doesn't jostle the larger bat resting close to the lip of the ledge. He dumps his load of hay, immediately jumping off the stone edge to get more. Hay rains down on the wounded bat from above as Moonshiner unloads while airborne.

> *Stop that.*
> *Land next time.*

The shy bat gives one squawk of acknowledgment before turning for another trip. Decker stretches out a wing to nudge the lump of hay off his unmoving brother. Rocks is in bad shape, and has used most of his energy hiding the agony he's clearly in from his girlfriend. Decker had hoped when Connie agreed to return him that it would've been sooner. Once he's made Rockland comfortable, he'll organize a feed. The little one-eyed bat hovers just below the ledge, her wings pumping hard from exertion.

Hurry up, Bailey.
Drop it.

The little bat puffs as she beats her wings, slowly rising up to reveal claws full of ... not hay, but one hot pink, well-loved seahorse.

For you.

She looks at her big brother, but he has closed his eyes. She's happy he's not panting like he was earlier when Miss Connie put him on the rocky outcrop. His wing is tied to his body with cream-colored bandages, and she knows her little seahorse will take the pain away.

No seahorse.
Straw!

But ... she replies.

No.

The large bat opens his eye and looks at his brother hanging above. He communicates that the seahorse can stay, before closing his eyes again. Letting Connie think he was fine took more from him than he had to spare. He had to be strong for her or she would worry for two months. The thought of staying trapped in this animal form for eight long weeks makes him want to roll off the ledge. How will he survive this torture, let alone the pain every time he tries to move?

She said the pain will ease in time and so did that doctor, but he's not convinced. His thirst is greater than he's ever experienced. He fed from that sleepy beast only twenty-four hours earlier. How can he need more blood already?

The little bat sets the seahorse down beside him. He doesn't want her to fret either; she's been through enough, and that pink lump might make a comfy pillow once the straw is settled.

Decker leaves his brother to find their mother. The Sire summoned Zada shortly after the patrol was given their instructions. He doesn't wish to face Strickland any more than he needs to in case he admits to the lie. Letting his brother take the blame for disclosing their roost weighs heavily on the young male. The Fold will judge Rockland harshly for the crime, but what choice did Decker have? He would have promised Rocks the world to ease his pain and suffering, but little did he know how hard it would be to fulfil the promise back at the roost, surrounded by the not-so-subtle judgments echoing back and forth across the cave. Judgments that his brother does not deserve.

Graceland informs him their mother is still with the Sire when he stops by the Land wing. Taking flight, he gets as close to the den as he's comfortable with, but he can't see the female. She's still inside, so he heads back to check on the progress of his siblings. He apologizes to Rocks for not feeding last night, and therefore not being able to offer the wounded bat a meal. Jeremiah fed, but can't help since he won't be back from patrol until dark.

Wake up.

His brother stirs, slowly trying to lift his head.

Need blood.

It's coming, Decker confirms.

The stream of aerial traffic past the ledge is increasing. Decker wants to shoo the gawkers away, but the bandage and splint on Rockland's wing is a sight to behold. If Connie is right, and it's true what the animal doctor can do, then he knows the colony needs to witness the spectacle first hand, yet he can't help but feel for his brother on display. If the judgment for breaking the blood oath is put to a colony vote, Decker knows the only thing that might save Rockland is if the members witness the cure for certain death. No Camazotz has ever survived a broken wing. It's a slow, nasty death every member secretly fears.

Several years ago, Decker remembers the agonizing death of his uncle, Shepard. The Camazotz was feeding under the cover of darkness on a small, sleeping deer and didn't hear the sly bobcat stalking up behind. Whether the cat was hunting the bat or the deer they'll never know, but in the struggle that followed, the bobcat snapped both of Shepard's wings. The staggering pain caused the male to flip, scaring the life out of the cat before it fled into the underbrush. Shepard managed to walk back to the roost by dawn.

The brave Camazotz sheltered under the great pine as members of the Trade wing fed him for three days, but his wings were completely mutilated. On the evening of the fourth day, when they left the roost at dusk, Shepard was gone. The Sire ordered no member of the colony to search for the wounded Camazotz. During the day, Shepard had turned into a man and made the decision to leave. Once he found a secluded spot, he no doubt flipped and waited till dehydration claimed him.

Rockland will not suffer that same dreaded fate.

The excitement of Connie and her father visiting, and Rockland's return has woken most of the usually sleepy bats. When the Camazotz aren't on market duties, they tend to prefer a more nocturnal routine—sleep late, flip to make goods for sale in the afternoon, feed at dusk, fly hard till midnight embracing the call of the wild, then return to the roost several hours before dawn. Decker scans the sea of moving bodies for Zada.

When he told his mother of Connie's plan, she was as highly skeptical as he was, but in preparation, she stayed well fed—if only he had done the same. He curses his decision to stay in last night. If he had access to a phone like Rockland, Connie could have texted him so he would have known his brother was returning today. One day, he will own a device too. He's saving his earnings from his metal work, and

Rockland knows Connie will take him shopping when he has enough saved.

The Sire's voice echoes for a second time inside his head. He calls a dozen young females to the den—immediately. That command silences the exuberant colony members. Decker watches the young bats congregate in the middle of the open space before heading toward the den. The girls are no doubt nervous about the unusual summons. Rebekkah, Phoenix, AuburnSky, Violet, Lavender, Macantia, Madison, RedFaith … Decker loses track of the young females as they enter the den. What is the Sire doing, and why does he still need Zada?

Trying to be patient, he flips onto the tiny ledge, careful not to stand on Rockland's good wing. The dizzying height doesn't bother him, and using just the tips of his fingers against the rough stone, he balances himself with ease. Picking up his brother as gently as he can manage, he arranges the straw bedding.

"I'm so sorry, brother. I should have been prepared. Just wait a little longer, and Zada will be here. She's the only one Jeremiah and I could trust with our plan. If Strickland had heard we were letting Connie bring you back, we'd be wolf bait," he whispers.

I know.

Rockland flinches as his brother lays him back in the soft dry grass. His wing is throbbing and his thirst is the worst he's ever known. All he can think about is feeding; gorging himself on whatever beast is dumb enough to stay still long enough. He wishes Decker had snuck him to feed from the goats first, but Connie only had minutes before her father would get worried, and too many eyes were watching them.

When the shaman cursed the Camazotz, the magic used was dark and powerful. Rockland has often wondered about the villagers of that time, and what they were like because the terms and conditions that came along with the spell were complicated. No Camazotz can stomach the blood from another Camazotz. Were his ancient ancestors prone to cannibalism? Or did the shaman not understand the magic he was weaving?

As bats, they can feed from run-of-the-mill, weak, little aeronaughts for a powerful snack, but they can never drink the blood from their own kind. When the Camazotz feed each other, they regurgitate the blood of the animal they fed from to the bat in need. They never actually allow their own blood to be consumed. If Decker could, he'd slice open his vein now, but it would be a useless gesture. With his fast metabolism, his meal from the night before last is long gone. He weighs up the risk of being seen heading to the goat keep. The goats are for emergencies only, to see the colony through harsh, winter storms. And feeding from them is only allowed once the Sire commands it.

Zander re-appears from his patrol with news that the colony is safe and secure—the aeronaughts have left the mountain. He disappears into the den to give his full report in private.

Strickland emerges later followed by Zada and the young girls. They glide down to the cavern floor while Zander does the rounds collecting other Camazotz to join them. When the whole Land wing take flight, Decker gets nervous. Before he can figure out what the Sire is up to, he's summoned along with all of Rockland's siblings and closest cousins from other wings.

Strickland waits for quiet before making his announcement. "These females," —he points to the twelve— "and ONLY these females will be responsible for feeding and nursing Rockland."

"What the—" Decker starts, but is stopped by the ice in Strickland's glare.

"No arguments. Are we clear? They have their duty. Matter closed."

Decker eyes the group of girls, trying to hold back his curse of horror. This is a low blow even for Strickland, and his brother will never agree to it. He finds Zada in the group, her eyes red from crying. She's watching him because she knows he will guess how Rockland will react to this decree. She shakes her head once, the smallest movement—a warning.

Decker feels his blood pounding through the vein in his temple. He respects his mother greatly and knows she's the only member of this colony to truly understand their Sire, but this is wrong. He bites backs the words, trying to keep control.

"Decker, fetch a goat. The girls have my permission."

Decker takes three steps away from the group, before his feet won't shift. Rockland would defend him—his brother *does* defend him, forget about would.

"He'll never agree to this." His comment is greeted with utter silence. He turns slowly to face the anger he knows will be written clearly across Strickland's features. "You know this."

"He will do as I command or suffer."

"Or die, you mean?"

Several members of the group gasp at his bold honesty, but he's right. The only option the Sire is giving his own flesh and blood is to feed from the chosen females creating a blood bond—or die.

"That will be his choice. A bond isn't the end of the world, Decker. You should be so lucky to ever experience one. I am giving Rockland a great honor."

Decker's whole body is taut as a wire, the anger seething below the surface of his skin. He knows his argument won't help his brother, but saying nothing feels like a betrayal.

Zander steps forward and lays a warning hand on Decker's arm. "Sire, I feel Decker is worried by the numbers. Surely, you are giving Rockland a choice from these females?"

"No. Rockland will bond with each and every one of them."

"But, Sire, that's ... that's unheard of, and he—" Zander replies.

"Zander, do not make me repeat myself."

"Yes, Sire." He bows his head and steps back.

The Sire walks forward and stops inches from Decker. He slowly folds his arms over his hard chest, using up the little space between them. Decker stands his ground, waiting. "Just so ALL understand. Rebekkah will feed him now; later tonight he'll need more blood so Phoenix will do her duty. They will rotate, and continue to rotate until he is well. If he refuses *one* of them, he won't be offered any more blood from *any* of them."

Decker steps back, lowering his head. It isn't a sign of respect, but one of resignation. The Sire has cornered his own son—bond with a dozen Camazotz females, or forfeit his life. Zada takes the young male's hand and gives it a squeeze. Her comfort does little to ease the situation.

"Bring the goat!"

Decker flinches at the command, drops his mother's hand, and looks the Sire directly in the eye.

"You know this won't *cure* him, don't you? Trap him all you want, but he won't let her go."

7

Selfie

Connie

THAT night sleep evades me. I don't even attempt to guess who those men are, but my gut goes psycho every time I think of them. Poor Tiff knew I was lying when I told her on the way to the mall that those men had nothing to do with me. She asked if I'd seen the van again, and I barely managed to keep my Honda from mounting the curb. If only she knew how closely I'd seen that van.

Turning on my lamp, I retrieve the red velvet pouch Rocks gave me. Tucked away inside is his eyebrow bar. Pulling my knees up to my chest, I balance the red metal on my kneecap. It's a weird connection to him that my earrings, hair clips, and necklace don't give me. He'll come back for this—I'm sure of it.

Never in a million years did I think I'd turn into one of those boy-obsessed girls. I used to be so carefree and happy. Then Josie's letter turned me into an angry, confused liar. Now I'm wandering around lost and without any focus. Discovering my birth parents has left a shadow over who I am. I don't want to ever be like them. Not that I know anything other than what the media reports on my father, but I don't want to be like him regardless.

What does Rocks see in me? He must be crazy to think I'm good girlfriend material. Those Camazotz girls share a side to Rocks that I will never understand. I don't know what it feels like to fly, or flip, or need blood. And no matter how hard I try, I'll never comprehend that. I squeeze my eyes shut trying to prevent more tears. I hide the piercing back in the pouch and shove it under my pillow.

No more crying.

Get it together.

God, I miss him. Pinching the bridge of my nose, I will myself not to cry over a boy that can't help the fact he's not visiting because he can't fly. His absence doesn't mean the Camazotz have won. He's injured. The end. I wince and rub my aching abdomen, then roll my eyes. This week should be a real winner. I'm not losing my mind over a boy—I'm premenstrual. *Awesome.*

Tap, tap, tap.

My eyes flick to the window, and I fill my lungs with air in prep for my horror-movie-girl scream. There's a shape looming in the darkness. Before I can go into full-blown panic mode, Decker's face appears against the glass. What the ... he's flipped on the tiny ledge of roof outside my window.

"What are you doing here?" I whisper as the bitterly cold air hits my exposed flesh.

"Sorry." He sits next to the opening with his back against the wall. "Didn't think you'd be awake at this hour."

"Get in here."

"No, I'm good." I eye him, but he just smiles. It reminds me so much of Rocks. "No really, it's fine. Feel a bit odd coming in your bedroom at night without your boyfriend here."

My eyes widen. "Gimme a second." I duck back inside and grab my coat, gloves, and scarf. Popping my wool-covered head back out the window, I continue. "You know?"

"Are you kidding? He couldn't wait to tell me about the mistletoe, and you don't think he collected all that on his own do you?"

I feel my ears heat up under my beanie. A moment ago, I was doubting Rocks, only to discover he's told his best friend about us, and how he planned our second kiss. Not only am I the worst daughter in the world, but I can add worst girlfriend to the list.

My cheeks join the pink party. "So whose idea was the whole 'drink from my neck thing' back at the blood ceremony?"

The moon has risen and is a few days away from being full. It lets me see Decker's face although not well. I'm pretty sure his cheeks match mine.

"I knew he'd never ever be that forward with you, even though he wanted to. So I thought I'd help him along a little. Sorry." His sheepish grin is so familiar.

"Don't be. I was an idiot for not remembering he couldn't drink from me as a human."

Decker chuckles. "You're all right, Connie. You really don't judge us. And you've risked your neck for us, too. I'm ashamed to admit this, but I never thought I'd see the day where an aeronaught cared so much."

We're silent for a few minutes because I don't know what to say. That's the nicest thing a Camazotz has ever said to me, other than Rocks.

"Rocks asked you to fly by?"

"Yeah. He's worried, and I needed out of there."

This is new. Decker loves his colony and being a Camazotz. "Are you allowed to be here?" Another sheepish grin is his answer. "Decker! I don't want you in trouble too because of me."

"It's not you. It's me. I said some stuff to Strickland, and let's just say he hasn't forgotten." He sighs, staring up at the moon. "I honestly don't know how Rockland keeps his cool with that man."

"I know right."

"But I didn't come to talk about Strickland. How are you?"

Decker has proven he loves his brother and doesn't mind me, so I might as well be honest. "It's been a long two weeks. I miss him so much. Is he getting better?"

"The cast is still on if that's what you're meaning. He's doing ... okay. He's alive."

"Oh." I'd imagined him healing well. My heart stutters at the thought of some unknown complication. "I was hoping you'd say he was better than okay."

"If Rocks heals, he'll be the first bat ever to have survived a broken wing. He hasn't said, but I think he feels trapped."

"How?"

"I can't remember him being a Camazotz for this long without flipping. I think it's messing with his head, and well, ... yeah, just bat stuff." The sheepish grin returns, but I'll give him a pass on the bat stuff remark. I have more important questions.

Poor Rocks. The Camazotz that loves being human is forced to remain as a bat for eight long weeks. The worst of it is his bat form is going to save his life. If he thought he could remain human with me, this will let him know he can't. It will prove to him that he can't pick one side of himself.

"You okay?" he asks, studying my face.

I nod. "Tell him not to worry. I'm fine."

"Good. Those men come looking for the money?" I indicate no and Decker lets out a deep breath.

"I never got a chance to thank you and Jeremiah for saving me. I owe you both my life."

"No, you don't. You saved my brother and risked the wrath of Strickland doing it. I owe you."

We agree that each life debt cancels out the other so we're square. I sneak down to the kitchen and heat Decker some leftover mac and cheese. I remember it's his favorite and try not to laugh when I see his nose twitch before I pass the bowl out the window. This is my chance to get more information while he's distracted with cheesy goodness.

"Care to tell me what you know about Alex Green?"

Decker chokes on a mouthful of hot pasta. He coughs and splutters, smacking his chest, and I worry the noise will wake my parents. I hand him my water bottle, and he gulps it down between coughs. It's easy to forget he hasn't had much practice eating and talking at the same time.

"Rocks said you were the most determined girl he knew, and he wasn't wrong. Man, you don't let anything go." He smiles at me and wipes his chin. "What do you want to know?"

"I'm surprised she had an aeronaught boyfriend."

He snorts. "So was Strickland. We all were. Celand started disappearing a lot, always having an excuse for not being were she was supposed to be. Turns out she was sneaking off to see him."

"How did they meet?" I rub my cheeks with my gloved hands, trying to prevent them from freezing.

"Apparently, she found him lost on our mountain. She told Rocks he was 'alternative.' Whatever that means."

"What did he look like?"

"Covered in tattoos and pierced all over. His hair was half red and half black." Decker laughs. "I thought he blended right in with us—not like someone I know." He side eyes me with a smile. I silently curse being blonde for the millionth time. "I don't know much, but I know she left with him. We never saw her again. There's lots of rumors, but she wanted to be with him, and she paid for that with her life."

I suck in a breath. "How do you know she died?"

"A group was sent to look for her—daughter of the Sire and all. They questioned Alex, and he swore she hadn't met him where they'd arranged. Never saw or heard from her again."

This explains so much about what I've experienced at the colony. The other members are watching and waiting for me to lure their next leader off into my world and are worried it will kill him. Strickland must want to strangle me. I also understand why Rocks never told me. He didn't want me to feel sick with second-hand guilt like I do now. One of my kind was responsible for his sister's death. I think of Mini and how I would feel toward the Camazotz if one of them were responsible for her death.

That thought leaves a bitter taste in my mouth. I'd want blood, and I wouldn't care whom it belonged to. How can he look at me and not feel some kind of animosity?

"You okay?" Decker's voice brings me out of my head. I seem to disappear there too often these days.

"Rocks, he ... he doesn't ..." I sigh. "The other Camazotz blame me because I'm an aeronaught. Rocks doesn't think like that."

"That's our boy. Rockland's the most level-headed, reasonable bat I know."

Decker clicks open his silver pocket watch and sighs. "I should let you get some sleep."

"I'm wide awake. It's okay." I lean on the windowsill next to him in silence. Decker sits, staring at the rising moon, but his fingers tap out a beat on his thigh.

"Your lap computer handy?"

My brain had drifted to Rocks and his struggle with staying as a Camazotz while his wing heals. "Um, no, it's in the TV room."

"Oh, no matter." Decker looks back at the sky, folds his arms and then unfolds them again.

"I can search anything you need to know on my phone." I slip it from my coat pocket and unlock the screen.

"No, it's okay. It's silly really."

Nothing Decker has ever said has come close to silly. In fact, using silly in the same sentence as Decker is laughable. "I doubt that. Spill it." I lean further out the window and rest my elbow on the roof, facing him. "Tell me."

The hint of pink has returned to his cheeks, and he's studying his hiking boots. Boots that I know were once hanging in a tree. "Rockland showed me the photographs you made on the computer. I thought … ah, I'm going to sound so self-centered. Forget it," he huffs, crossing his arms again.

"You've flown how many miles tonight to check on your brother's girlfriend? Hardly the actions of a self-centered man."

A little smile plays at Decker's lips. He looks at me sideways briefly before a full-blown smile appears. "Don't tell Jeremiah, or I'll never hear the end of it."

I cross my heart, but my gesture confuses my Camazotz friend. "I promise," I explain.

"I've never had a photograph of myself. I was wondering if … but the computer is downstairs. Told you it was silly."

These bats live so far removed from us that some days I feel as though I'll never understand them. I try to imagine no photographic evidence of Mini's short time on this planet. Every single milestone in her life has been photographed and videoed to excess, but at the age of seventeen, Decker has never seen one photo of himself.

Aiming my phone at him, I try to focus at the odd angle. "Smile."

Decker shifts away from the device as though it's going to stun him. "What are you doing? That's a phone."

"And a camera too." I turn the screen toward him and watch the wonder set in as he sees the dark trees in the moonlight fill the screen.

"Does Rocks know about this?" He's frowning. "Does his have a camera too?"

"Yeah." Our technology lesson the day my parents left after Christmas was cut short. It was the first time we were home alone after getting together and spent most of the day cuddled up on my bed making out. I'm grateful my beanie is pulled low over my ears. With all the drama that followed, we never got around to using his camera.

"I do not think he knows he has his very own camera."

"I think you're right. Smile." The first one I snap is too dark. Nervous about the flash drawing attention to the boy on our roof, I insist Decker must come inside. I take four pictures of him and then explain the emergence of the selfie. His hesitancy evaporates when he looks at his image on the screen. Slinging an arm around my shoulder, he pulls me in, and since he's got longer arms, I let him press the button to capture us grinning.

PREVIOUSLY, SCHOOL DISTRACTED me from dwelling on my identity crisis in the hunt for my parents. Now, it's an alarming reminder of what I discovered. Rambo and his buddy have been sitting in some sinister-looking car every day when I leave school. They simply sit and stare and occasionally comment to each other as I exit the parking lot.

The parking lot at school is short about twenty car spaces. Late students are forced onto the street. By Thursday, I was leaving for school so early that both Dad and Mom commented. There was no way in hell I was parking near the gate or on the street with those two suits lurking.

Friday, I beg and plead to convince Mom that I don't feel well enough to attend class. She's not working and sets me up on the couch wrapped in a quilt with hot tea, freshly baked banana bread, and the remote control. I spend the morning feeling safe from men-in-suits and drug lords. What on earth am I going to do if they ask about the money? I don't have it, and I certainly won't be sending them to Blood Mountain.

Or should I?

Ash could get a fix of aeronaught blood—

Sugarplums! What the hell?

Am I really plotting a bloody end to two men who technically haven't done anything to me? Good lord, I am Enzo's daughter!

The three slices of hot banana bread I scarfed down swirl around in my stomach. I rub my temples and take a deep breath. This is a new low even for me. What would Rocks think of me sending aeronaughts up the mountain for the Camazotz to "take care of?"

Mom calls from the kitchen, and when I enter, she's got Mini in her highchair and is rolling out cookie dough. "Want to help Mini make animal cookies?"

Mini grins. Two more teeth have come down, slowly filling in the gaps in her precious smile. I pinch her rosy cheeks and pull up a stool. Family time will distract me from my fudged up thoughts. I dig through the drawers searching for the animal cookie cutters. Mom and I work well as a team in the kitchen, but it's been too long since we've done this. I know she knows I'm not really sick, and I'm grateful for her not asking why.

While Mom patiently assists Mini with cutting out the cookies and laying them on the three trays, I start the frosting. By the time the oven dings, we have pink, yellow, green and blue icing, and half the counter is covered in bowls of decorations—mini marshmallows, sugar stars, chocolate chips, crushed candy—it's a feast. Mini's jigging up and down in her chair in anticipation. She's going to be covered in more frosting than the cookies shortly and can't wait to get started.

The next hour, I'm lost in decorating heaven. Three distinct cookie styles cover the counter. My mom's cookies resemble their real life animal counterparts so well they could be photographed and used as characters in a children's book. My cookies—while pretty—contain copious amounts of my favorite toppings—lots of 'spotted' marshmallow farm critters. And Mini's are decorated with the kind of enthusiasm that only two-year-olds possess when given free access to frosting and candy.

"This is fun," Mom comments, smiling. She reaches over and wipes something off my face.

"It's been a while." I want to return to the old days before the letter when Mom and I hung out all the time.

"I missed us."

"Me too. I'm sorry I've been such a pain lately."

"I've been worried. I don't know what's been going on, but I'm glad whatever it was is over." She's not upset; she's just being honest.

"Got time for a movie?" I ask, trying to select which cookies to devour.

"I'd love to. By the way, I chipped two nails." She holds up the evidence, and I can tell she's hoping I'll offer to fix them. The look on her face says she doesn't want to push the mother/daughter time quota.

"Let me get my polish."

THE MARTIN LUTHER King Jr. holiday gives me four men-in-suits free days in a row. By Tuesday, I've slept well and am ready to confront them. Well, maybe not them, but I'm telling a teacher. I want to know why they lurk by the school, and I'm sick of being afraid. What sort of men intimidate teenage girls? Then I think about the sort of men that kidnap teenage girls. My bravado deflates quite a bit, but not enough to stop me. I want answers to the questions that are slowly driving me insane. After spending an awesome weekend with Mom, Dad, and Mini, I will not risk anything happening to the family that I'm desperate to keep.

My plan should not endanger my girlfriends either. I say goodbye to them at the lockers, explaining I've got books that need returning to the library. When I'm sure they'll be well on their way home, I march to the front gate.

I'm slightly disappointed to find my stalkers waiting in their usual spot. Part of me had hoped that my absence would have solved the problem, but they're staring at me like usual. So much for vigilant teachers monitoring student safety! These thugs could be extras in *The Godfather*. Placing my hands on my hips, I summon my most defiant glare, and then yell at the top of my lungs. "Principal Skenner!"

The school entrance isn't overly busy. A few kids are still chatting by their cars. All eyes are on me—particularly two blood-chilling glares. The men advance before I have a chance to call out a second time.

Since the principal's office is in the corner of the building closest to the gate, I know he'll have heard me. The Rambo-wanna-be grabs my arm while the other dude covers my mouth and shoves me behind a parked car.

"Shut it now, Contessa."

Oh, fudge me.

The remaining students can't see what's going on, and I can't see anything but a wall of giant man in front and behind me. I struggle and bite down hard on the sweaty hand over my mouth. I will not be dragged into another car. Not now. Not ever. I dig around in my bag for the pepper spray that I pray is still in there. Daddy gave it to me years ago, but I've never had a need for it.

My fingers curl around a canister and in a flash I'm pressing the pump repeatedly at head height. Both men take a step back letting me go, and one laughs.

"Feisty like her father," he mutters, looking at Rambo.

Father?

I can't breath, and my head starts to spin. They aren't after the money. My fingers press down again as my brain slowly processes the fact that mace doesn't smell—at all. *What?* Then I realize that I've just sprayed them with my inhaler. *Awesome.* Apparently, Ventolin to the face is quite the deterrent ... who knew? I rub my arm where that monster grabbed me.

"Get away. Leave me alone." I focus and stand tall, not wanting to act the victim. "Stop following me," I command. I ready my lungs for a scream.

"You that keen to be snatched by the Vipers again, little girl?" The fair-haired one asks.

"Maybe she wants to give 'the Finger' back his money."

"What? How do you— Who the hell are you?"

They know about the money the boys stole from the Vipers. That's not possible.

"We're all that's keeping you out of a shallow grave." Rambo frowns and indicates toward something behind me. "You need us. Be smart and tell your teacher all's cool."

Over my shoulder, I see Principal Skenner and two juniors talking to him, pointing my way. The alarm has been raised, but now what ...

THE WORDS "SHALLOW grave" haunt me day after day. I don't think I'll ever be calm enough to eat anything again. The week is a blur. My first instinct is to text Rocks, but I decide against it before hitting send. He can't check his phone, and if by some miracle someone checked it for him, he'd freak if I told him the Vipers want their money back, and two of Enzo's meatheads are keeping me safe from having to return it. He'd flip to be by my side, and since his wing has only been in a cast for just short of a month, that would be an epic disaster. What's the probability that members of the two biggest rival drug gangs in Atlanta know who I am?

Enzo knows about me.

And, he's protecting me.

Where's my inhaler when I really need it? I thought I'd closed the lid on the emotional pit when I discovered my parents' identities. I was dead wrong. It's a whirling cesspool of confusion that's bigger than ever. Since finding out about Enzo Ascari, I've felt nothing but loathing and revulsion to think we share the same genes, but now he's keeping me alive. Why? The idea of banging my head against a wall until I suffer from amnesia is looking more and more appealing. These questions are piling up and pissing me off to no end.

Since my confrontation with his men, I get a slight head nod when I leave school. I've noticed black Town Cars everywhere, but have no idea if I'm merely being extra paranoid or whether I've got a constant tail.

Screams and squeals from the gaggle of two-year-olds drift in from the backyard. We're celebrating Mini's second birthday with a dozen of her closest daycare buddies and their parents. The feast is spread across two folding tables on our back patio, and I'm officially off duty and hanging with the girls in front of the TV. I don't give a sugarplum who the quarterback is dating this week, or if Parker is ever going to talk to me again. I tune out the girls' voices and retreat into my gloomy question corner.

A handful of Swedish fish hit me in the face. "Hey!"

The girls laugh and eye each other. "Are you even listening?" Tiff asks, shaking her head. Brandy is on the floor sitting crossed-legged behind Mary Lou with a curling iron. They're all staring.

"What's the Rocks update?" Mary Lou repeats, twirling one of the soft curls.

"I told you he broke his arm. Haven't seen him."

"But you're still texting, right?" Brandy asks. "Broken arm doesn't mean he can't call you. He's into you. I thought for sure you'd hook up over Christmas."

Maybe I should tell them? Why haven't I? Us hooking up was brand spanking new and then BAM! I get mixed up with the Vipers, and Rocks gets hurt. I guess I just wanted more time to adjust to the thought of having a Camazotz boyfriend and exactly what that entails.

"Call him." Brandy dumps the curling iron and lunges for my phone. "See if he and the boys can come over. Tiff would looooove to see Jeremiah again, wouldn't you, girl?"

That gets my attention. Tiff blushes and it's such a rare look on her. Her confidence with guys used to drive me crazy. "You like Jeremiah?" I ask. "Since when?"

"Honestly, Connie, do you ever listen," she asks.

Later that night at the hotdog stand, I focus all of my attention on my best friend. Tiffany is right; I'm totally clueless about what's been happening with my friends. My head has been so crammed with my problems that I've completely ignored everything else. It feels good to stop the internal chatter and listen.

"Has Rocks ever said if Jeremiah's got a girlfriend?" she asks. Her anime blue eyes are hopeful.

A girlfriend? As in singular? Nope. A dozen of them? Probably, if he's half as popular as Rocks. I think the universe is trying to drown me in my emotional pit. I finally manage to claw my way out of the Enzo-Vipers-being-stalked-over-money-I-didn't-technically-steal hole, only to be shoved into the Rocks-Camazotz-girls-mating-bats-what-does-our-future-hold abyss instead.

"No, but, um. I don't know if you two—"

"What?" She puts her hands on her hips and faces me.

Crabapples. A good friend would tell the truth, but the truth involves secrets that aren't mine to share, and I'm pretty certain letting another aeronaught into the fold—so to speak—would be all it would take for Strickland to send his bat squad my way.

"I don't know. He's, um, sort of intense." What I don't say is he drinks blood and kinda hates our kind. She frowns. "Calm down. I'm not saying you wouldn't be good together, but ..." Sometimes telling the truth sucks balls. Fudge this. "He did ask about you one night when we were hanging out." Her frown melts away and that dreamy eyed state she gets when reading replaces it.

"Really? Tell me *exactly* what he said?"

A customer at the window saves me from more white lies. Jeremiah did ask, but that's all I've got, and she wants minute details. The fact that his face was smeared with *my* blood at the time probably isn't what she's after. Looking out the serving window, I wish I hadn't.

"Fuc—" My hand flies to my mouth.

I'm looking into the dark-rimmed glasses of Enzo—freaking—Ascari.

8
Harem

ALL I can hear is the pounding of my heart. I'm positive it's relocated to somewhere between my ears because the thumping beat is deafening.

A quick glance at Tiff tells me she has no clue about the identity of my customer as she moves to check our wiener numbers. Thank God, she doesn't watch the news much either.

My eyes flick back to Enzo—my father. He's middle-aged and kinda pleasant-looking. Talk about never judge a book by its cover. Enzo could pass for a regular businessman, but he's anything but regular. His shoulder-length, blond hair is pulled back in a low ponytail. My fingers grab the end of mine, before I realize what I'm doing. His green eyes roam over me with the same scrutiny that I'm sure he can see in mine. I'm curious which of my features strike a chord with him.

"One dog, please."

On autopilot, I prepare his order. He knows where I freaking work. Why this surprises me I have no clue. The mute, teenage girl that has difficulty talking to boys other than Camazotz also has nothing to say to scary, biological fathers. My hand shakes a little as I pass him the hotdog.

The note he hands over is a fifty. "Keep the change." His eyes flick to the money briefly.

When I look, there's a slip of paper inside the folded bill.

Tell Miss Tiffany Jenkins you won't need a ride home tonight.

I close my eyes. I want to be sick. What did I ever do to the universe to deserve this? He knows her last name, and I'm guessing that's not all he knows. I nod once to confirm I understand his message and watch as he walks away, handing the hotdog to a dark silhouette in the shadows.

I tell Tiff that my father is taking me home—not a lie. But comparing Dad V2.0 to that man makes me understand how Judas felt at the last supper.

Two sinister-looking vehicles wait across the road near the dance club. My feet have the sudden urge to run, but then I think of Tiff. Are they watching her head to her car? If I make a run for it, will she pay for my cowardice?

"You wanted to know who he was," I mutter, crossing the road. "Now's your big chance."

The back door of the first car opens and Enzo emerges. His smile sends a shiver up my spine.

He buttons his navy blue suit jacket and runs a hand over his hair, before gesturing to the open car. "Get in."

"No."

The smile fades. "I said get in!" His voice is as effective as liquid nitrogen. My spine stiffens instantly, but I don't care. I'm not getting in that car. I know what happens when girls get shoved into cars.

"And I said, NO!" I yell. If he wants a scene, I'll give him one. He knocks on the hood twice. A large gentleman exits the driver's side. He straightens his tie and casually places a hand on his hip, pushing his suit jacket open to reveal a holstered gun.

Fear envelops my entire body as the memory of Mullins and his revolver rush to the surface. My eyes dart to the clubbers across the lot. Enzo can't shoot me with this many witnesses—surely. If he wanted me dead, he would have left me to his rivals—the Vipers.

I swallow and lift my chin. "My answer is still no. Your thugs don't scare me."

Liar, liar, pants on fire.

Time seems to stand still. I turn to leave, but Enzo's laughter roots me to the spot.

"You are delightful," he chuckles. "Positively delightful, child."

Without thinking, I know I've pulled my 'what the fudge' face. I turn back toward him. He closes the door and leans against the car, crossing one ankle over the other.

"You're an Ascari all right."

"What?"

"You can't be told what to do, and you don't intimidate easily. That makes me very proud, Contessa. If you did whatever a man with a gun told you to do, you'd be of no use to me."

If only he knew how close to collapsing I am right now. And hearing my name on his lips makes me want to shudder. I am not his.

"What do you want?"

He smiles again and places his hand over his heart. "I should thank your mother. I always dreamed of having two girls and two boys. I told her what we would name them, and even though I didn't know of your existence, she followed my wishes and named you after your Grandmother."

A month ago, I would have killed for this kind of information, now it turns my blood to ice.

"What do you want with me?" I snap.

He has the nerve to look taken aback at my tone. "Isn't it obvious?"

I stare at him without answering, but he simply laughs, shaking his head. "Ah, Contessa, you are the spitting image of your mother when you try to be so serious. A pussy cat trying to be a tiger." He steps away from the car, reaching out to touch my face, but I lean back out of reach. "I want us to be a family."

"Are you crazy? I have a family thank you very much, and I don't need a new one that breaks the law." Last year, I wanted nothing to do with my fake family—that's how I saw them for a while—now I cling to them with everything I've got. I know who my family are, and who they aren't. And Enso Ascari is not my family.

"Breaks the law?" The liquid nitrogen tone is back. "And how would you describe taking money that doesn't belong to you?"

Despite the evening's low temperature, a trickle of sweat runs down my temple. I am not like him ...

Enzo studies me, then opens the door again. "This time it's not a test. Get in." My feet won't move. He sighs. "I don't have time to follow you home on foot, and I'm not convinced they still don't want to harm you."

They?

The Vipers?

Fudge.

I slide as far across the leather as possible. Enzo joins me and we head toward my house without a single instruction uttered. The car pulls up three houses down. I'm grateful he's not so keen to be seen by my parents because I have no doubt he knows exactly which house is mine.

"Any concerns. Call." He hands over a crisp white, embossed business card with a cell number scribbled on the back. "We'll be in touch, Contessa, darling. You can count on it."

"Why?"

"You need to pay more attention to the news. See if you can figure it out."

The second I'm out of the car, I sprint to my door. I can't stand knowing he's watching me, and I doubt he'll drive off until I'm safe inside.

I would never have believed that Dad V1.0 would ever imitate Dad V2.0. *Watch the news.* You've got to be kidding me.

DAD DOESN'T SAY a word about my sudden interest in current events. I'm on the couch daily, glued to whatever channel he selects. I'm sure he's curious about why I no longer barter for the remote. Hopefully he's enjoying our new hang out time.

Hardly any news reports cover the Vipers trial. Now that the date has been set for March, there aren't any updates, but I watch religiously on the off chance. *See if you can figure it out.* For every question I get answered, a dozen more appear.

"Vampire bats attacked a group of school children in Floyd today," the newsreader reports. The footage shows a group of ten-year-olds with cuts and scratches to their faces and arms. "The teacher accompanying the children witnessed three giant bats bombarding the kids. A local employee was shoveling snow at the time of the attack and came to their rescue."

I'm on the edge of my seat and even Dad has lowered the newspaper to watch the footage.

The screen shows a massive bat on the snow-covered ground—dead. I cover my eyes sending up a silent prayer. I tell myself to listen and calm down. It absolutely, positively is *not* Rocks. The reporter says the appearance of vampire bats this far north has wildlife experts totally perplexed. The previous victims weren't able to identify a species, but authorities are looking into the matter.

My fingers run over my phone screen. The urge to text Rocks is overwhelming. He should know about this. He should also know about Enzo. I chuck my cell back on the couch and sit on my hands. I will not risk him flipping on my account.

"You don't know what type of bat attacked you, do you, sweetheart? Did it look like that?"

All I can see is that dead bat when I close my eyes. That is a person, and nobody except me seems to know that fact. I don't understand why that Camazotz was attacking those innocent, little kids, but a colony member is lying dead in the snow at the hands of an aeronaught, and I know precisely how the Camazotz will react to that.

"It was too dark." Not a lie.

THE NEXT MONTH passes without any news reports that give me cause to sweat profusely or feel faint. Nothing on Enzo, and thankfully no new bat attacks. I hang with the girls after school without looking over my shoulder too many times. On two occasions, I've spotted Enzo's thugs watching me from a distance. Apart from that, my life almost resembles that of the carefree girl I was this time last year. I play with Mini; I paint mom's nails and watch the evening news with dad every night.

The only hump in my almost happy routine was Valentine's Day. Talk about torture. The sight of hearts, flowers, candy, and cute, cuddly toy animals almost had me in the car and heading for Blood Mountain.

It made the ache in my chest intensify as though my heart was trying to burn its way free. I wondered if we would have gone on a date, or if Valentines' Day and its rituals would have been as foreign as mistletoe. I know it's a first we could've shared together, but didn't.

Each night, I open my window no matter what the temperature. It's been eight long Rocks-less weeks. The absence of any text messages has my blood pressure on the high side. Surely he'll text the second he's a human again. I push the thought of where we stand aside, now that he's been a bat for this long. I can't go there, but I also can't forget the look on Decker's face when he said he didn't think his brother was coping.

"We should go to the movies next week," Tiff suggests. She's adding extra hotdogs to the pot since a load of college boys almost cleaned us out.

"Sure. I'm dying to see—" My heart rate spikes the second my eyes land on the black leather vest through the window. However, it's not the Camazotz I've been looking for. Ash and his creepy fang tats peer in the serving window.

"What do you want?" I ask under my breath. Tiff is still stocking up on hotdogs.

"Missed you too, naught. Where's Rockland?"

My breath catches. "He's better? He's—" I stop myself from asking if he's able to fly. "Tiff, I need a minute."

Stepping outside, I notice that Ash isn't alone. A boy with the same cold, hard eyes is talking to my cheer squad. Freaking awesome. Zabreena grins as the whole group approach. Rebekkah, the girl with the stars tattooed around her eyes, and the little one who was attacked by the owls are all present. Two other girls stand behind them with a mean-looking boy. I'm desperate for information about Rocks, yet I know these girls will not give me anything without a fight.

"His arm healed?"

Ash nods. "He left the roost alone. Strickland sent us to find him."

Rebekkah steps forward. The scarlet dress she's wearing looks as though it's made from crushed silk. If she's not feeling winter's bite, then she's had her fill of blood recently. "We came searching for lover boy to make sure his wing is holding up." She smiles, playing with the end of a long, black, satin ribbon that's been braided into her hair.

"Well, it did last night." Zabreena winks at me. "If you get what I mean, naught."

Double fudge with a serving of crabapples.

"Wouldn't you say being in his *true* form these past two months has brought out Rocks' animal instincts, Phoenix?" Rebekkah looks at starry-eyes.

The girl blushes. I grab my stomach. *Please no ...* "He just lets go now. Can't control himself around us. I've missed that side of him," she replies, grinning at Rebekkah. Her eyes never leave mine, and I try to fight the urge to scream. My worst nightmare is coming to life in front of me, in clothes I wouldn't step out of the house wearing.

"He's proven to be a Land wing male, all right," Zabreena adds. "He'll take after Strickland for siring pups."

I will not dignify their words with a response. Turning on my heel, I head back inside to Tiff before the tears that are burning behind my eyes dare to escape. My fear of what would happen to Rocks after being trapped as a bat has just slapped me hard across the face. Maybe the fact that he's denied himself his animal side all these years has only made it harder for him to control it now. Is this the end for us? I scrunch my eyes shut willing my tears into non-existence.

"You okay?" Her wide-eyed stare speaks volumes. No, I am definitely not, I think. Rocks has been flying with those girls and hasn't come back to me. The animal inside of him isn't interested in me. I'm the biggest idiot alive.

When Tiff drops me at home, I listen carefully as I walk up the path. A slight wind rustles the leaves in the holly tree, but all else is quiet. My disappointment spikes when he's not waiting on the porch swing.

Heading to my room, I collapse on my bed. Anger and hurt bubble and hiss like hot lava in my bottomless pit. I will not cry. I check my phone for the five millionth time and hate myself a little more. After an hour of stewing on his whereabouts, I close my eyes and try to sleep.

Connie?

"Sugar!" After almost falling off the bed, I race to my window. I know that voice. "Rocks?" I whisper.

EEEEKKKK!

My jaw clenches and my teeth grind together. He is so *not* coming in my bedroom if he's been 'bonding' with those bat *biatches*. I pull the window closed, grab my jacket and sneak downstairs. The TV room is quiet so I'm hoping that means the folks are sound asleep.

Crossing the lawn, I stop near the trees. A second later, Rocks steps out from under the low branches. He looks amazing, but I will not let the sight of him in my favorite velvet vest distract me from finding out the facts. The way he smiles makes my heart shatter.

"Don't," I say, stepping back. His arms drop to his side and he frowns. "All this time, I'm missing you like mad, and I think you're resting and healing, but then I find out you're flying with those flippin' girls!"

His eyes widen. "Connie? What—"

One second I'm looking at Rocks, and the next, he's surrounded by those flippin' girls again. The Camazotz that visited me earlier are now on my front lawn, standing way too close to my boyfriend. If I'd known they were hanging around, I would have screamed my lungs out to knock them out cold.

"Did she really think he was just hanging around doing nothing for the past two months? Oh God, that's so adorable," the little one says.

Rocks moves toward me and away from his little harem. I cross my arms over my chest and soak up everyone's body language. "Violet, don't lie—"

Phoenix speaks before Rocks can finish. "Humans are so optimistic. You gotta give them that."

If the little one's name is Violet, then she's from the same wing as Ash. No wonder she's not a fan.

"Yeah, it's 'cause of their lazy lives. They don't understand that every mouth in the colony has to earn its keep—one way or another," Rebekkah says with a sultry wink at Rocks.

"Connie, ignore them," he pleads. "You lot, go. You're not supposed to be here."

"No one is above the Sire's law. Strickland sent us to get you. Besides we missed you, big man," Rebekkah adds. All the girls laugh.

My face is burning up despite the cold. It's a combination of thinking about Rocks being with them and why they're calling him 'big man.' He is very tall, but—

When I look back at him, his breath is coming out in hot puffs against the cool air. He reminds me of a fire-breathing dragon. Is he angry because his secret is out? Or is he angry with me? Or at these annoying girls?

I look from Rocks to the group, unsure of what the hell is going on. Have they just played me again? My teeth grind together.

Rocks asks if I'll give him a moment to deal with the Goths on my lawn. I scrunch my eyes closed and bite my tongue. I stalk back to the porch stairs and wait. Rocks has to bend over to whisper furiously at the girls, and I can't hear anything he says.

The boy with Ash comes out of the trees and approaches the group. The set of his shoulders tells me he's not happy with Rocks. I cringe expecting punches to be thrown any second. Rocks points a finger at the guy, causing him to halt in place before returning his attention to the girls clustered around him. Their body language alters as he continues his rant. All of them, except Rebekkah and Zabreena, look down as if in apology, or some sort of surrender. Rebekkah folds her arms and to be honest, I'm glad I'm not on the receiving end of the glare he gives her. In a moment of clarity, I see the potential Sire in the making, but the thought makes me want to tear out my hair, and punch several of those *biatches* in the boob.

"Go!" Rocks points to the sky.

"Or what?" Ash takes several steps toward him, and I can't help biting my lip. "You lecture them for not showing you enough respect? Why should they? I'm the one that's going to be leading us into the future."

Rocks walks over and the height difference between the two males is almost laughable. He leans over Ash and once more I can't hear what's being said, but the two argue back and forth. It ends with Ash swearing loudly and I worry the folks will stir, but if there were sounds from within our house at least one of the Camazotz on the lawn would have reacted.

The next minute, they all flip—except Rocks. My eyes dart up and down the street, praying the neighbors aren't about to call the cops. The Camazotz can hear when the coast is clear a lot better than I can see it. The bats fly low and all of them buzz past within inches of my head. It takes every ounce of bravery I possess to hold my ground and not duck out of their way. I watch them until they disappear into the darkness.

"I'm sorry," Rocks says. His eyes are sad and make me want to reach for him. He's standing at the bottom of the stairs, hands in his pockets. "They're just trying to make trouble. You have to believe me."

"Zabreena was looking at you ... well, she was looking at you like Tina Jeffries started looking at last year's quarterback, and she only started looking at him like that after they ... you know." I can't bring myself to say the words 'had sex' because Rocks told me he'd never done it as a human, and I absolute cannot describe the act as mating. Will. Not. Happen. That makes me want to hurl, followed by kicking him some place he would really rather I didn't.

"Zabreena is a liar, and I'm not really sure what this Tina girl did to her back."

Rocks' not understanding my football reference makes my heart melt a little. My 1860s boy is back—but he's not exclusively mine. "Tina had sex with a football player."

"What exactly are you accusing me of?" He folds his arms.

I remember the last time those girls got inside my head. Am I letting my fear of the Camazotz girls being better than aeronaught me cloud my judgment? I fold my arms, mirroring Rockland's stance. I've come this far; I might as well voice what's been eating me up inside for the past few hours.

"Doing that with all those girls!"

"I had a broken wing!" His voice is loud against the silent night, and he glances up in the direction of my parent's bedroom.

"So?" I whisper yell. "Sounds like you had pretty *personalized* nursing care. Does that mean you tried to ... you know ... but failed? They all visited me at Bun Lovin' earlier, and Zabreena made it sound like you were gonna be a father soon. Don't suppose you need your wings to do that!"

"Ugh, this is unbelievable." Rocks throws his arms in the air and then paces back and forth. He looks flippin' furious as though he's trying to stay in control. "Give me a moment before I say something a gentleman would regret." He turns away and looks up at the cloudy sky.

He speaks quietly, still not facing me. "I told you once before Zabreena and I would never mate, didn't I?" He looks over his shoulder.

The weight of this conversation is too much, and I sink into a heap on the steps. At the sound of my movement, he turns and holds out a hand to help me, but pulls it back. He sighs.

"I guess I should have explained why and saved you all this worry. Connie, you have to pay more attention. What wing is my mother from?"

His mother? What the— "Um, the Z wing." He raises an eyebrow at me like it's obvious. "So?"

"So that means about fifty-five percent of the females from that wing are off-limits. And if half the wing is off-limits, to make life easier, the whole wing becomes off-limits."

I have no clue what he's going on about.

"Zabreena is my second cousin."

"Eeww, gross." That lying little … little guano!

"I agree. She and I will never be like that. And the idea of me being able to do that with any of the girls is absurd. I know because I've seen other males and females with broken wings in the past. It is a death sentence—usually. I was lucky because of you! You got me back to the colony safely. If not, I would have died trying to get back there like every other bat does." He sounds forlorn. "And let's not forget the pain I was in most of the time. You saw me. I was trying not to show you how much it hurt, but believe me when I tell you I was not in the mood."

When I called myself an idiot earlier this evening, I wasn't wrong. "Why do they say that stuff?"

His lips curl up to give me the tiny hint of a smile. He tilts his head to one side and looks into my eyes. "They want to make you jealous. They want you to push me away. And they know your weakness."

"What's that?" I don't trust my own brain to put the puzzle pieces together.

"You don't like to share."

I think back over all their remarks—all innuendos and snide suggestions only sending my brain in a downward spiral of jealousy. He's right. They've worked out my biggest fear and are using it against me. Those girls are playing to win, and they mean business.

"Last night, I flipped for the first time. Tonight is the first time I've left the roost since I saw you, and the first place I came is here. I tried to get to the hotdog van, but I'm a bit slower than I was even though my wing is fine." He holds out his arm to show me. "I'm so unfit. It took me much longer to fly here, but ... well, I'm not sure why I bothered. I thought ... I thought ..."

"You thought what," I whisper from my seat on the stairs. Rocks kneels down on the bottom step so we're eye to eye.

The heavy crease that has dominated his brow for most of the conversation lifts. His eyes soften as they roam over my face and land on my lips. "I thought you'd shower me with kisses." He smiles, the anger from earlier gone.

I let out a very unflattering, unladylike snort before launching myself at him. The megawatt smile that lights his face melts away all the lies those girls tricked me into believing. You would think by now I could recognize a liar at five paces with all the practice I've had. Rocks stands, pulling me up with him. His hands cup my face.

"I've been waiting for you and only you," he says.

I reach up on tippy-toes and grab the back of his neck. "A little help here, bat boy," I say, trying to pull his lips into range.

Rocks straightens to his full height and glances around the garden. He's feigning disinterest, but the smile he's trying hard to conceal gives him away. I punch him lightly in the ribs.

"Owwf, I'm an injured man remember. Watch it, Beans."

He leans forward, the look in his eyes is serious again. Running the backs of two fingers down my heated cheeks, he whispers. "I missed you so much. Being stuck with the Camazotz for eight long weeks has driven me wild. The fact I was so far away from you consumed me. Yet, it was thoughts of you and of us that kept me going. Are we good?"

He's still mine. I never lost him. All I lost was my faith in him, believing their stupid, ugly lies. Rocks chose me—and still does. I'm so happy I could fly.

I nod and kiss him, unable to contain myself any longer. I sigh at the warmth of his lips and body against mine. Stopping for a second, I step back up onto the steps so we're closer in height. Rocks wraps his arms around me and pulls me against his chest. He's midnight. He is my moon, and I am his sun. I can feel the smile on his lips when he kisses me again, making me giggle. He deepens the kiss as I open my mouth. I'm alive in his arms after hibernating for too long.

Gripping his velvet waistcoat, I yank him toward the porch swing. Rocks trips on the stairs. It's so unlike him. He's always so measured, in control. Maybe he's as happy to be back in my arms, as I am to be in his.

"Easy there, Beans. Just recovered from a broken arm. Don't need a broken leg to match."

The porch swing creaks and groans as we fall into it. The sound is too loud against the Sunday dawn. I have no idea what time it is, but I know it's really late, or crazy early.

"Shhh, you'll wake them up," I admonish with a grin.

"We can't have that. I've got to make up for lost time." He leans over and nibbles my bottom lip.

A buzzing energy is trying to burst out of every atom in my body. His touch makes me tingle to the point where I might explode. Before I overthink my actions, I scramble onto his lap. I need him close after all that doubt. Rocks holds me tight against his chest. He rests his chin on my head as we swing back and forth in silence.

"This feels good," he says. I feel his long fingers rub down my back. The connection I'm sharing with my midnight boy is going to be the death of me. "You're so precious to me. Don't ever forget that."

I kiss him again—and again—and again. In fact, we sit and kiss and whisper quietly to each other until sunrise. The sky slowly changes from grey to pink, and I imagine what someone passing by on the street can see and blush—the tall, lethal-looking dude in black sitting with the pretty-in-pink, pajama-clad midget on his lap. Thank goodness the neighbors are late risers.

"Are you going to be in trouble when you go back?"
Rocks snorts. "Yep, but what's new."

9
Gypsy Wagon

ROCKS doesn't return until Tuesday after school, and those two and a half days felt like forever. I wasn't able to text him because he hasn't been back to the market to charge his phone. Since the whole colony are still living in the cave, he would get into even more trouble for using aeronaught technology in the open, especially with the broken blood oath hanging around his neck.

"You really are back," Mom sighs as Rocks enters the kitchen. I barely manage to refrain from rolling my eyes. She engulfs him in a hug and pushes him onto the nearest stool. All his favorite treats cover the counter. "You've lost weight, dear boy. We can't have that."

"Good to see you, Mrs. Phillips." Rocks glances around, and I die a little inside knowing who he's looking for.

"I'll get Mini." He smiles and the twitch of his nose tells me he's famished. "Start without me," I suggest, heading to the doorway.

"Mrs. Phillips, do you mind if I stay for dinner too?"

The answering squeal from my mother—the born again teenager—I assume means yes. For the first time in two months, there's a lightness to my step. Rocks being back hasn't changed or solved any of our problems, but I'm not dealing with them alone. I have help shouldering the burden, and that makes my spirit want to sing. Watching the Mini/Rocks reunion causes my cheeks to hurt from smiling so hard. He noticed her new teeth and every changed detail about her, prompting Mom to hug him again.

Since he's staying for dinner, it was easier to escape Kelly's attention and head to my room. There's so much I need to tell him—my brain *so* wasn't thinking about this stuff the other night on the porch swing. Rocks sits in his chair, and I'm opposite, cross-legged on the bed. I plug in his phone just in case he gets a minute to himself at the roost and begin my tale.

"You met Enzo?" he half yells. "Why didn't you tell me? Are you all right? Did he threaten—"

My giggle leaves him totally perplexed. Enzo Ascari in my life is no laughing matter, but Rocks being back has made me deliriously happy.

"This isn't funny." His eyebrows dip together under his hair.

"I'll tell you what isn't funny—bat attacks."

I fill Rocks in on everything that has happened since he left. He insists I show him the news articles about the bat attacks. The look on his face when he sees the dead Camazotz I'm sure mirrored mine when I first saw it. According to him, this is bad on so many levels. He paces around my room, frowning or rubbing his temples, and has no clue about who is behind this, or what they're trying to achieve.

Next we discuss the burning desire I have to tell Parents V2.0 that I know about Parents V1.0. Since Enzo found me, I've wanted to come clean. I don't understand why the urge to tell them won't leave me, because deep down I'm truly petrified of how they'll look at me once they know. Yet, I hate the feeling that I'm kinda lying to them by keeping it a secret. Rocks weighs up the pros and cons, and in the end, can't decide if I should tell them or not.

"You'll need this." I throw the velvet pouch at him. His red eyebrow bar falls onto his palm, and he smiles before shoving it in his front pocket.

"You're not going to wear it?"

"I'll get Decker to help me." My frown earns me an eye roll. "If I want it to be visible when I'm a bat, then I have to put it in while I'm a bat. Otherwise, if I put it in as a human, it will vanish when I flip like my clothes do."

Ha, how interesting. I wonder if there will ever be a day when I know everything there is to know about my supernatural boyfriend.

"I can help."

Surprise flashes over his features. "You won't mind, um, while I'm a bat?" His eyes dart to the doorway and back to me.

Tiptoeing to the door, I quietly close it. Mom and Dad have an open door policy that I'm starting to hate. Facing Rocks, I notice he's fidgeting.

"Why would I mind?"

Standing near my window, he looks at his scuffed boots and shrugs.

"Rocks?" Stopping in front of him, I take hold of his hands to stop their circuit from his front pockets to his back ones. I receive the most adorable shy smile.

"It's been a while since I've been around and, um," —he shrugs again— "well, as a bat."

I huff. "You honestly don't think I'm still freaked out by you when you're a bat, do you?"

His hair falls over his eyes. "Well, last time I flipped you had to watch me feed. I worried you might have thought about that while I was gone."

Silly Camazotz.

Rocks is usually so confident—or appears to be anyway—that when he has moments of vulnerability it catches me off guard.

"I've done nothing but think about that, and about how much trust you had in me to help you when you weren't sure it would all work out. What I witnessed was amazing—just like you. So flip and let's get this piercing back where it belongs." I hold my palm out waiting, unable to stop my smile.

Rocks shakes his head, grinning down at me before leaning over. His lips hover just out of my reach. "You're the amazing one, Miss Connie Phillips," he whispers, before kissing me softly three times.

LATE FRIDAY NIGHT, his text requests my presence at the market on Sunday. That's the day the Sire will decide if they should re-open for business or wait a bit longer. Rocks hasn't resumed his Bun Lovin' Barn escort duty since he's under surveillance, so I hope the Sire consents to opening the market.

Rocks is leaning against their rusted van when I pull into the parking lot.

"I think you should talk to Strickland about your parents and Enzo," he says the minute I'm in his arms.

"What?"

"It's all I've thought about since you said you wanted to tell them, but I don't know if you should or not. My father might be wrong about a lot of things, but he does give good advice—so long as it's not to me." Rocks smiles, but he can't hide the sadness in his eyes. His hair falls over them when he looks down.

"Talk to Strickland? Really?" Having a heart-to-heart with the Sire is not exactly high on my list of things to do—ever.

"The colony—we're like a little village. Villagers share their problems and work everything out together. That's part of being a community."

"But I'm not a village member." I raise an eyebrow.

Rocks chuckles. "You are to me."

I feel my ears heat up and am glad I wore my hair down.

"Besides he owes you for saving me. He'll listen. Don't mention the bat attacks. I want to do my own investigation on that without anyone knowing."

My shoulders tense at the thought of sharing my fudged-up family tree with Strickland. Then again, he should hardly be one to judge. Rocks peers around the end of the van and scans the sky and branches above us. I follow his line of sight wondering what he's doing. A second later, his hand slides into my hair, and he pulls me in for a kiss. Sneaky bat.

We find Strickland and an army of Camazotz in human form down near the dairy. Even if I didn't know Strickland was their leader, just watching him issuing commands and surveying his territory, I'd know he was powerful and not to be messed with. A deadly focus almost oozes from him. Camazotz approach him with a certain amount of caution and scurry off the instant he dismisses them.

The market is a hive of activity. Rocks explains they're going to open up for business by the end of this week, and every member is on clean up duty. It's funny how I'd never noticed how few people were at the market each time I visited. Now that most of the Camazotz are here, it's teaming with activity. They really do avoid being human whenever they can.

"It's pretty busy. Is this a good idea?" I can't help but notice the stares and glares coming my way. I like visiting the market but would prefer to not be the focus of everyone around me. The strange thing is the stares don't seem so sinister now. Maybe not everybody wants to do away with me and hide my body.

"Ignore them. I do," he replies.

I know that's not exactly true. Rocks hungers to be accepted for who he is by his colony, but that's a conversation for another time.

Strickland strides toward us the moment he notices me. His scowl does nothing for my nerves, and I still have the strongest urge to curtsey when he comes to a stop before us.

"Hello, sir." I look away from his hard stare. He crosses his arms over his muscled chest, but doesn't issue a greeting. *Great.* "Um—"

"Miss Phillips, I'm a busy man. Are you going to tell me what your problem is or not?"

Trying not to annoy him any further, I launch into my tale about my adoption and discovering the identity of Parents V1.0. I go off course a little trying to explain exactly why Enzo is such bad news because I'm not sure how much the Camazotz know about illegal drug trafficking.

His scowl deepens, and I feel like that poor minion hit with Gru's shrink ray. "*These* are the kind of aeronaughts you expose my son to? That nearly kill him?" he snarls.

I stand tall and meet his eye. "A *Camazotz* is the kind that tried to kill him. Do not blame that crime on us!" I don't like thinking in terms of 'us' and 'them,' but I will not have the human race blamed for this one. I look at Rocks. "Did you ask her?"

He nods. "She was no help."

"Who?" Strickland asks.

"Zabreena knows the bat that did it," I explain. "He told me crushing Rocks' wing was a death sentence. He did it to Rocks on purpose. He knew all about—" Sugarplums, maybe this is stepping over the line. Strickland is waiting for me to finish. I swallow. "He knew how you view your son." There. Interpret that as you will, Mr. Judgy-McJudgypants.

Strickland holds up a hand and snaps his fingers. An enormous, young man with shark bite piercings materializes at his side. I can't help but think that the two rings piercing his bottom lip on either side of his mouth remind me more of vampire fangs, and not shark's teeth. The dude's chest and shoulders are so broad it's kinda scary. I find it hard to imagine him being able to fly carrying all that muscle bulk.

"Bring Zabreena. Now." The man flips and flies off as fast as his wings will carry him.

"Do not tell them," he commands. "Your parents," he clarifies.

"But—" Strickland holds out a finger, and I snap my mouth closed. *Fudge.*

"The less people that know of the Camazotz involvement, the safer it is."

"My parents do not *know* about the Camazotz, and I wasn't going to mention that part."

"Your parents are now connected to the Camazotz whether they *know it* or not. You have three lives to worry about. I'm responsible for a hell of a lot more, and until I'm satisfied there is no danger, you will not say one—single—word. Clear?"

"Crystal." He frowns. "I mean, yes, sir."

Zabreena flips and knocks me sideways. Rocks grabs my arm to prevent me falling over and steps between us. I'm impressed he noticed my clenched fists so fast. Strickland questions her, and her almost submissive body language reminds me of the night on the lawn after Rocks spoke to the girls.

"His name is Joey," she replies.

I snort, then wish I hadn't. Strickland is one step off furious, and I have a feeling my presence has shortened his fuse.

"I can't believe she fell for that," I explain. The look in three sets of eyes tells me they have no clue what I'm talking about. "You seriously didn't believe that was his name, did you? I mean he wouldn't exactly be the first Camazotz to tell a lie. Right, Rocks' little *cousin?*" I glare in her direction.

Anger flares for a brief second across her face. Then I notice Strickland's face and wish I'd kept my mouth shut.

"From your story, Miss Phillips, it seems you also are more than capable of telling a lie," Strickland points out.

"Ah, yes, aeronaughts are nasty liars. I was just surprised that Camazotz lower themselves to our level since you're so superior in every other aspect." I keep my tone even and hope the sarcasm doesn't register on his radar. I notice Rocks wince in my peripheral vision, but it's Strickland that my eyes never leave.

Camazotz understand sarcasm all right.

Tiff once forced me to read this werewolf book, and the young men had trouble keeping their temper under control without shifting. Right now, I imagine Strickland flipping and flapping me to death in a fit of rage.

Crabapples. I shouldn't be disrespectful, but his lack of respect for his son makes me want to go all Kung Fu Panda on his butt.

Rocks frowns at me but tries to bring us back on topic. "Why wouldn't that be his name?"

"It's not like this place is crawling with names like Tom, Dick or Harry now is it?"

My logic is clearly lost on the bat population that is staring at me like I'm a fish out of water, or maybe I'm the aeronaught up to her eyeballs in bats. "Those names are very common in my world, and if I didn't want to be tracked down, that's the kind of name I'd use. It doesn't exactly sound like a Camazotz name, does it?"

Even though my logic on the matter is sound, Strickland still seems to be holding me personally responsible. I want to scream in his face that I don't know that freaking bat, but a member of his own colony does.

"Which colony?" Strickland asks.

"Duskwing," she replies.

"We will pay them a visit." The Sire has spoken. A quick head nod and Zabreena flips and departs. "You will be leaving us *immediately,*" he says to me before glaring at Rocks.

Rocks takes my hand and pulls me in the opposite direction. I assume he's escorting me to my car, but we don't turn off the path at the signpost. Instead, he leads me up past the apothecary toward his shop. Before we get there, two figures step out of the apothecary and head toward us. I recognize Zada immediately, and even though Rocks says she likes me, I'm still not convinced. The other is a tall man, maybe in his mid-thirties. It's hard to tell because he's dressed kinda like a punk rocker in full leather, and there's something about him that seems more modern. Maybe it's his black, shoulder-length hair, but for an old dude, he's kinda good-looking. Then I realize he has the same bone structure as Rocks.

"This is my brother, Zander," Zada says. She still has that 'off with the fairies' vibe about her. If I didn't know any better, I would say she'd recently smoked something that's illegal in this state.

"Hi Zada." I meet Zander's eyes and then remember he's also a Fold member. "Hello, pleased to meet you." I dip my head in acknowledgement. I don't want to piss off every member with power at the colony.

The surprise I'm not expecting is that he smiles, and it's a warm, genuine smile. *Holy crabapples*. After standing next to the Sire, and the anger he was radiating mostly at me, this is a welcome reprieve.

Zander extends his hand, and I step back on instinct causing Rocks to snort. "He wants to shake your hand."

What the?

Staring at his outstretched hand, my ears start a slow burn. "Sorry." We shake once, and his grip on my hand doesn't break any bones as I was expecting. I think I've been in the presence of anti-aeronaught Camazotz far too much.

Rocks explains that we were just dealing with Strickland, and Zander nods in understanding. "He can be pretty intimidating—even to me." He smiles again, and I hope my face isn't showing my total and utter confusion at his lack of scare-off-the-aeronaught-bitch-itude.

"I wanted to thank you for saving Rockland and returning him to us."

At that, my jaw drops open before I can stop myself. Some alternate universe has swallowed me whole. "Um, oh, yeah sure." Smooth. I need to calm down. "You're welcome, sir."

His mother and uncle turn with another smile and head back into the store. I stare at Rocks who is grinning like the cat that ate the canary. "Did I imagine that?" I ask.

He laughs. "No, my uncle is serious. He's really grateful. There was so much death last year, you know, and you performed a miracle by preventing mine." He tells me that for seven grueling hours last night the Fold and Clip members voted on his broken blood oath.

Rocks says that he stood before the group and told them he only disclosed the roost location because he wanted them to witness his recovery using special aeronaught animal healing. He said that if he stayed with me while he healed, most of them never would believe he had a broken wing. When I raise my eyebrows at him, he turns slightly red. We both know Rocks wasn't convinced he would heal, but he figured this version of the truth was the only way he would be allowed to live. Zander and Judge both stood by his side and spoke in his defense. In the end, the vote was close, but enough members voted in his favor because they were so shocked to see him fly when the cast was removed.

A wing break is their worst nightmare, and for the first time in their history, a member has survived imminent death. He explains there's a rumor going around that I'm a descendant from a powerful shaman.

"They think I did magic to heal your wing?"

Rocks smiles and I'm relieved to know he thinks the rumor is crazy too. "Sylvana is not happy."

"Oh sugarplums!" I do not like being on her radar—ever. "So they're not going to punish you for telling me about Blood Mountain? It's over. You're in the clear?"

"They're not going to put me to death, but they are punishing me." He rolls his eyes and won't say anymore about it, apart from it's nothing he's not used to anyway. "Having two Fold members vouch for me was what saved me in the end, I think."

It suddenly occurs to me just how high up the ranks Rocks is. His mom has kids with not one, but two Fold members, and her brother is in power too. If the Camazotz had royalty, Rocks would no doubt be the crown prince. No wonder the other bats get out of his way.

"Is Zander okay with you being human so much?"

Rocks shrugs. "Not sure."

"Which way did Strickland vote?" I don't want to ask, but I need to know.

Rocks scans the sky, and I wonder if he's looking for little batty eavesdroppers. "He voted last and sided with the majority." He looks down and kicks a stone into the garden opposite us.

Fudge me, Strickland's a hard ass. I don't want to think how he would've voted if it wasn't going Rocks' way. Surely as the Sire, he could spare a life if he wanted to, but he'd have to want to …

Rocks takes my hand and we keep walking, but I'm surprised when we don't enter his workshop. When I point to his closed store, he smiles and leads me around the corner down behind the building. Opposite the back entrance, sitting under a massive tree is an old-fashioned, gypsy wagon.

"What's that?" I can't take my eyes off the mystical, horse-drawn carriage before me. I feel as though I've been transported back in time. I let go of his hand and move closer. "Oh my …"

I've never seen anything so beautiful but so old world at the same time. The wagon has a rectangular base that's at least seven-feet wide across. A horseshoe-shaped dome sits on top. It's made from dark, brown wood, but the front door is paneled with carved ornate patterns in rich, glossy colors. Blood-red, deep purple, and forest green engraved patterns cover the entire front wall. All the railings and trim are painted in shiny silver that outlines all the panels making them pop. Staring at the patterns makes me imagine dark-haired gypsies traveling under the stars. A short, curved ladder of five steps leads up to the ornate door.

"This is home."

My mouth drops open for a second time. "But …" I shake my head. "Wow, but … some days I honestly don't know you."

Rocks takes my hand and walks over to the ladder. "You know me better than anyone."

The inside of the wagon is even more spellbinding. The space is small, yet every inch is put to use. The far end of the wagon houses a plush double bed, covered in pillows. A large window—surrounded by an ornate frame that matches the design on the front door—dominates the back wall. Red velvet curtains are tied back with thick coils of golden cord to let the sunlight in. Rocks' bedspread is made from a green fabric that is so dark, it's almost black, and the edges are embossed with heavy, gold thread.

Running the length of the right side of the wagon is a cushioned bench seat. Lined up on the bench in ridiculously neat stacks are Rocks' folded clothes and few precious possessions. Above the seat are cupboards with sliding glossy, wooden panels. Between two cupboards is a tiny little window. I stand on tippy-toes to peer out and am stunned to see a dozen or so goats under the same massive tree that protects the wagon. Two large animals are butting heads while the rest stand half asleep.

"Your goats?"

He nods and a little tinge of pink colors his cheeks.

The left side of the wagon houses a turn of the century iron stove. Looking up, I follow the silver chimney until it vanishes amid the most jaw-dropping ceiling I've ever seen. One long, arched panel covers the center of the roof. Carved into the wood is the Milky Way—the moon, distant planets, silver stars, a comet, and flying bats—feature on the artwork. Beside the stove, there's a sink and strange wooden dresser that can only be described as a miniature, turn-of-the-century kitchen. It's plain and ancient, and clearly hasn't been used anytime in the last fifty years. Instead of pots and pans, the bench is filled with jewelry-making supplies and tools.

"What do you think?" I jump at his close proximity behind me. Being here is like stepping into another world.

"It's freaking incredible. Wow!"

Rocks smiles. "You really like it? You don't think it's … stupid?"

"Stupid? Are you crazy? Look at this." I gesture to everything around us, turning in a circle as my eyes soak up more details.

"But it's not modern like your house."

"I'd feel like a gypsy princess if I lived here. This is way cooler than my house." He motions for me to take a seat beside his precisely folded shirts while he reaches up and digs around in a small cupboard above my head. He pulls out the e-reader my folks gave him for Christmas.

"I think it's broken. It says it holds three thousand books, but I can't find any."

I bite my lip, but my smile escapes regardless. We never got a chance to have a lesson on the e-reader with the craziness that was post-Christmas.

"I'll take it home and download some for you."

Since we finally have some real privacy, I grab his vest and pull him down toward me.

Before I can kiss him, Rocks jerks up, looking toward the door. Little Bailey's head appears as she climbs the steps into his wagon. Her hot-pink seahorse is tucked under her arm, and she's now wearing a leather eye patch. A miniature Goth pirate in the making.

"Did you bring them, Miss Connie?" Her good eye sparkles.

I have no idea what she's talking about and look at Rocks.

"Bailey, how many times do I have to tell you it's rude to ask? How about starting with hello?" He sighs and lifts her onto the cushions beside me. She straightens out her long skirt and places the seahorse on her lap.

"Hello, Miss Connie. How are you?"

"Fine, thank you, and you?"

"Fine, except Odelia doesn't have a baby to love," she explains, looking at me, and then up at her enormous brother.

Crabapples.

My mind rewinds back to the blood ceremony and meeting her little Goth friend that didn't get a Beanie baby. Bailey had requested that I bring more babies that could fly—like her. Her and her little friends have been waiting patiently ever since.

"Oh, sweetie, I forgot. I'm so sorry." I try not to look at her eye patch, but into the deep blue eye that's watching me so intently.

"That's okay. I know you'll be back," she says with a smile. "Do owls ever attack you, Miss Connie?"

Sugar. That's not a question I would have expected her to ask. Rocks rubs his eyebrows, half covering his face with his hand, and leans his hip against the counter opposite us. I don't like the slump of his shoulders.

"No, they don't."

"Just us then?" She's waiting for an answer.

I nod. My gut is warning me to keep my opinion on the safety of being human to myself. After all, she's just a kid—a pup.

"They're dangerous. I worry about my family every night." She looks up with tears forming in her good eye. "But I don't have to worry about Rockland as much."

This is one smart kid, but these sorts of conclusions are not what the Sire would want her making. "I'll bring you a new baby soon," I say, trying to change the subject. "I'll bring you lots of them." Her face lights up and reminds me that she's still a child regardless of how mature she seems.

She hops off the seat and heads out the door. I stare at Rocks. He simply shakes his head and shrugs his shoulders. "She's got a point."

"How's she doing with—" I point to my eye.

"Good, I guess. Adjusting."

"Yeah?"

"It's affected her flying. She's covered in bruises, but she's getting better at it. It's messed with her depth perception. She'll eventually adjust."

That poor little poppet. I imagine myself in gym trying to do that stuff with only one eye. I can barely manage with two as it is.

"She was spending a lot of time in the shop with me before we closed for winter."

"That's great. I know how you miss the little ones." I stand in front of him and take his hands.

"It's not great when she's scared to flip. I thought she might have forgotten about it since we've been away, but she asked you about the owls." He turns and watches her through the windows behind the stove. She's chatting to her pink seahorse, and it looks like a serious conversation. "If the wrong wing heard that …"

"What?" My hackles rise.

"They'll think I'm trying to brainwash the pups that being a Camazotz is dangerous." He shakes his head and sighs. "The problem is I don't trust them not to make an example of her."

"What are you saying …" I can't even bare to voice this crazy notion that the leaders of this colony might single her out and punish her after what she has already endured. Bailey is Judge's daughter, but her mother is Zada. Would Strickland punish the daughter of the woman he's had children with when Judge is a Fold member too? This is getting beyond absurd.

"I don't know," Rocks replies. He looks tired—that bone-deep tired that comes from too many worries and is usually only seen on overworked adults. "I don't know anything anymore, and that's half the problem."

10
Camping

BAILEY'S questions have left Rocks flat. He tries to smile, but nothing about his body language is happy. He's worried, and that makes me worried—and I'm worried enough already. With Rocks trying to find the rogue bats on his own and Enzo always in the back of my mind, I don't need anything else to stress about.

"We need to have some fun."

That gets his attention. "What do you have in mind?"

"Can you get away from here? I know everyone has work to do."

"Lead and I'll follow. When it comes to hours at the market, I more than pull my weight."

My idea has me practically bursting with excitement. This is exactly what we need. "How about a driving lesson?"

The weight from earlier vanishes as the most blinding smile crosses his features. "Yes!"

He's such a teenage boy. I forget that when I see him so serious and responsible here. I explain since he doesn't have a learner's permit we can't get caught on the road. He says there's a high school one county over from Helen that has a large parking lot and a road that rings right around the buildings and sports track. Having an aerial perspective can be handy.

My old Honda is an automatic so Rocks won't have to worry about gear changes—not that I would be much help in that department. Seeing him behind the wheel and so excited makes it hard for me to concentrate. The first time he hits the gas, I'm thrown back in my seat. Talk about beginner to NASCAR driver in two nanoseconds. His eyes are so wide, and after he quickly slams on the brakes—confirming that seatbelts do indeed save lives—he throws his head back and laughs.

"Sorry." His apology does not match his earsplitting grinning. "You okay?"

"Just ease your foot onto the gas pedal, Speedy."

It's been too long since I've seen Rocks this laid-back and content. In no time at all, he's doing laps of the school grounds, steering straight and generally trying not to age me or the Honda. In the confines of my car, all I can smell is that moonlit night scent that is all Rocks. It's doing strange things to my insides, which gives me an idea for lesson number two.

I get him to pull over behind the school, where the parking lot backs on to the forest. It's away from the main road and private. Perfect.

"What are we doing?" Even though the daylight is fading, I can see the excitement almost glowing in his eyes. I pull the handbrake on and turn to face him in my seat.

"Um, teenagers do lots of stuff in cars that don't have anything to do with driving."

His frown makes me giggle. I can't help myself. Mr. Old-Fashioned gives me a confidence that simply vanishes when I'm around the boys at school. "Like what?"

"Like this." I reach over, grab Rocks by the collar and pull him toward me until my lips touch his. Rocks has always been a fast learner, and in no time at all, we're a tangle of limbs, making out like it's our last hour on earth.

A text from Mom separates us, and I realize it's dark. I'm late and have a long drive ahead of me.

"I gotta go."

Rocks cups my face, he's mere inches away from my lips. We sit and grin at each other in silence until my phone beeps again.

"Driving is my new favorite thing if this is what happens." He winks, and I lean in to kiss him quickly before he climbs out of the car.

Instead of walking around to the passenger side, he just stands there.

"Aren't you coming?" I say, sliding into the driver's seat.

He shakes his head. "I'll be fine. You get going and *drive* safely." His raised eyebrow makes me laugh, and I know he's never going to think of driving the same again. The last thing I see is him give me a quick salute before flipping, and his bat silhouette disappears into the thick line of trees.

BACK HOME, I seek out my family. Mom is reading to Mini tucked up in her little bed, and Dad is in his armchair watching a game. I think of Strickland's command to not tell them, but the desire to share my secret is still strong. I can't explain the sudden urge to include them. Maybe it's simply hanging out with them so much and knowing they love me that I don't want anything between us. I try to find the words, but they die on my lips at the thought of telling them Enzo Ascari wants to get to know me better.

Flopping onto my bed, I'm convinced confiding in them is a really stupid idea. I know they wouldn't want me anywhere near that man, and the thought of Enzo 'insisting' he see his new daughter makes my stomach lurch. I send a quick text to Rocks telling him I'm home safe. He replies faster than he flips.

When can we go driving again?"

I stifle my laughter in my pillow. Boys! I reply ...

You alone?

When he confirms the coast is clear, I call him.

"Connie?" I can hear the shock in his voice. We've never called each other before even though he's had a phone for so long.

"Can you talk?"

"Yeah, nearly had a heart attack. The phone started barking at me, and I dropped it."

I cover my eyes in the crook of my elbow and try not to laugh. I used to change Dad's ringtone if he left his phone unattended for any period of time. I guess Dad eventually gave up in the end and that must have been the last crazy ringtone I'd chosen for him.

"Where are you?"

"In bed," he replies. I grin. I picture exactly where he is lying in that amazing wagon behind his shop, looking up at the carved night sky on his ceiling.

"Me too. I still want to tell them, but I think Strickland's right and I shouldn't, so I called you. Distract me."

"Strickland wants us to visit Duskwing. He'd never say it, but I know he's secretly seething about one of their members trying to kill me."

That's a distraction all right. Finally, his Sire is having the correct response to what happened. Rocks says the Fold had another meeting, and a group has been selected to drop in on them. He also explains that since too many of their members have died, Strickland is reluctant to fly there in case of another surprise attack. They would be forced to fly over miles and miles of residential land away from the safety of the National Forest.

When I ask about the owls, he explains that so far they've been safe. Levi, the oldest Fold member, thinks that since they headed to their roost for half of winter, the owls that were released have probably moved on in search of better feeding grounds. However, the Sire is still wary, and members aren't supposed to be out alone after dark. I shudder at the thought of owls eating them.

"If that colony is called Duskwing, what's yours called?" I meant to ask Rocks this when we were questioning Zabreena, but as usual I got sidetracked.

"We're known as the Shadows colony."

"Cool." I'm thankful it doesn't have anything to do with blood. "What about the third one?"

"They're Vuelo de la Muerte."

"Sounds Spanish." I wish I wasn't on my phone so I could check Google Translate. "What does it mean?"

I hear Rocks sigh down the line. "Death Flight."

Charming. There's the sinister, Goth presence I was expecting.

"So will you help us?" Rocks asks quietly.

"Me?" How on earth can I help the Camazotz? "Sure, how?"

"Can you drive us to their farm?" At Rocks saying the word drive, I blush and am so thankful we're not on Skype.

Rocks explains that Judge isn't fond of driving on the interstate. He enjoys coming down the mountain to Helen once a month, but Rocks says he barely reaches the speed limit. The interstate full of heavy trucks would be a disaster, and they would draw attention to themselves that they do not need.

"There is no way Strickland is going to agree to this."

"I told him I'd ask you. It might be another good way for them to see an aeronaught do something good for us. It might help them forgive you for entering the roost."

Hmmm … he's right. Camazotz/aeronaught relations aren't exactly in a good place. I did save Rocks when he had a broken wing, but they all view me as being responsible for that mess. This might be seen as me helping them for nothing in return. It makes me sad that Rocks is thinking the same way. It confirms my suspicions that he does still care what they think of him and his friendship with an outsider.

During dinner the next night, no moment feels right, so I dive in.

"Can I go camping with Rocks and his family this weekend?" The silence that follows is not what I was hoping for. I look back and forth between my parents.

"Ah," Dad finally speaks. "Sure, but I'd like to meet them first?"

Oh, hell no! My ears are instantly flaming hot. If I'm not careful, they'll singe my hair. The image of Chad and Kelly being introduced to Strickland and Zada with Rocks and I standing in between makes me pray the ground will open up and swallow me whole before that *ever* happens. "Well, um, ah …"

Mom comes to the rescue and asks me questions I actually have pre-prepared lies for. Where are we going? Blah, blah, blah. I take a deep breath, answer, and look back at my father helping Mini with her peas.

"Honey, with a boy that has manners like Rocks, his parents must be delightful," Mom comments to Dad, then smiles at me for confirmation.

I cover my mouth because the idea of Strickland ever being described as delightful makes me want to cry with laughter. I don't expect he'd be pleased with that description either.

"Truly delightful," I say, nodding. "And can I borrow the van?" Dad frowns. "With all his siblings, they need an extra car to carry the camping gear." I struggle to keep my tone light, and hope my glowing ears stay hidden by my hair, lest they out me and my growing list of lies.

The look in Dad's eyes tells me he knows Rocks and I aren't just friends, and giving us the van for a weekend is a bad idea. In reality, he can't possibly know. As I feel my cheeks heat, I'm grateful when Mini drops her fork. I duck under the table and take three deep breaths, trying not to think about making out with Rocks in my Honda, or where the hell I'm going to sleep on this little trip with my brand new boyfriend and his scary-as-fudge father. It's not like we're going to get any alone time. Dad honestly has nothing to worry about.

Mom is my savior and convinces Dad that no harm will come to his precious work van. He grunts a yes but eyes me for another solid minute.

"So what happened in world news today?" I ask, hoping to distract him with his favorite topic.

INSTEAD OF OPENING the market on Saturday as planned, it's decided we'll drive to Duskwing's farm. They're a smaller colony and don't have an organized market for income like the Shadows. Rocks had whispered to me that this colony believes the Mayan story, and they view what the shaman did to them as a curse rather than a gift. The Duskwing would frown upon how Strickland treats his firstborn son. They understand and share Rockland's desire to be human.

The sun is high overhead when I arrive at Sanguine Mountain Market. Strickland and Rocks are waiting under a pine tree. A screech from high above has me looking up to find fifteen or so bats hanging in the lower branches. When I take my place next to Rocks, he doesn't lean in and kiss me, but his index finger slides into my back pocket. I don't care that our relationship isn't in the open here, because I haven't come clean to my folks either, but the fact that he gives me a connection to cling to means the world.

"You don't have to wear black all the time," he says in my ear. "I like your bright clothes. Be yourself."

I shrug, looking up into his gorgeous, blue eyes. "Just trying to help." He smiles.

My Camazotz passengers consist of four Fold members and their sons—Strickland and Rockland, Judge and Decker, Cypress and Ash, Levi and Mazal—and four other males. Guess that makes me lucky number thirteen.

While the Sire is away from the Shadows, the three other Fold members will guard the colony and market. Mazal is Jeremiah's older half-brother. They share the same father, Levi, and Mazal looks like he's seen some action. He's probably in his late twenties, but his face is weathered with deep-set age lines making it hard to be sure, but that's not what grabs my attention. His hair is trimmed close to the scalp, and across each temple coming from his hairline is a tattooed point that thins down to touch the side of his eyes, turning into thick tattooed eye liner. When he turns to speak with fang-face—Ash—I get a look at the whole design. The back of his skull sports a gruesome bat tattoo, and the wings wrap around his head ending with the wing tips lining his eye sockets. The bat isn't anything like Rocks' gorgeous ink. It's creepy and makes me want to cover my neck on instinct.

The other four males are Jeremiah, and Rocks' cousin Harland—who helped me when the Vipers were caught following me. Malachite—the guy with the big nose from the Blood Ceremony, or as Rocks would say Graceland's batfriend. And lastly, the enormous, broad-shouldered dude I saw at the market last weekend. As he lumbers toward me wearing nothing but a black vest, I can't help but stare at his bulging biceps.

Rocks introduces him as Pegasus. Yep, if he flipped into a horse, he'd be a Bud Clydesdale for sure. Seeing how Rocks is being treated by the colony has given me a keen interest in the hierarchy of their politics.

Wings vote together and support each other. Pegasus comes from a small wing that is named for flying creatures and is the older brother of Phoenix from Rocks' old harem. They apparently vote with the Z wing, and the Z wing vote with the Land wing, which explains why this dude isn't snarling at me. I'm seriously going to need notes to keep track of these pesky, power-related bloodlines.

Rocks whispers that since Zander has sired only female pups, he's grooming Pegasus to take over his Fold position when the time comes. Pegasus grunts a hello and immediately turns to give the Sire his attention. He's got a large tattoo high on his shoulder—a knot of three interconnected crescent moons with large feathered wings sprouting from them.

Harland gives me a grim smile. His viper bites glint in the still-rising sun. As the Fold members stand together discussing today's plan, Jeremiah and Decker stroll over to join us.

"Good to see you, Beans." Decker smiles and leans in closer. "Any chance you can get one of your pretty friends to teach me to *drive?*" His cheeky comment turns my ears into an inferno. I punch Rocks in the arm, and the boys—including normally silent Jeremiah—all snicker. Strickland's frown turns us all to stone.

Cypress turns his cold stare my way. I'm thankful he's covered his blood-sucking tats with a dark, silk shirt. "She shouldn't be with us."

Rocks steps forward before I can stop him. "Her *name* is Connie, and she's the only ride we've got. But if you want to risk flying solo …" All I can see are Rocks' straight, hard shoulders. "Show her some respect."

Cypress glares past him to me. "The day I listen to a naught-lover will be a sad day indeed," he scoffs. Jeremiah grabs Rocks' arm and pulls him back between us.

"These are secrets that she should not know," he continues. His hands are on his hips, and if what I'm reading from his body language is correct, he is definitely not happy with his Sire.

"It's not like I'm marching into their secret roost." I regret my words the second I speak. Reminding them of that time my dad and I did march right into their top-secret roost isn't going to win me any favors. I'm guessing if the Plant wing had their way, Rocks would be history.

My stomach rolls. How can he live with such hate and animosity day and night? "I might be able to help."

Ash steps up next to his father. "You do not get to have an opinion on Camazotz matters."

That's when I see red. His smug, fanged face makes my hands clench into fists. If anyone should be going on this inter-colony excursion, it's me. I'm the only one present who's seen the face of that drug-dealing, wing-crushing Camazotz we're searching for.

"Really? We're headed to where they sell stuff, right?" Judge nods his head in reply. "And that's where aeronaughts are allowed to come and spend their money, right? Well, I don't see you turning away aeronaught dollars here, so I'm pretty sure my money will be welcome there!"

"Watch your tone, naught!" Cypress spits out.

"How many times do I have to tell you that humans are not *nothing*?" Rocks growls. "We were once just like them, and you would do well to remember that." The stare-down between Rocks and Cypress cools my temper. I do not want trouble this early in our big day.

"How's the nau—aeronaught going to find it? I'm betting her sense of direction is as weak as she is."

"I don't need a good sense of direction," I say, smiling. "I've got GPS." I want to stick my tongue out, but I know better. I should not be goading these bats, but their attitude is making it very hard for me to remain respectful.

The Duskwing farm is located in Floyd county. Rocks gives me the address, and as I punch the details into the GPS, I see his long fingers grip his knees. He wants to play with the gadget, but the back of Dad's van is full of watchful, judgmental eyes. Jeremiah, Decker, and Harland all choose to remain in human form and are sitting on the floor chatting. The rest of my passengers are hanging upside down from the cargo straps Rocks strung across the space. I can feel their eyes scrutinizing my every move.

The first thirty minutes of the trip, I'm sweating like a marathon runner at the Olympics. I don't know why having these bats watching me drive is affecting me this way. It's not like they know if I'm a good driver or not. I try to avoid looking in the rearview mirror, seeing their bodies swinging with the motion of the car every time I hear a male voice in my head. They aren't communicating much thank goodness, but they still manage to make me squirm. I remember how hard it was for Rocks to 'talk' to me telepathically at first. Maybe since my brain is used to him poking around in there, it's easier for me to plug into all the Camazotz frequencies now.

Rocks slides a hand over the bench seat and taps my thigh. "You okay?"

I swallow and nod, glancing in the rearview mirror yet again. "I know," he whispers and starts fiddling with the radio. Dad is a classic rock fan, and Rocks leaves the radio set to that station. At first, I panic that aeronaught music will piss them off more, but when no complaints echo inside my head, I relax into the drive. It's only three hours, but that's long enough with my cargo.

Stopping for an early dinner was interesting to say the least. Rocks, Decker, Jeremiah, Harland, Judge, Levi and Pegasus all kindly accepted my offer of buying them burgers at the truck stop. The waitress who took our order didn't know she was in the presence of Camazotz, but from her expression and the way she practically threw our food on the table, she had picked up she was in the presence of something. I wanted to strangle her because her rudeness only confirmed the opinions of the bats still hanging in the car.

Judge loved his first taste of sweet potato fries, and in the end, I piled my portion into his plate. Decker has a new appreciation for bacon since I convinced him to try the BBQ bacon cheeseburger. He whispered to me he's never been that keen on pigs before, and half the guys agreed. It's not the tastiest blood around apparently. Then Rocks swiped my bacon and announced it was a new favorite. Harland wasn't keen on the burger at all. I think it was the onions, but he did drain three cans of grape soda and stood eyeing the other flavors in the fridge, while the boys finished their meals. Pegasus made short work of Harland's leftovers and announced the market needs to invest in a device to create thick shakes.

Twenty minutes later, instructed by the GPS, we pull off the highway.

"Almost there," I report. The farm is located on a quiet road outside the abandoned town of Livingston.

Flip!

The chorus of loud thuds makes me swerve slightly as the men hit the floor of the van. Entering enemy territory is more dangerous as a bat, so Strickland isn't taking any risks. Funny how it's suddenly safer to be a human, but I bite my tongue.

A small sign advertising fresh honey for sale is all that marks the driveway to the Duskwing farm. I remind myself to pick up some for Mom as proof of our trip. The entrance winds through dense trees blocking all the farm buildings from the road. This place is secluded and safe from aeronaught eyes.

The two-story main house has a large verandah, which runs the length of the lower level. The building is neat and in good repair with a fresh coat of paint. This place does not have the feel of the Shadows' market at all. Wandering around Sanguine Mountain makes me believe I've stepped back in time—it's rustic and tired, and has a strange darkness that clings to it. This farm makes me expect a fresh-faced, young couple might reside here.

"Drive around back," Strickland orders.

The tires crunch on the unpaved drive as I slowly head behind the large house. Hiding behind it is the biggest barn I've ever seen. It could house a Boeing-747 and then some. The doors to the barn are closed, and I'm itching to see what's hidden inside considering this colony prefers to be human.

The place looks completely deserted—not a soul to be seen—but I sense we are under heavy surveillance. I look over at Rocks and watch his Camazotz senses come to life. His eyes dart around, and I don't even want to breathe in case he misses an aural clue.

"Wait here." Rocks jumps out of the van and is joined by the others. I notice how the men surround Strickland. Are they protecting their Sire? I rub the scar above my brow. Fudge, these bats make me nervous some days.

Movement in the grey shadow of the looming barn catches my eye. Three men step out into the light from the setting sun.

"Strickland?" one calls. "What do you want?"

Strickland steps to the front of his group but doesn't move any closer. The heat radiating off my body makes me want to wind down the window, but instead I leave my hands glued to the steering wheel, ready for a quick escape.

"I mean you no harm, Nighthawk, unless you are harboring the Camazotz responsible for the attempt on my heir's life. If not, I come in peace."

Nighthawk—dressed in denim overalls and a black shirt—speaks to a thin boy who runs back into the shadow of the main barn. "Agree to stay human?" he requests. Strickland grunts what I think is a yes. Nighthawk steps forward with his hand outstretched. "Forgive me, old friend, but these are dangerous times."

By the time Strickland has grasped his forearm, the small door set in the large sliding barn door opens, and several dozen people step outside. Many are dressed in simple, plain aeronaught clothing. They could pass for farm folk and not raise any kind of suspicion. The other half favor black fabric and scream Camazotz to the trained eye, but none of their outfits are as sensual or Gothic as those at the Shadows. As the tension dissipates from our group, I make my move and step out of the car.

My blonde hair garners quick stares, but there isn't the hatred I'm used to when the Shadows' members look my way. Nighthawk indicates to me with a polite jerk of his head. "Not your usual style."

Strickland barks out a short laugh. "As you said, dangerous times. Calls for dangerous methods."

I am not dangerous I want to yell. That stupid witch pointing her ringed finger at me and stating I was a danger to the colony is still haunting me.

I lean against the van and watch my Camazotz passengers move forward, grasping arms in greeting with the Duskwing members now they don't fear attack. As the tension eases out of everyone present, the welcome Rocks receives is no surprise. They all appear to have met him before and seem happier to stand with him than Ash, Malachite, or

Cypress. I breathe a sigh of relief. Strickland nods to Rocks and Decker, and the boys leave the group. Rocks takes my hand, and we all head toward the barn.

"Connie wants to buy some honey," he explains, when instantly wary bodies block the entrance.

A young woman, with two long plaits, smiles at Rocks before nodding her head. A path immediately opens for us. "She'll have to come inside because we closed our stall for the evening. It's a bit chaotic."

Access to their barn is exactly what Strickland had hoped. My job is to scan as many faces as possible to find Joey.

Entering the structure, I'm blown away. Ninety percent of the Duskwing are in human form, and the barn is a hive of activity—literally. The rear section is home to all their active beehives placed near large open sections of the back wall that allow breeze and sunlight into the huge interior. In the center of the open space is all the equipment needed to bottle honey for sale. Crates of glass jars both empty and filled are stacked high.

To my right, several antique sewing machines are whirring away as older women sew denim clothing. The barn has three split half levels, which you reach by climbing ladders that have seen better days. A group of kids, three stories up in the rafters, are playing on one of the wonky looking ladders, and I have to remind myself that if they fall, they can flip and fly back to earth.

I try not to stare as I scan face after face in the open area. Dozens of hammocks hang on the first open level, and I notice some of the Camazotz resting in them are heavily bandaged. I wonder how so many of them could be hurt when they all seem to prefer being human. Glancing up at the rafters high above, not one single bat is anywhere to be seen.

Rocks and I are guided to a small counter behind a makeshift wall. There's a group of teens working on hand-sketched labels for the jars of honey. It's a labor-intensive job, and I wish I could show them the efficiency of modern day printing. These Camazotz might not be against being human, but they're just as stuck in the past as the Shadows.

"You're pretty," a slender, young girl says with a smile.

I almost want to pinch myself. These Camazotz are so different from the Shadows.

"Yes, she is," answers Rocks, slinging his arm around my shoulders—a move he would never do at the market. "Connie, meet Moonlight. She's Moonshiner's first cousin."

At the mention of Rocks' half brother—little Moonshiner—her eyes light up. "You know Moonshiner?" she asks me.

I nod. "Yeah, he's a sweet kid."

Several others join the conversation as Rocks tells them how he's doing. I continue to scan the sea of faces, but Joey isn't among them. I spy Decker leaning over to whisper in a very pretty girl's ear. She blushes and giggles behind her hand before nodding her head at whatever he said. If they weren't Camazotz and just normal kids at school, I'd guess they were a hairs breadth away from ending up behind the gym.

By the time we leave the barn, I'm loaded up with more honey than even my mother will be able to use, and all my money is still in my wallet. The second they discovered I'm 'with' Rockland and I know little Moonshiner my money wasn't accepted. When I hugged Moonlight in thanks, the surrounding gasps shocked even me. Rocks murmured on our exit that I'm probably the first aeronaught she's ever had direct contact with, and even though they don't hate aeronaughts, the fact I treated them normally was a welcome surprise.

Back outside, a small group has formed to the side, including Strickland, Judge, Levi, Cypress, and four of the new Camazotz.

"Connie," Strickland summons.

When I reach the circle with Rocks on my heels, Strickland squints at me in question. I shake my head and try not to take his scowl personally. Strickland presents me to Moondust—the Sire at Duskwing. Again I'm overcome with the urge to curtsey, but I hold still and give him a slight head nod. Next I'm introduced to their Fold members— Nighthawk, Ganymede, and a woman—Starjewel. A female Fold member surprises me as it's forbidden in the Shadows. She has brilliant blue eyes and offers me her hand causing my breath to catch at the icy, cold temperature of her fingers.

Her touch makes me notice how most of these people are in long sleeves as I am. Moondust—probably in his early thirties with spiky, black hair—is the only member with bare, muscled arms. He must have fed recently and is warm enough to reveal his full sleeve tattoo, which covers his left arm. It's the solar system in swirls of black and grey, and high on his shoulder is a large crescent moon with a bat flying through the middle.

The backs of Ganymede's hands show two blazing sun tattoos. The difference between the Shadows and Duskwing members is night and day—it's me and Rocks. They don't ooze darkness and night like I'm accustomed to, and I wonder if they spend more hours in the sunshine. I would certainly recognize them as Camazotz, but they aren't anywhere near as intimidating.

"Tell them," Strickland barks at me, and I instantly notice Starjewel's frown.

I describe the Camazotz who attacked Rocks because, as suspected, no member here goes by the name Joey. All the wings in this colony are named for elements of the evening ... moons, stars, planets, and darkness. I resist the urge to mention if they truly want to integrate into my world, then these names have to go.

Tempers flare when Moondust realizes Strickland thought the killer was among them and sent me scouting behind their backs.

"You think I would be involved in the murder of the Camazotz that protects my son?" he growls.

Son?

My eyes dart to Rocks, but he's focused on the angry man before us.

"I don't know what to think after the losses we have suffered." Strickland shakes his head. "And, I resent your implication. We *all* take care of Moonshiner. He's one of us."

The way the 'us' is spoken speaks volumes. So this is the sire of little Moonshiner. Jeepers. Strickland is face-to-face with yet another of Zada's lovers! I wonder if the tension in his shoulders is due to that, or simply the stress of being here under these circumstances.

Moondust's eyes zero in on Strickland. "You're not going to blame us for the attacks as well, are you?"

"I do not suspect you of releasing those owls, unless you give me reas—"

"Not the owls, Strickland," Moondust continues. "We've suffered from those beasts as well. Twenty-seven dead, thirty-five seriously injured. That's not what I'm talking about."

Rocks takes a step closer to me, and when I look up, his eyes are full of worry. *Oh sugarplums.*

"The Camazotz attacks on the aeronaught children? Tell me you know of this."

Strickland's usual mask of control slips for a second, and he glares from Rockland to me and finally back at Moondust.

"When are you going to get with this century and take an interest in their news?" Moondust points at me. "They are not the enemy, my friend."

A yelling match follows with Cypress expressing his less-than-flattering opinions of me and my kind.. My respect for Judge grows when he steps between the two men and states that fighting amongst the colonies when a force is trying to weaken us is exactly what whoever is behind this wants to happen. He calls for respect, peace and trust.

"Why should we trust you?" Moondust asks. "Two years ago, we gave refuge to a medicine woman. The next thing I know a large number of our fledgers chose to be fixed. Suddenly, she vanishes—along with our young."

The lines around his eyes suggest he's as stressed as any member of the Shadows. "We can't afford another hit to our numbers. We won't survive. So if you have no information on the rogue Camazotz, then this conversation is over. Leave."

11
Blood Bonds

AFTER we left the Duskwing farm last night, Rocks and I got an earful—make that a head-full of abuse—from the Sire. He was livid he hadn't been informed about the rogue bat attacks, and discovering an aeronaught knew more about what was happening in the Camazotz world than he did wasn't pretty. Since I was exhausted from being under constant anti-aeronaught scrutiny, and from the responsibility of having a load of Camazotz in the back of the van, we ended up at a nearby campground for the night. Strickland bombarded me with questions well into the night, acting as though I was responsible for the attacks.

Once I had finally assured the Sire he knew everything I did, he left me alone in the back of Dad's van. Sleeping in the pitch-black darkness alone while a dozen bats roosted in the tree above—including Rocks— was a totally surreal experience. I had hoped he would send me mental messages, but then remembered all the bats would be listening to our not-so-private conversation.

When we return to the market on Sunday, there's a welcoming committee waiting for us. Zada and all of Rocks' siblings are milling around the parking lot. I watch Ezra greet Jeremiah with a slap across the shoulders before Bailey tugs on my hand.

"Did you bring them, Miss Connie?" she whispers. Rocks is busy hugging his younger brothers and talking to his mother. Moonshiner is standing to the side, waiting for his chance to say hello, and I wonder how well the young boy knows his father at the Duskwing colony. Is he allowed to visit him? Or will he one day in the future be looking for answers about his bloodline?

"I did. Meet me at your brother's wagon." I wink, making Bailey giggle.

Strickland walks up, eyeing little Bailey. I worry by talking to her he'll think she's on Team Aeronaught. "Thank you," he says, with a frown.

Holy sugarplums!

I gape because I'm sure my ears are playing tricks on me. Strickland just thanked a *human*. "You're welcome, sir. It's a shame it didn't give us answers."

He nods once. "You will return with that information?"

"Yes." I swallow.

Strickland leaves me to join his family. I watch him wrap an arm around Zada's waist and pull her close. Affection and the Sire seem about as compatible as fire and ice. Maybe there's more to the man than how he portrays himself as their leader. Zada kisses him briefly on the lips and smiles before moving off to the side. I watch as Strickland places a hand on little Ireland's head. I keep forgetting that, although Ireland is Strickland's daughter, she's not one of Zada's children. I look around to catch a glimpse of her mother.

Grabbing my backpack, I say a quick hello to Zada and the circle of siblings clinging to Rocks. Baxter is still pretty shy but politely says hello. He's nothing like his chatty older brother, Decker, or little Bailey. A second later, they all flip and fly off. We head to Rocks' wagon for a moment before I head home.

Bailey is waiting on the top rung of the ladder when we approach the wagon. Rocks offers a hand to help me up the narrow steps, and I accept purely to have a moment of physical contact. He smiles, knowing I know why he offered his assistance as I'm more than capable of climbing a five-step ladder. Bailey scoots over to make room as I unzip my bag, and the look on her face, as I pull out *Scorch The Dragon*, is priceless.

"What is *that*?" she says, looking at me in awe.

"A dragon." Her wide-eyed look tells me she's never seen one before. I want to smack my forehead realizing Bailey hasn't been exposed to storybooks or cartoons and probably knows nothing of these creatures. All she knows about are real animals that she would encounter on the mountainside.

I dump the contents of my backpack on the carpeted floor—a brightly colored rooster with a pink comb, a startling blue-jay, a proud peacock, the prettiest hummingbird I've ever seen, a scarlet-red cardinal, an orange lightning bug, and a pastel butterfly—all flying creatures as requested.

"I'm going to keep the dragon, but I'll share these with the others. Can you tell me about him?"

"Well, he's magical." I've positively made her day.

"Like me?" she asks.

Oh, fudge. These kids think … no, they know magic is real. How the hell do I explain this? Wait. Maybe dragons were real back in the witch-burning days too. Isn't that what knights were for? Slaying dragons to rescue the princess.

This is messing with my head. Bailey is waiting patiently for an answer. "Yeah, a bit like you, but the sad part is nobody has seen a dragon for hundreds of years."

Bailey looks at the creature in her hands with a renewed awe. "This is very special then, Miss Connie. I will take extra good care of him so he knows someone remembers him."

A commotion outside has Rocks stepping around us and exiting. Once Bailey has all the babies tucked under her arms, I help her down the ladder before sitting on the top rung myself. There's a small group of teenagers surrounding Rocks and a group of bats hanging in the lower branches of the nearby tree. The kids range in age upwards of thirteen or so. Rocks is standing tall with his arms folded over his chest, listening to two boys talking over each other. Decker flips almost on top of me, and I barely manage to stifle my scream. Wouldn't I be popular if I knocked a bunch of them unconscious on their own turf?

"God damn you, Decker." I go to punch his arm but stop. He squeezes into the space next to me, resting his boots on the rung with mine, and chuckles. He holds out his tattooed bicep for me to line up my hit.

"Go on. It was rude of me to almost land on you. Some days, I forget you aren't one of us."

The Camazotz have a much smaller body space requirement than aeronaughts. I remember seeing how closely they snuggle together on the ceiling of the roost. Warm bodies crushed up against one another in total harmony. I move over to give him more room and decide not to thump his offered arm. The fact Decker is so comfortable around me makes me happy. Grabbing my backpack, I slip the envelope onto his lap.

"What's this?"

"Our secret." His eyes light up with recognition. He pulls the four photos out and sits staring at his own image. I can't comprehend seeing myself for the first time in print at this age.

"Wow, will you look at that." He instantly blushes a little and ducks his head. "Thank you." Decker shuffles through the pictures repeatedly, a smile tugging at the side of his mouth the entire time.

"What's going on there?" I point at Rocks surrounded by the teens.

He smiles. "Rockland has been missing for two days, and a lot can happen to the fledgers in that time." He explains that every wing has a leader known as a Clip. From the Clips, the Fold members are voted into power. And from the Fold, the Sire is selected. He says when disputes occur who sits in judgment is determined by the seriousness of the dispute. Fledgers are young bats that are out of their pup stage but still too young to vote. When Rocks turned nineteen last July—officially becoming an adult Camazotz—the fledgers started bringing their quarrels to him for resolution.

"Seriously?" I gape. If I had a dollar bill for every time Rocks shocked the absolutely sugarplums out of me, I'd buy a new car.

"I told you, Jeremiah and I are betting on him being the next Sire." The photos get tucked back into the envelope. He leans back and slips them just inside the wagon doorway, explaining he'll pick them up later.

"I thought the others hated him being human? I can't imagine they'd want him influencing the next gen," I say.

"True, they don't like it. The problem is Rocks will always make time for the little ones. The Clip and Fold member are so consumed with defending us, and now they have the rogue bats to deal with too, these kids never get heard."

The young boys shake hands with each other, flip and fly off. A group of three kids take their place, and Rocks begins again.

"What did Moondust mean when—"

Decker turns to face me. "Stop right there, Beans. I know where this is headed, and I'm not going there."

"Decker!" Moondust mentioned some fledgers getting fixed, and when he said it, Strickland flinched. I can't imagine much in their world making that hard ass react.

"Nuh-uh, not telling. Oh, shit. Here's trouble." Decker points to the small gap between the buildings. Lurking in the shadows is their healer, Sylvana, with two boys.

"Did Rocks tell you about Elm and Oak?" He takes out his pocket watch and checks the time. "They're twins."

"Cool. I go to school with identical twins."

"Not cool around here. They're the only other members that were born human like our boy here. Twins are considered bad blood—too human."

This information makes me really want to swear, but I hold back since there are so many young bats around. "It's perfectly natural," I grit out between my teeth.

"No, to Camazotz, it's not."

"Bet Cypress *loves* them." How ironic that my biggest hater has sons born in human form. I instantly feel sympathy for the young twins.

Decker snorts. "That's one way of putting it."

Sylvana wraps her arms around the boys' shoulders and leans in close to whisper to each of them. The whisper continues until she pulls something from the folds of her skirt, but we're too far away to make out what it is. The boys take one look at whatever she's holding and then stare straight at me. Sylvana meets my eye and sneers. Her lip actually curls up to bare her teeth.

What the—

"Did you see that?" My arms break out in gooseflesh.

"Yep, but doesn't half the colony look at you like that?"

Decker has a point. "I don't know. That seemed extra nasty. She's up to something."

"She's always up to something, but stay out of her way. Do not mess with her, Connie." Decker's voice has a solemn tone that adds to my nerves. "I gotta fly. See you around."

Before I can say goodbye, Decker's flying up into the setting sun above Rocks and his little gang. When I look back at Sylvana, she's pointing at me and whispering to the boys. I watch as they leave her side and slowly walk around the group Rocks is presiding over to stop a few feet from the wagon steps.

"Hi there." I smile.

The twins are identical except for their scars. The angry red lines indicate they were probably attacked at the end of last year by the owls. The boys notice me looking.

"I'm Elm," the one on the right says. He has three parallel scars that run from his chin, down his neck and into his shirt. Talon marks I'd bet.

"I'm Oak," his twin adds. Both boys have shoulder-length black hair and fine-boned faces. They'd be picked on at school by the bigger brutes that roam the halls if they were educated alongside aeronaughts. Oak has two parallel scars that run from his elbow to his wrist.

"That must have hurt," I say, pointing.

They nod in unison as only twins can. "It did, but we were lucky," Oak replies.

"I'm sorry." The boys shrug together making me smile. "I go to school with twins just like you."

Their eyes widen at the concept. "Really?" they say together. I bet they've never met any other twins and believe the BS that they're doomed, or cursed, or evil—whatever the colony infers.

I describe the pranks the twins at school pull on the teachers every other day. The boys edge a little closer, and their eyes keep flicking to my hair. The golden blonde is such a contrast to the sea of raven-haired kids. "Want to touch it?" That earns me two ear-splitting grins.

Jumping down from the wagon, I flick my ponytail over my shoulder and kneel down. The boys are more timid than mice, but eventually get within range.

"What were you talking to Sylvana about?" I ask in my best casual voice.

"We want to get—" Oak's hand flies over Elm's mouth, and he vigorously shakes his head.

"We just need to practice," Oak says to me, slowly removing his hand from his brother's mouth. Elm won't meet my eye.

I dig around in my backpack and pull out my Snoopy PEZ dispenser. My hope is to distract them into telling me more about what that creepy witch is up to, but it fails. Oak is tight-lipped and seems to catch on to what I'm doing. I give them the dispenser when they leave and hope that gesture doesn't come back to bite me later.

Rocks looks over his shoulder and mouths the word sorry. I point to my watch and wave him over.

"Don't worry about it. They need you, but I've got to get moving. The folks'll be worried, and I've got school tomorrow. What days will you visit?"

"The market's opening tomorrow, so I doubt I'll be able to get away. Once things settle down again, we'll pick up our old routine?"

"Okay. See you on Saturday then. I'll bring all the info I can for Strickland." I want to kiss him so badly, but we have a massive audience scrutinizing our conversation.

"*Drive* safely," he says, with a wink. His eyes flick to my burning ears. "You want me to walk you to your car?"

"Nah, stay here and sort this out. Your eReader is on your bed. Enjoy it."

Night has fallen and I pick up my pace heading to Dad's van. I don't feel quite so vulnerable around the Camazotz any longer, but at the same time, I never like to push my luck. When I round the end of the van to get to the driver's door, Rocks' old harem is waiting in ambush.

I sigh—so not in the mood to deal with these girls.

"Here she is," Zabreena announces. "Have fun with our boy?"

"Leave me alone." *You little guano!* "I know, as his cousin, anything you say to me is BS." I try to get past them, but they won't budge.

Zabreena points to surrounding members of the harem. "He owes them all blood bonds. No lie." The face she pulls reminds me of playing card games with Mary Lou. She gets this smug I've-beaten-you look alerting us to her awesome hand. The only problem is I have no idea what "blood bond" means—but it can't be good.

I look to Rebekkah, little Violet, and finally Phoenix. When our eyes meet, she looks away and shifts back a step.

"We should thank you. Talk about a gift, giving us Rockland to feed." Rebekkah's smile turns my spine to ice. She flicks the tangle of long, black, satin ribbons over her shoulder and juts out her chin.

Stay calm. They're trying to ignite my jealousy. I chant to myself to trust Rocks as my brain tries to interpret what she's talking about.

"Feeding him was magnificent, wasn't it, girls? Being that close … Sharing blood … Something you will never understand."

Oh, God. My stomach heaves at the thought. Why did I never wonder who fed Rocks while his wing healed? Real vampire bats do feed each other. I recall what I learned researching bats when I was trying to save Rocks.

They're quite complex little blood-suckers as it turns out. Since their diet is liquid, it means they need to feed regularly. If they miss only a couple of feeds, it can be deadly, and I saw how quickly Rocks turned a weird grey color after he broke his wing. To solve this problem, the bats willingly feed their friends. Any hungry bat can go to any fed bat for a quick snack. The impressive part is that the bats remember who fed them in their time of need and who refused.

If a bat who refused to feed them asks for a free meal down the track, the other bat will remember and turn them away. They evolved this way to prevent lazy bats from not going out and even attempting to hunt and simply relying on others to keep them nourished instead. How freaking clever is Mother Nature? Except now I'm thinking about my boyfriend being fed, Mother Nature sucks. For some reason, I just assumed it would be the Land wing, but obviously not. *Fudge.* Their laughter confirms my face has betrayed my thoughts.

"He fed from you?" I don't want to ask, but I need confirmation—not more innuendos that these girls are experts at delivering.

All of them, except Zabreena, smile and nod.

Oh, crap!

"Let me share my favorite part of being a female Camazotz with you—you know, girl to girl." Rebekkah places a hand on her slender hip. A blind man could see the diva vibe she's sending my way. "I can feed any male bat I want with my life sustaining blood. And, you know what that means?"

I don't answer because I know she can't wait to enlighten me.

"It means he owes me. And, when we call in a blood favor, they get answered."

My lungs open again, allowing oxygen back in. Phew! So Rocks has to feed these little *biatches* at some point in the future. For a moment there, I was getting worried. I have to remember that without them feeding him, he wouldn't be alive. As much as it pains me to admit it, they saved him way more than I did.

Zabreena adds. "You don't get it, do you?"

"So he fed from them. They saved him. Thanks, and one night when they don't feel like going out, they can ask him for a feed." I shrug like it isn't a big deal, but the way she smiles again makes the hair on my neck stand on end. I don't want to imagine Rocks feeding any of these girls, but if that's what he has to do, then I'll try to be mature about it.

She laughs and raises one eyebrow at me. "I can almost understand why your sweetness attracts him. No, naught, those favors aren't *only* returned in blood if you know what I mean."

Where's my inhaler? What the fudge is she talking about?

"I'll make this real simple for the simple-minded, little naught—" Rebekkah says.

"Don't call me naught! I'm *not* nothing."

"Oh, yes you are. How much time has Rockland spent with you since he's healed?"

I turn away. Not that much. If it weren't for me doing the driving this weekend, I wouldn't have seen him at all. He's only visited me twice at home in the last two weeks.

"I know where he's been, and it hasn't been with you, so that means you've got nothing. You are nothing to him. His time as a bat—unable to flip—was good for him. It made him see what matters. Blood matters. He's back where he belongs in the colony surrounded with love."

That gets my attention. "Ah-huh, you can't have everything. Last year when you paid me a visit, I distinctly remember you laughing in my face about bats falling in love, so you either love him or just want to …

you know … with him." I can't bring myself to say it because then my brain thinks it, and I've already thought too many times about Rocks getting busy with these girls, and that's an image I do not need in my head. "So cut the bullshit."

"Okay, I'll cut the bullshit and tell you the facts," Rebekkah cuts in. "A blood bond means you are owed a life. He can feed me, or he can give me a life—a pup. A life for a life. That cutting the bullshit enough for you?"

Little Violet steps in. "And since you've got him hooked on that aeronaught food of yours, he's not going to be able to feed any of us without blood, so that doesn't leave us much choice really." Violet says with a wicked gleam in her eye.

"That's enough," Phoenix mutters.

Zabreena turns on her and I'm glad for once not to be on the receiving end of the hatred in her eyes. "Do not tell me you feel sorry for *her*? You be careful. You need us. That weak little wing of yours isn't good for much."

My heart skips a beat and my knees buckle as the implications set in. I grab the side of the van for support. No. No. No. This cannot be happening. Oh my God. They can each ask him to mate with them, and he can't say no? My eyes land on Phoenix.

"This is pathetic to watch. She knows all she needs to. Let's go," Rebekkah says before flipping. Violet and Zabreena copy, and one of them flies so close, their claws tangle in my hair and yank it painfully.

"Ouch!" I should scream, but I bite my tongue, rubbing the side of my head. "Is this all … true?"

The stars around Phoenix's eyes are pretty, but her features are filled with a deep sadness. She nods at me. "It's true. He owes a dozen blood bonds."

"What?" It feels like my chest has been ripped open, and my heart has been pulled from it.

"Some of the smaller wings, well, it's the only way they would get attention from someone like Rockland. Having a Land pup raises their standing. Everything is about power and votes. He wasn't really in a position to say no."

FUDGE ME upside down and inside out.

"Will you ask him to mate" —I swallow— "when you call in your bond?"

She looks at me without saying anything for what feels like an eternity. "No, I won't."

"Why?"

"I know what they said, and they will. Trust me. But ... I care for Rockland a great deal. He's kind to our wing. We're small and need the protection of a bigger, powerful wing. He gives that to my brother and me. But, because I care for him, I would never ask him to do something that would upset him. The others know calling in the blood bond as a mating will hurt him because of you, and it makes it all the sweeter to them. That's not me."

"Why are you being nice?" She was part of the posse that came visiting the Bun Lovin' Barn both times.

"Pegasus has wanted to try aeronaught food since forever. You know it's forbidden. He told me you introduced him to it. Tasting it made his night—probably his whole year."

My phone ringing makes both of us jump. The parking lot doesn't have any electric lighting so when I pull it from my pocket it lights up the whole area. Mom wants to know why I'm not home yet. Before I can get Mom off the line, Phoenix vanishes. Our conversation is clearly finished.

I want to storm back to his wagon and confront him, but I'm exhausted and confused. My folks are expecting me, and the drive will give me time to think. I need to think about what this means, and whether I can stand by and let it happen.

They saved his life, but at what price to us?

12

Dragons

"OU look like crap," Brandy says, sliding her lunch tray onto the table. "Like the worst case of Monday-itus I've ever seen."

I take a deep breath. After my encounter at the colony, sleep was so not going to happen. Rocks and those girls—fudge!

"Couldn't sleep." I shrug.

"Tell me all about 'camping.' I want the juicy details, girl." I hear Tiff's overexcited voice before I see her. She practically sits on top of me and throws an arm around my shoulder. "Oh my God, you look like those girls on MTV after their first night of Spring Break." Her eyes change from concerned to wicked. "Does that mean you and Rocks?" Her eyebrows dance and her elbow finds the soft flesh of my side.

The sound of my head hitting the table followed by a groan is the only answer she's going to get.

"What did I miss about Rocks?" Mary Lou chimes in, joining us. "I ship you two SO hard."

"Con went camping with him and his family on Saturday night, and I want *all* the deets."

What on earth am I going to tell them? I need help. This bat-blood-bond business is doing my head in.

When I finally raise my head, all eyes are on me. "We kissed, but—" The squealing and subsequent rapid fire questions drowns out my words. I stay silent until they settle down, and the other students turn back to their lunches.

"There are other girls … that … *hang* around. I can't even deal right now."

Fudge me. My stomach rolls the small amount of food I've put into it up and down like an angry ocean wave. The thought of telling my best friends this stuff stinks of betrayal. Talk about complicated. I wasn't going to mention any Camazotz secret, but it's all interrelated. It wouldn't make sense without it. "I need to talk to him this weekend, so until then, can you guys just drop it?"

Tiff's big, blue eyes turn sad, and her arm returns around my shoulders. "You okay?"

"I will be. I need to tell him it's me and only me, or …" I shrug. A second wave rolls through my gut at the thought, but deep down I know it's the right thing. I cannot and will not stand back and have my boyfriend do *that* with other girls—no matter what the reason. I'm not a Camazotz. I can accept Rocks is, and I have no problem with his supernatural alter ego, except when that part of him makes me feel bad about myself. That isn't right.

Before the bell rings, I tell Tiff I'll meet her in English and head toward the exit. Sitting still is the worst. My brain has lodged itself into overdrive and won't shut off; it makes it impossible to sit still and not do something—anything. I need to walk before I have to sit in class again, going over and over what Phoenix told me.

"Hey, Connie!" A voice echoes across the cafeteria. Turning around, I scan the sea of faces and finally spy him. Parker is standing near the emergency exit doors behind a folding table. Two of his wrestling buddies are beside him. "Come here!"

The table is covered in papers, and Parker lifts a clipboard as I approach. We've avoided each other since the dance—even in English class—but I guess I can't avoid him forever.

"Hey."

"Hi Connie, how you been?"

"Oka—"

"Wanna sign my petition to kill those bats?"

My stomach hits my lungs as though I've jumped off the edge of a thousand-foot cliff. "What?"

"I'm gonna get those rabid—"

The papers covering the table—now I'm really looking at them—show the faces of those little kids I saw on the news. And photos of bats—lots and lots of bats.

I grip Parker's t-shirt and yank him half way over the table so our noses almost touch. "What the hell are you doing?" I can hardly breathe.

Parker's eyes go wide for an instant, but then he gets this weird look. Ugh! Don't even go there! Our proximity has given him a bird's eye view down my top. I let go of him as though I've just touched an open flame and step back, crossing my arms. Parker blinks twice before meeting my glare.

"I'm doing what the county needs to do," he says, holding up the petition. "The attack yesterday made me want to do something."

"Yesterday?" I miss the evening news for two nights, and they report on another attack. I rub my scar, but stop when he notices.

He scavenges amongst the printouts and shows me a picture of three teenage girls crying, and one of them has a cut above her eye. I want to be sick because she looks like Horror Movie girl's body double. That's what Mom and Dad would have seen when they opened the door to me that night—rivulets of blood dripping down my face. Poor girl. Fudge! My hands clench and unclench. My heartbeat starts a double-time rhythm, which almost hurts. I feel for those poor girls, I really do, but under no circumstances can the county go to war against the Camazotz.

"They're a danger!"

"They are not!" Stay calm.

"They tried to rip my eyes out."

"Parker, there wasn't a scratch on you. I was there. I was the one you left behind when you ran away screaming. There was no danger." I mean I know I wasn't in any danger, and those bats weren't going to lay a claw on me, but Parker doesn't know that. Maybe if I make him feel bad, he might end this madness. Big wrestling hero he turned out to be.

"What are you, an expert?"

"Yes, I am. I was attacked too; remember? But the difference is my attack ended with two stitches above my eye. You, however, not one single mark, so trust me, if those bats had wanted to, they could've done some damage."

"You're talking like they have brains and decided not to hurt me."

Fudge! He's right. I'm going to get Rocks and myself in big trouble if I don't act smarter.

"They're just rabid, stupid, blood-sucking vermin that need to be disposed of." He holds the pen in my face. My eyes land on the bottom signature making my heart skip a beat. Fifty-seven idiots attending this school have supported his madness already.

DURING THE WEEK, I spend my time focused on digging up every detail available about all the attacks on the aeronaughts. I print out newspaper articles and maps showing where each attack occurred. I download several news reports to my phone, scanning the Internet constantly.

Thankfully, Friday is a student-free day because we haven't had much snow this winter and don't need to make up for snow days. I'm free to head to the market to make my report to Strickland on the bat attacks, and then confront Rocks. We need to have this conversation face-to-face because I simply couldn't stomach doing it over the phone. The lead weight in my gut needs to go—one way or the other.

Dressed in all black, I stride through the market, but before I make it to the jewelry shop, I almost have a heart attack. Two women—one reminds me so much of Mom—exit the candle shop with a large Sanguine Mountain shopping bag. I spin around and notice several other shoppers strolling along—their bright colored clothing a shock to my system.

When I enter Rocks' shop, it takes a few seconds for my eyes to adjust to the dimness. He's leaning over the bench that lines the far wall, inspecting something. He grabs a hammer, adjusts the tongs resting on the anvil and whacks it three times. Holding up the tiny square of silver sheet metal, he inspects his work closely. Suddenly his eyes flick to me, and the smile that will break my heart today appears across his face.

"Hey, I wasn't expecting you." He carefully places the tongs and hammer on the counter and skirts around some equipment to get to me.

"I need to talk to you about—"

Rocks places a slender finger over his lips shushing me and winks. The same finger points upward indicating to the ceiling. My gaze follows …

"Shi—sugar!" I gasp, grabbing my throat. Dozens and dozens of little bat faces stare back at me, hanging from the roosting bars that cross the airy space of his ceiling. "Wow."

Good Morning, Miss Connie. Good Morning, Miss Connie.
Good Morning, Miss Connie. Good Morning, Miss Connie …

The chorus of young voices rings between my ears making me flinch. I try to smile, but know it probably looks like more of a wince of pain. A moment later, I'm surrounded by what must be every single pup in the colony. I glance over my shoulder to look out the window, but the coast is clear.

"Hi, kids."

The whole group giggles before Bailey steps forward. "We're not goats. We're pups." Her leather eye patch has been engraved with a bunch of flowers.

It takes me a second to work out what she's talking about. I guess the goat population to feed the colony would have to multiply. She probably gets to play with the kids each spring. It's yet another reminder these children are so isolated.

The sea of mini Goths crowds closer, and then the requests begin. There are forty little girls—without beanie babies tucked under their arms—looking at me with hopeful eyes.

I look at Rocks. "I'm gonna be in big trouble, aren't I?"

"Not gonna be—you are!" Rocks takes charge, and before my eyes, these tiny girls in the cutest Goth dresses you can possibly imagine all form organized groups. "Raise your hand if you would like Miss Connie to bring you a Bean's baby to love?"

A quick hand count, then he instructs them *not* to tell anyone before shooing them out the door. They can't flip outside since there are unsuspecting aeronaught customers on the prowl, so I watch as they skip or run off without a care in the world.

"Come see me before I leave, Bailey." She smiles over her shoulder as she skips off with her friends.

Rocks explains it's the first time he's ever seen all the girls together without the politics of the wings getting involved. He reiterates how certain wings stick together and vote, but the new fascination with aeronaught toys has bridged all divides, even at this young age. He says Bailey would never spend time with some of those pups before this and offers to give me some money to help pay for their orders. The pups have been hanging in his shop for three days when they heard I was due to visit Strickland.

"Don't worry about the money. It's fine."

Movement at the back of the shop causes me to jump again. Rocks just smiles. What I wouldn't give for his senses some days.

Moonshiner is standing alone in the shadows. He gives me the tiniest hint of a smile before turning an impressive shade of scarlet. I'm guessing he's glad the army of girls has left.

"Come closer," Rocks encourages. The boy's eyes turn the size of dinner plates. "Don't be shy."

Moonshiner has the same high cheekbones and chin as Rocks. I realize it must be a trait they get from Zada. I bite my tongue to resist telling him I met his father. Nobody understands the longing for discovering your family better than me, but he's so young …

"May I … may I …" His eyes dart up to Rocks.

"Go on."

"May I touch your hair?" he finally whispers.

"Of course." Kneeling down to his height, I have the strongest urge to hug this boy and tell him everything will be all right.

Stepping closer, his fingers stroke down my ponytail. "It reminds me of dawn. The first golden rays that break the night."

That does it. I can no longer keep my hands to myself. "Can I have a hug?"

The look on his face is priceless and reminds me so much of the shocked faces at Duskwing, when I hugged his cousin. If my hair is the first rays of dawn breaking the night, then his smile is the explosion of light when the sun breaches the horizon in a glowing red orb.

He wraps his arms tightly around my neck as his raven-haired head rests on my shoulder. Rocks frowns, as though in pain, before turning away.

When Moonshiner eventually lets go, his eyes are sparkling. "I want a hug every time I see you, okay?" I add.

He turns bright red again, but grins and nods before shuffling out the door.

Rocks still has his back toward me, and my instincts have no clue why. They're too overloaded with feelings and emotions to possibly stand a chance at interpreting this. "Why did you say that to him?" His voice sounds tight.

"Because as the only member of his wing, I'm betting he doesn't get enough hugs."

Rocks moves so fast and has engulfed me in his own bear hug before I have time to protest. "Thank you," he says quietly in my ear. "That will mean the world to him ... and to me."

His words make my chest ache. I have to ask about the blood bonds.

A throat clearing behind us forces Rocks to let go, and we turn to face his father.

"You bring that information?"

Well, hello to you too, Strickland. I'm very well. Thank you for asking.

I trip getting to my bag, but feel Rocks' fingers at my waist to steady me. They send a shiver up my spine I simply do not need right now. Handing over the stack of information, I grab my phone. My lungs begin to wheeze.

"Do you want to watch the television reports?" I hold up what Strickland considers the spawn of Satan and his reaction is as predicted.

"We do not have access to those televi—"

"Sire, it's a yes/no question." Rock interrupts. "Do you want to see it or not?" I'm pretty sure my eyes match the size of Moonshiner's. Rocks has never spoken to his father that way around me. I wonder what's happened in the last five days.

Mini was mesmerized by *Road Runner* on our TV when I left this morning. Wile E Coyote's plan was foiled yet again. Strickland is channeling that crazy, pissed off coyote to a tee. His eyes look feral, and his shoulders have bunched up so high they've completely swallowed his neck. I actually check to see if steam is coming out of his ears.

"Here." I shove my phone in front of his face. I do not want to be part of any more arguments. Pressing play, Strickland jerks with surprise when the newscaster fills my screen and starts speaking.

He requests I play each news report twice. I'm guessing the aeronaught magic made it hard for him to concentrate on the information during the first go. The maps with the attack sites I have marked are handed over next.

"They lied," he growls. If I thought he was upset before, that was nothing. The muscles of his arms almost ripple with tension, and the map he's holding crinkles in his fist.

Rocks pries the paper from his father's hand and studies it before swearing quietly.

"What?" I look to each of them.

He looks to his father who gives a quick nod of his head. "These locations point to Duskwing being responsible," Rocks says.

Holy fudge sundae.

"I'll assemble the Fold and all the Clip. We need to make a decision," Strickland says. "Contact Rockland if you hear anything more."

Bailey chooses that exact moment to return to the store. My teeth worry my bottom lip as Strickland tracks her movements. She smiles up at everyone before she sits on the bench seat next to my handbag, patting Scorch on his head once she's settled him on her lap. When Jeremiah taps on the door, getting the attention of both men, I use the distraction as my chance. I slip the picture book about the dragon who's allergic to fire out of my bag and under her arm.

I move back to stand next to Rocks. He's listening to Jeremiah and his Sire. I study his face while he's occupied. He's so good-looking it's no wonder half the girls here are after him.

"What is *that?*" Strickland snarls, making me jump. All eyes are on me. Bailey is sitting flicking through the pages with the biggest smile I've ever seen on her little face. "Enough!" He takes two strides and ends up way too far inside my personal space. I step back seeing nothing but his furious eyes. "No more toys. No more aeronaught influence. En-ough!" he booms.

Before I can defend myself, Bailey is pushing between us. Her little fists thump on his rock-hard thighs. "You can't tell her what to do. You're not her Sire," the tiny spitfire announces.

Crabapples.

"Bailey—" Rocks tries, but Strickland quiets him with a raised hand.

"Go to your mother immediately, and I will deal with your impertinence when I'm done dealing with the cause of it."

"No." She rests her tiny fists on her hips. If this weren't so serious, it would be freaking adorable.

"Go!" he shouts, pointing to the door. Her bottom lip quivers, as she follows his command.

"What are these *dragons* she keeps talking about? Are they a threat to us?"

He can-not be serious. My eyes flick to Rocks, but I get nothing from him. The fact a grown man is acting as though dragons are real is too much. "You seriously have never heard of them?"

"Are—they—a—threat?" he snarls.

"No, of course not. They aren't even real."

His eyes narrow. "Then what is this nonsense you're filling our pups with?"

"It's … well, fun." I swallow.

The stare he levels on Rocks makes me quiver. "This is what you're after?" He points at me. "Fun?" He shakes his head. "Fun?" he yells, and I curse my frayed nerves for jumping a second time. His venom gets turned on me. "You expect me to know about 'fun' when we're under attack not only by the force out to weaken us, but now your government is going to study us and do heaven only knows what if we're discovered. You think I have time for games? If dragons can't feed, clothe, or protect my kin, there is no room for them in my life— or our pups! Are we clear?"

"Father, she was—"

"You will refer to me as Sire. Right now, the last thing I want to be reminded of is you being my son. A disgrace to the blood we share."

Rocks doesn't even flinch at the insult, but my blood is beginning to boil.

"You've always told me that aeronaughts would never accept us, but here is Connie doing just that—showing kindness and love to our pups—and yet you push her away."

Strickland simply glares at us both, turns on his heels and strides off. Just the angle of the Sire's shoulder blades tells me either of us would be crazy to go after him. Yet again, I've made life in the colony more difficult for Rocks.

"Sorry—"

"Don't. Just don't. You know this isn't about you, or the fucking dragons. It's about me. It's not your fault. You do not need to apologize."

I beg to differ. This has everything to do with me and my aeronaught self. That's why those wings are in the Sire's ear about Rocks—because of me. My gut tells me this is a battle I won't win, and given what Rocks said on my previous visit about him influencing the pups, Strickland's outburst isn't good.

Rocks is pacing back and forth. The tension in his shoulders and his clenched fists an indicator that he's as furious as Strickland.

"Give me five minutes" —he says striding toward the door— "I need to check what's going to happen to Bailey."

He's gone before I have time to answer. Taking a seat next to the door, I try to sort out how I'm going to broach the subject of his blood bonds. I close my eyes and focus on breathing in through my nose and out through my mouth three times.

"Where's Rockland?"

Opening my eyes, a girl—clearly several years older than us—is giving me a look like I'm dog poo on her new shoes. Pissed off from Strickland, I give her my the-feeling-is-mutual-sister scowl. The tattoo patterns that cover both hands remind me of Indian henna designs. Only I know better. They must reveal their pattern when she's a Camazotz.

Before I have time to answer, she adds, "It's about last night and my blood bond." Her shoulder-length hair is fine as silk and moves with the breeze coming in the door.

Crap!

No!

He didn't ...

If I wasn't already seated, I know I'd be a crumpled mess on the floor. Pain like nothing I've ever felt rips through my entire body. The day I read Josie's letter didn't even come close to hurting this much.

"Well?"

"The Sire," I whisper, pointing down the street. What they did last night is the final nail in our couple coffin. We are done. I bend over my knees to help get oxygen to my lungs. The air slowly seeps in so I rest my head on my hands.

"Connie? What's wrong?" Those long fingers rub my back.

"Do not touch me," I hiss, sitting up. "You got your *rocks* off last night, and think you can touch me today?"

The venom in my tone makes his eyes widen. "Get my what off?"

"You know!"

"Get me off what?" He frowns.

"Oh fudge your 1865 language skills. Open Urban Dictionary Mr. Techno-pants and let it explain." I, then, have to explain what Urban Dictionary is, and Rocks is delighted to have access to a dictionary of modern terms. I study his face as he reads the definition. The anger from a moment ago creeps back into place.

"That is not funny."

"Tell me about it!" I yell.

"What's going on with you?" He stares down like an avenging angel in black, but I return his glare with the most menacing stare I can muster.

"Did you ... did you ... with, ugh, I don't even know her name! Keeping track of your bonds is getting out of hand." I stand so he isn't looming over me. Rocks' mouth opens slightly, and it confirms to me he didn't know I knew about the blood bonds. "Did you sleep with the girl with swirls tattooed on both hands?"

The immediate denial I was praying for doesn't come. He looks up at the ceiling for a brief second. "I haven't slept with anyone. I told you that."

"Yeah, as a guy, but what about as a bat?" I need to be crystal clear here if I'm going to end the only relationship I've ever wanted with all my heart. "Did your dick … bat or other … go anywhere near that girl? Did it? Tell me?"

Rocks winces at my wording, and I can't blame him. I could have phrased that soooo much better, but I need to get this out in the open once and for all.

"It hasn't, but … I owe her a blood bond."

"Why didn't you tell me about those?" My eyes fill with tears. I dig my nails into my palm as a distraction. Pain other than what's crushing my heart might prevent me from crying. "I tell you all my secrets, but you're still picking and choosing what you think I can handle. When are you going to trust me with who you are completely?" It's a fair question if he wants to be my boyfriend.

"It's not that simple." He pauses, and to say he's looking wary is an understatement. It's as though he recognizes just how close I am to exploding. "I do trust you. I swear, Connie. There is nobody I trust more."

"Yet you keep vital stuff from me! Were you ever going to tell me about the matings you owe all over the freaking colony?"

The pain in his eyes makes me feel slightly better—I'm not the only one hurting. "I didn't know how. I'm sorry—so sorry I didn't tell you first."

"What about the blood bond you owe me?"

He looks confused, hurt, and worried all at once. He takes my hand and indicates for us to sit, but it only annoys me more that he can tell my knees are about to give out.

"I got you back to the roost so you could live. Don't you owe me one too?"

Rocks' chin falls to his chest. "Of course, I do. Connie—"

"So at any given moment *any* of those girls can ask you to … and you will? You have to?" Tears well up again as I imagine him with that girl, or Rebekkah … not me … but one of them. I know they won't sleep together as humans, but it's the only image my mind can conjure, and my stomach churns each time I witness that scene in my head.

"I can't say no. It's more about my bat … essence."

"Gross!" That makes me want to shove my fingers in my ears. I let go of his hand and slide further away down the wooden bench.

"What?"

"I'm sure you love spreading your *'essence'* around."

It takes him a second to react. "No!" His eyes are so dark and livid. "That is not what I'm talking about. What I mean is … like an essential part of me … my essence. Those instincts I was telling you about."

"What. Ever." I have visuals I need bleached from my brain. Boys are so gross.

"No, Connie, I'm serious. Please. This is who I am."

I take a second to rein in my anger. "Sorry." I can't turn into a hypocrite now. I'm always asking him to share this side of himself, and now it's freaking me out. I need to listen and try to understand.

"I have this creature—this wild animal—inside of me. While I was unable to flip, it was strange. Almost like the bat in me was getting stronger or something." He doesn't look happy when he admits this. "He's an animal driven by instinct and nature. But then there's me, the guy. Of course, I can make moral decisions, but sometimes as a bat, I don't want to. Nature isn't right and wrong. It's good, pure, and raw, and it can take over. Yes, I know what I'm doing, but it's not always bad. It just is, and animals don't overthink stuff. That's a human brain at work." His hair has fallen over his eyes. I want to comfort him, but his words have wounded my heart.

I want to love this boy with everything I've got, but I can't let myself do that.

Silence envelops us both. I try to imagine if Feathers lived inside me and how that would feel. What would she make me do that I would be ashamed of as a human? "You need to understand that's all I've got to work with, Rocks—a human brain."

"Don't you see? I'm not going to be scoring with girls and putting a notch on my belt. I'm just trying to sustain my species. It's not emotional." His voice is raw making me wonder if this is hurting him as much as it is me. He adds softly. "It's not how I am with you."

I squeeze my eyes shut. I will not cry today—I will not. His words are spinning around in my head. I understand—sort of—but I cannot share my first boyfriend. I will not become someone I'm not—or do something that I hate the idea of—just for the sake of a boy.

"I'm not trying to make you jealous or hurt you. I swear. It's my duty."

"I get it. Okay? But that doesn't mean I have to like it. You have debts, but I can't sit by and watch. I can't … I don't care what form you are in. We can't." I don't want to say these words, but I must. I will not have more than one female—bat or human—in this relationship. It feels as though I've been struck by a wrecking ball. Somehow I got in the way of the giant swinging ball on it's way to demolishing a building, and now I'm the one that's been demolished. "We're done, Rocks."

"What does that mean?"

"You aren't my boyfriend any longer, okay? We—are—done."

"But I didn't mate last night. I'm in massive trouble with the Sire today because I told her I couldn't until I had discussed it with you. I swear, Connie, I just didn't know how to tell you. You saw how angry Strickland is with me. Like I said to you earlier, it's not about you at all. It's about me delaying my first blood bond. I did it because … because I love you."

The tears escape at last. He's making enemies here because he loves me, but that doesn't solve our situation. He's only delaying what must be paid back for him to stay a member of his colony.

"I know you do." I sniff. "That's why I'm doing this—"

A mob of bodies in leather, lace and velvet enter his small shop. These aren't aeronaught customers. The scent of sage hits me, and then I see Sylvana in the middle of the horde. She steps forward and points that blasted ringed finger at me yet again.

"She is to blame. I saw her. I saw her give them aeronaught temptations. She is behind this!" she screeches.

Rocks is on his feet, blocking me from the angry mob. I spy Strickland, Macallister, Cypress, and his sons—Ash and Cedar. Half a dozen other Camazotz I don't recognize surround them, but it's the young woman crying that gets me to my feet. I stand next to Rocks in front of the mob.

"Where are they?" the woman yells at me, swiping tears from her face. "What did you say to them?"

As the crowd moves closer, I step back. Rocks holds out his arms as though to protect me and try to stop their advance.

"Sire, what is this? What exactly are you accusing Connie of now?"

13
Job Offer

THE angry mob want answers. All I can think of is the crowd of little girls swarming around me earlier. I didn't tell them anything except I would bring more toys. How can this be the cause of so much anger? Yes, I gave her a book and some toys— hardly a crime. Then, I remember Bailey's attitude toward the Sire. Maybe some of the other pups have rebelled against his 'no more aeronaught toys' command too.

"I saw her telling them aeronaught lies!" Sylvana screeches again. She's standing closer to Rocks but facing the crowd. Her arms are out wide and her gnarled, crooked fingers wave in front of their faces. I have a clear vision of her hunched over a bubbling cauldron casting spells. Her skirts rustle and jingle as she moves. "I foretold she would be a danger to the Shadows. I foretold it!"

Strickland leaves the group and eyeballs his son. I'm glad Rocks is providing a wall between them and me, but we're outnumbered. Strickland eventually looks at me over Rocks' shoulder, breaking the staring competition. "What did you tell them? Where are they?"

"What's this about?" Rocks demands.

"I promised them I would bring more," I admitted quietly.

Strickland frowns. "More what?"

"Toys. The little girls that don't have one."

"I'm not talking about the dragon nonsense. I want you to tell me where Elm and Oak are immediately!" His voice echoes off the hard surfaces of the shop.

"The twins?" I confirm. How would I freaking know. "I don't know. I haven't seen them."

"She lies!" Sylvana yells. "I witnessed the aeronaught giving the boys some evil from her bag."

"What evil? I gave them candy—"

"And now they are gone! Did you help them leave? Did you tell them where to run to?" Her eyes are open so wide I can see the whites all around her irises.

My brain is not processing this madness fast enough. I gape for a moment, looking from face to face. The mob is still waiting for an answer. "Tell them where to run to? I don't know what you're talking about. It was just candy."

"Evil modern treats are an easy lure for pups and fledgers," Sylvana announces like it's written in stone. "Her aeronaught ways are evil."

"Evil?" I try to keep my voice even. "My *evil* modern ways saved him." I point at Rocks. "Modern medicine allowed him to fly again after having a broken wing. How can you seriously think it's evil?"

Several members of the group stare at Sylvana waiting for her to counter my argument, but she can't. She's got nothing, and she knows I know it. I stare her down not breaking eye contact until Rocks speaks. I hope the others think about what I said later.

He tells the posse he noticed the boys were staring at me last year at the blood ceremony, and they followed us back to his shop on foot through the woods. "Didn't you see them?" he says to me. "They were staring at you—like really obviously."

"No, it was a bit hard to tell those two were staring at me when the whole freaking colony was staring at me." I fold my arms over my chest.

"I do not believe it was candy she gave them," Witchy-pooh announces.

My anger bubbles above the disbelief that is brewing in my stomach. I push between Rocks and Strickland. "I'm not the only one that gave them something that day," I argue.

I explain that I did talk to the twins after returning from Duskwing, and I gave them the candy dispenser—nothing else. It takes a moment to describe a PEZ to the gathered Camazotz, and more mutters and grunts follow.

"Sylvana was whispering in their ear about me," I say, looking from their crying mother to Strickland. "She was pointing at me and then they came over. Ask her what she told them. I did, but the boys refused to tell me." I don't know why I'm bothering to speak. These aeronaught-haters are never going to believe my word over one of their own.

"Where are they?" the young woman, Hannah, begs. "I want my boys back."

"How would I know where two young bats would fly off to? Like seriously?"

Rocks steps forward so I feel his body against my back. "When were the boys last seen?" he asks.

Several voices speak at once. Eventually, it's established that the twins have not been seen at the market, or the roost, for two days. Cypress doesn't take his eyes off me as I swear I have no idea where the boys are, and that I didn't help coerce them into leaving the Shadows.

"Why on earth would I lure them away from here?" I argue in utter disbelief. I feel sick. How can they honestly think I am involved with this?

"The last time one of our own went missing an aeronaught was involved," Cypress says between gritted teeth. "And, we all know how that ended."

Strickland and Rocks both flinch at his words. "Connie had nothing to do with Celand going missing, and she has nothing to do with this," Rocks says in a calm voice to the group. His eyes move to Cypress as he continues. "If you weren't so prejudiced about your boys being born human, they would still be here. Maybe if you'd treated them like equal members of your family, they wouldn't have left."

A yelling match ensues between all the males. I slump down on the bench and press my cool fingers to my temples. "What about the owls?" What if they got caught flying back to the roost by an owl? It wouldn't be the first time one had gotten too close to them.

Silence follows my suggestion. Macallister—the Fold member who usually only speaks about me, rather than to me—comes closer. "What do you know about that, little naught? Are you upset the owls have moved on after winter? You planning on releasing more?"

His implication slams me like a punch to the stomach. The air in my lungs slowly evaporates. I blink. "What?" I gasp; glad to be sitting down. "You think I did that?" Is he seriously blaming me?

Rocks has him by his leather vest and is leaning over nose-to-nose with the much shorter Fold member. "How dare you—"

Strickland and Cypress pull him off Macallister before he can say anymore. They shove him back next to me, and Strickland points at him to stay put. The disgust that Rockland would raise a hand to a Fold member is evident on all their faces.

"Taking her side over your own blood. You are a disgrace," Macallister adds, spitting at Rocks' feet.

I will not allow them to punish him anymore on my account. Standing, I look at the whole red-faced group. "I guess you're going to accuse me of flipping and scratching those school children next? Blame it *all on me*," I say, my voice rising with my temper. "I am in *love* with one of your own. Why would I ever want to hurt any of you? Don't you see that would only hurt him?"

Several people gasp, and Rocks' fingers grasp my elbow, but I pull away. "I'm leaving. I will not stand here and be accused of total bullshit. You can blame me all you want" —I stare at Sylvana— "but I had nothing to do with it, and blaming me won't bring those poor boys back." I turn to face Cypress next. "And you, you have always stared at me with utter loathing and hatred. I can't even imagine how your poor boys coped with that level of disgust their whole lives. Your prejudice is to blame."

Grabbing my bag, I swing it over my shoulder, but the door is blocked, and my nerves aren't up to getting closer to these pissed off Camazotz.

"Ban her!" Cypress cries.

The muscles in Strickland's jaw tighten. "Do not return."

"No!" implores Rocks. "Sire—"

"Let her pass," Strickland states. The sea of bodies separates the second their Sire speaks. The loud roaring between my ears blocks out the protests coming from Rocks. Maybe this is perfect timing. Maybe this is a sign from the universe that I shouldn't date a Camazotz.

As I unlock my car, Rocks flips next to me. I scan the half-empty parking lot, but no shoppers are present to witness his magical transformation.

"Connie, please. Wait."

My pounding heart isn't helping my frayed nerves. "This is it. We're done."

"But, you love me."

I can't look in his eyes, just the sound of his voice tells me what I'll see there if I dare. Having never broken up with a guy before, I had no idea it would hurt to this degree.

"And because of that, I won't share." I sigh. The pain in my chest almost numbs my heart. "Goodbye, Rocks."

MY SHIFT AT the Bun Lovin' Barn is the only reason I stopped crying. My sinuses are blocked; my temples are pounding, and no amount of makeup will conceal my puffy red eyes or nose. I tell Tiff that Rocks and I are no more. The conversation is short because the tears threaten to spill again, and with the heavy foundation I'm wearing, that will be a disaster. Tiff makes me a sweet iced tea, points to the door, and insists I take a break.

The worst of winter finally seems to be over. I sit on the milk crate and stare into the trees next to the van. The streetlight shows a hint of green starting to bud on the branch tips. Spring is breaking through at last—a new beginning. Maybe it's time for a fresh start for me as well.

I sip the tea and close my eyes. The look on Rocks' face when I closed my car door and drove away will haunt me always. Devastated, crushed, betrayed—but he's not the only one.

"You never called."

The tea falls from my hand as I jump three inches into the air. Enzo Ascari is standing with one hand on his hip and the other leaning on the closed door. He steps over the river of tea and ice running toward his shiny shoes.

"Stay away from me." I scramble to my feet to escape, but he's blocking the door.

"Now, Contessa, that's no way to speak to your father."

"You are not my dad. I have a dad. Thank you very much." I'm positive he can see my heart thumping against my chest. Enzo chuckles, shaking his head.

"I have a business offer for you. Remember? Did you figure it out?"

"Why on earth would you think I want to do business with you?" I make a mental note to check my horoscope later. I'm betting my planets are in 'fudge with Connie' alignment this week.

"Now, now."

"You sell drugs to kids—KIDS—just like me." I whisper/yell at him.

"No, I don't—"

I give him the biggest eye roll I can muster without getting dizzy. "Do all adults lie so easily?"

"You never let me finish. What I was going to say is that I don't sell drugs to kids like you because you, my darling daughter, are too smart for that."

"Don't call me that." The irony of me being desperate to find my real dad and now being desperate to lose him again is not lost on me.

"Whether I call you my daughter or not, the fact remains that you are my flesh, dear child."

Yeah, like I need to be reminded of that horrifying fact.

My feet are itching to climb the steps and get away from him. "My break's over. Move."

"Wait!" His tone has gone from silky smooth to deadly. My sneakers are cemented in place as my heart rate rockets out of control again.

"Do not waste my time," he says a little softer. "I have decided it's time for you to join the family business. The timing couldn't be better. You will take over from Sophia while she is away."

What the—

For the second time today, my brain is having trouble processing the crazy that's being spouted at me. "Join? What? Work for you?" A nervous giggle escapes. My head feels weird and I take a deep breath. "You are like totally cray-cray! You should have told me this last time 'cause I would've said no and saved you the visit. Work for you? Nah-uh, no way."

"I don't make a habit of disclosing my plans until I know who is with me … or against me." The look in his eyes chills my blood to the bone.

"Why me?" I swallow the lump in my throat. "I don't know the first thing about your business, and I don't ever want to either."

"Come now. I have copies of all your school records starting with first grade and know you have perfect grades in Economics and Accounting. It pleases me you share your sister's talents."

I stare at him, trying to close my gaping mouth. How much does he know about me exactly?

"A car will be waiting to pick you up Monday after school. I suggest you don't give the men in my employ any trouble. They're loyal to me. Upset them, and you will be sorry. Understand?"

"No, I don't understand any of this! Me? I can't."

"Can you count money?"

"Yes—"

"And you wouldn't dare steal from *me*, would you?"

My eyes widen at the ludicrousness of that idea. "Pfff, I'm not an idiot." As the meaning of 'me' becomes clear my ears burn. "Technically, I didn't take that money, just so you know."

"Perfect. The job is yours."

"I don't want the job. I'm sure you are inundated with wannabe gangstas that would be thrilled with your offer. Me? Not so much." He frowns but doesn't say a word. My skin crawls and my gut is screaming at me not to sass him. Giving attitude to Mom and Dad is one thing, but I doubt Enzo will be so forgiving. I swallow. "Why now? Why me?"

"Had I known of your existence sooner, I would have come for you. Blood is blood after all."

Fudge no! Blood? That's the last freaking thing I need to hear about. The pang of hurt that rises at the mention of blood is all I need. I pray Rocks hasn't been punished too badly because of me. He refused his first blood bond because of his aeronaught girlfriend—not to mention almost assaulting a Fold member—and now I'm not his girlfriend any longer. Fudge.

"Monday. Do not test me, Contessa." Before I can protest, or refuse, or even beg him to leave me alone, he turns and walks swiftly to the car waiting in the darkness. I guess Monday I'll be studying in the library.

SATURDAY MORNING, DAD has the paper spread across his knees and is fast-forwarding through last night's late news report. My folks went to a fundraiser, which explains why Mini is little Miss Cranky-Pants today. That babysitter never follows Mom's instructions. I collapse into the chair and stare blankly at the images zipping past.

"You want to come rappelling tomorrow?" Just the invite makes me smile. Nothing good has happened to me in forever so it's a pleasant change.

"Yeah, cool." The grin Dad gives me indicates I've made his day. When I look back at the TV, my moment of happiness vanishes.

Dad rewinds without me saying a word. "The trial of Vipers' leader, Mitchell Jones, and his right hand man, Raymond Ramirez, has finally begun. The pair are charged with first-degree murder of two police officers, and the daughter of rival gang leader, Enzo Ascari, is said to be taking the stand some time in the coming weeks ..."

This is why he showed up last night. Sophia will be in a safe house through WITSEC until she gives evidence in the Vipers' trial. I pull my legs up and hug my knees. Enzo was serious. The urge to text Rocks is so strong I end up sitting on both my hands. He isn't my boyfriend and does not need to know this.

Mini comes barreling into the room and gets her sticky fingers on Dad's phone before he can stop her. As she runs off with her prize, Dad dumps his half-read newspaper on my lap before pursuing her. A black and white photo of a bat dominates the page. Smack bang in the middle of page eight is an article about the recent bat attacks. I swear I'm cursed. If that blasted witch made a voodoo doll with blonde hair, then she's better at magic than I suspected. I must be cursed. Seriously. It's the only explanation for the cluster of fudge that is my life.

Scanning the article, I grab my stomach to hold back the tidal wave of nausea that wants out of me. The local county has decided to begin steps to eradicate the rogue bats following the overwhelming number of groups lobbying for action. Parker and his dumbass petition is probably one of them.

Dad returns with Mini tucked under one arm as he tries to extract his phone. The wailing that ensues forces me to the sanctuary of my bedroom. I pace back and forth across the rug. I open the window all the way, and let the cool, crisp, spring air try to calm me.

After several minutes, I decide the Shadows and Rocks need to know this information. My arguments for not contacting him are weak and selfish. Finally, the fear that the council will eradicate the wrong Camazotz sends me sprinting downstairs. I snap a photo of the article while Dad is trying to wrangle Mini into submission. All his usual tricks—like tipping her upside down—aren't working. The girl has her eye on his smart phone, and nothing will substitute for it. The fact that I never taught Rocks about the camera in his phone niggles at me. He would love it. I hope Decker told him he has one, and I pray he works out how to open the picture I'm about to send.

Thought you should know this.

The lack of emotion in my words makes my heart sink and my gut twist. I head to the bathroom and splash cold water on my face. My brain chants two important facts—I'm not welcome at the colony, and Rocks has blood bonds to take care of. This is for the best. My head knows it, but the rest of my body is refusing to listen. The silver bat dangles from my ear in our illuminated bathroom mirror. Crabapples! Slowly I remove both earrings, and my necklace. As the filigree bat that hasn't left my neck since Christmas falls into my palm, I burst into tears.

Rocks and I are done.

Back in my room, I place all the jewelry he made into the velvet pouch. Searching for a hiding place, I spy my boots in the corner and stuff the pouch inside. Since spring is in the air, I shove my snow boots to the back of my closet and slam the door. Sliding down the wooden frame, I sit on the floor and let my emotions erupt. The tears run in constant streams down my face, and I don't even care. The only good side to us not being an us is that Rocks won't be risking his neck flying down to see me three times a week. Now the bats are under scrutiny by my kind, he'll be far, far safer.

ON SUNDAY, I'M convinced my alarm clock is possessed. The hands speed around the dial toward Monday morning at an almost supernatural rate. Hours feel like minutes. I spend most of the day pacing my room with Feathers chirping at me to let her out, but I'm in no mood to play. I need a 'how to avoid working for a drug lord relative' plan. I wonder what Google would suggest.

Late in the afternoon, Mom brings a piping-hot salted caramel bun up to my room. Sitting on the bed cross-legged, I tear sticky strips off and shove them in my mouth.

"So goot," I mumble, chewing.

"You're not wearing Rocks' necklace."

The caramel suddenly tastes bitter, and it's hard to swallow my mouthful. "Cleaning it," I lie. The wound inflicted from breaking up with Rocks is still bleeding, and under no circumstances will I discuss it with Mom. I have a feeling she'd be as heartbroken as I am, which makes me feel a smidgen better. I'm not the only one that will genuinely miss him.

"I see you got a few college envelopes downstairs. Could be an acceptance letter." She smiles, sitting on the edge of my bed. "You nervous?"

I shrug and jam more bun in my half-full mouth to avoid talking. If you could measure just how nervous I am, it would be completely off the charts, but it's not the idea of college causing it. Thinking about my plans after graduation is the last thing on my mind. My focus is staying as far away from Enzo and his business as possible. Kelly would have kittens if she knew what I was thinking.

Mom inspects her nails. "Loads of people complimented me on these," she says, holding out her fingers. Her nails are jet black with a sprinkle of gold glitter on the tips. They matched her black and gold evening gown for the fundraiser.

"You can't go wrong with glitter."

"Do you think Rocks will stop by tomorrow afternoon?"

I sigh. Mom is missing her favorite mouth to feed. "I don't think so. He's got lots of work to do with his family business. They're preparing for the summer tourist season." Not exactly a lie.

She's going to keep asking though. I need to tell her something better, otherwise I'll be lying about his absence every week.

"And" —I swallow the last bite of caramel bun— "he's sort of got a girlfriend now." The image of Rebekkah, Violet, Phoenix and that new girl floats into my head. It's my turn to study my nails, and I pray the tear I can feel stays put.

Mom leans over and rubs my arm. "Oh sweetheart, I'm sorry. I thought maybe—"

I look up and share the pain that's inside. "Me too, Mom. Me too." I swipe the single tear and push out my bottom lip the same way Mini does when she's told no. Mom smiles and offers to get me another bun, or make whatever I want. She says she knows it won't replace Rocks, but nothing chases the blues away better than freshly baked treats drizzled with hot caramel.

The doorbell chimes and Mom disappears to find out who's visiting on a Sunday afternoon unannounced.

"Connie, sweetheart, it's for you," she calls from the door.

Half way down the stairs, I spy his unevenly laced boots. Rocks is in our entryway taking up way too much room and bringing with him his shadowy darkness that suddenly feels odd. My heart flips at the sight of him, until I force myself not to get excited. His eyes go straight to my bare neck, then flick to my ears, and finally meet mine. What I see stuns me until his hair falls down as he looks at the floor. I straighten my shoulders. This isn't fair. I shouldn't be made to feel like the villain.

"Come up." I turn and head for my room, then spin around on the stairs. "Mom made caramel buns if you want."

I know his nose knows what's in our kitchen already. His eyes flick in the direction of the tempting aroma, then to me, before he stuffs his hands in his pockets. This sucks. The awkwardness between us seriously sucks. I order him up to my room, making the decision for him, as I head to the kitchen. He won't have easy access to aeronaught food anymore, so I'll let him indulge while he can.

The three warm, sticky buns hardly fit on the plate. He's perched on the end of my bed and not in his usual spot in his chair. He rests the plate beside him and watches me as I sit at my desk.

"Why didn't you text me you were visiting?"

"I knew you'd tell me not to come."

I nod. Yep, I so would have. It occurs to me he probably doesn't know a damn thing about breakup etiquette. The bats don't date, and I've never felt any tension between Zada, Strickland, and Judge. Their open relationships are just accepted as normal.

"I need you to print out the newspaper article please." His voice is soft and laced with sadness. I know how he feels. The fact he's ignoring warm, baked goods speaks volumes. "If the government comes after vampire bats, it's a disaster." He shakes his head.

"I know. I can't even bear to think about it." Opening the laptop, I find the article, and the only noise in the room is my printer clicking to life. I watch him from the corner of my eye.

He goes to pick up a bun, changes his mind, and rests his head in his hands. A second later, he looks at me as though he knew I was studying him.

"Connie—"

"Don't. Please don't. I know what you're going to say. The girls are right. I won't share you. I'm sorry."

The printer whirs and stutters before spitting the page onto the floor. I hand it to him but don't meet his eyes. "Can I have another driving lesson, but this time just the driving part?" he asks quietly.

Oh, fudge no!

Rocks in my car is going to have my senses on high alert. That midnight smell is the last thing I need in the confines of my car.

"Um."

"You promised."

"We broke up." My fear of him not understanding what happens when an aeronaught ends a relationship is confirmed. He frowns.

"I'm well aware of that, but what does that have to do with us being friends?"

"Doesn't it, like, hurt to see me?" I ask. I know it's killing me having Rocks in my room and knowing he is not mine anymore.

"Yes, but it hurts far more not seeing you." Knowing Rocks is feeling our separation as much as me helps. Technically, it's only been a day since we weren't an item, but he's struggling too.

"Usually when aeronaughts break up, they don't tend to hang out much for a while, but you're right. You promised me you would help me find my parents, and you did. I promised you I would teach you what I know of my world and driving is part of that promise, so let's go."

Mom wraps up the caramel buns, and I drive Rocks to Dad's work for a driving lesson on private property. I don't broach the fact that without a birth certificate he's never going to get his license because that's no longer my problem. When the lesson is finished, he hands me a crinkled envelope stuffed with one-dollar bills. He explains that the Sire has stripped him of all privileges, and this was all he had in his tips jar at the shop.

The money is for his phone account because he doesn't think it's right that I pay for his texts now. I don't have the heart to tell him the amount in the envelope won't last long, but since we aren't texting so much, maybe it will. The silence between us is foreign and makes me want to cry. Rocks and I have never had trouble talking—ever.

"Guess I better get going. Thank you." His face is blank and masking his emotions. I hate seeing him that way, but I know I'm doing the same thing to him. If he really wants to learn about my world, then it's time for a really hard lesson.

"Rocks, we need a break. Okay? I need you to stay away for a bit."

14
Envoy

Bat POV

THE great, black bat swoops in low over the mountain, following the rise and fall of the land. No owls have been sighted since the market opened, but he stays on high alert. Listening. Sensing. Watching for movement in the foliage below. The nocturnal creatures are slowly awakening. The forest smells clean and crisp after the overload of suburbia, which Connie calls home.

Connie.

We need a break.

The pain those words send through his system cause the bat to call out on the wind—one lone, piercing cry. He knew this day would come. It was a matter of when—not if. How could an aeronaught ever truly accept the ugly, dark creature he becomes every thirty-six hours? No control over what form he takes when the animal breaks out, and the curse controls his wants and desires shoving them aside. He's a freak of nature forced to fight against the animal urges hidden within.

Blood bonds.

Duty.

Family.

What does it all mean if you can't be the real you? Why honor bonds when his own kin consider his human side an indulgence and a disgrace to the blood in his veins?

Blood.

The life-force that drives the universe. The substance he longs for, but hates himself for wanting the very next moment. Connie witnessed the animal in him feed. He drank from her neighbor's beloved pet. *I am a monster.*

Hoo-hoohoohoo Hoooo Hooo

The bat dives for the cover of the nearest, tall pine. He twists in a dizzying turn to come in low under a secluded branch to take cover.

Look left. Check right. Deep breathe. Scent … Birds!

Stinky bird. Find bird. Scent of feathers. Listen. Wait.

Rockland hangs perfectly still, listening. After a moment of silence, he wraps his wings tightly around his body, waiting for another call to confirm his fear. The fear his colony will not be pleased to hear when he reports—the owls have returned. He would bet everything he owns—including his precious phone—on that call belonging to a Great Horned Owl. It's the sound of death, but these forests are filled with dozens of owl species, and not all of them are his enemy. Maybe he's mistaken; maybe he didn't catch the correct cadence of the call. He was distracted, and he knows better than to fly alone distracted.

He scents the familiar stench of a feathered creature—birds stink. The scent is weak indicating it's either a small species, or it's far away, but the difference could mean his life—or death.

As the sun sinks below the horizon, he watches the purple sky for movement. No Camazotz should be this far south, so any large wing span silhouettes will mean only one thing. He closes his eyes to prevent his vision distracting his ears from a subtle call on the wind.

He waits.

He senses.

He watches.

Patience is survival. The patience he depends on waiting for his prey to fall asleep before he feeds—No! Don't think about feeding. The aroma of the sweet buns Mrs. Phillips had made awakened his appetite. The boy flipped feeling hungry so now the bat demands a feed. He should have eaten those treats in Connie's car, but he didn't want her thinking he was only visiting for food. He was visiting for information, well, that's partly the truth. Her text was the excuse he was waiting for to see her.

The last vision of her leaving the colony on Friday will haunt him forever. The sadness and disappointment in her eyes is what he's used to seeing from the Sire. Seeing it in his girlfriend's eyes confirm what a failure he really is in this world. He let down the one person he swore he never would.

The pink and purple canvas above is turning a deep indigo. He needs to keep flying, but his instinct—that animal he loathes—is telling him danger is close.

Silence.

He takes another deep breath analyzing the scents, discovering a new visitor is close—a raccoon. Hanging upside down, he scans the forest floor. Leaves rustle to his left, and through the dense branches, he spies the fat, grey, fur ball waddling along.

Letting go of his hold, his body plummets, until he snaps his wings open wide. They fill with cool, night air and he evens out, gliding to the forest floor.

Flip!

The pine needle bed softens his heavy landing. With his instincts sure an enemy is close, he's safest in human form. He'll walk up the mountain until he's sure he can fly again without detection or threat.

The exercise will do him good and might keep the bat quiet. Without his long, regular flights to Atlanta, the animal becomes restless, but only since he spent those eight long weeks trapped. Thankfully, the market will be empty by the time he returns, and he won't have to face any consequences of his unauthorized excursion. Pushing through the dense underbrush, his mind wanders to his—no, not his—*the* golden girl. Connie would be tripping and stumbling along in the dark, clutching at his elbow to stay on her feet. He wonders for the millionth time if aeronaught eyesight is really that atrocious. Sometimes, she acts half blind. He smiles at the memory of her mud-covered feet the night they first met—the night his life changed forever.

"WHERE HAVE YOU been?" Strickland demands the moment Rocks arrives at his wagon. The Sire steps out of the darkness causing several of the goats in the adjoining pen to bleat. "Should I be surprised you're ignoring my orders?"

Rocks' boot freezes on the bottom rung, and the argument fades from his lips before it's given voice. He pulls the folded printout from his back pocket and hands it to the rigid man before him.

"There was another attack. Connie did some research."

Strickland reads the article despite the fact it's pitch dark. He frowns before staring back at his heir but buries the growl of distaste that the knowledge of his son fraternizing brings. He needs access to this information, but since he banned that strange girl from their presence, he had hoped his son would choose to stay with his own kind. This twisted fascination with them needs to be bled out of him if he's to lead the Shadows one day.

"Hmph," the Sire grunts, slipping the folded paper inside his cracked, leather vest. He wants to ban his son from traveling to her, but the alternative is worse. Without visiting the girl, Rockland would resort to using that device she gifted him with. The less his son is seen by the fledgers and pups with that thing, glowing in his face and barking in his pants, the better. "Keep me updated," he growls, turning.

"Wait."

Rockland notices the tension ripple across his father's shoulders. He senses the Sire considers being in his son's company a form of punishment. What will the Fold say? What will the lower Clip members think? Why isn't what his son thinks and feels of any importance? Rockland winces, trying to gain control of his emotions before his father sees his weakness and adds it to his list of sins. Connie's words have set his emotions on fire, burning the calm control he needs when facing Strickland.

"A quarter of a mile from Wolfpen Gap, I heard an owl call. It sounded like a Great Horned."

Strickland finally faces him. "You sure?"

"Not a hundred percent. I couldn't sight the beast, but I sensed the danger." He swallows, waiting for the repercussions of his admission.

Strickland shakes his head. "And I'm to trust *your* instincts? Instincts you never let free for fear of it making you less of a man!"

Rockland looks away, sighing. "Whether I'm a man or a bat," he whispers in a harsh tone, "I'm still a Camazotz, and I would never endanger the colony—ever!"

"You told those aeronaughts where we roost!" the Sire yells. "The one promise a true Camazotz would rather *die* than break. Yet, you blurt it out like some feeble female."

Rocks' fists form at his sides. His father is out of line in so many ways, but he doesn't miss the sting in his words. Maybe Strickland would've preferred he died? The insult to him is yet another to add to the pile. But females have worth, and just like the aeronaught population eventually allowed them to vote, the Camazotz need to as well.

"What my mother sees in you I will never understand," Rocks growls. "Doesn't her opinion—"

"Enough!" the Sire roars. "You need to keep quiet and obey my commands. That aeronaught is not to enter here without my prior knowledge. Clear?"

"She has done nothing but try to help us."

"Are. We. Clear?"

The beast inside Rockland wants to go for his jugular. Instead of pushing down the anger and resentment, he lets it loose.

"Why should I listen to you or any of the elders here? You never listen to anyone else. Maybe if you had listened more, you'd have known your daughter didn't think aeronaughts were the enemy either. Maybe she'd have told us she was getting fixed. But she was so scared of the consequences because of you!"

Strickland is on his son and has a fistful of his shirt, pulling him down closer to his height. "How dare you put that on me—"

"Well, who else should I blame? Zada? Judge? Zander? Do you think it was them that made her so secretive? Now Elm and Oak are gone too. Do you really not see the pattern, father?"

"Do not speak to me in that tone!"

"Why? Who else is going to stand up to you if I don't? They were born human, and I'm guessing—like me—they felt more comfortable in this skin." Strickland jerks back, letting go of his son as though touching the naught lover might be contagious. "But I was never allowed to talk to them because of Cypress. That man is so full of hate and anger—Macallister too. How can you not see it? Their dislike isn't about what's best for this colony. They're afraid."

"How dare you say a Fold member is afraid! What in heaven's name did I do to deserve your disrespect and insolence?"

"Nothing, father," he says quietly, turning to walk away. "You've done *nothing* for me my whole life, except hope I'll grow out of my *human phase*."

Rockland stalks off into the night leaving his father silent in the darkness.

DECKER'S FEET DANGLE high above the ground. He's straddling a thick limb in the ancient fir tree, picking at the smooth bark between his legs while watching his brother. Rockland is sitting below, leaning his back against the round trunk in silence with his legs stretched along the solid branch. He hasn't said a word since he flipped. They're waiting for Ezra and Jeremiah to return to the roost before the meeting commences.

Decker plucks a cone from the branch above, spinning it in his fingers. "So LittleStar wants to go for a moonlit flight later tonight."

He waits for his brother to respond to his big news, but after a minute, pelts the cone at Mr. Selective Hearing instead.

"Hey!" Rocks rubs his skull where the missile made contact, looking up at his best friend.

"Did you hear me?"

"What?"

"Earth to Rockland, a female asked me to go flying tooo-niiight!" He rubs his hands together, trying but failing to hide his excitement.

"Are you ready for that? How old is she?"

"Turned nineteen two nights ago. Now she's an adult, she's getting busy. I'm trying to work out how I can persuade her to flip for a bit."

"Why would you want her to flip? Don't tell me nobody explained to you what those flights are about, little brother."

The evening sky doesn't hide the blush on Decker's cheerful cheeks.

"Ha-ha. I'm perfectly aware, thank you, but you know why I want her to flip?" He waits a second. "So I can experience making … What does Connie call it? Making up?"

Faster than he flips, Rocks snatches three pinecones and fires them directly at Decker. His brother ducks and weaves the incoming projectiles trying not to fall off the limb. "I told you NOT to tell anyone about that! God, Decker! Connie would kill me."

"I haven't! Well, I won't be until later when I'm trying to convince LittleStar," he jokes. "You never give me any of the juicy details, brother. Who else is going to guide me into adulthood?" He winks.

Decker watches the sadness fill Rockland's eyes. When his brother notices his stare, the vacant look from earlier returns to match his sour mood. If it's possible for Rockland to avoid contact with the colony even more than he already does, then that's how he's been for the past few nights.

"You gonna tell me who drained your best goat?" Decker waits. "You don't think the Sire was serious when he banned Connie, do you?"

Rocks sighs and looks back up at his brother. "I do, but her ban isn't the problem. She ended it."

"Ended what?"

"It's called breaking up. We aren't dating any more. She asked me not to visit."

"Ah, shit, man. I'm sorry. You serious? I mean, you have seen how that girl looks at you, right? If LittleStar looked at me with even half of that, I'd be sweet."

"You know LittleStar's Daddy looks at you with that and more. He's after the blood in your veins. Figures if his little girl can't be a Fold member, then she might as well mate one."

"Yeah, yeah, I know what he's planning, but, hey, I might as well enjoy the ride."

DEEP UNDERGROUND, ROCKLAND leans against the limestone wall, waiting for the last few Camazotz to arrive. The match in his fingers sparks to life, illuminating the damp walls. The sacred meeting cavern is lower than the main cave the bats use to roost. It can only be accessed as the bat flies, down a thin fissure in the floor, and entrance is by invite only. This ground is strictly reserved for Fold and Clip matters.

Strickland takes his human form a second later, calling the meeting open. "Flip."

Rockland lights the ancient glass lantern that hangs permanently in the cavern. The Camazotz don't necessarily need the light to see, but all past generations and hopefully future ones have lit the single lantern for meetings. The flickering, golden light signals proceedings have begun. The shadows of the members dance on the cavern walls making it seem like twice their number are present.

Meetings of this nature require every Fold member with his heir, and each Clip member and his heir to be in attendance. More than a dozen men take seats on the stools carved from the remains of stalagmites so the rows standing at the back can see their leader.

"Volunteers for the envoy to Vuelo de la Muerte?"

Rockland eyes his father in the center of the circle, arms folded—a man of few words and even less emotion. He wonders if the Sire warned the others the owls may have returned. Rocks has avoided any and all contact with his father and the Fold since they had words, and he hates himself a little more for even worrying about their argument. Deep down, he knows he owes his father the respect his position demands, but the arrogance the Sire exudes drives Rockland beyond control, not to mention the fact his father never talks about anything emotional—particularly Celand.

Pegasus is the first to volunteer, and his sire, Peryton, pats his broad shoulder. The pride is evident across his features making Rockland look away. Cypress steps up, looking at his son. Ash jumps off the cold, stone seat he's slumped in and nods once at Strickland, trying to act cool.

"Of course, you'll go. Thank you, Cypress. Speak directly with your mate if you can," Strickland orders.

"I'll go," Levi announces. "Since Mazal has another pup on the way, I put forward to have Jeremiah accompany me."

"Done," Strickland replies, looking around the circle of remaining members. Five is not enough to send safely by air. "Any Clip?" He ignores the hiss of surprise from certain wings. On envoys of this importance, the Clips stay on duty at the colony, but drastic times call for drastic measures.

"Foxfire and I volunteer, Sire, with honor," Foxhunt's voice booms from the darkness at the very back of the large circle. The two men step into the light.

Rocks smiles seeing the look of excitement on his third cousin's face. Foxfire has always been ambitious, but their wing doesn't have the numbers. The young Camazotz with shaggy hair and a tattoo of a small bat with three stars trailing in its wake high on his cheekbone stands tall. Relations between Rockland and Foxfire have been strained since his regular visits to an aeronaught were made public knowledge. Rockland wonders what their wing think now having seen his miraculous recovery.

"Count me in, Sire," Rockland says behind his father.

"That's eight," states Strickland.

Cypress surges forward demanding Rockland is left at the roost to babysit the pups. He states he should not be trusted since he couldn't be trusted to keep their location a secret. Rockland waits—not daring to move—watching for his father's reaction, and wondering for how many years he's going to pay the price for Decker telling Connie about their roost. He's desperate to look at Decker to make sure his brother doesn't open his big, honest mouth, but he focuses on the hard shoulders of his father instead. Cypress stands facing his fellow Fold members and continues his rant.

"Why should he be sent to represent the colony? Only the most worthy members should be given duties of such importance. It misleads the lower wings into thinking that he" —Cypress jabs a finger in Rockland's direction— "might be worth voting for one day. Sends conflicting messages."

"What do you mean by lower wings, Cypress?" Rockland asks, moving out from behind Strickland.

"Watch your tone, boy!" Cypress puffs out his chest trying to look as big as the tall male challenging him.

"Forgive me, *sir*. But could you please explain, because I thought we referred to them as smaller wings. Aren't all the members of this colony on the same level?" A rumble passes through the meeting, but nobody speaks up. "Father? What do you say?" Rockland's eyes never leave Cypress.

"Quiet. I don't have time for this. Back to the volunteers. Who else feels Rockland shouldn't represent us?"

Rockland doesn't miss the subtle movements in the outer circle. His father should have addressed Cypress' choice of words and reassured the Clip that they matter. Every single member matters when numbers are threatened. Rockland closes his eyes and takes a calming breath. Always disappointed by his father's leadership; will there ever be a day he isn't?

"I refuse to listen to my nephew's honor being debated again. We voted, and he was cleared of his crime—allowed to live amongst us." Zander's cool voice echoes around the high chamber.

Rockland's eyes move from Fold member to Fold member watching for a reaction to the use of the term nephew. A not-so-subtle reminder that the young man's veins carry more than one powerful wing's blood.

Levi speaks next which leaves Rocks quiet. "He is the biggest and fastest flyer. If we are attacked, he has a better chance of leaving the envoy to reach help. I want him by my side, and I know my son will agree."

"Yeah, he's good at leaving his own kind. He's proved that time and time again," Ash sneers.

The Sire turns his back on Cypress and his taunting heir. "Pegasus? Foxhunt? What do you say?"

The vote is a landslide, and Rockland becomes the eighth and final member to accompany them.

ROCKLAND IS RESTLESS and annoyed by the time the envoys land at the Vuelo de la Muerte compound. He likes Pegasus a lot, but flying with the muscle-bound giant is painfully tedious over short distances, and downright torture over long ones. He's possibly the slowest flyer at the colony. Cypress commanded they remain in official formation for the whole journey, leaving Rockland no choice but to distract himself from the boring flight with images of the golden girl.

Thinking of Connie leads him to the one place he tries to avoid—the pit of self-loathing and hate. He spent so many of his fledgling years feeling guilty and confused by his need to be human, and yet, as an adult, he's no closer to understanding what's right. Being a bat saved his life when his wing healed, but his Camazotz duty lost him the only person he's ever fallen in love with. The one person that's ever made him smile everyday and allowed him to embrace his human side. The one person the animal he battles with was able to save, only to lose her later because of it.

The group transform in the trees by the side of the empty road, no fear of their miracle being witnessed at this early hour. Pegasus is red in the face and wipes sweat from his forehead, gulping the cool oxygen. Foxhunt checks that the young male is all right, before stepping in next to Cypress.

Large, silver metal gates block the once open entrance. "These are new," Levi comments, eyeing the eight-foot high barricade. "Should we flip on the other side?"

The group stills, their Camazotz senses checking the surrounding area. "Something feels wrong," Rockland says just above a whisper, cocking his head left and right. He wonders where the colony got the funds to install fencing of this quality as he eyes the solid steel running down the length of the perimeter for as far as the eye can see.

A series of metallic clicks followed by a low whirring has the group of men stepping away from the heavy gates that slowly begin to open of their own accord.

"What—"

"Aeronaught gadgetry?"

Rocks gives Jeremiah a quick glance. Connie had explained the magic of remote controls late one night, when Rocks saw the neighbor across the road stop his car in the driveway. Nobody got out of the vehicle, but the large door panel that was illuminated by the bright headlights began to open—seemingly by magic. He was fascinated, and the boys have witnessed the phenomenon on several occasions when they've been hanging outside her room.

Halfway open, the gate stops with another click. "It's all right. I've seen similar to this before. It's safe," Rocks explains, stepping through the gap into the compound.

The group makes their way on foot up the long, asphalt drive. It's been laid recently and still has a strong odor that tickles the Camazotz's keen senses. Waiting on the front porch of the wooden house, which seems out of place surrounded by low concrete buildings, are two Vuelo de la Muerte Fold members dressed entirely in black—Océano and Sandía. Standing as guards on either side in the shade of the porch are two tough-looking youths.

Océano manages a weak smile. "Greetings to you, Shadows. I hope you had a safe journey." Her eyes check each member is in one piece. The owls are clearly still terrorizing this colony too.

"Greetings, Vuelo de la Muerte. Lovely to see you again, Océano," Cypress replies with a curt head bow. "Sandía. Is your Sire present?"

He explains they have come to discuss the matter of the bat attacks on the aeronaught population. Rockland studies the sentinel guards behind them. Neither of these two are the heirs of the Fold members. Although he's rarely by Strickland's side when colony business is conducted, he's the oddity. Most Fold members have their heir close to use any opportunity to teach them what will be expected should they be voted into leadership.

Stepping around the Shadows and Muerte Fold members, he approaches the pair.

"I'm Rockland, son of Strickland," he announces, holding out his arm in the Camazotz formal greeting style. The male stares at his offered hand, raising an eyebrow, and then grinning to the female on his right. He eventually grips Rockland's forearm with enough force to break it again and shakes once.

"Temblor."

The skin on the back of both hands of the big male is covered in thick ink. The Camazotz has tattooed the anatomically accurate bones that lay beneath his skin over the surface, but it's the freshly heeled scar across his face that interests Rocks. The puffy, pink gash runs from high in the center of his forehead, across his left eye before disappearing into the scruffy hair somewhere near his ear.

"You're lucky you didn't lose that eye," Rockland comments.

The thickset shoulders of the talkative Camazotz lift briefly. "Some might say lucky, although you probably wouldn't." The look in his eyes is a cross between defiant and smug. Since he clearly isn't going to elaborate Rockland focuses on the other sentinel guard, trying not to let how odd he thinks these interactions are show on his face.

"And you are?" Rocks asks, offering his arm to the bone-thin female.

"Tromba, daughter of wouldn't-you-like-to-know." She stares at his hand, but doesn't move to take it.

Rockland drops his arm and is instantly flanked by Jeremiah and Pegasus. The bone-thin female looks both new males up and down before smirking. She flicks her long hair over one shoulder revealing shiny, gold hoop earrings that match the bangles and bracelets which adorn half her arms.

"You, I don't know," she says to Pegasus.

While Pegasus gives her minimal information in return, Rocks scans his memory of the power structure at Muerte. He's not as familiar with their wings since he rarely visits, and regretfully was too busy playing the rebellious fledger to remember Strickland's lectures on who is more powerful than whom in their world. This colony emits warm and fuzzy feelings—which rival the Shadows—toward members who prefer to be human. They would embrace Connie as enthusiastically as someone hugging a cactus.

Quickly translating the pair of names just given to him, Rockland realized that Earthquake and Whirlwind are obviously related, but he can't recall a wing named for natural disasters. If the Muerte are suffering losses similar to that of Duskwing, then it would explain why members of a smaller wing are helping keep the colony safe. Everyone steps up for duty when danger lingers.

"Nice tat," she says to Pegasus, studying his wing's symbol displayed high on his shoulder. Since the guy's biceps are too bulky for standard sleeves, his arms are bare. "You don't belong to a Fold wing, so why are you here?"

"You're not a Fold wing either, so let's just leave it at that," Rockland replies, straightening to his full height.

No Camazotz will intimidate a member of his colony while he's present. Strickland wouldn't allow it and neither will he. He turns his back on the two guards and joins the Fold members—as is his right—knowing Jeremiah and Pegasus won't leave his back vulnerable.

The conversation ends with Sandía stating their Sire will join them shortly. He looks behind him at Temblor, who flips the very next second.

"Are Mantarraya and Concha around? It's been a while since I've seen them," Rockland asks Océano. Her once beautiful, brown eyes have thin wrinkles starting to appear. He knows she's only a couple of years older than Zada, however she's aged in the past year.

She frowns, looking past him. "No, unfortunately my heirs are at our roost. Away."

"Please tell them I was asking after them. I hope they're safe and well."

"Yes, me too." Her sad smile doesn't reach her eyes. Rockland wants to ask if her wing has suffered recent deaths and offer the Shadows' condolences. The scar on Temblor's face would suggest such, but he doesn't wish to upset her more than she clearly is.

His concern is warranted a moment later when the Vuelo de la Muerte's Sire walks—or hobbles—around the corner. Saturno—the man who once emanated power only Strickland can match—is hunched over a walking cane and being assisted by a small woman. Rockland looks around for Asteroide, his heir. If Strickland was ever this weak and injured, Rockland wouldn't leave his side for a second, particularly if another colony showed up at their market unannounced.

Levi steps forward to pay his respects to their Sire. "Sire, what happened?" he asks, taking hold of the older man's elbow. The age different between the two men is only five years, but tough Levi makes the Muerte's Sire look geriatric by comparison. The injuries must be deep. Rockland regrets their need to speak with the leader, and wonders why he isn't recovering in the safety of their roost.

Would Strickland cower in their roost if wounded?

"Those beastly creatures!" Saturno replies to Levi.

"Jeremiah, fetch a chair," Levi commands, scowling at the female Camazotz on the porch.

"Not necessary, I can't stay long," Saturno interjects.

He informs the group the owls hunting these Camazotz never left the area for winter, and Saturno was attacked one evening—barely surviving. The Shadows' members question the Sire in much the same way as they did visiting Duskwing, before Cypress requests to see Venus.

The sister of the Sire is walked out accompanied by Temblor and runs forward, throwing her arms around Cypress' neck. He picks her up and walks several feet away, kissing her openly in front of the group. The look Jeremiah gives Rockland needs no explanation. How hard-edged Cypress could land the female that suits her name perfectly in looks and demeanor is a modern mystery.

Her silky, black hair is worn in two braids that fall in thick ropes over her breasts. Once Cypress lets the woman breathe on her own, she plays with the ends of her plaits while they talk quietly. But with Camazotz hearing, they might as well join the group because everyone present can hear their whispered conversation.

"Where's my son? I wish to see him." Cypress asks.

Venus glances at Temblor before answering. "At the roost. It's so dangerous now."

Cypress bristles in a way only a male that once mated with her would. "Why are you here? You should be with him. Protected. Not here, alone," he growls. She drops one plait to rest her hand on his forearm.

"We will be fine."

Cypress further questions her about the attacks, the owls, and how the Muerte are responding. She swears on their bond that the attacks on the aeronaughts have not come from their members, and that the Camazotz Strickland is looking for is undoubtedly from Duskwing. Her tears seal her oath as Cypress cradles her to his chest.

The envoys fly straight to Blood Mountain. Harland and Decker are hanging on watch duty at the top of the twisted pine when they arrive.

> *Welcome back.*
> *All safe?*

Cypress confirms and asks for the Sire's location as Rocks swoops in to land upside-down beside his brother. When the other members of the envoy dive into their roost, Rockland communicates with his brother.

> *Come to meeting.*
> *Need to hear.*

Decker replies he'll be there as soon as he can find someone to cover his watch duties. The larger bat, unhooks his claws and drops, barely missing the twisted, gnarled limbs as gravity pulls him toward the cave entrance.

His head fills with greetings as his vision adjusts to the near blackness. A tiny bat with one eye stitched closed joins him on his way to the crevasse opening.

> *Missed you.*

> *You too, Bailey.*

> *Can I come?*

> *No, stay here.*

Knowing his little sister will be annoyed by his response, he lifts one wing tip sending him gliding under her. With another flap of his great wings, he rises up, forcing the tiny creature to land on his back. She folds her wings in against her body and clings to her big brother.

Ready?

EEEEKKKK!

With one eye gone, her depth perception is still lacking so Rocks happily gives her a joy ride—way faster than the little bat would be capable of flying herself. He circles the huge stalactite that has almost reached out to touch its sister formation below, zipping around and around the limestone teeth in tight, dizzying loops, then bottoming out flying inches above the gravel floor. At the end of the cave, he goes vertical, heading higher and higher. At the highest point of their roost, he orders her to hang on before twisting into three continuous summersaults ending in the death dive. Wings tucked tight and with her extra weight, the bats hurtle toward the narrow fissure.

Be careful.

Zada's voice is the last thing the pair hear before vanishing out of sight. The trick is a favorite of all fledgers, but little Bailey will probably never master it. With the opening barely a square foot wide, there is zero margin for error.

Her whoops of joy edged with terror echo inside his head as he pulls out of the hair-raising dive with only two feet to spare. He U-turns heading back up the crack in the stone to return her to the main cavern.

When Rocks enters the meeting chamber a few seconds later, all are gathered around their Sire. Levi and Cypress are giving the report, so he flips and waits his turn. When neither Fold member mentions that none of the younger Camazotz were present, Rocks speaks up. Cypress turns on him, shutting him down.

"Venus swore they were trying to protect their future generation by keeping them at the roost. She swore a blood oath on it."

"It didn't feel right," Rockland counters, trying to stay calm.

"What do you know about right? You don't know right from wrong because if you did, you would respect our ancient blood bonds."

"I do respect them."

"Well, prove it," dares Cypress. "Go to AuburnSky now, and fulfill your duty to her. Prove once and for all to the Shadows that you are grateful for the life-giving blood you received."

Rocks turns to Strickland. "Sire, this isn't about my blood promises; it's about what I saw at the Muerte. Don't you agree it doesn't add up? Would you send all of us" —he points to the next generation of fold— "into hiding? Or do you need us more than ever to watch out for and protect the smaller wings?"

15

Surely Not

Connie

WHEN the school bell rings, my stomach threatens to eject what I struggled to swallow for lunch. Enzo's men are going to be waiting in that car—and I'm not going to show. His advice about not upsetting them releases a tidal wave of acid in my already upset belly.

Implementation of my plan for 'not joining the money laundering business' began earlier with parking my Honda three blocks from school and cutting across several backyards to enter the school behind the gym. Part two involves staying in the library until his thugs give up. If they can't find my car, I'm hoping they'll think I'm not here and leave me the hell alone.

I wipe the sweat from my neck when the librarian, Mrs. Batch, shoos me out the door so she can lock up. My sneakers squeak on the linoleum in the halls. Every sound echoes and reverberates in my rib cage, and I feel as though the school marching band might as well announce my exit for all the noise I'm making.

Peering over the windowsill next to the entrance, I scan the parking lot and street.

Empty.

No sign of ominous looking Town Cars or men in suits. I take a deep breath and push out the door. Still nothing. The street is quiet, and by some miracle, I'm in the clear.

It is Monday today, right?

My skin prickles as I sneak back to my hidden car. I don't feel like I'm being watched, but my gut is still warning me that all is not right in my world. I glance around one last time before getting in and starting up the Honda. I guess defying a crime lord comes at a price. Maybe I'll be looking over my shoulder for the rest of my life. College in another state is looking more and more attractive by the second.

The street outside my house is suspiciously empty. No unusual vans or cars. Mom is home, the house smells of lasagna, Mini is giggling loudly, and a newsreader's voice drifts softly from the TV room. Normal. All appears fine, despite my gut telling me to panic.

By nine, I'm exhausted. My senses have been on high alert listening for footsteps, or car doors slamming, or gunshots. Good grief! Not only do I cry at the drop of a hat now, I'm a drama queen to boot. Nobody is coming for me during the night—Camazotz, or other. I'm safe. Enzo, no doubt, has far too much on his plate to worry about a teenager that never showed up. I have the urge to text Rocks. But to tell him what exactly—I'm safe in bed? Taking three deep breaths, I turn off my lamp and hope sleep will come.

School the next day is almost too quiet. No tinted dark cars were waiting by the front gate when I arrive, yet the feeling of doom persists.

When I get to my locker after last bell, Tiff grumbles and moans about my snail-like speed. She's updating me on all the gossip that has occurred since lunch because my cell phone battery died, but I can't focus on her words. Sitting inside my locker is a picture of a tiny child's coffin. It's pure white, like the soul of the little angel who would rest in it for eternity. Glancing up and down the corridors, there are only a few lingering students left for the day. A shiver tingles my spine and the hairs on my arms stand up. Who would leave a picture of a coffin for me? I root through my backpack for my inhaler.

Surely those brutes don't know my locker combination too.

"Have there been any pranks going on?" I ask Tiff, as I fold the picture in two and slide it into my back pocket.

"Not that I know of. Why?"

"Just curious." My gut is telling me this isn't a coincidence. Last year, the football team thought putting disgusting items—like their sweaty, worn jock straps—in girls' lockers was hilarious. Yet this doesn't feel the same. Then the worst thought of all slams my frayed nerves.

The Vipers are back.

This is their little hello message informing me they want the money back the boys took from their van.

Closing my locker, I rest my forehead on the cool metal. I can't seem to win. Yesterday, I trick my father's men into leaving me alone, and today his deadly enemies have come to pay me a visit. This school needs to invest in some serious new security monitoring.

"Come on, girl. Let's get the hell out of here. School finished almost half an hour ago and lurking here when the mall is calling my name is all kinds of wrong," Tiff says, her brilliant blue eyes dancing with mischief. "Besides, the others will have eaten all the donuts if we don't hurry."

Stepping into the afternoon light, my intestinal friend stops its slithering, when the coast is clear. No thugs from either organization are waiting. The universe might be giving me a small reprieve. Maybe the picture in my back pocket is purely some stupid student chain letter. A school joke, and I'm supposed to slip it into someone else's locker to creep them out too.

But something stops me from showing Tiff.

We meet Mary Lou and Brandy by the donut stand, and for the first time in forever, I feel the need to shop to distract my brain from everything I've been obsessing over. I start with a Boston Crème, then buy three bottles of nail polish, and a Sven and Olaf Beanie Baby for Mini, before adding the stack of dollar-bills to Rocks' phone account.

"Did you see Parker staring at you in English?" Tiff asks. Brandy raises an eyebrow at this new information.

"Yeah, so what?" A blind person wouldn't have missed Parker staring at me, but Tiff did miss the fact that I was giving him my best how-dare-you-sign-a-petition-to-kill-my-ex glare. If anything comes from his bat cull petition, I'll wear his nuts on a necklace. He might have to give up wrestling and join the girl's choir instead.

"No second chance?" Brandy asks.

"Nope. He's signing petitions to kill innocent animals. I'd hardly be an animal lover if I dated someone like that."

"I better get going." Tiff sighs.

Glancing at my watch, I realize I'll make it home just in time for dinner. On the way to my car, I dump the folded picture in the trash.

I'm letting my imagination run wild. And that's a dangerous thing these days.

Considering I know that magic is real and can turn people into bats, it's no wonder I think this stupid school prank is a message from the Vipers. Retail therapy and girl talk really can fix anything.

Driving down my street, I can't miss the police cruiser parked roughly where my house is. The eel pokes his head out to see if it's worth stirring up my guts again. When I pull up, I not only confirm the cruiser is parked outside my house, but there are another two police cars in the driveway where I usually park.

What the fudge?

It can't be Enzo. It can't be Enzo, I chant entering the house. Would he really take out my Dad so that he can replace him? I shudder at the vile thought and curse the snarky attitude I gave him.

The Vipers? Surely this isn't to do with that coffin picture—surely! The reprieve my nerves had this afternoon at the mall vanishes as my blood pressure picks up the pace once more.

My living room resembles something from that crime show Mom watches religiously. There are men in uniforms and others in suits standing in groups. Mom is on the couch rocking back and forth crying. A man is perched opposite her on the coffee table asking questions about someone's appearance for something called a BOLO.

Where the hell is Dad?

I scan the groups of strangers and sigh in relief when I see Dad frowning and nodding at one of the plainclothes policemen speaking with him.

My keys hit the tiled floor making everyone look my way.

"Connie," Mom wails, her hands reaching for me in the air.

Dad pushes through the bodies and comes to my side, telling me to take a seat next to my mother. My lungs feel as though they've shriveled up entirely. "What's going on?"

I look from one policeman to the other. The split-second fear that Enzo had done something to my parents vanishes as fast as it appeared, but I don't like the grim faces staring at me.

With my backpack still on and shopping bags in hand, I'm pushed onto the couch next to Mom. The sadness and fear in her eyes is like a slap across the face. "They've got her," she moans between sobs.

"Kelly!" Dad snaps. He looks back at me. "You didn't answer your phone."

"Battery died."

What the hell is she talking about? My eyes scan the room quickly before landing back on Dad. "Who?" I whisper, not wanting to acknowledge what my gut is screaming at me. There is one little person not present.

No!

"Jasmine."

"What do you mean? What? Mini?" My lungs constrict. I grab my chest. My pulse thunders in the vein in my neck as my mind pictures that little white coffin.

Oh fudge. Not now.

An officer starts speaking. I can see his lips moving, but I can't hear anything past the wheezing in my lungs. I try to drag in more air. My vision flickers. There's a sea of swaying bodies crowding around me, and I feel like I need to punch my way free. I can't breathe. I can't breathe. Air. Not enough air.

I never leave the house without an inhaler in my backpack, but my arms won't co-operate with the shoulder straps. I'm trapped. I sway on the couch and feel hands on my shoulders.

"Step back."

"Give her air."

"She's having an asthma attack," Mom screams.

Dad's calm tone fills my ears. I look toward the sound and try to focus on his face. He shoves my inhaler between my lips and orders me to take a puff. One pump, two pumps, three …

Cool air rushes down my windpipe as my lungs release and open. Gasping, I close my eyes and center my energy on simply breathing. Stay calm. Take a breath—do it again.

"Are you all right?" Mom's cool fingers press against my cheeks. "Look at me." The high-pitched frequency of her tone makes me wince.

She's just lost one child—somehow—and now she's panicking over her other.

"Sorry," I gasp. Dad holds up my inhaler again, but I push his hand away. If I have too many puffs, it will make me dizzy, and I need to focus on what the hell has happened to Mini. She's only two years old—just a baby. Oh my God. They wouldn't, would they?

I take my inhaler from Dad and decide I need more. I hold my breath letting the Ventolin do it's work. Dad is still kneeling at my feet, and I notice he's holding my other hand.

"Your mother was carjacked coming home from daycare."

"How?" I look across to see she's crying silently beside me.

"She stopped for gas. Two hooded men pushed her to the ground, grabbed her keys and stole the car. The police are sure they didn't know Mini was inside. It sometimes happens," he explains in a calm voice. He tells me the police are confident our car will be found with Mini safely inside it in a shopping center parking lot. This kind of thing has happened before, and once the car thieves realize they have an extra passenger, their joy ride loses its appeal.

I squeeze my eyes shut. This really can't be a coincidence. But what do I tell them? I wish I hadn't thrown that picture away.

Oh God, this is all my fault.

"What if they don't find the car?" My chest is tightening up again. I try not to panic so my lungs will continue to function. The look on the nearest detective gives nothing away.

"We have our teams on it. Don't worry. We'll bring your sister home safely. It's only a matter of time."

Leaning back against the couch, I close my eyes. Maybe this isn't Enzo's doing. Maybe this really is just a carjacking gone wrong. Surely. Oh please. Poor little Mini. I pull the shopping bag off the floor and let the fluffy reindeer and snowman fall into my lap. When Mom sees them, she starts howling loudly and mumbles something about kind big sisters.

Dad moves to rub her back, and then the man with the notebook is back with his questions. Mom didn't get a clear look at either of the men because it happened so quickly. They're trying to trigger her memory of any small detail that might help them catch these sugarplum heads!

"What can I do?" I can't sit around here doing nothing. "Can I drive around ... looking ... something?"

The police within hearing all shake their heads. The search is in their hands, and they'd rather I didn't get in the way. Dad suggests I make Mom some coffee as it's going to be a long night.

By the time the late news airs, we're crowded around the TV. The police have released the footage from the gas station security video, and it plays out like a horror movie. Recognizing Mom on the late news is creepy. I'm so used to watching terrible things happen to somebody else—never people I know. It's a nightmare.

The scene unfolds exactly as Mom described to the cops. Two men approach her, shove her to the ground with bone-crunching force, wrestle the keys from her fist, and speed away with my little sister. I'm in tears by the end of the short clip from the relief that it wasn't either of the two thugs who kidnapped me last year, or Enzo's goons that hang out near school. Maybe this really is a freaky accident and has nothing to do with me.

The worst part is seeing Mom crawling on all fours, scrambling to get to her feet to pursue them even though the effort is futile. As the men speed off, she collapses on the concrete, and even without any sound, I can tell she's screaming. My emotional pit is a raging storm-tossed sea that's trying to spill out of me.

As the helpline number runs across the bottom of the screen, I send up a prayer someone will have seen something to help the police bring Mini home. However, each hour that ticks past feels more desolate than the previous one.

Dad sends me to my room around midnight. He promises to wake me if there's any update on Mini's whereabouts. My fingers twitch as I contemplate calling Rocks. He loves that kid and will be as devastated as we are, but I just asked him to stay away and give me time to get over us. Pulling him back in so soon isn't right.

I dig around in my bookshelf and place the white business card on my quilt. I eye it gingerly, trying not to touch it. Surely Enzo is not involved—surely. But if it's the Vipers, then maybe he knows how to help. An hour later, I shove it back inside a book and stare at the ceiling. I feel sick to the bone.

I wake with a jerk still in my jeans from yesterday. Blinking, I look around my room and my stomach churns. My sister is missing and I'm sleeping! How could I? Jumping out of bed, I race down the hall. Mom and Dad's bed is untouched, confirming what I already know. Stumbling down the stairs, I find them both in the TV room glued to the news.

When I look to Dad, he shakes his head and looks at the carpet. After the turmoil of last year, I realized I know my parents better than I thought. I'm betting he feels as though he's let Mini down by not finding her, or at least joining the search.

Walking over, I rub his shoulder. "It's not your fault." Tears build at the corner of his eye until he blinks them away. His hand covers mine, but he doesn't say a word.

I take a seat next to Mom, alarmed to see she's aged overnight. Her usual perfect, crisp appearance is ruffled to say the least. Her hair isn't done, and she too is still in yesterday's dress, but it's her eyes that worry me—they're blank. Empty. Lost.

My hand wraps around hers and gives a gentle squeeze. "The police will find her," I promise.

I can't sit here and do nothing. Moving to the kitchen, I start a fresh pot of coffee. My stomach turns at the thought of putting food into it, but my gut tells me we all need to eat. Sugar. I might be able to handle sugar. Heating a pan, I decide on French toast, and lose myself in its preparation.

I carry the laden tray and place it on the coffee table before my folks. Mom starts crying and the sight of her anguish makes me wish I hadn't bothered. I never realized how much I rely on their strength. How safe and secure it makes me feel in this world. Seeing them frayed at the edges and barely holding on is something I pray I never have to witness again.

We nibble and pick at my offerings in silence, and Mom eventually drinks a whole glass of juice. The house is never this quiet in the mornings. It's eerie. My mind wanders to where poor little Mini is and if she's okay. Is she still strapped in her car seat with a wet diaper, crying, cold and alone? Or worse? I wince. I cannot afford to think that way. I want to mention the picture, but the words don't seem to form. How do I even start?

The phone ringing loudly causes me to spill my orange juice. Mom would normally rush to get a wet cloth but sits comatose, hardly even noticing. Dad moves faster than Rocks can flip, but the one-sided conversation only adds to my nausea.

"Thank you, Detective Williams. We'll be here."

His face crumbles as he disconnects. Mom leans forward and covers hers with her hands, but I want confirmation.

"What?"

"No leads. Nothing." He slumps into his armchair and closes his eyes.

"I'm going out to look for her."

That statement gets a response from both of them. They don't want me looking for car thieves or getting involved. If only they knew. I argue that more people searching for Mini would give us a better chance at finding Mom's abandoned car. Mom begs me to go to school where she knows I'll be safe.

"Please, sweetheart, I can't bear the thought of losing you as well. Please. Just go to class. Be safe."

"I'm not going to school when my sister is missing!"

Dad gives me a look. He's never one to use the evil eye—usually that's Mom's territory—so I heed his warning. I sense he doesn't want his barely coping wife upset by anything else. Thinking from their perspective, I'm instantly sorry for raising my voice.

"School? Really?"

She nods her head. "We might be called to the station again. I just … yes, go. Please." She sighs. "We'll call you the second we hear anything."

My heart wants me to fight this ludicrous idea, but my head tells me not to add to her stress levels. In truth, I wouldn't know where to begin looking for abandoned cars, but the thought of school makes me feel like a traitor to my sister.

At school, I race down the corridor to my locker and almost tear the door off trying to open it. If that picture is connected to Mini, then they might have left me another clue. Disappointment floods my system, followed quickly by relief when I find it exactly as I left it yesterday.

Principal Skenner calls me to the office first thing. His kind words and gentle tone make it hard not to cry. He says he wants me to focus on my studies today, but if it's too much to come and see him, his door is always open. I tell him my phone will not be switched to silent and will be in my hand during all classes, and if he can't make that happen with the teaching staff, then I'm spending the day in the library.

The girls are my support crew. They keep the other inquisitive students—eager to get up close to someone whose parent appeared on the late news—at a distance. It's surreal. I don't want to be famous for having lost my little sister, but their callous actions slowly morph my despair into anger.

Last class for the day is English. If I can survive this, I'm free. Parker stops by my desk and confirms the ugly whispers I've tried to ignore all day in the halls.

"Sorry about Mini, Con. She was a cute kid."

I'm out of my chair the second I hear my worst nightmare spoken aloud.

"WAS?" I scream. Tiff grabs hold of my belt to prevent me doing something I'll regret later when my parents get a call from the principal.

His eyes dart from me, to Tiff, to the rest of the room. The school cell grapevine is probably going ballistic. I'm giving the vultures gossip to feed on, but my sister *is* coming home. There is no 'was' about it.

"Sorry, you know what I mean," he mutters before retreating to the back of the classroom. I grab my books and head to the office. I'm done.

By the time I get to my car, I can't control my emotions another second. Tears flow freely down my cheeks. *Was.* It echoes in my head. What if they don't find her? What if it's too late already? I lean against the car with my face buried in my folded arms.

A throat clearing behind me causes me to wipe my eyes on the sleeves of my hoodie. If anyone snaps a pic on a cell phone of the big sister losing it, I will not be held responsible for what I'll do next.

"What the hell?" My lungs start to constrict. Before I go into another full-blown panic asthma attack, I dump my backpack on the hood and starting digging for my inhaler. My eyes don't leave the two suited men standing behind my car.

"Come with us," the sandy haired one commands. He steps back and indicates to a massive gleaming SUV by the gate.

"Today is not the day to mess with me. No!"

"I think we can change your mind." The Rambo wannabe slips a hand into his suit jacket and throws a ball at me. On instinct, my hand flies up to catch it, and then the bottom falls out of my emotional pit. It's not a ball, but a tiny pink and purple shoe. I know this shoe. The Velcro never sticks right and Mini always pulls it off.

My throat closes over, and I sway on my feet as dark spots appear in my vision.

Mini needs me.

The moment the thought enters my head, I upend my backpack on the ground. The inhaler is a beacon on cloudy day. Grabbing it, I pump three times until my lungs start to function. Standing up, my fists curl at my sides. They will pay in blood if anything has happened to her.

"Take me to my sister, you sick bastards."

16
Accounting

"TELL your parents you're hitting the mall with Tiffany," he instructs, sitting next to me in the back of the SUV. Rambo is driving. My fingers fumble across the screen—numb. How much do these strange men know about me and my family? I eventually type the short text, grateful that he didn't insist I call my folks. Dad would know something was wrong the instant he heard my voice. It only takes a second for him to reply.

Don't be late.

His message guts me. I wanted him to demand I come straight home, but at the same time, I need to find out where they took my sister. I just don't want to do it alone.

A blindfold is tied around my eyes, and the dark tint of the windows won't allow other motorists to see. The thug beside me takes my cell and backpack but gives me my inhaler when I ask for it. Channeling Rocks, I try to use my senses as Rocks does to work out where they're taking me, but I'm too on edge. These men are professionals. My father—fudge no—*Enzo* would never tolerate anything less. My mental slip-up has my heart skip a beat. He will never be a father to me.

The longer we drive, the more my hands shake, and I have to concentrate on breathing. The memory of the last road trip I did bound and gagged causes me to sweat. I can almost smell the stale, moldy bag that was over my head. The car slows, possibly exiting a freeway, and after a dozen stops and starts, a motor grinds above us. We drive forward a few feet before it sounds again, and I'm guessing the car is inside a building. The urge to scream is overwhelming, but I know nobody will hear. For Mini's sake, I have to stay calm—my panic will not free her. The horror of what happened the last time I was kidnapped and panicked comes flooding back to me. Rocks got hurt— almost killed. I will stay calm and do what I'm told.

I'm pulled from the car, but they don't remove the blindfold. The cool air reeks of strong, bitter coffee, and my nose wrinkles in disgust. Not a word is spoken as I'm led this way and that, but when the second door clicks locked behind me, the blindfold is removed.

I squint as my eyes adjust to the harsh, fluorescent lighting. Enzo is seated on a soft, leather couch sipping a steaming cup of coffee. "I'm disappointed."

"Where's my sister?"

"You should've obeyed me, dear girl. Now look at what you're putting your *parents* through." His stare stops my heart. For the first time since I came face-to-face with Enzo, I'm scared of what he's really capable of.

"What do you want?"

"I told you."

"Remind me." His glare hardens. "Please."

"You will work for me three days a week until your sister is finished taking care of our competitors." He sips his coffee and indicates for me to take a seat next to him.

I obey. "What can *I* possibly do for *you*?"

"Count money. Some of my associates occasionally succumb to temptation." He sighs. "And finding a replacement is a headache I do not need. It was your sister's job and now it's yours."

Each time he says the word sister, I think of Mini. I will do whatever it takes to get her back. Enzo and I are the only ones in the room. It's an office with two doors, and on each of the four walls, there is a large rectangular window covered with venetian blinds. His heavy oak desk dominates the middle of the space, and we're sitting off to one side on the lush, cream couch. Enzo informs me his men will pick me up three days a week—Tuesday, Thursday, and Saturday mornings—and bring me here to bundle up his takings. He explains that I will be in a room with his revenue, a counting machine and his books. Once it's counted, bundled, and bagged, his men will return me to my car—simple.

"What about my sister? I'm taking her home."

He smiles, but it doesn't reach his eyes. "Not an option. I gave you my trust, and you let me down. Now you must earn it back."

"What does that mean?" I lock my fingers together on my lap to prevent them from shaking. My questions are probably annoying him, but I want to be crystal clear on the situation. The stakes are too high for a misunderstanding.

"She stays until I know you can be trusted to obey me."

"No! No, you can't," I plead. My anger slowly bubbles to the surface. How dare he involve her? "She's just a baby," I snarl. My emotions don't know which way is up lately. "I swear I will do whatever you ask. I swear." Then, I think of that crime show Mom watches. They always demand to see the hostage no matter what. "I want to see her. I will not do a thing for you until I know she is alive and well." I swallow the lump in my throat that negotiating with this evil man gives me.

This time when Enzo smiles it does reach his eyes. "So much like your mother." Standing up, he walks to the window closest to the couch and beckons me to follow. It's double-glazed with the venetians in between the two pieces of glass. He slowly twists a knob, opening the blinds.

Mini is standing in a white, wooden crib, screaming her lungs out, but I can't hear a single peep. The room must have amazing soundproofing because I know how loud those little lungs can wail—as do our neighbors. As long as I live, I'll never forget the look of misery on my sister's face. My fingers slide down the glass. She's so close but so untouchable.

"Let me in there," I gasp, looking at the two exits on opposite sides of his office. Peering back in at Mini, I spy the closed door of her prison cell. It's on the far wall so there isn't direct access from this office. "Please, let me calm her. Please," I beg. My fists bang on the glass, but Mini doesn't look my way.

Enzo gestures to the couch and takes his seat. I can't take my eyes off her. Tears and dribble run off the end of her chin in long threads. She's been crying for a long time to look that upset. Out of every painful thing I have experienced in my life, nothing has ever come close to this. Leaving Rocks was nothing in comparison.

"I need to hold her."

"Sit."

I obey. I don't realize I'm crying until tears drip onto my hands. I'm perched on the edge of the couch trying to stay as close to Mini as I can.

"You will see her after your first shift. Be on time, do the job, and then you will be let in to that room for thirty minutes. Understood?"

"But—" The twitch in his left eye tells me to take the deal. "Understood." My heart shatters when I give up the fight to see her so easily. I can't risk him hurting her, but I can't help but feel consumed with guilt for complying with his demand.

The thugs from the car return, and I'm introduced to Johnson, with the sandy blond hair, and Rambo's name turns out to be Brick. They'll be my escorts from now on. Brick holds up the blindfold and without hesitating I stand. I take one last glance at Mini through the window, still screaming her lungs out. Enzo stands and before I can step away, he places a kiss on my forehead. He's caught me off-guard, and it takes every ounce of my self-control not to wipe the spot his lips just touched. I will do whatever it takes to prevent anything else happening to Mini including offending this hideous human being.

"You won't hurt her. If you really are my father, then you would never lay a finger on a little kid."

"I am your father, and I'd never lay a finger on *my* child, but ..." He looks through the window and frowns. "Earn my trust, and you'll free the little one." He leaves with a knowing look at my bodyguards.

Brick speaks. "Tell your parents about this, and you will never see her again."

I nod.

"Not only will you never see her alive, but the police will never find her body either," adds Johnson. "We'll be waiting at school tomorrow. For every minute we wait, it's a minute less you spend with her."

"I'll be there." My heart is thumping so hard against my ribs it hurts. How the hell am I going to face Chad and Kelly? Images of the little white coffin flit behind my eyelids.

My car has been moved to the park around the corner from home. The entire ride back, I sit blindfolded listing out loud all of Mini's likes, dislikes, and her daily routine in the hope that one of these gorillas will pass the information on to whoever is looking after her. When the car stops, Johnson hands me my backpack before threatening Mini's life again if I say a single word. He indicates that they *will know*, and I wonder briefly which cop is in their employ, but I have bigger issues to face.

My parents.

Opening the door, I hear the news and retreat instantly to my room. I'm a coward. Moments later, Mom is standing with her hands on hips in my doorway.

"Why didn't you come and ask about Mini?" she demands. Anger is an improvement on desolation. It's put color in her cheeks.

"Because when I walked in the door, I knew she wasn't here. And to be honest, I don't want to hear how the police have no clue."

The truth is I didn't want them to look at the person responsible for their daughter's disappearance. And I'm not sure how to hide the sadness, fear, and guilt from my eyes. I bite the inside of my lip. The words are on the tip on my tongue. I can almost feel them wanting to fly out of my mouth, confessing all my sins. But keeping my mouth shut will save my sister. Under no circumstances can I tell them. Enzo and his men made that very clear.

The pain I see flash in my mother's eyes reverberates inside. My selfish, fudged up desire to discover the truth about my birth parents has brought a world of pain onto everyone I care about. I want to scream and destroy anything and everything in my vicinity, but I fold my hands on my lap and force my features into a neutral look.

"They haven't found her, but the police aren't giving up hope yet," she says. "I'm surprised you went shopping at a time like this." The hurt is evident in her voice, and she stands waiting for an answer.

I swallow and bring the image of Mini's red, screaming face back into my mind. Her anguish will get me through this. I've told enough lies now that I should be able to do it when my sister's life depends on it.

"Actually, I didn't go shopping. I … I can't deal being in this house without her," I say, and it's the truth. I close my eyes for a moment. "Her not being here is killing me. I needed to do something, and the police won't let me help, so I joined the Library Outreach program."

When I dare to look at Mom, I let out my breath. Her face is scrunched up, and she's crying silently. Or maybe like me, she's just having trouble breathing properly. I walk over and put my arms around her. She leans against my body, and the frailty I feel under my fingers scares me.

"I know what you mean. It's killing me too," she sobs. "I'm useless. I let those men take my baby, and now I have to sit here doing nothing."

Rubbing her back, she slowly settles, and by the time she lifts her head, she's in control. "Tell me about the program. It will distract me."

We sit on my bed as I lie through my teeth. I do not deserve the love these people have given me. The program is three times a week, and I'll be helping little kids from poorer areas of the city learn to read. What I know about lying is that it's always easier when it's close to the truth, and my high school does have a reading program—I'm just not a part of it.

Mom says she's proud of me and that brings tears to my eyes. She would never say that if she knew the truth. A cold stillness seeps into my bones. The urge to call Rocks pulses through me, but I will not do anything to risk the life of my sister more than I already have.

"Is it okay if I go again tomorrow after school?" I ask not meeting her eye. "It will be Tuesday, and Thursday afternoons and Saturday mornings from now … indefinitely."

"Of course, sweetheart, and I'm sorry. I shouldn't be taking my frustration out on you. It's not your fault."

Yes, it is.

That night I cry myself to sleep as the image of Mini haunts me every time I close my eyes. When I can't stand lying in bed a second longer, I'm up and sneaking into her room. I need to take some supplies to her without mom knowing. I grab several changes of clothes, some diapers, her favorite toy, and the soft pink security blanket.

Then I put it all back. Mom will notice if her things go missing. In the end, I stuff the two new toys I bought her at the mall in my backpack. In the kitchen, I raid the pantry of her favorite snacks. Those will not be missed, and at least I'll know she's been given something half decent.

Dad is perched in his chair, and the sight of him worries me. I have a feeling he hasn't showered or slept since she was taken. The urge to tell him where she is sears the back of my throat. I want to reassure him that she's alive and not sitting stuck in the back of mom's abandoned car dehydrated.

BRICK AND JOHNSON are waiting as expected in another black car I've never seen before with the same blackout tinting on the windows. Instead of getting in with them, they instruct me to drive a few blocks away from school and park. Part of me had been hoping the principal would have noticed these guys, but they're one step ahead of me. I guess there's a reason Enzo's business has taken over the entire East coast.

The drive to Enzo's "coffee house" is identical to yesterday. I can't see and have no clue as to where they've taken me, and once I'm in Enzo's office, the blindfold is removed. He's sitting at his desk writing and ignores me. The blinds into Mini's prison are closed, and I command my feet to stand still and not run over to open them.

"Hello," I say after several minutes.

He continues writing. "Not the greeting I was hoping to hear. 'Hello, Papa.' Don't you think?" His hard eyes leave the document to study my face.

The urge to rush to his desk and hurl everything on it across the room pulses through my veins. My temper seems to have a hair-trigger since he entered my life. He is not my father, and if I utter those words, I'm betraying Chad and all the love he's given me. I glance at the glass window again and know what I must do.

"Hello, Papa." I swallow. Enzo raises one eyebrow in question. I might have said the words he wanted, but there wasn't a scrap of emotion behind them.

Silence follows and I don't know where to look. "Contessa, you're a problem." He steeples his fingers, half covering his face. "As my daughter, I want to welcome you, have you embrace the family business, but I know you're only here because of the child. That saddens me."

He hasn't asked a question so I remain silent. My gut is telling me to tread very lightly so I wait. He sighs, and I wish I knew what the emotions behind his eyes meant.

"I'm hoping it's simply a shock to you that I'm your father. I, myself, was stunned by your discovery, but it was a pleasant surprise. In time, you will see this is as your family, so I'll wait." He gets up and walks around in front of his desk. "Do you want the tour?"

Fudge no, I want to yell. I don't want to know anything about you or your business, but Mini is depending on me. If he wants a daughter, then that's what he'll get—a pretend daughter. This time I say it with feeling.

"Yes, please … Papa." His face shows the tiniest flicker of emotion before he locks it down. I can do this. I can lie my way into his trust. "I'm sorry for disobeying you Monday. I, well, my parents aren't strict. Not like I see you are, and I thought I could treat you the way I treat them. I was wrong. Can I see where I'm going to work?"

He smiles his half smile that doesn't show his teeth. It's the same smile I stared at day after day in the Polaroid I stole from Josie. Bingo! He was happy then, so I'm finally on the right track. If I can get Enzo to smile *that* smile, it's my ticket to Mini.

Enzo stands and ushers me to the opposite doorway. The tour begins with a walk through the shipping warehouse. I expected to see bags of white powder, but all I find is crate after crate of coffee beans. The coffee distribution is the front for his real moneymaker, and he explains the aroma ensures any whiff of cocaine not dealt with by the air-conditioning will be hidden from the outside world.

As we wind our way deeper into the rat's nest, more and more oversized, armed men are present. Most are dressed in suits, but a couple could be mistaken for construction workers. I notice how they all lower their eyes when Enzo passes by. He's definitely the biggest fish in this pond, and everybody knows it.

Outside a door with a coded entry pad, Enzo asks if I truly am prepared to join the family business.

I swallow and nod my head. His eyes narrow. I need to explain. "This is all a massive shock" —I indicate around me— "plus meeting you and finding out … um, like who I really am," I say. I swallow down the bile caused by my lies. "If I'm going to learn the business, then I guess I need to know."

He unlocks the door, and I try not to gasp. I've been teleported inside one of those trafficking movies—except this is real—not some Hollywood take on the drug trade. A dozen young men and women are in nothing but their underwear. There's a strange haze in the air, and it smells harsh, but unlike any chemical I've ever smelt before, almost a cross between gasoline and the marker pens we use in art. My hand covers my nose, but I force it back by my side when I notice Enzo watching me. The workers are wearing facemasks as they weigh and bag up the white powder. This cannot be real.

Enzo closes the door again. "The product."

He leads me further along, and I'm trying to keep track of where I am in relation to his office and Mini. We pass several doors on the left and stop outside a plain white door on the right. No key pad on this one, and as it turns out, it isn't even locked. A little way down the hallway, there are two men sitting on stools. Each has an automatic assault rifle resting between their legs. My heart starts to flutter, and the muscles in my neck and shoulders feel like they've turned to stone. I remind myself that Enzo will not hurt me unless I give him a reason to. Right now, he needs me.

"Boss," one of them acknowledges.

"This is Contessa. The daughter I was telling you about." He turns to address me. "When I'm not in my office, they keep an eye on things," he explains.

Enzo opens the door, and the instant I see what it hides, I can't believe he doesn't have a keypad and twenty-five dead bolts on the door. Entering the room, the smell is unmistakable—money—and lots of it.

Black duffle bags are stacked four or five high along the length of one wall. A long table occupies the center of the room holding three sets of books, a laptop, some small device, and a counting machine. A pile of papers is wedged under one of the books, and a box of rubber bands has spewed its contents over the end of the desk. Large clear, plastic bags, paper clips, brown envelopes, a box of latex gloves, and empty duffle bags sit at the opposite end.

One puff of my inhaler opens my lungs enough as I scan the room. To my right, there's a window of mirrored glass. My guess is his office is on the other side. Even though I'll be alone in this room, I'll be under his surveillance. The lack of obvious security on the door settles a cold, stark reality deep in my bones.

You don't mess with Enzo Ascari and live to talk about it.

"Sit." Enzo grabs a journal and starts my first lesson in money laundering. "It's a good thing you have perfect grades in Accounting and Economics."

My job is to track all his incoming funds for this part of his operation and to ensure his buyers are delivering their agreed sums. It astounds me that it's only a portion of his illegal income. Opening a duffle bag, I gasp when I see it's jammed full of US dollars. I can't even fathom how much money surrounds me, or the fact that Enzo is leaving me in here with it alone. I guess in his sick, twisted mind, he has something of equal value of mine. I'd be marking her for death if I stole any of this. Panic seeps through my system at the responsibility he's just handed to me.

"I have five dollars," I say, standing up and turning out my pockets. "See." The rumpled bill I didn't spend at lunch sits on the table. Enzo chuckles and squeezes my shoulder. I try not to pull away.

"You will have more than that in your pockets once you prove I'm right to trust you."

"Why are you doing this if you think I took that other money?" I hate to mention it, but the fact that Enzo knew I had stolen from the Vipers has bugged me. But what's bugged me more is why he needs me to count his money. It doesn't make sense. "Why me? Why go to all this trouble?"

Enzo is silent for several minutes. His scrutiny makes me want to squirm, but I will my body to stay still. I can't show him the level of fear he instills in me whenever we're together. For the life of me, I can't work out why he'd go to so much trouble to get me here a few hours a week. He's a powerful man with an army of thugs ready to step up to do his bidding—surely.

"Because my biggest weakness is what's written in those journals." He points to the three books sitting on the table. "Contacts, figures, product, distribution … the whole Ascari enterprise is hidden within those pages. The reason I'm successful is because I never show any one person all my cards. Sophia is the exception. If one of our competitors got to me, she would know what to do to take my place. Never trust anyone like you do blood. Even your mother, after all these years, never turned me in, and we were only family by marriage. I needed someone I can trust, and there is nothing stronger than blood. In time, you won't only be working the books, Contessa, you will join Sophia, and when the time is right inherit all this."

"But …" I can't tell him I don't frigging want any of it. I want my sister and to be left the hell alone.

"I know nothing about this … business."

"Irrelevant—"

"But you know nothing about me. You're risking an awful lot by me being here."

Enzo gives me the tiny hint of the smile that occasionally crosses his face. "When you escaped from the Vipers and then had the audacity to steal from them—knowing full well what they would do to you—it impressed me. It showed me you really did have Ascari blood in your veins, and with a little help from your true family, you will come into your own and be one powerful young woman—like your sister."

I flinch at the word sister. If two sisters are going to take after each other, it's going to be Mini and me. No matter what I'm required to do, I'll do it to give the Phillips' sisters that chance.

Rocks would turn rabid if he knew rescuing me, when I was kidnapped, made Enzo think I'm an Ascari. And I'm going to thump those clueless bats when I see them next for taking the money from the van. I knew I would pay for that stupidity; I just didn't expect it to be like this.

"The Vipers was dumb—"

"Don't say luck." His eyes are hard. I sense his anger has a hair-trigger too. Maybe that's a family trait I didn't know about. "I heard the details from those two myself. You fought back and succeeded. That was all I needed to know. You saw an opportunity and took it. Impressive under the circumstances."

Crap. He thinks those bats entering the building were a distraction and I took the opportunity to escape!

"And for the record, you don't need to worry about those amateurs. It was a pleasant surprise the machinery at the chicken farm still worked. The feds won't find pieces of them big enough to identify."

The faces of the Vipers men who kidnapped me come to mind. I hated how weak and vulnerable they made me feel, but is hate enough to justify the outcome? Is this how Enzo became who he is today? I swallow. Just thinking of that equipment turns my stomach. The relief that they won't be waiting for me ever again is immense but it soon sours. They're dead because of me.

Fuck!

I swallow. His eyes scan my face, but I know a smile is impossible. I bow my head. "Thank you, Papa."

My brain is scrambling. He just admitted to killing two men for me. I drag air slowly into my lungs and push the thought away. I don't want to know these things, because I can't do anything with the information without endangering Mini. But now I know those thugs won't be showing up at Kelly and Chad's house ever again. I'm safe—for now—because of Enzo.

Enzo teaches me how to sort his takings. It turns out I'm the new payroll officer as well. One journal shows the money he owes his employees, one shows the money he's putting through the coffee business, and the third book accounts for the rest. The money in the bags needs to match a coffee invoice before I begin distribution. I try to concentrate as much as possible and ignore the churning of my gut.

A small black device I hadn't seen before is used to check for counterfeits. The UV light illuminates the hidden glowing strips in each US note. A hundred dollar bill has a pink strip on the left, whereas a fifty has a yellow stripe down the middle. I'm to check notes at random before I count them. He instructs me to wear two pairs of latex gloves at all times while in the counting room. Money is filthy and my hands will smell of it.

The zeros become a blur as he starts up the counting machine. I load wad after wad of bills, ensuring it purrs constantly. The side panel boasts it counts 1800 bills per minute. In one minute of my afternoon here, I'm holding one hundred and eighty thousand dollars fresh out of the machine. The panic rushes up my spine for a second time. I grab an elastic band and stuff the bundles of money into the correct bag. Fudge me, this is seriously fudged up, and I'm pretty sure my folks wouldn't believe me, even if I was stupid enough to try to tell them.

The books are complex, and to be honest, I'm pushing my accounting skills way past what we've been taught. I want to make notes to remember for Saturday, but Enzo says that's strictly forbidden. Nothing will come in or out of this room. No notebook. Nothing. I focus all my energy on memorizing his instructions. A mistake could cost me, or even worse, Mini.

By six p.m., my brain is fried and the 'washing' as I start to think of it, is done. My lips are again busting to say one word—Mini—but my head is telling me not to ask. If he sees she's my only incentive, he won't ever trust me.

"All done. I need to get going," I say, glancing at my watch.

Enzo is a man of few words. I'm learning his eyes are the key to what he's thinking, but he's the king of control. He stands and buttons his suit jacket before opening the door. The two guards at the end of the hallway are nowhere to be seen. I follow him down another new corridor to the door I've been looking for all along. A sticker with the word PRIVATE in red block letters taunts me. When my eyes land on another keypad, my hope fades.

Enzo angles his body so I can't see the code he enters. I need that number to have access to my little sister, and now I understand why Mom always says patience is a virtue. I'm out of it—not an ounce left. I push past Enzo the second the lock releases. All I care about is Mini, and to my relief, she isn't screaming her lungs out. Her little face erupts with joy the second her eyes land on me.

"Nee. Momma. Nee," she chirps, bouncing on her feet in the crib. Her little arms are outstretched, and I'm pulling her into mine the instant I'm within reach. She locks her arms around my neck as my legs crumble beneath me. I kneel on the floor, rocking us back and forth, telling her how much I love her. I try not to squeeze too hard, but I'm elated to finally touch her. She's real. I have her, and everything will be okay—eventually.

My backpack is still in the possession of Johnson. He has her toys and snacks. Pulling back, I do a mental inventory. She smells clean; she's wearing a strange jumpsuit, and there's no visible damage to her chubby little body or face. I try to make her stand, but she throws her arms around my neck like she's channeling a boa constrictor.

My heart shatters for the little poppet. She's missed me, and she's probably scared surrounded by strangers. Tears well in my eyes, but for her sake, I will not add to her worries by crying. I'm the closest thing she's got to an adult, so I have to shoulder that responsibility just as Mom and Dad would.

After a moment, I spy the mirrored glass panel and on instinct I shield her from whoever is watching on the other side. The thirty minutes is over before I'm ready to give her up. Brick opens the door and gestures for me to leave.

Oh God.

The only way I manage to return her to the crib is by focusing on what Enzo will do if I disobey. I can't break our first agreement. Reluctantly, I pry her clinging fists from my shirt.

"Momma and Dadda love you," I whisper.

Her bottom lip wobbles when I step out of reach. I turn my back on her before I grab her again and cause a scene. When I'm three steps away, her scream pierces my soul. Step after step, I ignore her pleas until the door clicks locked, and the soundproofing silences her.

17
Bad News

On my way home from school on Friday, I'm scanning the streets for black cars with dark-tinted windows. I want those thugs to be trailing me. It would give me a chance to beg them to take me to Enzo's warehouse to see Mini.

Not one suspicious car in sight.

Back home, I drag my feet getting ready for work. The Bun Lovin' Barn is the last place on earth I feel like being, and to add salt to my wounds, Rocks won't be waiting after I'm done. The exhaustion of the week is catching up with me. Shouldering the burden of what's happened to Mini and watching what it's doing to Mom and Dad is taking its toll—not to mention I've just gone through my first breakup.

The pizza box on the kitchen island announces my family's defeat. Mom has given up cooking, and Dad has resorted to take out. My parents are losing it, and I can hardly blame them. The doorbell chimes, and for a second, I want to rush to answer it, but then reality sets in. The cops will not have Mini in their arms. Mom flies through the kitchen, straightening her hair with her fingers as she beelines for the door.

From my spot in the kitchen, I have a clear view of the entryway. When she opens the door, the looks on the faces of the two detectives explain why she begins to chant the word no, before Dad is by her side and visibly keeping her on her feet. Once invited in, they all head to the living room. I stalk in quietly, monitoring each officer in turn. There is a rat in the employ of Enzo. If I can find out who he is, I might have a chance at getting Mini free.

Last year, I spent hours watching Mom and Dad for signs they knew I was onto them about my adoption. Those psychoanalysis skills are coming in handy. The problem is neither of these men might be connected to Enzo, and knowing what I do about him, I'd say Enzo has a much higher-ranking official in his pocket, but I study the men in my living room all the same.

"We're sorry, Mr. and Mrs. Phillips. The fire department has located your vehicle."

"Fire department?" Mom gasps. Dad grips her hand anchoring her.

"Go on, Detective Williams," he rasps.

"It was burned out, and forensics are still analyzing the vehicle. Doesn't appear that your daughter was in it at the time, but we'll know more shortly."

I grip the edge of the doorway. Mini was not in that vehicle. Yesterday, I did exactly as I was told. Enzo would never get another day's work out of me if he'd harmed her overnight. His agreement is all that's stopping me from collapsing on the carpet. He promised that if I do what he says, Mini stays unharmed.

Mom is in full-blown hysterics at the thought of Mini being in the car when it was set alight. I head to my room to escape listening to her pain. Every time she cries for Mini, I feel a piece of my heart fall away. The coldness is back in my bones, and I wish I knew for certain Mini wasn't in our car. Digging through my books, I grab his card and dial.

"Was my sister in the car?" I blurt, when his smooth voice answers.

Silence. I look at the screen to confirm it connected.

"Papa?" The word tastes worse than acid. "Please tell me she's all right."

"You need to trust me, Contessa."

"Trust? Trust a man who kidnaps little babies and uses them to get what he wants? Trust?" I wince. I can imagine the glint of rage in his eyes at my outburst. I need to be smarter. I let out a breath to calm myself. "Sorry. The cops just told us. I don't understand why you needed to trash their car." I purposefully choose my words. I want Enzo to think I'm distancing myself from my family and turning to him. Their car—not our car.

"As I said, trust me. See you tomorrow. Your sister will be waiting." He disconnects the line as relief floods my system causing me to smile and flop backwards onto my bed, but I need to get myself under control. If I thought my emotions were all over the place last year, it's nothing compared to how they somersault now. I close my eyes and take a second calming breath. I can't appear too happy about the car inferno when I join my folks.

When I poke my head out into the hall, I can't hear Mom any longer. On the stairs, the murmur of male voices indicate the police are still present and are asking my parents for a list of people that might have a grudge against them. I camp out on the stairs to eavesdrop. Dad's face shows he's lost for words, and I don't blame him. Chad and Kelly are model citizens, and the idea of someone holding a grudge against them is ludicrous. Staying on the stairs away from them will prevent me from admitting out loud that I know for certain Mini wasn't in our car.

My time with Mini on Saturday seemed to be up before it's even started. When I entered the room, I was pleasantly surprised to see the toys I'd brought for her the other day in the crib. She was also wearing another new outfit so my worry over her wellbeing eased a smidge.

The Saturday count took way longer than Thursday, and I'm dreading how many bags will be waiting for me on Tuesday. The weekends are clearly profitable for Enzo. My requests to visit Mini on Sunday or Monday were abruptly denied, but Enzo did say he was proud to report his examination of my work showed zero errors.

To avoid my rising guilt levels forcing me to come clean with my folks, I lock myself in my bedroom with my books. The pages I'm studying refuse to sink in, and my mind wanders to Rocks and how he's doing. What he's doing … anything about him at all. I miss him, and it's hard to believe it's only been a week since I gave him his last driving lesson. It feels closer to a year since he shared all my secrets. Stress makes time do strange things. The hurt I felt at breaking up with him has paled in comparison to how I feel about Mini being taken. But the moment I think about him and the colony, it pushes to the surface with the same ugly intensity.

Dad knocks before poking his head into my bedroom. He tells me that they're going down to see the car and talk some more with the detectives on Mini's case. When he worries over the phone, I assure him I'll be here to answer it. I don't bother pointing out that if they're with the police, then they're hardly going to miss their call. He's doing his best under the circumstances.

The layers of guilt I'm carrying are almost too heavy to handle. Knowing no new lead or information is going to show up adds one more layer to the stack. I watch from my window as Dad helps Mom into the car. Day-by-day, she's becoming a stranger. The feisty, independent woman I've always admired is fading into oblivion. If she were a photo, her color would slowly be leaching out.

I stare out into the trees wondering. Is there a way out of this? What if I tell the police? If only I knew which officer was the rat. My plan of attack is to study the payroll journal on Tuesday, but Enzo wouldn't have gotten this far by using real names.

Lying on my bed, I try to focus on my textbook. Schoolwork doesn't stop simply because your sister is missing. I'm behind in every subject and need to catch up, but I'm saved from repeatedly reading paragraphs that won't stay in my brain when my phone vibrates.

I'm on your porch.

The ache I was trying so hard to ignore erupts. My secret-keeper is here. Outside. I could tell him …

No.

I will not risk my little sister, and since I have no idea where that warehouse is located, he won't be able to rescue her anyway. I'm going to have to do this on my own.

When I open the door, Rocks and Jeremiah are standing with their backs to me, looking out over the porch railings. The set of his shoulders is wrong. Something is up …

It suddenly occurs to me that Mini's cheeky, smiling face is plastered over every surface the police have access too. She's on the TV, newspapers, and missing posters. Stepping out next to him, I swallow my confession.

"Hey."

"This a bad time?" he asks, still staring ahead.

Oh fudge!

I've never lied to Rocks, but how do I get around the truth now?

We're not together.

He has the blood bonds to take care of.

I'm not betraying his trust.

I suck in a deep breath. "The folks are out." Rocks turns his head my way, flicking his hair off his face, and I gasp when I see the sadness and pain in his features. "What's wrong?" I reach out a hand, but place it back on the wooden railing next to his. "You okay?"

He can't look this broken because of me ... because of us. I miss him so intensely it frightens me, but seeing him so utterly devastated scares me more. My controlled, mature, Victorian-era boy is gone.

Rocks' face crumbles. He turns away and covers his eyes with one hand. He's holding his breath, and I can't stop myself from placing my hand on his arm when I realize he's trying not to cry.

This is so not about us.

Rocks has folded in on himself, I think, to prevent me witnessing his distress. I look to Jeremiah, and again, everything about his body language is off. These boys usually have an animalistic stealth, but I can't work out what's missing. Jeremiah steps backward, shaking his head and ends up down on the grass, standing away from us. When his head lowers and he gasps for air, my heart stops. If Jeremiah is crying, it's bad.

I look from one broken boy to the other. "Where's Decker?"

Rocks flinches. His eyes meet mine, and I feel like I'm going to drown in the pain I see swirling behind his. "The owls ..."

I gasp. "What? Is he badly injured? Do you need me to take him to the vet?" My hand instinctively pats my jeans pocket for my car keys.

Jeremiah speaks from the lawn, his voice colder than I have ever heard. "He's dead."

Rocks can't contain his emotions. As his chin meets his chest, two tears spill over, running down his face. My brain struggles to believe what Jeremiah just announced. A numbing sensation seeps outward from my emotional pit. Rocks needs me, but I honestly don't know what strength I have to give. I've used it up dealing with Enzo, but I can't stand by and witness his agony without trying to offer the comfort I know he needs.

I pull him to me, trying to convey how sorry I am with my hug. I rub his back, finding comfort in his familiar midnight scent. "Oh my God. I'm so sorry." My voice breaks. "Decker was kind to me right from the start."

The cheeky, young Camazotz face dances behind my eyelids. Rocks slumps against me, and it's almost as though half his body is folding over mine and about to collapse. I can feel the defeat under my fingertips. His inked arms wrap around me, but there's no strength to his hold.

My excitable bat boy is broken, and he's not the only one. I absolutely cannot tell him about Mini because Rocks has enough to deal with. His best friend and half-brother is dead.

I invite the boys in, but I'm too embarrassed to admit the cupboards are bare. Jeremiah states he will not leave Rockland here alone—daylight or not. Rocks stands silent at the kitchen counter, having composed himself, but his new stillness makes me uneasy. He's a living, breathing statue staring at the pattern in the marble countertop.

Jeremiah settles in front of the TV with a plate overloaded with leftover pizza. He's never been much of a talker, but today I get more words from him than ever before. He is as affected by the loss as Rocks, and he doesn't move when I rest my hand on his shoulder. He's not one of the Camazotz I initiate aeronaught contact with, but I know it's right when I receive his sad smile.

"Thank you, Connie. Firstly, for giving Odelia that baby, and well, for … you have given us so much. Now, I will never forget. Please do what you can."

His words don't make sense, but I figure once Rocks and I are alone, he'll explain. I'm surprised to discover that Odelia is Jeremiah's little sister. I knew the pup without a Beanie baby was related to him from her name, but I had no idea how closely.

Returning to the kitchen, I stand at the open fridge listing its contents. Rocks shakes his head at all my suggestions. He says he's not hungry. My world has just been tipped upside down on its axis. The fact that Rocks' gloriously inked arms are on display makes me wonder how much he's been a Camazotz. But, that's none of my business. Grabbing a bag of pretzels, I pull him up to my room.

"Tell me what happened."

Rocks sits on the bed, and I'm torn about whether to join him. The breakup is still a raw wound, but Rocks would never abandon me in a moment of need. Sitting next to him cross-legged, I wait.

"The owls are back. They … he …" Rocks is studying his hands. His hair has created the shield that I detest so much, but I understand he's using anything to protect himself from the loss. "The Sire thinks these are new owls. Have been released since we've been back."

"Oh my God."

"Decker and a bunch of pups were flying back to the roost when two owls swooped down on them. One owl had two of the pups locked in its talons. Decker …" Rocks looks at me. He chokes so I take his hand. "Decker saved them. He wrapped his wings around the creature's head, blinding it. It let go of the pups, and they both plummeted down, twisting and turning. He let go and was winging it back to the injured pups when the beast grabbed him."

"What happened?" I don't want to ask, but I owe it to the kind Camazotz that befriended me.

"It tore him in two." Rocks sobs once, letting go of my hands to cover his face.

"No!" I wrap my arms around his shoulders and pull him in against me. My emotional pit was close to overflowing before, and now it spills over the edge. My tears join his as I try to push the horrific visual from my mind. Poor Decker—so kind, sweet, and accepting. The colony has suffered an enormous loss. Rocks says the owls eat their prey and my stomach churns in horror.

We sit crying together for I don't know how long. I know some of my tears aren't just for Decker. They're for Mini, what my parents are dealing with, and for Rocks and I. It's all too much. Rocks gets control of his emotions way before I can stop mine. Now that the floodgates have opened, it's hard to stop the flow. He sits up straighter and is suddenly holding me and giving comfort.

"I know you told me to stay away, but I figured you'd want to know," he says quietly. I nod against his chest.

"Thank you. Decker was my friend too."

Rocks pulls back and wipes the tears under my eyes with his thumbs. A faint smile pulls at his lips. "He was your friend. He never said a bad word about you—ever."

Rock shifts to the side and pulls out a piece of folded paper from his back pocket. I watch as he opens it and nestled inside is one of the photos of Decker. He's standing tall with a hand on his hip posing for the camera. Seeing his happy, carefree, smiling face tears at what's left of my heart. I bite my lip so I won't start crying again.

"You must have done this. It's your room." Rocks points to my lace curtains behind Decker. He frowns again, and I can't even begin to understand how hard this must be for him. "When did you do this? I don't mind. Honestly, I'm ever so grateful, but when?"

I tell him about the night Decker came to check on me, and that he refused to come inside my room because Rocks wasn't here. Rocks smiles and agrees it's so like his brother. I recall how shy he was acting when he made his request, and the only way I could lure him in was when he asked for a photo.

"Do you have the others?" I ask.

"What others? Jet found this at the tin shop hidden amongst Decker's tools at his workbench. There's more?" Hope fills his features, and it allows me to breathe deeper seeing him look more like his old self.

I grab my phone and show him the four photos—three of Decker, and the one of Decker with his arm slung around my shoulders laughing. Rocks takes my phone and flicks back and forth between the photos, a gentle smile on his face.

"Oh, Connie." He looks at me. "You've given us so much. Thank you. I can never repay you. Now, I will never forget my brother's face." My heart beats faster. I have given a gift to Rocks that nobody will be able to tarnish. Regardless of all the trouble I have caused, I have done another good thing, and Jeremiah's words suddenly make sense.

When I ask about the pups that Decker saved, the solemn look

Rocks gives me sends my emotions swirling. One of the two pups bled to death the next day. The other is badly injured but still alive. Swearing loudly, my hands fist as Rocks explains that the wings are divided. Judge wanted Rocks to bring the wounded pups to me so I could take them to the animal doctor. The Sire put his foot down and decreed that since I was no longer involved with Rocks, all aeronaught interaction was strictly forbidden—except with customers at the markets.

"Judge thinks you could've saved little Harper. She was his niece. His brother was killed last year in the first attacks, so his bloodline has come to an end."

"What wing is the wounded pup from?" I'm trying to work out how the wings are feeling about technology. Change might be in the air if modern medicine can save them, and that will make Rocks less of a target for their disgust and mistrust.

"Gems. Little Sapphire has some deep talon wounds. They're still bleeding. I think she's only got a fifty-fifty chance."

"What does Carnelian have to say about it?" Judge has always been on my side. I wonder what the Fold member of the gemstone wing is thinking now that one of his own is potentially mortally wounded.

"Not much. I think he might be siding with Judge, but he hasn't said. He's in a difficult place politically. For two generations, the Gemstone wing wasn't in the Fold. Carnelian—with the help of his father—got voted back into power like his great-grandfather was. He plays his cards close so he doesn't ruin Malachite's—his son—chance of taking over, allowing the Gemstone wing to remain influential within the colony. It's part of the reason the union between Graceland and Malachite is encouraged."

Malachite was the Camazotz sent to scare me away last year in the park. He's being politically aligned with the Land wing on purpose in order to gain votes when the time arises.

"So the, the" —I swallow— "*union* between two Camazotz is sometimes political?" I need to get over my aversion to the term mating.

Rocks nods. "More often than not. Because the Gem wing was out of power for two generations, Carnelian selected daughters of Fold members to mate with. The Little wing was a powerful wing, except they've been plagued with female offspring. As a result, they keep losing their Fold standing, but they're a well-liked, large wing. Carnelian had Malachite with LittleBee—her father was Fold member LittleSong. Next, he mated with Sawyer—Judge's sister and a daughter of Fold member Ranger—to sire Jet. To ensure long-term stability for their wing, he's given his offspring a good start politically because by blood they are aligned with two large influential wings."

"Whoa! No way." These bats mate for political gain.

I'm beginning to see why I'm such a black mark on the Land wing. Every time I'm at the colony, Strickland must be tallying up how many votes my presence will cost his son when the next generation vote.

"The smallest thing can sway votes," Rocks continues. "Judge is disappointed in Strickland. I can't ever remember a time when the Land wing and Trade wing were against each other. Judge wants to make sure the pups Decker defended survive so that his son—and wing heir—didn't die in vain."

I had no idea that Decker was destined for the Fold. He was always so relaxed about life and more focused on Rocks succeeding Strickland. But Decker and Rocks' mother—Zada—is the daughter of a previous Fold member, and her brother is a current Fold member. Decker's father—Judge—is also a Fold member and the son of a previous Fold member. Bloodlines like this made Decker a Camazotz prince too. Judge's anger at their lack of medical access makes sense, and I'd feel the same way. Rocks picks up my phone and flicks through the photos of Decker in silence.

"I'll get them professionally printed."

"I'll give you some money."

"Don't worry about it. I got this." Considering all Rocks has been through I can't take any more of his precious cash.

"But—"

I grin at him. "I know you usually win the yes/no game, but this time I won't budge. I'm paying. The end."

Rocks gives me the shy little smile that still manages to curl my toes. "Thank you."

"You have a camera you know." The fact that Rocks has technology he isn't aware of has been bugging me far more than I would have predicted.

"I do?" Rocks slips his phone from his other pocket and holds it out to me.

"I thought you would have hit every button by now and found it."

He shrugs and unlocks his screen. I hate the tension in his body, gone are the days of him lounging in his chair relaxed and carefree.

"What?" I ask. Rocks being guarded is bizarre. I don't like it one little bit, but I guess I'm being the same with him. "You came here to talk to me, so talk."

He sighs. "My phone isn't the same without you texting me, and some of the stuff on the Internet is not very nice."

I bite my lip trying to imagine what he's discovered, because he's right. There's some crazy, awful stuff on the net that would curl the wings of a technologically naive Camazotz. "What did you find?"

Color tints his smooth cheeks. "One day there was an advertisement with a cartoon lady, but she didn't look *anything* like the drawings in my Superman comic." His eyes flick to my chest so fast I almost miss it. It's the first time I've ever caught him looking. I try not to laugh when I realize why.

"Let me guess, she had big boobs and wasn't wearing very much?"

His eyes pop open wide. "You've seen her too?" he asks.

This time I can't contain my laughter. I nod, giggling. This lightens the mood, which is exactly what Rocks needs.

"When I clicked on it, there were more advertisements for lonely ladies waiting for me to call th—"

"Tell me you didn't? Tell me you didn't?" His credit won't last long if he calls those numbers.

"No, I ..." He looks away. "I wanted you to be my first."

Oh Rocks.

Now, I can't look at him, and wish my bangs were long enough to hide behind too.

"After more clicking, I discovered pictures of ladies ..." A heavy frown creases his brow, and I know he's considering his words. "Put it this way. If the Sire saw those photos, he would ban the Internet FOR-EVER." Hanging around Tiff at the hot dog stand has rubbed off on him.

"There're lots of websites on the net that you just don't click on."

"I know that *now*."

Pointing to the screen, I click on the camera and Rocks is back on a technology high. He goes to take a photo of me but stops. He gets up and walks over to Feathers in her cage. My heart initially skipped a beat, but now it's flopping around inside me like some dying fish. Not being together but still being around each other sucks and is going to take some adjusting. I join him at her cage and explain the zoom and focus.

"Can I take one of us? As friends?" His voice is low, and I'm guessing he thinks I'll say no.

I don't understand why I feel like a traitor in this situation. It doesn't make sense. Maybe all breaker-up-ers feel this way? Rocks—as the break-up-ee—wants to get back together. I'm the one that ended what we had, even though what was going on at the colony was the cause. The painful part is that I do want to be friends with him; it's simply that not being his girlfriend hurts too much still.

I smile, trying to hide the turmoil swirling inside. "I taught Decker how to take his first selfie, now it's your turn."

Rocks has to duck down to my head height and that causes both of us to laugh. It's so weird looking him in the eye. Having his lips so close makes my ears ignite as I remember how it felt to kiss him.

Focus on the camera.

What camera?

Fudge.

The skin on my cheeks is heating up to match the temperature of my stupid ears. I curse my choice of my usual high ponytail. Rocks is mesmerized by our image on the screen and thankfully doesn't pick up on my body screaming to reach out and touch him. Or maybe he does and is just being polite.

"You're not looking," he says as I drag my eyes off his mouth and look at our reflection.

The advantage of his long, strong arms is that they're perfect for a good selfie. Staring at each other on the screen, we laugh again. He's still Mr. Midnight, and I'm the golden midget. Our laughter makes it hard for the camera to focus. He snaps pic after pic until we eventually get one right, but I have a feeling he'll never delete the others.

As he flicks through the pictures, I push him into his corner chair. Just him being here has helped the tightness in my neck and shoulders ease up for the first time in a week. I feel almost normal. It's not that I've forgotten my little sister, but facing that dilemma seems easier with Rocks at my side.

"I'm going to take photographs of all my family." His eyes are filled with the brightness that I love.

"The Sire?"

He grins. "Yep, but that will be a stealth mission. Speaking of which, he wants to know if the authorities have said anything more about culling the rogue Camazotz—well, bats to them?"

"How come each Halloween the Camazotz don't make the news from your creepy attacks?"

"What?"

"You told me last Halloween not to go out because that's the one night the Sire won't get upset about the Camazotz feeding from humans. So how come that never makes the news like these bat attacks have?"

"Oh, that. No, when we feed, we wait till our host is asleep. On Halloween, you never want to go camping. I told you to stay inside because I didn't want to risk any of the less aeronaught-friendly getting any stupid ideas. It would've been hard for the Sire to punish them for attacking you."

"Hmph, so just because I know about you all, I'm fair game?" I cross my arms.

"No, you'll never be fair game because I will always protect you. They wouldn't have been trying to feed; they would've been trying to hurt you—very different. But even now, I will protect you from any threat I know about—us dating or not—and the colony knows it."

Oh Rocks.

My heart skipped a beat when he said he'd always protect me.

I hate to admit I have no clue what the government is considering, since all I've been focused on is Mini and Enzo. My guilt level rises, but I stomp it back down. There *is* a threat against Mini, but there only *might* be a threat against Rocks. I'm doing my best to deal with what I can. Opening Google, we start a search. As we scan the news items, I suggest Rocks needs an email account so I can email him anything I find. He stands behind me, leaning over and takes control of the mouse to click on the articles he wants to read. All I can smell is the forest on a moonlit night. It's a scent that will forever calm me, but I'm sad I don't get to be this close to him any more.

Despite the fact he refused all food, I open the bag of pretzels. I hear him take a deep breath—his senses analyzing the new smell. I hand the bag over my shoulder, and seeing no alarming headlines, I watch him return to his chair and dive in. He munches away constantly in the corner while I set him up an email account.

"Jeremiah would demolish these," Rocks says, holding up the packet to study it.

"He's probably finished the pizza. I'll go give him some." Rocks grabs a massive handful and hands me the packet back. "No, I'll get him his own. There's more in the cupboard. You want a soda?"

He nods, but as I go to leave, he grabs my hand. "Are you okay?"

I nod, but my skin begins to itch as though I'm going to break out in hives. He senses something's wrong.

"Just … you know … Decker."

His eyes roam my face. "You look tired." I don't know why, but him noticing I'm not fine squeezes my heart tighter than a vice. I pull my hand away before my confession spews out.

Jeremiah is entranced by cars that turn into robots. He's so lost in the action on our flat screen it takes a moment for him to notice me.

"Cars don't really do that, right?" His eyes are flicking between the screen and me. The Victorian-era gentleman inside of him wants to be polite and look at the lady that's talking, but the lure of Hollywood CGI is hard to ignore.

"Right." I grin, handing him two sodas and a full bag of salty pretzels.

"Was gonna say you need an upgrade bad." Chatty Jeremiah is as foreign as Rocks not being hungry.

"You dissing my Honda?" I raise an eyebrow.

"Dissing?"

"You know, disrespecting?" I explain.

"Nope, I'm pretty envious of that thing." His eyes flick back as rockets try to take out the good guy. His mouth hangs open, and I have to leave before the giggle I'm choking on embarrasses him. I can't imagine what I would think of some modern movies if I'd never seen any of this stuff before.

"You good for a bit longer?" I squeak. He nods, opening the bag of pretzels on autopilot, but then an ad break gives me his full attention. I watch his lungs fill with the aroma of his new snack exactly like Rocks just did, and he stuffs his mouth without waiting.

"Um, Rocks says you made that photograph of ..." He doesn't say his name, just swallows the mouthful he's chewing before stuffing more in. Rocks hides behind his hair—Jeremiah stuffs his gob. Boys and their emotions are so awkward at best.

"Yes."

Jeremiah chews for a second longer, then scratches what's left of his missing ear. When his shoulders relax, I know he's made a decision. "Could you make one of Rocks and me?"

Oh, God. He's worried he's going to lose Rocks—whether from the attacks or because of his aeronaught obsession, I don't know—but that makes me sad all over again. "Come on. Follow me."

Back in my room, Jeremiah doesn't know where to stand. I point to my bed, but his wide-eyed look tells me to find another chair. God, I've missed these well-mannered bats.

"You ask her?" Jeremiah questions as Rocks grabs the still full bag from Jeremiah's hold. My eyes flick from the scrunched up packet in my waste paper basket to the I'm-not-hungry boy.

"Not yet." Rocks notices my stare and his cheeks gain a touch of color. I vow never to listen to him when he says he's not hungry. "Judge wants you to research all the vet doctors near Helen. See if any know about bats."

"Seriously? I thought interaction's been banned? Holy sugarplums, should you two even be here?" Some days I'm so slow, it's mortifying.

"No, but I don't care." Rocks looks at Jeremiah. The pair seems to be communicating with their eyes, and I almost wait to hear voices in my head, but they're both human. "Judge came to me afterward. I think he knew I'd tell you about Decker, and he said a little research couldn't hurt. Strickland does *not* know about this. I've never seen the two of them face off like that."

I try to imagine Strickland and Judge up against each other, mad as hell.

Jeremiah nods in agreement. "Judge is always so calm. Restrained."

"He's feeling it. He wants Decker's death to mean something. You saved me from a death sentence, and I think Judge will always wonder 'what if' even though there was no chance for Decks." Rocks' face has lost its earlier joy. "Can you find out?"

I nod and start another search.

"Strickland is in a tricky position," Jeremiah adds, grabbing the bag of pretzels back. "He's got the safety of the whole colony to consider. If a Camazotz flipped from pain in front of one of your doctors ... Geez. Risk all of us to save one, but if I was injured ..."

"Would you want help?" I ask. "Modern medicine?"

Jeremiah looks at Rocks, his eyes travel down his healed arm. "Yeah, I would."

It's painfully clear that the colony needs their own vet—and one that's in on their mind-bending secret.

18
Rainbow

Bat POV

ROCKLAND is standing before the archaic anvil on his workbench. The weight of the steel tongs in his hands is familiar. Lifting the hammer, he positions the sheet of hot metal and strikes once, twice, three times before inspecting his aim. The gentle movement of air at his shop entrance causes him to glance up as the small bat swoops down low to enter.

Sire needs you.

"Everything okay, Graceland?" he asks, frowning. He misses her soft voice inside his head. They haven't spoken in weeks—or much at all—since his connection with Connie was exposed.

The bat does a circle in the lofty space above him. She doesn't land on the thin, wooden roosting beams positioned between the two sides of the slanting roof, but continues to circle. Her need to keep airborne is the cause for his question. Graceland has never enjoyed being in her human form. She prefers the agility and freedom of her animal side. She always feels cumbersome and clumsy in such an oversized body. But the reason she doesn't land might also be that she still doesn't approve of his relationship with Connie. With the loss of Decker so fresh, the distance between them feels like a gaping chasm that will only widen.

Sapphire died.

"Shit." Rockland rests the tongs and hammer on the bench, closing his eyes, and lowering his head. "When?" he whispers. Looking up, he tracks her movements in the small space, sadness filling his eyes.

Come. Now.

Without waiting for him to flip, she drops low and disappears under the doorway and out of sight.

Even though she didn't say, Rockland figures the Sire will be at their roost. Apart from him, when a Camazotz is injured, they head for the seclusion and safety of their secret cave to recover. Instead, Rocks retreats to his little wagon, but he's the only Shadows' member to ever risk sleeping as a human—injured or healthy. The others view him as reckless and insane, but he's given up trying to convince them that in human form, he's a lot safer when he sleeps. No owl or falcon would dare come near him, not to mention hungry coyotes or other scavengers. And, even if they were brave enough to enter his wagon, it's them that would get the scare.

Rocks scans the pink and orange skies through the back window of his shop. It's part of the Sire's duties to give comfort to a wing in mourning. With the recent attacks, it's been a ritual that's been repeated far too often. Untying his leather apron, he heads outside, the cool evening air calming him.

His mind turns to Judge, and how he's probably reacting to the death of the last pup Decker gave his life to save. If only Rocks could've convinced the Sire to let him take her to the vet. Deep in his heart, he knows the vet would have stopped the bleeding.

Connie had told him about the surgery her pet chinchilla Feathers had after she rescued her. The vet had amputated her leg and saved her life. The Camazotz need for blood every day or so means they're vulnerable to bleeding out. Without feeding when they're injured, death often claims them. It's another reason feeding each other is so vital to their survival. It's never about lazy bats that don't feel like going out to feed; it's about having the ability to save a precious life.

Habit causes the tall male to tilt his head listening for danger. He squints as he looks into the setting sun scanning for predators. His human brain knows that at this time of day at the market, he's perfectly safe, but the instinct to be aware of his surroundings surges up from the same dark place inside of him that houses the creature he battles.

Since being a Camazotz for two grueling months, the bat is restless. His long flights to visit Connie were perfect for keeping it at bay, but he doesn't fly down to the city now that she wants some space. He visited to tell her about Decker, but now he's keeping his distance as requested.

Connie.

What's she doing? Is she all right? Has she moved on with that rude boy from behind the gymnasium? His heart is sad enough without thinking of the girl he lost. His heart also senses there's something not right with her from his visit, but she said she was fine. Filling his lungs, his last sense does the final check, combing the air for scents that signal danger. All clear, as he predicted.

Flip.

Flap hard. Strong wings. Need height. Sniff.

Eeekkk!

Wait, son.

Turn hard. Beating wings below. Bat approaching.
Friend—not enemy. Together. Circle. Wait.

Zada, roost?

Yes. Sapphire.

I heard.

The small, slender bat joins him high above the little row of shops on the western side of the market. The shoppers have long gone, and only those preparing goods for sale tomorrow are present. His nose twitches with the scent of sandalwood and lavender as the little bat takes the wing position. The Z wing are candle makers. For many years, Zada had been too busy rearing pups to be able to contribute much attention to her craft, but since Bailey has been spending so much time in human form, it's allowed her to return to her trade. Losing herself surrounded by essential oils and colored liquid wax distracts her from the gaping wound in her heart caused by the loss of a second child.

The day the colony realized Celand was gone for good, something deep inside Zada broke. Her firstborn, sweet child—and the first offspring of their great and powerful Sire—was dead at 23 years of age, leaving no pups behind for her legacy. If only Celand could've mated younger. At least Zada would have the dear, little one to care for to keep her daughter in her memory.

And now, her first-born son to Judge has been lost as well. Always such a caring mate, Zada wishes she could offer comfort to the gracious Fold member, but she's barely coping with the absence of another of her brood.

The gods blessing her seven times with six bat pups and one boy child should mean she doesn't need to worry about the Camazotz legacy she will leave behind, but losing one of those precious pups—let alone two—is a devastation she's not sure she will ever recover from. She should be grateful she hasn't lost her only heir like Judge's brother, Shepard, did when little Harper passed.

We rest?

The voice of her boy brings her out of the misery that has swallowed her heart whole since learning the innocent, little pup, Sapphire, has departed this world to join her brave son. She needs to fly hard to get back to the roost to support another grieving family broken from loss, but her energy has left her along with her happiness.

No time. Fly.

The two bats flap hard to pick up speed. The larger male takes the airspace slightly above. He's protecting her blind spot, making sure no aerial attack will come from above. Yet, her need to protect the Sire's heir has her beating her small wings faster, harder. She slows to fall in behind him to take his vulnerable place above.

No, mother. Stay below.

Protect you, precious heir.

No. Stay below.

Without even appearing to exert himself, the great bat—with the largest wingspan in the colony—maintains the distance between them. Even though Zada wants to change places with her son, it's impossible without his co-operation. She knows he's flying slower for her. He could travel to Blood Mountain in half the time it takes her to fly the same distance. His younger, more agile body is able to duck and weave around the treetops faster than hers, but he stays to guard her—her gorgeous, human boy.

He's the colony misfit and a source of constant irritation to the love-her-of-life, Strickland. One day, her Sire will see the value of his revolutionist heir. Her blood and heart tell her all will be well whenever she begins to worry about Rockland's future, despite with his aeronaught fascination.

Eeekk. Eeekk.

Attention. Deep breath. New mammal scent.
Strange call. Scanning conscious thoughts.
Reach out. Communicate. Nothing. Little bat.
Not Camazotz. Not one of us. Ordinary bat.
Higher. Up. Cold air. Distance. Better protection.

Fly higher. Local bats.

Yes. They're sweet.

No. Bring owls.

The larger bat barely angles his wings, but in an instant, swoops down and takes a new position below his mother. The presence of garden-variety bats is a risk they don't need. These bats could lead the owls straight to them, too innocent and void of conscious thought to know any better. They don't know there are more deadly hunters in the area than usual thanks to a cunning plot to destroy the Camazotz slowly—one bat at a time. These creatures are just out in search of food, answering the call of twilight, as day becomes night. Their instincts should protect them, but every evening as the local bats take flight to become the hunter, they also become the hunted. It's nature; the way of the food chain.

The larger bat scans the highest branches of the trees below him. He searches for glowing, yellow eyes that can see just as far as he can. He sniffs the air. He can smell the familiar scents of the forest around his roost in the distance. The guard should be present to bring them in safely. With the recent deaths, the Sire has commanded a squadron of strong males to escort any small groups home.

Northwest. In oak tree.
Area clear.

The new voice gives the two flying bats the guards' location.

Coming, he answers.

With protective eyes below him, Rockland waits for his mother to take the lead. He will return to flying above and slightly behind her to keep her safe. The Camazotz guards have told him the area is clear, but he won't risk her life to anyone else's care but his own. Until she's human, he will have her wing.

As they descend toward the treetops, the patrol of bats rises up from the trees and surrounds them. The one-eared bat automatically falls in on Rockland's left wing—his usual position. The moment his friend joins his side, Rockland relaxes ever so slightly. Jeremiah would give his life for Zada in a heartbeat. He's a male of honor and is brave beyond his years. Rockland trusts his friend's sharp senses like his own.

The patrol, led by Harland, confirms in brief messages that Rockland and Zada have heard the terrible news. They reply that's why they are returning to the roost.

Graceland safe?

Yes.

Relief washes through him. Rockland pushes aside the thought that his sister would risk flying back alone rather than letting him accompany her. He's let her down, but how can being in the form that makes him the most comfortable be a disappointment? Why would she risk herself? Almost as though his friend can read his private thoughts, Jeremiah eases his internal battle.

Malachite and Jet escort.

Rockland doesn't answer. Knowing his sister didn't fly alone allows him to focus back on the task of getting Zada back in one piece. The group, slowly one by one, peel off and spiral down at a dizzying rate toward a gap in the foliage that wouldn't be noticeable to the untrained eye. To avoid their location being detected, the patrol split off—half taking the two bats deeper into the forest, the other circling back, staying hidden below the tree line to check for threats that might have tailed them—feathered or otherwise.

Rockland resists the urge to dart in and out of the gnarled tree branches. Only two things can distract him from the sadness of little Sapphire's passing. One is flying, and the other is most likely trying to ignore her baby sister while she attempts to finish her homework. The thought of Connie's outrage at another preventable death eases his anguish. She's the only one that truly understands because she knows about modern medicine. It's not evil; it's a miracle.

The large bat follows closely as his mother moves around tree trunks and under or over branches toward the entrance. It's a path all the Shadows' Camazotz could fly blindfolded. With the trees starting to show signs of new life after the long hard winter, Rocks keeps his senses on high alert. Flying is always safer during the summer months when the leaves offer protection from predators waiting to attack.

One lone, sentinel bat hangs in the great behemoth tree that stands guard over their secret underground cave. Two short mental messages later, confirming friend not foe, and Zada tucks her wings in close and disappears into the dark, gaping chasm. Jeremiah and Rockland circle around once before diving into the darkness one behind the other in tight formation.

HIS BOOTS CRUNCH on the sparse covering of gravel on the roost floor. Two braziers have been lit in the middle of the cavern space since so many Camazotz will flip to pay their respects. Next to the nearest fire, Sapphire's body lays at peace. Her eyes are closed and her hands are folded over her middle. The glow from the coals gives warmth to her face even as the color of life slowly drains away.

"Oh," Zada gasps, when she flips so close to Rockland he feels the swoosh of her long cheesecloth skirts against his leg. "She's—"

"Human. Yes," Strickland finishes in his rough, hard tone.

Zada's hands cover her mouth as she tries to hide her shock from Snowflake. Sapphire's mother is kneeling by her daughter's side. Her sobs are the only sound other than the gentle trickle of water from the underground spring at the far end of the cave. She rocks back and forth covering her face with her hands.

Zada's eyes dart from Snowflake to the Sire and finally back to little Sapphire. Her dress is wet with blood in several large patches from her wounds, but the dark grey fabric lessens the macabre sight.

"She flipped from some kind of muscle spasm and died a moment later," he explains softly.

Camazotz prefer to die in bat form so they can fly up into the next world to find peace. But sometimes the pain of death takes the choice from them. When they die in human form, there's a much larger body to take care of and hide from the aeronaught community. It's another danger that threatens their exposure, particularly when they die away from their hidden sanctuary.

Rockland walks over and kneels beside the grieving widow. Last year, Snowflake lost her mate Kyanite in the first wave of owl attacks, before the Shadows realized the deadly owls were released on purpose. He whispers words of condolence to her, his larger shadow thrown higher on the cavern wall than the small delicate shadow of the woman he comforts.

Carnelian emerges from the darkness and stands behind Snowflake. At thirty-three years of age, he's the youngest Fold member, but the recent losses have aged him past his years. His bare arms have only one tattoo high on his right shoulder—the Gemstone wing's crest. Inside a black pentagon are several geometric patterns that symbolize the faceted stones for which they are named.

Standing up, Rockland extends his arm to the Fold member. Carnelian grips his offered forearm, and the males shake once.

"I'll dig her grave," Rockland offers. Carnelian's features falter for a second before he frowns and nods once in confirmation.

"Your wing honors my niece. I thank you."

Without glancing at his father, Rockland leaves the group and heads into the darkness. He doesn't flip, but walks the winding, desolate path that leads deeper under the mountain following the underground stream. For occasions when a Camazotz dies as a human, the task of digging a human sized grave is arduous, and some of the more superstitious members believe it's a dark omen. As the misfit already, his position can't get any worse by adding gravedigger to his list of sins.

As a child, Rockland spent his winters mostly in human form, exploring the depths of their cave roost. Some of his favorite underground chambers he can no longer access because of his adult height, but he can always flip and fly into the narrow passages if he's feeling nostalgic.

The cool air moves his hair as he walks past an open fissure on his left. If not for his Camazotz eyesight, he could easily misstep and vanish into the bottomless abyss. From this location, their burial chamber is the second cave on the right.

As he enters the burial cave, a bat flies over his head. In the pitch darkness of this rarely visited chamber, he loses sight of his companion quickly. Although it's been years since he entered this area, he remembers where the tools he'll need are kept. Before he makes it to the alcove in the limestone, the glow and hiss of a match being struck stop him in his tracks.

Jeremiah's face appears as he touches the tiny flame to the oil lamp. It takes a second for the unused wick to catch, but soon the lower section of the chamber is bathed in a golden glow.

"What are you doing?" Rocks asks, as his eyes adjust to the light and land on the long-handled shovel.

"Helping."

"Don't. You know what they think of this job. I'm fine. Go back."

Rocks scans the soft muddy floor. This section of the cave isn't hard rock, which makes it perfect for their need. Six graves, covered in small, hand-painted stones, can be seen within the circle of light. There are more further back, hidden by the blanket of darkness, but he won't disturb those resting souls.

When death claims a Camazotz in bat form, they're buried in their wing's chamber, but for human deaths all Shadows' members rest together. He walks to the edge of the most recent mound and starts to outline the space little Sapphire will occupy.

"I know, but I don't believe in those crazy superstitions."

"Jeremiah, you know the power they hold when they want to."

He nods. "Yeah I do and it's time I stood up to them too."

"No, you don't want that kind of distrust and animosity. Believe me," Rocks says, starting to pile the dirt behind him.

"I should have stood with you more, like Decks did. He was never afraid, and I let him defend you for me. But I should have said something. Maybe if all the Camazotz who don't care about being in one form or the other stood up and said so, things would be different."

Rocks stops and watches the other male.

"I'm sorry I never said more before. But just so you know, I've never judged you for your choices. But from now on, I'm gonna stand with you 'cause I don't have votes to lose like you do."

Rocks sighs. The last thing he wants is for his friend to be tainted in the eyes of the colony too, but since Jeremiah's older half-brother—Mazal—is next in line to be the Hebrew Fold member, Rocks knows Jeremiah won't be targeted as badly as he has been. Picking up the smaller shovel, Jeremiah joins his friend as they begin their solemn duty.

At midnight, the funeral procession begins. Young Sapphire is wrapped in a blood-red, velvet shroud. The eleven-year-old's body is placed gently in the small grave. Since all the Camazotz cannot fit into the tiny cemetery chamber, only those closest to the Gemstone wing attend.

The Sire, his Fold members, all of their mates, and the eldest male heirs to each Fold are in attendance in human form. They stand around the grave in their wings with Carnelian and Snowflake in the center of the subdued crowd. Jet dips his head once at Rockland in thanks for the service he performed.

Snowflake's short, bobbed hair has been braided with dark, satin ribbons that shimmer in the candlelight every time she bows her head. Zada's hair is filled with similar ribbons for her son. They hang low below her hairline almost to her waist. Too many of the colony's females wear the black ribbon braids these days.

When all the Camazotz are positioned around Sapphire, the scent of sage fills the cramped space moments before Sylvana appears at the entrance. The grey smoke from the lit smudge sticks swirls up toward the ceiling in delicate tendrils. She chants and twirls for a moment, dissipating the fragile smoke before kneeling at Sapphire's feet. Pressing the bundles of sage into the soft earth on either side of the grave, Sylvana stills, silently reciting the ancient burial incantations. The only sound is the rustle of her skirts as she removes several small, glass vials of oils and liquid silver from her hidden pockets. After sprinkling the liquids into the dark hole, she begins to shriek at the heavens. Zada places a gentle hand on Snowflake's arm in reassurance as the medicine woman's shrill tones reverberate off the limestone walls.

Shoving her hand in the hidden pocket a second time, Sylvana pulls a handful of tiny bones free. She crouches low over the grave, her lips whispering against the bones before holding them skyward. "May she fly to her ancestors and be free."

The bones are thrown high, and everyone present watches as they fall over Sapphire's velvet shroud. Sylvana takes the nearest candle and peers deep into the opening to read the signs the death bones foretell.

She huffs and puffs moving from head to foot as the other mourners move out of her way. At last, she looks to Carnelian and Snowflake.

"The omens are good. Her human form will not hinder her path to the afterlife," she announces.

Snowflake sobs loudly, relieved that her daughter will be able to join her father in the beyond. "Thank you," she whispers.

Sylvana leaves the chamber without another word. Carnelian steps forward and removes the leather cuff on his left wrist. Strickland hands over the burial blade with it's ornately carved, bone handle.

"Blood o' mine I give thee," he says, raising his wrist and slicing open his vein. He holds his arm over the dark wound in the earth, and lets his blood drip down to bless her body. "Peace on your final flight, my kin."

Snowflake takes his place and the knife, but her hands are shaking too much for her to wield the blade effectively. Carnelian returns to his brother's mate and gently slices open her wrist.

"Blood o' mine I give thee. Peace on your final flight, my darling girl."

One by one, the Camazotz all step forward and make the blood offering as a final blessing to their deceased colony member. Their blood will aid her on her ultimate flight. Strickland is the last member to open his vein in offering. The Sire murmurs a last blessing that has been passed down from Sire to Sire over the centuries. Deepening the cut, Strickland catches the rivulet of blood in the palm of his free hand. Each member of the Gem wing and Snowflake kneel before him at the side of the grave as he draws a circle with three dots over it on their foreheads. They will wear his blood as a symbol of honor in their darkest hour.

Rockland silently joins the end of the procession, and when the last member has been marked in blood, he takes his father's arm and carefully staunches the bleeding. The final task is to bury her blessed remains. As the females present begin to sing the ritual burial lament, Rocks takes one of seven shovels resting in the alcove. Although grave digging is considered bad luck, the Fold heirs perform the actual burial willingly. It's a sign they are prepared for the hardest tasks asked of Fold members in their service to the colony.

Rockland, Pegasus, Mazal, Malachite, Mackie, and Ash all start to shovel the loose soil. Rocks hesitates staring at the seventh shovel unused in the alcove. Decker.

The Trade Wing has yet to select a suitable candidate to replace Judge's eldest son. Since Decker's younger brother, Baxter, is only twelve and not yet a fledgling, he is ineligible to be the next candidate. In the coming months, all wings will have the opportunity to recommend a member they feel is worthy, but selection will not take place until Judge announces his period of mourning has ceased.

"Was a pattern decided upon?" Strickland asks Snowflake, as the young men complete the mound of dirt in the center of the chamber.

Snowflake nods, but her voice fails her as they pat the soft soil into place.

"A rainbow to match her bright spirit," answers Zada.

Snowflake kneels by the mound and places seven hand painted flat stones across her daughter's grave—each one the color of the rainbow. Two of the flat river stones have stars painted in the middle of the bright colors. From now until sunrise, colony members unable to attend the funeral due to the cramped space will enter the chamber and place their hand-painted stones upon her grave to complete the pattern chosen by her kin.

Zada places a large candle at Sapphire's head and lights the wick. The remaining lanterns are doused, plunging the chamber into near darkness. All present flip and fly down the narrow passage to rejoin their wing waiting on the ceiling of the main cavern. By the time the lone candle extinguishes itself, the rainbow of colored stones will be the only reminder of little Sapphire's time in this world.

19

Ugly Truth

Connie

In my third week working for Enzo, I do a double take when my name is the last entry in the payroll journal. The figure beside it blows my mind. I stare over my shoulder into the mirrored glass for a few minutes. I have no idea if Enzo is in his office or not, but he's out of his mind if he thinks I'm going to pocket the wad of cash he believes I've earned.

I want my little sister back, not a trust fund.

A moment later, the door opens and one of the armed, hall guards hands me a folded piece of paper. The message informs me to check the contents of bag twenty-one carefully using the fraud machine. I glance back at the mirror and nod once. I guess I'm always under surveillance.

The names in the journal are all coded. I'm pretty sure Brick wasn't christened with that name, despite how much it suits him. A tornado wouldn't move that man. None of the entries say cop or dirty pig in brackets next to them. So my hunt for the informant is over before it ever began.

I stare at the words—Little Sparrow. Enzo started calling me that the last time I argued with him about more Mini time. He says I go off like a gunshot, and in Italian—which he's very upset I don't speak—it sounds similar.

Last year, my anger simmered on a low heat the whole time I searched for Parents V1.0. Parents V2.0 never made me erupt like I've done several times with Enzo. He manages to turn the heat up past boiling, and I explode. I never knew I had it in me, but then again I'm sure anyone in my shoes would have a short fuse.

That reminds me of breakfast. Mom and Dad are falling apart, and watching it is probably shortening my fuse by the day. I hardly recognize the once symbiotic couple. They yell and scream at each other more than they don't.

Mom hasn't left the house since Mini was taken. I don't know if she quit her job, or if they're being extra understanding. Admitting I have no clue hurts as it means I haven't been close enough to her to talk and find out, but my guilt keeps me locked in my room when I'm not at the warehouse. Mom reminds me of a living ghost. She's fading from this existence, trapped in a circle of what-ifs.

What if she didn't stop for gas …

What if she fought harder …

What if Mini never comes home …

Dad has lost all faith in the cops assigned to the Phillips' case. He's hired two private eyes in the hope they'll discover something the police have missed. I want to tell him to save his money, but it gives him a purpose. He checks in with them every morning, and that seems to keep his hope alive. Mom's hope went up in flames along with our car, which is why they argue instead of talk.

My Google searches on coffee distributors in Atlanta and Georgia haven't helped. All I know is that it takes between fifty-three and fifty-nine minutes for me to arrive at the warehouse. Getting home is another story. My car has never been parked in the same part of town twice, and heading home varies from under thirty minutes to close to an hour. I have no fudging clue where the warehouse is located, and that's exactly how Enzo wants it.

Each Tuesday, I've had to stay longer to get through the amount of cash crammed in each duffle. Dad will look up from whatever newspaper he's scouring, while Mom sits staring blankly in the direction of the TV not even noticing my late return. Sadly, this is the new routine at the Phillips household.

I pull my attention back to the payroll. Mistakes are not forgiven in the Ascari organization. Tidying up, I'm anxious to get to Mini. She's happy most days I enter her room. Enzo still won't tell me who looks after her, but there's a distinctly feminine feel. Today, she has little bows in her hair, and slowly but surely the number of furnishings and general comfort level has increased in her cell.

When I place her on the new rug, she runs back to her crib, shoving her pudgy arms through the bars to grab "Ocof and Ven." I smile watching her tuck the reindeer and snowman under her wings like a proud mother hen. I hold out my arms, and she tears back across the space, slamming into my chest. She nearly topples over, but I grab her before she hits the concrete.

"Fingers gone," Mini says, looking at my hands. Her little fingers move over my bare fingernails. I doubt she's ever seen them natural before.

"No painted fingers today," I reply. My heart isn't in it. Painting my nails seems so frivolous and narcissistic. "What should I paint on them, Mini?" One of her favorite pastimes is emptying my carry-on case of all the pretty colored bottles.

She grins wide, and I notice a new tooth coming in. Fudge! Mom would kill to know about this.

"Ooof," she says, shoving Olaf in my face.

"You want me to paint him on my nails?"

She nods. I grab the little snowman and make him cover her with kisses. My fingers reach for my cell phone, momentarily forgetting it's contraband during my hours here. I'd give anything to record her infectious giggle.

ON SATURDAY MORNING after I'm finished my work, the guard down the hall leads me into Enzo's office rather than to see Mini. Enzo looks tired, and that's not a look I'm accustomed to seeing on him. He's always smooth as silk—never a hair out of place. He makes it apparent that he commands his entire universe, and it always obeys.

My eyes spy the stacks of money sitting on the corner of his desk. He's leaning against the front of the smooth oak with his arms folded over his chest. His white dress shirt is unbuttoned at the collar.

"You forgot something, Little Sparrow." He lifts up his dark glasses to rub his eyes.

"No, I didn't." Mini's blinds are closed, but the one behind his desk with a view of the coffee facilities has been pulled up.

"Are you trying to insult me?" I sense he's not to be tested. His left eye tics, and something about his body language makes him seems harder than usual.

"I don't want that. I'll swap it for my sister."

Enzo doesn't even bother to acknowledge my request. "Don't tell your sister, but you're more efficient than she is, and she's been doing this for five years."

I blink. I'm forgetting my own game plan. How could I be so stupid? I let him know Mini is still my sister and not Sophia. During the week, I spent hours trying to come up with ways to get him to trust me more, and then I make a stupid rookie mistake.

"If you continue your good work, I'll increase this each week." He taps the pile of bills beside him. It shows how heartless the man before me really is. How could he think I give a damn about money when my sister is his prisoner?

"Papa?" Enzo looks up and frowns. I need to call him that more, but it sticks in my throat. I try to make my voice sound weak and needy. "Can you use that money to buy me something?"

"I'll buy you whatever you want. You keep this."

"No, it's … well, I'm sure it won't be cheap since it's not exactly … legal."

The man beams at me like I've told him I'm expanding his business into Canada.

"I need a couple of birth certificates and socials for some friends."

Rocks will never get his real driver's license without a birth certificate or social security card. It's a massive roadblock to him joining my world. I've never asked if Judge is legally licensed, and it's probably not something they'd share with the nosy aeronaught anyhow. Since I had no idea how Rocks and I could overcome this, I might as well use Enzo's dubious connections while I can. It might even help build his trust in me if he feels he has something over me.

I grab a pen and write down the details and names. Rockland Shadows. Jeremiah Shadows. I figure since Jeremiah said he's envious of my car that he'll be more than willing to get his license too. I thank the stars above that Strickland and Zada aren't the weirdest colony names. He could have been born to Pegasus and Honeysuckle. Having scrutinized my birth certificate last year in the hopes that it would magically provide the location of Parents V1.0, I add all the information the forger will require. I'm pretty sure Rocks won't be upset that I've made Jeremiah his brother.

Handing over their details, I cross my fingers that Enzo will make this happen. Since Rocks isn't in the system at all, I know Enzo will never be able to track him to use against me. Googling Rockland Shadows leads you absolutely nowhere.

"Ah, now that's more like an Ascari. Consider it done."

I've made Papa's day by committing my first felony.

Movement over Enzo's shoulder catches my eye. Through the window, I watch as one of the young men from the 'cut and bag' side of the business is dragged into view. Brick and another thug I've seen around but never spoken to push him to his knees. He's wearing only boxer shorts and is speaking frantically to the two men. I can't hear a thing, but I instinctively cross my arms over my chest grabbing my shoulders. This looks bad—really bad.

Enzo turns his head casually to follow my line of sight. Before I can do anything, Brick pulls a weapon from inside his grey suit and fires—point blank. My whole body flinches at the sight even though I don't hear the gunshot. The man's body disappears from sight.

"What the—" My hand goes for my inhaler, but I think I'm going to be sick instead. I freaking witnessed a murder—a freaking murder! I bend at the waist, resting my hands on my knees. I blink repeatedly, looking around for a wastepaper basket. Maybe he's not dead. Who am I kidding?

"In through your nose, out through your mouth," Enzo commands.

I can't focus on anything. This can't be real. I have to be dreaming. His shiny black shoes stop before me. He commands me to breathe once more. I close my eyes and listen to his voice. When the nausea ebbs away, I stand in time to see Brick look toward the window and nod. I have to remember that he can't see inside. He doesn't know I just saw him kill a man. Or maybe Enzo planned this exact moment? He weaves such a tainted web that I have no clue anymore.

"It's a shame you had to witness that, but it is a part of what we are forced to do from time to time. Thus, why I needed you to take Sophia's place. Stealing is not tolerated under any circumstances." He picks up the money and holds it out to me. "Take this and enjoy the rest of your weekend, Little Sparrow."

I HAD BEEN lulled into a false sense of security by Enzo's crisp appearance and manners, and the fact that he has made me untouchable. The Vipers couldn't exact their revenge on me. His men give me a wide birth and show respect that I never earned. I was fooled into thinking I was safe. For a moment, I'd forgotten the newspaper articles I'd read about him being behind a dozen unsolved murders. My focus was Mini and trying to have him trust me enough to free her. But, he's never going to do that. He's an evil monster that issues orders to do unspeakable things.

I drive home in a daze. Halfway there, I pull over and rest my head on the steering wheel and cry.

I can't take this any longer. Winding down my window, I throw the bundles of cash as far away from my car as I can. Ten minutes later, I'm out on the street, picking it all back up again. This is not a game. I can't do anything stupid. I dump it in my trunk, dry my eyes, and head home.

The Bun Lovin' Barn is my escape to avoid my parents, but I couldn't care any less about how some drunk college kid wants his hotdog. Spring break has started so the night is busy, helping to pass the time, but I keep seeing the man's body jolt and then drop out of sight.

The terrifying image plays on repeat in my head. Mini. He's got Mini, and he will not think twice about hurting her if I make one wrong move. The hope that I could take her home was shredded when that trigger was pulled. And living without hope, turns you into a ghost like Kelly.

"I said double onions, not cheese. Jeez, too dumb to remember a simple order," mumbles the drunk pig.

I shake the cheese off the hotdog, but he insists I give him a fresh one since he *hates* cheese. My fingers lock around the bun in my hand, pulverizing the dough and meat. Tiff pulls me out of sight and steps in to take my place. She's got her flirt-face on and hands out the longest wiener I've ever seen. I scowl at her for giving a prize dog to a dick.

"Here you go," she says with another Kodak smile. "It's an extra big one to remind you of what's missing in your pants."

He curses loudly, but she calls the next customer waiting with a smile. I slide down the van wall, trying to hold in my laughter. I can't. It erupts as I sink to the floor. I laugh and laugh, glancing at Tiff to see she's biting her lip preparing the next dog. Tears roll down my cheeks, but then my emotional pit takes over and I'm no longer laughing. I'm sobbing, and I can't seem to stop.

I tuck my head into my folded arms that are resting on my bent knees. I don't want to make a sound, but after a minute, I need to breathe and another racking sob echoes in the confines of the van.

"Shhh ..." Tiff rubs my shoulders. "Don't let him get to you."

"It's not that," I mutter. "It's ..."

Mini.

Murder.

Rocks and Decker.

Where does it all end?

"You're stressed over Mini. I get it."

"And Decker died," I sob. *And I witnessed a guy lose his life today at the hand of the man that has my sister.* Tiff is shocked at my outburst. I explain that he was killed in an accident. Lying about his death makes me feel like a traitor. I can't tell her the ugly truth, but I hate myself for lessening the loss. That owl murdered him. It was a crime that nobody will pay for, just like Enzo won't see the inside of a jail cell for the guy's life he took.

The world isn't made up of unicorns farting rainbows. I get it. I really do.

Tiff insists I leave early. I don't have it in me to argue and walk home via the park. I never used to enter the park at night without

Rocks, but I've come to realize that I'm under the protection and control of Enzo Ascari. I sit alone on the park bench in the dark unafraid. Nothing will happen to me unless Enzo permits it—of that, I'm quite sure. I might not see his men, but there's no way Enzo doesn't watch my every move.

The cold snap that has hit Georgia forces me out of the park thirty minutes later. When I open the front door, Dad is hugging Mom in the wide entrance to our kitchen. I can't hear what he's whispering to her, but as I stand and watch them, her shudders of sadness lessen. Mom opens her eyes and when she sees me, she flinches. It's the strongest reaction she's had to anything or anyone in weeks.

"Everything okay?" I ask, walking over. Dad turns and looks surprised.

"You're home early?"

"Yeah, I kinda had a meltdown, and Tiff sent me packing," I admit. I feel so far away from them, and it's slowly killing me.

Mom's eyes roam over me for a moment or two, and then she turns and heads for her chair by the TV. The fact she doesn't ask about my breakdown makes me wonder if she's currently suffering through one of her own.

"Mom all right?"

Dad shakes his head. "You?"

I shrug. "Rocks' brother was killed, and with everything that's happening with Mini, I just ..." I shrug again. I'm pretty sure I don't need to explain.

Dad covers his eyes with one hand. "Oh, God. That's awful. No. Oh, God. Shit."

I hadn't wanted to tell them about Decker because I knew the mention of someone dying—someone young—would make them wonder about Mini and if she's still alive. Dad moves further into the kitchen and asks if he can get me anything, but he won't look at me now. I tell him I'm not hungry, but there's something off about his body language all of a sudden.

"Have you heard something about Mini from those PI's?" I can't keep the panic from my voice.

Dad shuffles around, opening cupboards and then the fridge, but he still won't look at me. "No, we, ah, we went to see the police. We just got home before you."

"What about?"

The sandwich he's making does not need that much attention. I step closer, but he's still focused on cutting cheese off the block.

"Just new leads. That sort of thing. Don't worry about it, sweetheart." He's obviously keeping something from me. Maybe the police told them statistics on missing kids or something equally horrendous. He's probably just saving me from more bad news that isn't confirmed one way or the other.

Dad moves to the spread out newspaper on the other side of the kitchen island, with his sandwich in hand.

"You see the update on that Viper's trial you were so interested in?" he asks. I wince and hope he wasn't looking at me to notice.

I shake my head, but as suspected he's zoned in on the small print and doesn't see. "No, what's happening?"

"The Ascari girl gave her evidence today, and the press are speculating it will be over soon. They think without their leader this gang might implode which will decrease their distribution." His finger is skimming along the article that he's summarizing. "Imagine an Ascari being hailed a hero."

Fudge.

The eel inside my guts starts trying to bite its way free. I want to scream that Ascaris aren't capable of kindness, or doing anything good. Then it occurs to me that I am one. The blood in Sophia's veins is the same as mine. What will my parents think when what's going on with Mini comes to a head? Will they be proud of me?

Never.

This is all my fault. I slink out of the kitchen and head to her room. Sitting in the dark in the rocking chair, the room smells of my sweet baby sister. It hurts to breathe in deep with such a strong reminder. Each week after my Saturday shift, I've felt lost. Not getting to check on her for two whole days nearly does my head in, but then I think of Mom. No wonder she's coming apart at the seams.

The start of my spring break usually has the girls and I in a frenzy of shopping and movie dates, but I can't focus on fun. Tiff texts to make sure I'm okay and see if I want to hang with her tomorrow. I decline and don't even bother with an excuse. Like Mom, I prefer to be closer to home, even though it means locking myself in my room to avoid my parents. I know Mini isn't going to be returned, but having fun makes me feel even guiltier. I don't deserve fun.

Tuesday, I lie to Mom about meeting up with the girls so that I can meet Johnson and Brick. Enzo arranged for me to be picked up earlier today because I'm off school, and since it's spring break, business is booming. There are seven extra duffle bags of cash waiting in his counting room. As a reward he allows me to spend a whole hour with Mini.

My backpack is always full of supplies for the little poppet, but so far my escort has confiscated it every single time. When I entered Mini's room however, it was by the door. Looking at the glass window, I can only see my reflection, but I'm sure Enzo is in there. He's given me access to everything I brought with me, except my phone.

Mini is delighted when I hand over a pack of her favorite cookies. After she scarfs them, she sits as still as a two-year-old can while I paint her little nails. It's the calmest I've felt in a very long time.

"Little Sparrow," Enzo calls as I'm being lead back to the SUV parked in the warehouse. "Come."

Brick and Johnson look at their boss—clearly this wasn't in the plan for today. I follow Enzo back down the corridor that runs between my 'laundry' and the room where the drugs are bagged up for distribution. Turning to the left, we enter a small kitchen room, and I notice supplies that are clearly for Mini on the counter.

"You can keep your things here if you wish," Enzo says, pointing to the wall of lockers. He opens a locker on the bottom row that's empty. "You will hand over your phone, but your backpack can stay in here from now on. If you have things for her, you can get them before you visit."

I have to force my jaw to stay shut. Enzo is giving me freedom at the warehouse. "What about the guards?"

"I will inform them you know what you're doing now. Your work has impressed me, and I'm not easily impressed. You can go where you please." He smiles without showing his teeth.

"Thank you, Papa."

"I knew the Ascari in you would surface."

WEDNESDAY WHEN I enter the kitchen to scavenge for food, Mom asks why I'm not at school. Her face crumples with anguish when I explain it's spring break, and she mutters something about that not being possible. I make her a sandwich and leave it in front of her. She's hugging Mini's security blanket and doesn't notice the food. I leave it in the hope that she'll eat something.

Dad comes through the door as I'm cutting up my PB & J.

"What are you doing home?" I ask.

He doesn't smile. His eyes go straight to the love of his life, who even he can't save. "I try to swing by to check up on *things* if I can."

My guilty conscience has trouble dealing with Mom. Occasionally, I think she's onto me, and her silence is punishment for what I've caused, but it's not the case. She just isn't coping and blames herself. I grab the bread again and start on a sandwich for Dad, leaving it on the countertop when I'm done. He's by her side coaxing her to eat and give him the blanket. It breaks another chunk off of what remains of my heart.

Our doorbell ringing stops me on the stairs. I dump my plate and soda on the bottom step before heading to answer it. When I open the door, I'm met with the angriest pair of blue-black eyes I've ever seen.

Rocks isn't just mad; he's flipping furious.

Since I haven't seen him for over two weeks, I can't even begin to fathom what has ignited such a reaction in him. I step back, but not to invite him in. His venom is almost seeping out of his pores, and I don't want to get any closer.

"Why didn't you tell me?" he seethes between gritted teeth.

"Tell you what?" My mind is jumping from every secret I'm keeping to find a reason he could be this angry—with me. Did I miss a crucial news report about the bat cull? Has another attack happened that he found on the news? My guilt spikes because I haven't been monitoring the media like I promised.

"About Mini."

I gasp. "What?"

I push him away from the door, almost closing it, and step onto the porch with him. "How do you know about that?" My brain is overloading and can't process how he could have possibly heard about her. Her face is getting less and less airtime as the weeks pass.

"The police paid me a little visit this morning. I've got to tell you the Sire is pretty impressed with me right now." His eyes are cold and hard—emotionless—as he stares me down. "Why on earth would you think I would take her?"

My stomach lurches. I'm thankful I haven't eaten my sandwich or I know it would reappear. Once the initial shock passes, I mentally connect the dots. Chad and Kelly were avoiding eye contact with me and acting strange. Dad swore when I told him about Decker. They spoke to the police a few days ago ...

"They didn't!"

I spin on my heels and storm through the living room and stop in the kitchen. Mom is resting her elbows on the kitchen island with her head in her hands. The blanket and Dad are nowhere to be seen. She's a broken woman, but that is no excuse for accusing Rocks of abducting Mini.

"How DARE you!" I scream.

She jumps and looks up. Shock ripples across her features as her eyes first focus on me and then the giant boy I can feel standing close behind.

"How could you? Rocks? Honestly? Did you honestly think Rocks would have anything to do with this?"

Silent tears track down my face because my body needs to let out some of the emotions that are twisting and snaking their way through my internal organs. I'm so disgusted with them that my anger is morphing into heartbreak. Plus the fact the Sire witnessed a cop question his son about aeronaughts that think he's capable of child abduction. This sends my guilt levels to a ridonculous high. If you could measure guilt levels, mine are probably orbiting around Saturn.

Mom clasps her hands over her mouth and bursts into tears too.

"What's going on—" Dad enters from the living room still holding Mini's security blanket. His eyes land on Rocks, and he swallows.

I turn on him angry as a cornered bear. "This was your idea, wasn't it? You really believe he would do that to Mini?" Dad recoils at the sound of my voice. It's acidic enough to burn through steel.

Mini's disappearance is on Enzo and me—my fault. Now the police have questioned Rocks at the market in front of his father. I have given the Sire and the Fold another reason to ban aeronaught interaction and keep them locked in another century—well, my parents have.

What did the police think of the Gothic appearance of all the market inhabitants, I wonder? I cringe at the thought of them asking for official identification. Sugarplums.

Would the cops treat the Camazotz with respect or suspicion based on their freakish appearances and the darkness that surrounds them? My heart is racing, and I can feel the blood pumping in my neck. I have to fix this, but how?

"Sweetheart, Rocks ..." Mom's voice is barely above a whisper. She sniffs. "I—we—please understand." She bows her head in shame, and the gesture makes me want to reach out and hug her even though I'm crazy mad. Deep down she knows what they did is wrong, but she wants her baby back. I get it, but Rocks?

When she faces Rocks over my shoulder, the look on her face makes me dig my fingernails into the palms of my hands. I need a distraction to get me through this moment. I must stay strong, and I must do it for my little, innocent sister who is alone in that cold, stone room waiting for me to return to her tomorrow. The need to come clean is fighting for freedom. But, I'm doing this to keep Mini alive and to keep Chad and Kelly safe. Enzo could just as easily have taken my parents from me to force me to turn to him. I chant this over and over in my head. There's a dirty cop on the payroll. Telling them will do more harm than good.

"Rocks, I know you love her and would never ever harm my baby, but ..." Her eyes turn vacant. Dad steps in next to her and wraps a protective arm about her fragile frame. His touch rouses her. "But, we had run out of leads, and we were desperate. We hadn't seen you. You practically lived here and then you just … disappeared too."

As if that is reason enough to send the police.

"You know him!" I yell. "I told you he was busy! You know he would rather give his own life than harm a hair on her head. You know this!" My voice breaks on the last word. My own tears are choking me. I feel responsible for them doubting the most reliable person on the face of the planet.

"I know," she whispers. "I know. We're so sorry. Parents will do desperate things when … the police kept asking for names."

Rocks walks around the kitchen island as silent as a shadow. Chad tenses, but Kelly pushes to her feet and steps into his open arms. Her sobs are almost hysterical, and I can tell that Rocks is holding her upright. If he let go, she would be no more than a puddle on the tiles.

We're all seated around the island with fresh coffee and cookies from a packet. I saw Dad glance at the best-by-date since I can't remember ever serving a guest baked goods from the supermarket. Mom appeared shocked as she scanned the limited contents of the fridge to offer Rocks a snack. It's like the fog that has choked the life out of her lifted momentarily, and she's seeing our reality for a second.

Dad moves to the doorway of the TV room. With the remote control in hand, he scans for any channels playing local news. I don't understand why this gives him hope because it's not as though Mini's going to appear on TV in the arms of a police officer safe and sound. It's never going to happen. She'll be stuck in her jail cell with Enzo until Sophia returns when the trial ends.

Rocks and Mom are talking quietly next to me. Her repeated apologies make me want to cut myself. The pain from my fingernails is barely registering. I need a bigger form of punishment, although watching the horror and torment in both their eyes is brutal enough.

I try to take a deep breath, but the air barely fills my lungs. There is no way in hell that Rocks could possibly connect Mini to Enzo. It was almost two months ago when I confessed to Rocks that Enzo had found me, but he doesn't know anything that has happened since. I pray he won't ask, but that boy rarely misses a clue. Mom smiles a sad smile and nods at whatever Rocks is saying to her. The look she gives me makes my chest constrict.

"I'm sorry again," she says before shuffling into the TV room to sit with dad.

Rocks turns his blue eyes on me, and I gulp. "We need to talk."

20
Revelations

ALONE in my room, I'm relieved to see that Rocks is no longer spitting mad. His anger has become disappointment, and I'm not sure which one I'd rather face. Letting Rocks down is my least favorite thing to do—ever.

"I'm sorry for yelling at you," he says from my bed. I'm sitting on the floor giving Feathers her treats.

Crap. He's apologizing? My guilt complex just shot past Neptune, but I have to be strong so he doesn't get suspicious. I have proven time and time again that telling lies causes bad things to happen, maybe not immediately, but eventually they catch up with you. If I tell him the truth—if I tell anyone the truth—then something horrible could happen to poor Mini. Whatever lesson the universe is trying to teach me, I'm not following.

Flicking his hair out of his eyes, he continues, "Why didn't you tell me? I adore her. Is it because I'm not your boyfriend anymore?"

I'm scared my voice will break and give him a clue that I'm lying. I nod my head because I don't know what to say, and I shift my focus to the fur ball jumping up and down over treat time.

"Connie, I consider your family *my* aeronaught family. I was so stunned when you accepted me after discovering what I am, but when your parents opened their home to me? God, I can't even begin to describe what that felt like. They let me in, fed me, included me at Christmas." He shakes his head, and his hair falls over his eyes. I'm glad because the pain I can see in them is making it hard to keep my mouth shut.

"Did you think because we broke up I wouldn't care about Jasmine getting kidnapped? If so, you're really making me feel like a monster."

Oh, God. That is the last thing in the world I ever want to do. I had no idea he considered my folks his aeronaught family. I know he adores Mini, but ... I think of how grateful I was for him telling me about Decker. I would be totally cut if I discovered he'd kept that a secret.

"I'm sorry," I say. I can feel the tears starting to build. I've turned into a girl that cries every five minutes. I want to go back to a time when I never had a need to—when my life was easy, and my sister was safe. "Can you forgive me?"

"Why didn't you tell me?"

If I lie, he'll know. I need to stick to the truth as much as possible. "I didn't want to add to your burden the day you told me about Decker. I didn't want you to worry when you have so much going on at the colony. I didn't think it was fair. Plus, you've kept serious secrets from me when you thought it didn't concern me." I wipe my eyes before the traitorous tears run down my cheek. What I said is true. It's not a case of me not telling him for bitchy ex-girlfriend reasons. Mini's safety is dependent upon me.

Rocks snorts. "I guess I deserve that."

He leans over and pulls me up off the floor and onto the bed beside him. He holds out his linen handkerchief, and the sight of it takes me back in time to the first night we met. So much has happened since then. Everything is so twisted and complicated.

"I've done nothing but think of you, of us ... of what I stuffed up since you've been gone ... since Decker." He sighs.

I can't look at him. I stare at his hands resting on his dark jeans, but command myself not to reach for them. "I'm sorry I never trusted you with my secrets. I should have told you everything about myself and the Camazotz right up front."

I squeeze my eyes shut. This is too much to add to my emotional pit.

"You always handled the gruesome truth about my Camazotz side so well. I—"

"I did not. I freaked out more than once, and I was totally grossed out over the whole blood drinking thing for ages," I admit.

He smiles, but I look away quickly. "I would have freaked out too if your parents and friends viewed me as a juicy Halloween snack." A cross between a laugh and a hiccup escapes me. "All my life, the Fold has preached how dangerous your world is. They said your fear would lead aeronaughts into persecuting us into oblivion, like with the witches and shaman of old. That's a hard lesson to forget, and even though I trusted you since the night we met, I guess deep down I was still protecting myself. I'm sorry. You know I'm still discovering who I am, and where I belong, but I made a big mistake not telling you everything, like the blood bonds. I should have trusted you—completely."

I look up and Rocks slides his hand over mine and squeezes lightly. "I swear to you, Connie Phillips, I will never keep a secret from you again. Never."

The tiny chunk of my heart that had survived my guilt attacks is eviscerated. I fold over my knees, covering both our hands with my body and cry. I can't stop. I have no idea how I'm going to lie to Rocks now.

Rocks pulls his hand free and rubs my back. "There is something you aren't telling me," he says.

My spine stiffens. I can't help it, and I know he felt it. I try to sit up and move away, putting some distance between us, but his bat sense never misses a beat.

"Tell me what's really going on, Connie."

"Nothing," I splutter. "The cops told you." He grips my wrist, pulling me back to him, not allowing me to escape. I stare at Feathers gobbling her treats.

"When I came to tell you about Decker, I sensed you were hiding something. I assumed, well, I thought it was you protecting yourself from your emotions since we weren't dating, but now I know it wasn't that. What is going on? Where is Mini?"

Again, I flinch before I can stop myself. I can't believe he's asking me these questions that require a direct lie.

I pull away and walk to the window. "I don't know."

Rocks is off the bed in an instant. I feel his body behind mine and know he won't move until I face him. His tall frame looms over me, but

I will not let him intimidate the truth out of me. This is about protecting my sister.

"You are lying. I know you. Look me in the eye and say that."

I look up, but my eyes fill with tears as I try to form the words. He cuts me off before I can even try. "What I don't understand is why. I know I kept secrets from you, but doing so cost me everything. It cost me you." His thumb delicately wipes under my eye, catching the next teardrop and the gentleness of the gesture is at odds with the feral anger oozing from him. "I'm going to give you time to think, but I'll be back. If there is anything I can do to find your sister, consider it done."

Without another word, Rocks flips and flies out my window.

ON THURSDAY WHEN Johnson removes the blindfold, we're still sitting in the town car. He opens my backpack and scans the contents, pockets my cell phone, and gestures for me to get out.

What the?

My frown must tell him how confused I am.

"The boss said you don't need an escort. You know what to do, where to go. If he trusts you, I trust you." He points to the hallway on the left. Usually I'm guided to the door of my 'laundry' before they remove the blindfold. "The break room is the third door on the right."

I cannot fudge this up. Enzo has given me freedom within the warehouse—publicly. A smile replaces my usual frown as I exit the car before they change their minds.

Scanning the stack of fat duffle bags, I know I'll get through them quickly and hope the extra time can be spent with Mini. It's payroll Thursday, and the figure beside my name this week rivals my guilt complex for magnitude. Enzo has lost his freaking marbles. But I will not offend him and risk my privileges being revoked. I put aside my cut and return to the whirring counting machine. At least now I can hide it in my locker instead of my trunk.

I close up the last journal and wonder for the millionth time how I could copy it. That sort of evidence would send Enzo to prison for the rest of his days if the IRS got hold of it. Forget murder charges, I could take Enzo down on tax evasion—and I'm sure he knows it. There's a reason he keeps everything old school—no digital files to be copied or emailed. One set of books kept under surveillance—the end.

"Sparrow, it's time you learn the other side of things," Enzo says quietly from behind. He must have been watching me from his office to know that I had just finished. It bugs me to not be able to tell if the blinds in the adjacent room are opened or closed. "Come."

"Thank you for the raise, Papa," I answer, bundling the wads of cash into my arms. His eyes look happy for the first time ever.

"I never told you that we move our operation every ten weeks or so. It won't be long before we set up our next warehouse. There may be a delay before there's work for you, but I'll let you know."

Holy shitballs.

The urge to ask what that means for Mini nearly cripples me, but I won't mention her and spoil his good mood. No wonder the cops can never get a lock on him.

After I shove the cash into my locker, I follow Enzo to *that* room—the underwear-only room. I resist the urge to check if my bra is decent, because whether it is or not, I'm not stripping. I chant that to myself preparing for the argument, but my breath hitches as we stop outside the door. I do not want to enter that room clothed, let alone half-freaking-naked. Witnessing the young guy in his boxers begging through the window haunts me. Being trusted with Enzo's cash flow is one thing, but the product is more than my nerves can handle.

A wisp of a girl with long dark hair exits, pulling the solid door closed behind her. Dressed in only her bra and panties, I try not to stare, but my eyes can't help themselves. *Pretend she's in a bikini.* She holds out a facemask for me and has one resting around her neck. Her smile seems so out of place in this prison of surly, sour faced men.

"Hi, I'll be showing you how things are done."

The smile fades when Enzo clears his throat behind me but doesn't say a word. She lowers her eyes and gives him a small nod. Certain ranks of employees obviously aren't allowed to speak with the big boss directly.

Turning, I point to my t-shirt and raise my eyebrows.

One side of Enzo's mouth turns up. "You, Little Sparrow, do not have to remove your clothes. I trust every ounce will be accounted for when you leave."

"Pffft, duh." My nervous eye roll gets another small smile.

"I'll leave you to it." He turns and both of us watch him stride down the corridor out of sight.

"That kid is so smart," she whispers.

"What?"

"It's the best part of my day, but we're not supposed to talk about her."

Her eyes travel up the empty corridor as though Enzo will have heard. My heart is beating faster than a hummingbird's wings. Finally, I know who is looking after Mini. These young girls are an army of willing babysitters.

"Thank you. Take care of her for me, please." I squeeze her hand and she nods.

The facemask does nothing to prevent the acrid odor burning my nasal cavity. It's almost a mix of old newspaper and something like gasoline. Gross. I doubt I'll be able to smell anything ever again. How do they work in here for hours on end? I wonder, taking my place at the cutting table. I've been given the easy job—working the scales.

I take a brick of pure product and weigh out a pound. The girl next to me takes it and adds the glucose to cut it down. The guy opposite me takes every third pound I weigh out. He's bagging up the good stuff—so I'm told—for high-end customers who want it as pure as they can get. That stuff goes into little snap-lock bags sporting a black pentagram.

The semi-naked staff seem to enjoy their work. There's music pumping from speakers above, and they all sway and move along to the beat. Nobody talks, but they remind me of the Camazotz. They seem to communicate without uttering a word, and the occasional laugh rings out.

The guy opposite me winks when he takes the next pound of powder from my scales, and the look that follows makes me uneasy. It's strange only seeing everyone's eyes, yet still being able to understand so much. No wonder Rocks knew I wasn't telling the truth.

The guy's flirtatious attitude causes my eyes to dart to the mirrored window. Only someone with a genuine death wish would flirt with the big boss's daughter under his watchful eye. Maybe they don't know it's Enzo sitting on the other side of the window.

None of these workers have probably seen the inner circle of his office. That mirrored glass haunts me everywhere I enter, but they don't seem bothered by it. Maybe it's because they aren't planning to spring their baby sister from her jail cell.

I watch as the powder moves down the production line—from my bricks to little baggies—but the crazy part happens at the far end. The bags are bundled up and hidden inside various household items. One girl is sliding a knife along the seam of a tissue box. Once the end pops open, she pulls out the folded white tissue, removes the bottom three-quarters, fills the gap with individual portions and slides it all back into the box. A glue gun takes care of the end. Simple.

The boy next to her is placing two hits inside hollow tubes designed to look like lip balm. He smears a glob of pink balm over the end to seal them in. *Genius, Enzo.* If the cops picked you up on a Friday night outside a dance club, having four lip balms in your pocket is hardly a crime. The more I witness, the less I want to know.

THE WIND WHISTLES through my hair as I drive home with my windows all the way down. The stench is probably only in my nasal cavity, but I want to give myself the best airing out possible. When I open the front door, two things surprise me—the house smells like cinnamon, and Rocks is back.

Shit. Shit. Shit.

I'm not ready to face him.

Walking into the kitchen, Mom is channeling her old self. She's done her hair, and there's a tray of snickerdoodles on the counter. The cinnamony sweetness washes away the acrid stench from earlier. I beeline for the baked goods, glad to have something other than the boy in leather to focus on. My growling stomach proves I've missed her 'Kitchen Goddess' skills more than I realized. Before I've finished shoving chunks of hot cookie in my mouth, Rocks is scowling at me from the far side of the bench. My cookie freezes midair. His eyes narrow and I watch in horror as his lungs expand, taking an excruciatingly slow, deep breath.

"Kelly, thank you for baking. Connie promised me another driving lesson, and we should get going." He's around the island and dragging me by my bicep toward the front door. I snatch two more cookies for the road.

On the porch, Rocks drops my arm as though I'm contagious.

"Where have you been? What is going on?" His body language is a hairs breadth from seriously pissed.

I narrow my eyes back at him, shove a whole cookie in my mouth, and shrug. His response is a wicked smile that I do not like one little bit. He leans in low, his nose next to my neck and drags the air into his lungs. His proximity is doing odd things to me, but my guilt complex kills that train of thought. If the universe is on my side, he will have no clue what cocaine smells like.

"You stink of money and some chemical I do not like. Do not tell me you were with the girls. Unless that involved rolling around in a bank vault."

The cookie turns to sawdust on my tongue. No lie will ever get me out of this.

His nose knows.

"Not here," I whisper, suddenly nervous that Enzo not only knows my location at all times, but is also monitoring my conversations. The totally freaked-out geek in me opens the front door and places my cell phone on the side table. The colony's zero technology policy might be right for once.

Rocks follows me to the car and gets in the passenger side. Reversing out, I scan every vehicle on the street—both sinister looking and mundane. I head out of Atlanta and drive until we hit farmland. Subconsciously, I've driven halfway to Helen and the market. When we find a country road that's deserted, I pull over. For as far as the eye can see, there isn't another soul around.

Rocks is still sniffing the air. His brain must be going through its catalog of scents.

"What I'm about to tell you could kill Mini."

He stills. It's almost like the bat in him is on high alert mode due to some unseen danger.

My need to share the worst secret of my life is let loose, and the words spill out, recounting every detail of what my life has become since Enzo Ascari entered it. Rocks' eyes are a maelstrom of emotion. Shock. Alarm. Hurt. Fury.

"So three times a week, I work for him to keep her safe. I have no choice, and with the dirty cop on his payroll, I can't risk telling anyone."

"Fucking hell! That Goddamn bastard."

I jerk at his harsh words. Rocks rarely loses his cool enough to swear vividly.

"I'm going to get her out of there. I swear to you."

My worst nightmare has become a reality. "No, you are not! No! I will not let anything happen to you again. Are you forgetting what happened the last time you got involved with my family drama?"

The hard look is back in his eyes. "I don't care what they do to me—a broken wing is nothing. Your sister is coming home no matter what."

My face scrunches up, but I manage to hold in the tears. "No. I would die if I lost the only other person I love as much as Mini. No way!"

It's Rocks' turn to look taken aback. But before I can regret telling him how I feel, his hand grabs my neck, and he pulls me to his lips. For the first time in forever, I decide not to think. I've thought myself inside out trying to work out how to rescue my sister, and it's gotten me nowhere. Right now, I just want to let go and feel, and Rocks feels so warm and safe I have to restrain myself from crawling into his lap to hide there forever.

I return the kiss, wrapping my arms around his neck. His midnight smell calms my racing pulse but sets a fire deep in my belly. There is a strange urgency between us that I've never felt before. I want him so much it almost hurts.

"God, I've missed you," I whisper when his lips move to my neck. He groans in agreement. A second later, he rests his forehead on my shoulder. His ragged breaths match mine and I can only imagine his heart is beating as fast as mine too.

"I'm sorry. I shouldn't have done that, but it's been hell without you, and knowing you still care … I … I couldn't help myself."

My fingers run up into his hair, cradling his head to me. "I missed you like you wouldn't believe," I admit. "I never stopped loving you. It's just those bonds."

Rocks straightens up, cupping my face in his large hands. "I haven't fulfilled a single one. I couldn't do it. I won't do it. AuburnSky is the only female to have asked. She's twenty-three so … kinda keen." He shrugs. "Anyhow, you saw how the Sire reacted when I said no. The others … well, blood bonds can take years to be called upon. When they call, I will deny them, and I'll deal with the consequences of that when it happens. All that matters is being with you. It's what I want."

"Seriously?"

"It's all I've thought about. Losing Decker made me realize that life is too short to live by other people's terms and conditions. Will you have me back if I'm faithful to you as both a Camazotz, both bat and man?"

I grin, biting my lip. The happiness inside feels so foreign. It's fireworks after a thunderstorm. It's hot, salted, caramel buns on a chilly winter's morning. It's Rocks asking to be mine and only mine.

My answer is to kiss the living daylights out of him. I feel his lips curl into a smile, and we rest our foreheads together. "Your car is turning out to be my new favorite place."

We both laugh. Rocks slumps back onto his seat, his long fingers drumming out a beat on his knee.

"We'll work this out. Now tell me everything again from the start. There has to be a way for me to get in there," he says.

We use the privacy of my car to catch up. Rocks tells me that the colony hasn't seen or heard from little Elm or Oak, since I was there last. That sends a shiver up my spine. The colony is experiencing the anguish of missing kids as well. When I ask him if Sylvana is still preaching that my evil ways are to blame, he goes quiet. I eye him before we both focus on the pickup truck rumbling toward us.

"I promised no more secrets," he admits with a grin after the ancient vehicle drives past. "She's been cursing you for weeks. It's a miracle your hair hasn't turned green. Maybe you're out of range?" He reaches out and runs two fingers through my ponytail. God, I've missed those cheeky eyes and that beautiful smile. "But seriously, she has half the pups scared out of their wits. One of them cried when an aeronaught customer told her she had a pretty dress."

"That wicked hag!"

"You should hear what Bailey says in your defense. She won't stand for a single bad word to be uttered about you. And her dragon threatens to char-grill anyone that disagrees with his mistress." He winks.

"How is she?"

"Good. Flying better, but she also had a thing or two to say about us breaking up. She's going to be a force to be reckoned with when she's an adult."

"Are you allowed to be here? What about the owls?"

"I snuck out since it's daylight. Even I won't go out alone at night since … you know."

I nod and breathe a sigh of relief. Rocks is being careful, and that's all I can ask for. He also updates me on the Duskwing drama. The Shadows sent another envoy to find out if the Duskwing are behind the aeronaught attacks. According to Rocks, relations between the two colonies have gone from frosty to arctic.

The Duskwing claimed they aren't behind the owl attacks because they have suffered losses from the barbaric creatures too. Strickland doesn't believe them. Rocks said the really odd part of their second visit was that there were hardly any Camazotz present. He knows they prefer to live at the farm rather than their roost, but it was a ghost town.

I lean forward, peering out my windshield, trying to locate the sun. It's behind the tree line so I start the car. Rocks cannot be out alone after dark.

"Let me out here. It's not far as the bat flies." He points toward the trees on the horizon. "I'll see you Saturday. Text me." Rocks leans over but then stops. My heart beats like it's sprouted fairy wings.

"You can." I bite my lip. I don't know why I'm back to being so nervous at the thought of Rocks kissing me. But then again, Rocks and I didn't have a lot of time *together* together before his wing injury.

"Yes!" He leans over and kisses me three times. "Keep me updated. Any time, just call."

My guilt complex has returned from the outer reaches of the galaxy. Sharing my load with Rocks has helped. I might just get a decent night's sleep later.

My mom is waiting when I arrive home. The house smells of lemon bleach, and I trip over the vacuum cleaner cord on my way to the kitchen. Seeing the vacuum out adds to my happiness. Kelly is really coming back to us.

"I saved you some dinner," she says, pushing the foil-covered plate my way. Her dishcloth stops wiping the countertop. "Do you think he'll forgive us?"

Knowing she feels bad for sending the cops after Rocks makes me close the distance between us and hug her. "You know the way to his heart is through his stomach. I'm sure he'll forgive you in no time if he gains five pounds. His father though will be another story. He's pretty upset."

"You must invite his parents down, and I'll apologize in person."

Yeah, nope! Never gonna happen.

"No, they just need time. You look better." Her face crumples as though she's going to cry, but she doesn't.

"I'm so sorry, sweetheart. I just … I vanished for a while there, but I'm okay. Your poor father. He's been coping with all of this on his own. I feel terrible. When you yelled at me about Rocks, it woke something up inside. I saw your disappointment and realize that I deserved it, but not for letting Mini be taken, for letting this family down since."

I rub her back. "We were so worried about you."

"You and Rocks going to be okay?" I can see the worry in her eyes. It's the first time she's looked at me with concern since Mini vanished.

I nod. "He's coming around on Saturday. He wants to help any way he can."

That makes her cry. She tells me what a wonderful, young man he is, wanting to be here for us during such a trying time. I can think of more colorful words to describe this situation than "trying." I also want to tell her that Mini is fine. Lonely, but okay, and with Rocks on board, we're going to bring her home.

Mom returns to the vacuuming while I eat dinner. Home-cooked food is the best. My mind drifts to Mini—if she's tucked up asleep, if she's alone. I'm so grateful Rocks is going to help. There has to be a way for us to save her—Rocks and I—together. The feel of him kissing me makes my fingers drift over my lips. God, I missed that. I want to kiss him for hours on end, but that can wait till we rescue Mini, and I feel so bad enjoying myself while she's still a prisoner.

His promise to me plays over and over in my head. I feel my lips smile, but it fades when I think about the blood debts still hanging around his neck. I believe Rocks when he says he won't do anything about them if he's asked. I just worry what the Sire will do to him as a result. Will he be put on trial again for refusing a blood bond? I sigh, wishing I had more answers than questions for once. I guess we'll deal with that when it happens. For now, I need to focus on a plan to rescue my little sister.

21

The Plan

"ARE you sure you won't be in danger?" I ask.

"You forget how good I am at keeping out of sight, and this is about getting Mini, so it's worth it. Plus, I'm not planning on attacking anyone and ending up on the television. Relax." He runs his warm hands up and down my arms.

Rocks is standing in my room. My worry is preventing me from focusing the way I'd like to on his tight, black t-shirt and bare, inked arms. I swear his muscles are even more defined since I last saw him. The plan is for him to be my aerial escort when my human escorts take me to Enzo's in an hour. I'm worried, with half the population on bat alert, that he shouldn't risk being seen flying over the city during the day. It's one thing for him to visit me in the 'burbs, but who knows where Enzo's warehouse is located?

Opening my desk drawer, I grab the envelope I've had for a month. Getting emotional before meeting Johnson and Brick probably isn't the best idea, but I want Rocks to have those photos. He drops onto my bed when he sees Decker's smiling face in the first picture. I sit beside him and rest my hand on his thigh as he flicks through the rest of them.

"These are even better printed. Thank you." He leans over and places a kiss on my forehead. "Thank you." Holding up the photo of his brother and I, Rocks says he wants to frame it.

"Hey, did you get a pic of Strickland?"

Rocks clicks open his silver pocket watch to check we have time. He opens up his photos' folder, then hands me his phone. Strickland is standing with his arms folded across his chest, looking as cranky as I've ever seen him. His forehead is furrowed so deeply he's practically got a unibrow.

"I stalked him all over the market to get that. Fitting, don't you think?"

I grin. "Strickland on a good day. Does he know you took it?"

"Nope." His wide smile tells me exactly how proud he is of his ninja photography skills. He indicates for me to look through his photos. "Oh my God."

Bailey is on his shoulders with her pink seahorse and dragon sitting on Rocks' head. Their smiles could light the universe. I want a copy. I flick through photo after photo of Rocks at the market with different Camazotz.

There's a heap of him with his siblings—Baxter, Moonshiner, Ireland, and Bailey. Graceland doesn't feature in any, and I guess she shares her father's disdain for technology. I doubt her feelings toward me have improved much as Rocks has been in even more trouble since I saw her at the blood ceremony.

Surprised doesn't even cover how I feel looking at the picture of Rocks with Judge. The Fold member with the deadly scar down his face is smiling and has an arm slung around Rocks' shoulders. If I didn't know better, I'd swear he was Rocks' father and not the angry man in the other photo. Judge clearly views Rocks as family—since technically he is Rocks' stepdad—and it's nice to know that one leader in the Shadows has Rocks' back. I show Rocks the picture on the screen.

"Yeah, he was happy to have his picture taken after I gave him the photo of Decker. I've never seen Judge so open to what your world offers than when he was looking at the image of his son."

Rocks admits that he thinks Judge will stand with him if the Sire decides Rocks isn't allowed to see me. Apparently, I'm still banned from the market. When I go to protest that he should not be here, he says Mini comes first. I hate that I selfishly need his help so I let my counter argument dissolve on my tongue.

"Check out the videos," he says, oozing with pride.

The angle shows he's standing at the bottom of an enormous tree. The trunk is dead straight, and the branches all seem to be growing from the other side, off center—a freak of nature. There's movement high in the branches, a short squawk, and next thing a dark shape is zooming straight toward the camera. It's body barely an inch from the rough bark, and wings tucked in close to its side, the bat's face gets closer and closer until its nose slams onto the screen before the camera drops to the ground.

The phone keeps filming, and I can see grass and one of Rocks' black boots. The sound captures Rocks laughing and swearing at Jeremiah about getting close, but not *that* close. A second later, Rocks rights the camera, and it zooms in on Jeremiah—as a human—rubbing his sore red nose. It's flight school for daredevils.

AS THE AUTOMATIC roller door rumbles down, closing on the concrete, I listen as hard as I can for any calls from Rocks.

Nothing.

Trying to stay calm, I head down the hallway to the waiting duffle bags and pray that he knows my location. Locating the warehouse is step one, and without it, Mini won't be coming home. Inside my laundry room, I get to work opening the top journal. I grab the first heavy duffle and lug it over. As I heave it up onto my desk, I glance at the ceiling.

I feel as obvious as the sun coming out at night. Rocks wants details of every room inside the warehouse. He needs to know what weaknesses his Camazotz-sized self can take advantage of, but whoever is watching behind the mirrored glass cannot know I'm mentally taking notes.

High above me is the grill of the air duct. Of course! With the distinct smell of the product only a couple of rooms away, and not one window in the place, all the rooms are vented.

This is good news.

"Hello, Papa," I say, walking uninvited into his office later.

His back is to me, and he's looking through the open blinds into the cutting room. The young girl who explained production to me is working today wearing bright red, lace underwear. I use the chance to look around. Enzo's office has a vent high in the false ceiling too, and I can't see any alarm panels or sensors.

"I'm glad you came to see me," he says, walking to the enormous slate grey safe in the corner. Opening it, he hands me a large, yellow envelope. "Check the details, and let me know if there are any problems."

Rocks has a birth certificate and social security number. There are documents for Jeremiah too. My smile is real. Mini is usually the only recipient of genuine smiles when I'm stuck here.

"Thank you. Thank you so much." Enzo opens his arms, and the gesture almost wipes the smile away, but I force myself to step into them. His hug makes me want to grab Mini's baby wipes and shower with them.

"Bring me photos of the two if you would like other documents."
Over my dead body.

He will never lay eyes on Rocks. It's the only reason I risked getting these. His name, which isn't in the system anyhow, is one thing, but his photo is totally out of the question.

Rocks is sitting on the edge of the porch swing when I pull in. He's by my side faster than my eyes can track, asking if I'm okay. Before I've had time to close my car door, his hands run over my body to make sure I'm in one piece. I don't miss his nose twitch as he picks up the unpleasant aroma of my job.

"I lost you. I'm sorry."

Dumping my cell back in my car, I give the street a quick scan before speaking. "Let's go inside."

Rocks paces my room while he explains how he lost sight of the SUV. He says the vehicle entered a six-level parking garage just south of downtown, and he needed to wait a second before he could swoop down and follow because a family of four had just exited through the open boom gate. He didn't want to get too close and risk unwanted attention.

By the time he entered the garage, he couldn't see the car, and after searching every row, he realized there were two other exits onto the street behind. My suits took a detour through the building to lose any tail, or in this case—wing.

"We're gonna need help. I'll ask Jeremiah and Ezra. They can wait by each exit to see which one they take."

"No way! Nuh-uh. Not happening." I fold my arms.

"Ah-ha."

"Nuh-uh. No."

"Connie, we can't do this alone. You saw a man murdered. We have to get Mini out of there, and we're gonna need help."

"No."

"You need to tell Kelly and Chad what's happened to Mini."

I nearly fall off the bed at his ludicrous suggestion.

"Have you suffered a head injury I don't know about? I *cannot* tell them. They'll go straight to the cops!"

"So we're just going to bring her home, and the cops and everyone will celebrate the case getting solved? Where exactly are you going to tell them you found her?" His red eyebrow bar rises up under his hair. He's thought long and hard about our plan. My eel comes out to party in my guts—it thrives on misery. It astounds me how stupid I can be at times. All I was focused on was getting my sister away from Enzo, but bringing her home is just as complicated.

"Fudge me! Fudge Enzo! Fudge, fudge, fudge!" My fist slams into my mattress.

Rocks pulls me in for a hug. I listen to his steady heartbeat then take a deep breath. My heart rate slows to match his. "We need a way to make Enzo stay out of your life for good. I have an idea, but you're really gonna have to trust me."

ON SUNDAY, ROCKS pays Josie Hendersen a house call—alone.

As much as I hated to admit he was right, the risk of me being followed to my birth mother's house is ridiculously high. This all started with that stupid surveillance van outside her place anyway.

All morning, I try to stay calm, but the longer I wait, the more I sweat. I've cleaned my room, the bathroom and the kitchen. Twice.

Josie has a plan.

It's a good one.

My fingers fly over the keys trying to reply. Josie has a plan? That concept is hard to fathom. The woman that practically slammed the door in my face, telling me to get lost, wants to help? I don't think I'll ever understand how adult brains function.

You sure we can trust her?

I hate to ask, but Josie doesn't care about me, let alone Mini. Rocks thought Josie might be able to convince Chad and Kelly not to tell the cops when I come clean about Mini's location. He's right. If we're going to rescue Mini, my folks need to be in the know. But the thought of telling them who I am sends the eel ducking for cover.

As I wait for his reply, I ignore twelve other text messages, six Facebook alerts, and four snapchats from the girls getting ready for school tomorrow now that Spring break is over. The text I'm anxiously waiting for finally beeps.

She wants him behind bars too.

She feels responsible.

Good! That letter was the start of a landslide of events that just keeps on coming, and we need a way to stop it—forever. I want my old life back and the sooner the better. The ways that I have let down Dad and Mom make me ashamed to be called a Phillips. Lies, deceit and dishonesty are the trademarks of an Ascari. My old worry that I won't be welcome as a Phillips once they find out bubbles to the surface. Mini is only in danger because of me, but if I want to make this right, then I have to risk never seeing Mom smile at me with love ever again.

Ultimately, the risk is worth it to save the life of my baby sis.

It makes me think of Rocks, and what he's risking by choosing to date me over the Camazotz. The Shadows could kick him out because he wants to date aeronaught-style. He's risking too much but appears so calm about it. I really need to talk to him about those 'consequences' he said might happen, but first Mini.

Even though the thought of telling Mom and Dad everything sends me into a tailspin, I know deep down that's what we have to do. The truth needs to be heard. I need to be honest if I want to have a shot at being the old me. Last year, lies got me results in finding my birth parents, but they're the cause of everything that has gone wrong since. If I had talked to my real parents from the start, I'm betting I wouldn't be in this position. The truth would have saved us all this heartache and pain. So no matter the cost to me, I'm spilling the beans.

The only thing that calms me is that I've got Rocks. He knows who I am and what I'm capable of, and he says he still wants me. I won't be alone even if Chad and Kelly do disown me.

Rocks flies in my window, late Sunday night. The sudden echo of Jeremiah and Ezra's voices in my head scares the crabapples out of me as they say hi from the trees outside. My paranoia is at an all-time high. I didn't even want Rocks sharing Josie's awesome plan over the phone. Mom and Dad are sleeping, so we sit in the dark on my bed facing each other, whispering back and forth.

Step one: Find that warehouse.

Step two: Josie pays the Phillips a visit and convinces them to keep the cops in the dark.

Step three: Get dirt on Enzo to put him away for the rest of his days.

Step three is reliant on step one. Without Rocks finding the warehouse, he can't copy the evidence we'll need to give to the police—Josie's bright idea. I'm confident he can use the air vents to gain access to each room, but we won't know for sure until Rocks can check it out. Rocks says he'll be waiting for me at school on Tuesday while the boys will be stationed at each of the two exits of that parking garage. I need to hold it together until then. Rocks kisses me briefly aware of his listening friends hanging outside, but when he moves to the window, Jeremiah's voice in my head makes a request.

Bring pretzels.

Being surrounded by hungry teenage boys helps keep me grounded.

I DART AROUND the group of sophomores clogging up the exit. Going left, as three members of the football team go left, my pencil case snags on something sending the load I'm clutching skidding all over the concrete—books, phone, and a crap load of paper litter the exit. The sophomores barely glance my way, too focused on the close proximity of senior jocks as I rescue my junk.

Next thing I know, the last person I'm in the mood to face is reaching for my phone. Parker stands up as I continue shoving my stuff in my backpack, like I should have done at my locker.

"Please sign my petition. I'm handing the last one in today as the county is set to make a decision, and every voice counts."

I stand and try not to snarl at him. Parker hasn't given up his kill-innocent-Camazotz campaign.

"What do you mean 'make a decision?'" This is the last fudged up thing we need. The hairs on my arms stand on end at the thought of the government after Rocks. I rub my scar and when Parker's eyes follow my hand, I want to slap myself.

"Concerned citizens have rights—"

My brain is having trouble believing this is the same boy who couldn't write his own Economics essay six months ago. Then again getting signatures isn't exactly the same as arguing a side of an essay question and involves no typing skills at all—not that he has any.

"Just because it isn't in our county, doesn't mean we should ignore public safety for—" Parker continued.

"Parker!"

He stops talking and stares at me. I'm very aware that he still has my freaking cell. "What—vote?"

"To see if the cull will be paid for by the government."

"What do you mean 'to see if?' Isn't it a question of if the cull will happen?" I glare at him.

His smile sickens me. "Oh, it's happening according to my group, it's just a matter of who will pay—"

Before he finishes speaking, I snatch my cell and his clipboard. Parker's grin has an air of triumph about it. Shoving my phone in my jeans pocket, I tear the sheets from the clipboard and rip them to shreds before he can stop me.

"Shit, Connie, what the hell?" he yells as I throw the paper in the air making it rain confetti signatures.

"Cruelty to animals is never okay!"

On the drive to today's meeting point, I wonder if Rocks witnessed my Parker encounter. I have to watch the late news to find out about this vote he's so sure of. Strickland might not be as prejudiced as I've always thought. Imagine what the local residents would do if they knew those bats could shape-shift? I almost miss my turn off and the blaring honk from the car behind me tells me I need to shove the Camazotz cull to the back of my brain for later.

Brick is leaning against a gleaming BMW. Maybe Enzo should move into the car rental business, he's practically got a fleet of them. I slide into the back noticing the leather smells new, and Johnson is waiting with my blindfold.

"Afternoon, gentleman." My tone is light because my gut is telling me Rocks and the boys are going to succeed. Fifty-seven minutes later when I step out into the warehouse loading bay, I have to do everything in my power not to break out in dance moves.

Look up.

Nine o'clock.

High in the rafters, next to an open louver window is a black bat hanging upside down. The loading dock doesn't have a ceiling, and in this area only, you can see the metal roof and iron support beams. Rocks is in! He's here!

Enzo, you are going down, dearest Papa. You're going down.

When I hug Mini goodbye, I whisper in her ear that she'll be home soon and kiss the top of her head. I have to refrain from skipping down the hallway. Back in the loading dock, the frustration of not being able to communicate back to Rocks is pissing me off. I can't risk staring at the rafters either, so I focus on my scuffed boots.

Staying to watch.

Call later.

I nod my head and send up a prayer that Rocks will be safe.

THE NEXT DAY at school, Tiff elbows me three times during English when I'm called to answer different questions, but haven't heard a single word Mrs. Yamaguchi's been saying. I'm running on nervous energy and caffeine—okay, and a packet of Swedish fish and three of Mom's orange and poppy seed muffins. Sugar is going to get me to the finish line.

Tiff scrawls a message on her book.

Fudge! I bite my cheek and glance her way before picking up my pen and assuring her that I'm fine and not about to assault Parker if I see him in the halls. I should have known that display would have hit the cell network in seconds. I'm amazed I'm not viral on YouTube.

Her next message asks if there's any news on Mini. I shake my head. Tiff reaches over and squeezes my arm. It's as though she's squeezing my heart. She's a good friend—much better than I have been—and I don't know what I would do without her.

If she thought I was ignoring her last year, then that's nothing to how little I've spoken to her recently. I can only handle lying on so many fronts, and the folks take precedence. Sometimes, it's best to keep your mouth shut. But being the trouper she is, she's not upset.

Rocks is in the kitchen with Mom when I eventually make it home. She's baked. I'm glad because that means she's doing well today, and I need her at her best to cope with the bomb I'm about to drop on this household. When I ask her for the third time if Dad will be home on time, Rocks grabs my wrist and pulls me up to my room.

"Calm down. She'll be here. It will work."

Depending on Mom V1.0 is not something I feel comfortable with at all. This is the woman who gave me away. My feet start pacing the tiny circuit of my room. Rocks follows me with his eyes.

"Sit down. You've got three hours before she'll be here. Why don't you paint your nails?"

"I can't." So much rests on Josie convincing my folks to trust a couple of teenagers to secure evidence on the most successful drug supplier on the East coast to free their kidnapped daughter without the dirty cop finding out about it. "Crap! We are never gonna pull this shit off."

I breathe out through my mouth, trying to stop my heart from doing the rumba in my chest. Totally loco is what we both are for thinking this could ever work. Delusional. Cray-cray. Locney tunes. Take your pick.

"Calm down," he says from my bed.

"Distract me."

Faster than Rocks can flip, he has me pinned against my wardrobe door and is kissing the life out of me. All I can feel are his hands and body pressing against mine. He's taking charge, and after a second, I let him. I give in, moving up onto my toes to wrap my arms around his shoulders. Both his hands slide down into my back pockets and he gives my butt a slow squeeze. It's a bold move for the 1865 boy and sends my heart rate rocketing in the best way possible.

Rocks straightens up, ending the kiss. The lazy smile on his face I know matches mine. "Josie will show," he whispers.

"Who?"

Laughter fills the air, and then Rocks attacks my ribs with his long fingers. I'm screaming and squirming trying to get free. His arms seem to be endless, but I dart left and make it to my bed. Grabbing my pillow, I spin and whack him hard across the chest. I manage two well-aimed thumps with my pillow before his long arms circle and pull me against his chest. He turns and collapses backward onto my bed so I'm not crushed under his weight.

Rearranging ourselves, I'm snuggled into the crook of his arm as his hand plays with a couple of long strands of my hair. It's the safest I've felt in months.

My chest aches that I feel so happy lying in his arms when my baby sister still isn't safe. But I can't help enjoying this selfish moment. My stress levels have been beyond insane, and I need a small break to prepare for what we're about to do. I must be calm when I face my folks. Whether I'm a rocking mess in the corner, or smiling at the most amazing guy who has his arms around me, Mini will still be locked in her jail cell alone.

As though Rocks can read the turmoil I'm experiencing clearly on my face, he smooths out the frown I wasn't aware of.

"It will be all right."

We stayed entwined on my bed in silence until Rocks hears Dad's van pull into the drive.

He sends *the* text.

Rocks and I are waiting on the porch swing when Josie's beat up hunk-of-junk pulls up. She parks on the street and watching her walk up the drive is a scene I try to memorize. Each time I see my birth mother, I want to preserve every miniscule detail about her because I never know if it will be last time we cross paths.

"You certainly have her looks," Rocks says behind me.

Two of his fingers are in my back pocket. I think it's his new favorite. I know it's mine because the connection helps me to stay present instead of flipping out again.

"I'm sorry it came to this, Contessa. I really am," she says, stopping on the bottom step. She's wearing a blue cotton shirt, tucked into jeans with sandals that show her black painted toenails.

"So am I, believe me."

For some reason, I don't want this to happen around our kitchen island. It's the heart of our house where so many good things take place. Tainting it with my biological blood, and what it's done to this family seems wrong. The formal living room it is.

"Mom, Dad, can you come here please?" I call.

I usher Josie around the corner, and she stands beside me in silence.

Kelly enters first and stops on a dime when her eyes land on Josie. I watch her facial features as her eyes roam from head to toe. She gasps, stepping back, and collides with Chad rounding the corner. She's using both hands to cover her mouth as her eyes dart from me to Josie and back again.

She knows.

"What's going—" Dad starts before he sees an older version of me in his living room. "Who's this?" He steps around Mom but wraps an arm around her waist. He frowns when he sees the look of shock written clearly across his wife's face. "Connie?"

Mom swallows her shock and drops her hands. She steps up, straightening her already pristine dress. "I'm Kelly Phillips, Connie's moth—" Her eyes dart to mine.

"Yes, my *mother*. You're still my mother, but I know now." Dad's looking from me to Mom to Josie and doesn't have a clue. Men. "Dad, this is Josie Hendersen." I let the name linger in the air, but he still doesn't tweak. "My birth mom."

"What? Kelly? How did she find out?" He's more upset than I expected. And startled is not a look you see very often on Chad Phillips.

"We're about to find out," Mom replies.

Josie takes a seat, and I begin my crazy, hard-to-believe tale. It starts with the letter, and my awesome detective skills. Mom comments that it explains why I suddenly turned into a scowling teen for the best part of last year. When I tell them how I felt lied to and lost about who I was, Mom bursts into tears. Dad gets indignant, but I explain that he stopped kissing me when he came home at night. He would kiss Kelly, then Mini, but not me. That one harmless gesture added to my feelings of not belonging—of not being the child that mattered.

"Because I thought your head was going to shoot off your shoulders if I got too close," he explains, rolling his eyes. "You started staring at me with this crazy look. I thought it was your way of letting me know you weren't a little girl any longer and didn't want to be treated as such. It's why we let you take that job." His eyes are sad when he finishes explaining, and another layer of guilt joins the heap. I'm definitely guilty of watching him like a hawk.

After that, I soldier on because we aren't anywhere close to the part that's going to freak them out forever. I refrain from telling them the Vipers kidnapped me. That's something they cannot change, and since the Camazotz came to my rescue, it involves details that I don't want to lie about. When it's time to explain who my biological father is, Josie gives me a nod of encouragement.

"I want you both to know I'm so sorry for everything." I glance at Josie before focusing on my parents. "I'm sorry I opened that letter and didn't talk to you about it. I love you, and I hope you'll still love me too."

"Connie, don't—" Dad says.

"—be absurd," Mom finishes. "Of course, we love you. And will no matter what."

Three deep breaths later, bombs away.

"Enzo Ascari is my Dad, and he's kidnapped Mini to force me into working for him. There's a dirty cop on his payroll so I haven't been able to tell you any of this because I was scared of what he would do. Rocks, Josie, and I have a plan to bring her home safe, but we needed you to be in on it," I blurt.

My parents, who never swear, teach Rocks a few new phrases with their colorful response. Mom's tears have moved from sprinkler to water fountain setting, and Dad is pacing the living room, talking loudly but not making much sense. After several minutes, he sits down, rubs Mom's back until she gets herself under control, and then makes a move for the phone.

Thank goodness Rocks is here and moves like a Camazotz. He wrestles the cordless from Dad's hands before the man manages to dial those three vital numbers. Rocks looks like a cross between alarmed and guilty at getting physical with my father, but Dad cannot call the police. With no phone, his worry morphs into rage, and he starts to yell—at me. I flinch, but have to admit, I expected this reaction. His little girl was kidnapped, and I've known all along. The stress and sleepless nights they've experienced are all on me.

His face is bright pink from lack of oxygen. He's hardly taken a breath since his rant began. "How could you let—" he continues to roar.

Josie is on her feet. "Enough!" Her stern tone silences my father. "Sit down. I would like to remind you that my daughter has kept your daughter safe by following strict instructions issued to her by a man who is capable of murder. Have you thought for one single second how stressful that has been on a teenage girl? Would you have coped as beautifully as she has knowing her sister's life is in her hands?"

Dad starts to argue about there being ways to tell the police, but Mom places her hand in his and pulls him down onto the sofa.

Josie continues. "You've never been alone in a room with Enzo Ascari, have you? I know you haven't because if you had, you would know that when that man threatens a life, he means it. You should be applauding your daughter's strength of character and tenacity to do whatever it took to keep her little sister safe and well. You should be proud, because that man did not get to his position without shedding a lot of innocent blood, and Connie was smart enough to recognize that keeping this a secret, from everybody in her life, was the only way to protect Jasmine. I understand what she's been through because I was married to that vile excuse for a man."

Dad sits and looks suitably ashamed. He goes to speak several times, but nothing comes out. His eyes meet mine, and I try to convey that I understand. I get it. He has every right to be flipping mad.

Josie apologizes very sincerely for setting the wheels in motion that led to us all being here having this conversation. She continues to dismiss each and every suggestion Dad has for getting his little girl back. Josie knows Enzo better than anyone and is adamant that the only way to take control is by getting the evidence the Feds have been after for years to lock him away forever.

Josie has not one, but three Federal police contacts that have been waiting for the day when she gives them a call to help take Enzo down. If there's a dirty cop in the nest with Enzo, then Josie is guaranteeing a way around that lowlife. But under no circumstances are any of us to barge into his operation and steal Mini back. The Feds must rescue Jasmine, and then child abduction can be added to Enzo's long list of sins.

Some time during the second pot of coffee, my parents both promise Josie they will not go to the police. It's agreed that Rocks and I will obtain as much evidence about Enzo's current operation as possible, and then Josie will hand over the information. All the adults present are concerned about how Rocks is going to get this done. Our silence doesn't help, but he promises my parents he will get what is needed on Enzo. I tell Dad we're gonna need his GoPro camera and some rappelling gear.

"Afterward, I'll take the recordings to the police," Chad offers.

"No, it's best if you're not involved in this part at all, so you won't be called to give evidence in the trial, unless it's in relation to Jasmine. You'll get to walk away with your daughters safely."

"And you won't mention Connie?" he asks Josie again.

She swears that she will take full responsibility for Enzo and that I will not be involved. Dad relaxes as much as a man that's just found out the kidnapper of one daughter is the father of his other. I eye him wondering how he's feeling about me now.

"Good, because I want her safe. I want them both safe." He turns to me and continues. "I'm your father, and that's how it's going to stay. If you think for one second I'm going to have it on official record that Enzo Ascari is your biological dad, you're dead wrong." When he's calm, he's the best dad in the universe.

I launch myself off the couch and into his open arms. "I love you."

"I love you too, and don't ever, ever forget that. Sorry about earlier." I get wrapped up in one of Dad's hugs—the kind that only awesome dads can give. He makes the worries of the world disappear, and inside his arms, the silent promise is made that he'll make everything right.

With the hard part out of the way, it's time for some happy news. I kneel in front of Mom and take both her hands in mine.

"Mini's got a new tooth."

22

I Spy

"**O**h my god, you're safe," Mom wails as I walk in the door late Thursday. For my whole shift at the warehouse, I was waiting for one of Enzo's thugs to drag me by the hair into his office and play a recording of the plan we've all been hatching.

But my imagination has obviously hooked up with my guilt complex—it's completely out of control.

Enzo gave me yet another pay increase, and today I took the cash stashed in my locker and added it to the heap in my trunk. If Enzo's going down, then I might as well keep what he thinks I'm owed. The colony, or my college education, will benefit from his generosity.

Mom and Dad look as though they've aged ten years. I still feel responsible despite their repeated objections. Dad apologizes again for his outburst and insists that if I'd have known what would happen, I would never have looked for Enzo in the first place. He's right. I would have burned that letter and had hypnotherapy to make sure I forgot I knew I was adopted. No lie.

Mom is looking way too closely at her chipped nails. Tears fill her eyes, but don't spill over her smooth cheeks. "I can't help but think if we had told you from the beginning you were adopted none of this would have happened."

"What's done is done," I say, trying to ease her guilt. I know how heavy that burden can be, and to be honest, I'm so relieved to not be alone anymore. My parent's approval means the world to me and having them on board with all that has happened is surreal.

She smiles and dabs her eyes. "Tell me everything."

I give Mom the full Mini report—three times. Last night, she baked animal sugar cookies with marshmallow eyes for me to take to Mini. Mini spent three minutes reciting all the animal noises in her rather large repertoire—I felt it my big sister duty to pass on my animal obsession—before demolishing the lot. It was a joy to witness, and when she's back, I'm going to spoil that little poppet rotten.

The knock at the door surprises me. Rocks used to come straight in but has returned to waiting outside. I guess he hasn't forgotten the cops showing up on his doorstep. When I explain that to my mom, he gets an earful about always being welcome in this household, and that he really should have his own key. I stifle a laugh at the look of outrage that flashes over Dad's face at the thought of a teenage boy having 24/7 access to his teenage daughter. Then my ears burn, and of course, Rocks notices that.

"I don't understand why you're risking your life after what we put you and your family through," Dad admits.

I watch the weight of his words sink in. Rocks nods. "I know I look different. People have judged me—and my family—for the way we look for a lifetime. But I would never let something so petty stand in the way of doing what's right. We need to bring Mini home, and I can help do that. Those in the world that are judged are rarely what they are conceived to be."

Oh, Rocks. Now that we're getting closer and closer to bringing Mini home, I worry about what will go wrong for us next. Will the colony welcome me back? Will the colony kick him out? It reminds me of Parker and that vote. I check my Gmail account on my phone and wish I hadn't.

Dad shakes hands with Rocks and tells him that his father should be proud of the man he raised. My heart jackknifes in my chest. That's the one thing I know deep down Rocks is desperate for—the Sire to tell him he's proud of who he has become.

With the GoPro in hand and a mountain of abseiling equipment by the door, Mom and Dad leave Rocks and I to talk alone. I'm going to the market tomorrow instead of school to help Rocks prepare. Josie had made the folks promise they wouldn't grill us for details of the warehouse. She said from her years of dealing with the cops and Enzo, it's easier to be convincing if you simply don't know what's happening. The location of that warehouse and what it contains has to be news to my parents when Mini is returned and the police brief them.

I leave Rocks at the kitchen island, in heaven with a new gadget to learn, while I follow my folks upstairs. Dad is already in bed, and Mom is in their bathroom when I poke my head around the corner. Dad pats the bed beside him, and I'm catapulted back to my childhood. A quick run and a good jump has me nearly knocking him out the other side as I land on their king size bed. Our laughter causes Mom to see what's happening.

It's been too long since I've been this happy and carefree in my parents' company. I need it like oxygen if I'm going to survive what's coming, and I sense my folks need a break from the constant anguish they've lived with since Mini was taken. This light moment won't change Mini's situation, but it'll give me the strength I need to get her back.

"Sweetheart?"

I sit cross-legged in the middle while Mom gets into bed. "I have two questions."

"Shoot," Dad says.

"Can Rocks stay in the guest room so we can drive up to the market together tomorrow?" I don't mention it will prevent me from staying up half the night worrying that he'll get back there without encountering any owls.

Chad barely flinches at my idea. He's getting better, but he looks to Kelly for the answer. "Of course, I'll go make up—"

I grab her wrist before she gets one leg out. "I'll take care of it. You stay in bed."

"You sure?"

I nod. My blood pressure is on the rise, but I've put this question off for far too long. It's time. "Why did you adopt if you could have kids?"

The happiness that was on Mom's face a second ago at the idea of having an extra mouth to feed at breakfast vanishes. Her eyes show concern and a touch of guilt. Dad reaches a hand over and takes hold of hers.

"It's okay. We knew she would have to know one day," he says, looking at her. Tears well up in Mom's eyes, but not enough to spill over. Each second of their delay is freaking me right-the-fudge-out.

"Your dad is a cancer survivor."

My jaw opens, but I have no words. Not in a million years would I have guessed that was the reason. "But? What? When? Are you okay?" I focus on Dad's smiling face.

"Of course, it was when I was in college." He sighs. "I never thought I would see my twenty-first birthday."

Dad and Mom take turns sharing their explanation for why they kept my adoption a secret. Well, not so much a secret, they just didn't want the cancer to be their focus. It was about being positive and living a healthy lifestyle. Mom didn't want to give any energy to the cancer cells, in case it came back.

They wanted to enjoy life and really live without a cloud hanging over them. Mom apologizes profusely for the worry and hurt she caused me. It was her idea, but each milestone I hit seemed to arrive before they were ready. When I started school; when I became a teenager; when I turned eighteen; when I hit twenty-one ...

The Specialist that saved Dad had him store a sperm sample in case the treatment left him sterile. There was a mix up at the donor bank and I block my ears and sing loudly not wanting those particular details in my mind. When it's safe to listen again, I sit quietly and Dad continues. His Specialist then suggested they put their names on the adoption waiting list because it was likely Dad would never be a father naturally.

Six months later, they were called to collect me. The agency had said the wait would be years, and even though they weren't ready to be parents, they looked on my arrival as another miracle. It wasn't until Mom got pregnant that they discovered Dad could be a dad. For whatever reason, the universe had prevented them from having a child until then.

The questions fly from my mouth. I need to know the whole story or I'll never sleep. It turns out Mom fell in love with Dad while he was really sick. She used to visit him everyday after he had to drop out of college, and she would read the newspaper to him from cover-to-cover by his bedside. When he got better and was cancer free, Dad took over reading the paper as a little sign that he could do it—I've finally got a reason for their daily news-hour obsession. A miracle I have witnessed my whole life but never knew the significance.

"And that's why you go to those fancy fundraisers?" The truth has been right under my nose. Mom smiles.

"And why we never miss the reunion weekend," she adds. "That group all watched your father's recovery, and each year, without fail, we get together to celebrate another year of life together."

"I never knew. I would have come—"

"It's all right, sweetheart."

"And you're sure you're all right?" I ask Dad. I have to, but my worry is exactly what they were trying to avoid. He assures me again and kisses me on the forehead.

There's one more thing I need to discuss and now's as good a time as any.

"It's time I'm allowed to swear." Mom goes to speak, but I soldier on. "After the shit I've seen and experienced, I think I'm old enough to know when I can and can't cuss. Mom, you need to trust that I never want to hear Mini repeat any of those nasty words. I think I've proven I'd do anything for that kid."

"Yes, you would. You're a good big sister to her," says Dad, with a sad smile. Mom covers her mouth, clearly moved.

"And I'm sorry for lying. For all the lies I've told you. They complicate life in ways that don't make you a better person, so I want you to know how sorry I am."

"Honey, we understand you did what you had to do for Jasmine."

"But I lied to you last year too." I look away suddenly ashamed of my childish behavior. Her soft hand covers mine forcing me to look into her eyes. She's not upset.

"We understand, but we're glad you see it's not the only way."

A weight lifts after my admission. I never knew how much lying to them really cost me until now. It's almost like I've been given a new start. They know who I am and what I've done, but love me anyway. After hugging them both hard, I grab the laptop and head for the TV room. My family is even more amazing than I realized.

The Google alert I spied earlier does not sound promising. Rocks takes possession of the remote super excited for TV time and starts watching a news report about astronomy geeks getting their geek on over the lunar eclipse. I don't have the heart to stop him until I confirm if the sinking feeling in my gut is justified. The title of the video link leaves me both speechless and wanting to hurl.

"You're going to need to see this."

Rocks sits close, ignoring the TV and places the laptop on his knees. I try to keep still as the video buffers, but the words in bold across the top make it hard.

Go Ahead For Bat Cull.

The news reporter is live outside the Mayor's office. A group of men in suits deliver the worst news possible for the Camazotz. There's a representative from some nature/wildlife society, one from the National Parks, and three city officials. They all agree that due to public safety concerns, they will humanely euthanize the rare vampire bat colony that has been discovered in a Floyd County wilderness area. The reporters hit them with questions, and they decline to say the exact location, or when the cull will take place to prevent 'tree-huggers' from interfering. It's reiterated that the secrecy is in the interest of public safety, but that without the help from a vampire bat expert, they never would have found the mysterious roost.

The video ends, and I have no idea what to say to Rocks. He sits staring at the screen. I take his hand and run my fingers along his. Those amazing digits give him the capacity to fly.

"Vampire bat expert." I repeat. "If it's Floyd County, then they've found the Duskwing!"

"Let me watch it again," he requests quietly. One click later, and the deadly news still hasn't changed.

"What the—" I hit pause, drag the cursor back a minute and pause it again. "That fudged-up freak is involved. What the hell is going on?"

Rocks isn't following, and then it hits me—he doesn't know what he looks like. I point to the dark-haired guy standing behind the suits being interviewed.

"That's Joey!" Clear as day, the bat that broke Rocks' wing is on camera. "Some effing expert!"

"Are you absolutely sure?" Rocks is peering at the screen squinting. I wish it was better quality, but I print a screen shot anyway.

"It's him. I would recognize that, that …" I really want to swear now I have permission to, but nothing seems evil enough to encompass all that he's done.

"Why would he be supporting a Camazotz cult?"

ROCKS DOESN'T SPEAK as I drive up into the mountains. I guess his brain—like mine—is trying to connect the dots and work out what hidden agenda Joey has going. Endangering the Camazotz and risking their discovery does not make sense. He's ratting out his own kind.

"The others don't know yet?" The second I ask, I realize how stupid my question sounds. It's not like Rocks could call or email any of the Shadows members overnight. "Sorry. Stupid question."

He reaches over and places a hand on my knee. "It's okay. You're used to instant communication. Now you see how backward we really are. It's so *dangerous* being uninformed." He huffs and fidgets, and I can tell he's trying to keep his annoyance under control.

Within twenty minutes of arriving, there's an emergency Fold meeting that includes all the Clips as well. Each wing has a right to know what's going on, and how it will affect the safety of their members no matter how small they are.

Cypress hisses, when I open the video on the laptop, and makes quite a performance of stepping back a safe distance. He's wearing nothing under his leather vest, and his blood-gushing tattoos only add to my dislike of the man. When the group gets over their aversion to my technology—like the electricity is going to reach out and fry them all— they gather around closer to listen and watch the report. Despite the seriousness of this, I can't help but imagine some of these members wrapping their skulls with tin foil before answering a deadly cell phone.

When the video ends, their reaction isn't what I was expecting. A divide occurs between the wings. Half the wings argue that Duskwing have this coming to them for attacking those humans so blatantly. The other half think we need to warn them because this isn't an aeronaught problem and should be dealt with by the Camazotz instead. Strickland is alone in the middle, listening. He hasn't committed to one side or the other.

I sit back and try to ignore the aeronaught insults that are being hurled back and forth. They are not talking about me. And if I'm really honest, I'm angry at my own species too. Rocks takes a step away from the tight ball of muscle, black leather, and tension. He grabs my hand and heads for the door. Over my shoulder, the Sire's eyes track our movement. He was not exactly overjoyed to see me, but at the same time, my information gives him power to protect his colony. Even he knows continuing my ban at a time like this is suicide.

Rocks sits on his bed after we climb into his wagon. I notice immediately the starry ceiling above him has all the photos of us and the ones of Decker stuck to it. He rubs his temples, and I don't like the sag of his shoulders.

"They could be at that for hours."

I pick up his phone and forward copies of some of the pictures to my email. His ceiling has room for his whole family if I print them out. His arms have been bare every time I've seen him lately. I take a moment to study this boy from the Shadows sitting in his room. Rocks has had hundreds of hours to do the same to me. His black velvet vest is my favorite, and I look around for his wardrobe, wondering where he keeps his clothes, but he's only got small sliding cupboards crammed here and there to maximize the space.

Sticking out from under his mattress between his legs is a corner of paper.

"What's that?" I point.

His cheeks get a slight dusting of color as he pulls it free.

"My old comics."

He hands over the ancient and extremely well-loved comic books. One Superman. One Batman. The pages are faded, and two of them have come loose from the staples. I imagine Rocks reading this over and over in secret. This is highly contraband stuff, and considering his older sister had just gone missing, I'm sure the Sire would have set them alight if he'd known.

Rocks takes the comics and slides them back under his mattress, this time making sure no corners are visible. He frowns when a text from me arrives but smiles as he looks at me. I need to cheer him up a bit. He's been literally my rock since he found out about Mini. I'm positive I would have had a stroke the way my blood pressure felt, but he's calmed me down beyond words. And now I can return the favor.

"Why are you texting me? You're right here."

"Click on it, but you can't read them until later."

Quietly, I open my camera and zoom in. I want a pic of his blissed-out-on-technology smile. Three, two, one … bingo!

"No way." The stress has left his eyes and been replaced by awe. I'm so happy I could fly. "I can read these for free?"

"Yep, just click on the ones you want." I've sent him the link to read more of his favorite DC heroes online. There aren't many for free, but there's more than the two old comics he has memorized.

When he reluctantly closes the link, we get started. We need a harness for the GoPro to fit around Rocks' chest—his little batty chest. He's going to fly in, and video all he can from either the rafters or the air vents. We actually don't need Dad's abseiling gear at all, but asking for it prevents a line of questions that we can't answer honestly.

It's a good thing I got over my fear of Rocks as a Camazotz with his leathery wings and claws. The afternoon is spent with him flipping and me trying to size up the harness. I'm careful not to catch anything on the membrane of his wings. Rocks complains several times—inside my head—that I'm tickling him as he flinches and jumps while I adjust the straps.

He flips back, just as little Moonshiner comes knocking.

"Hi there." I smile.

Moonshiner still blushes violently in my presence, but he gives me a bear hug the second he's in the door. He remembered my request, and I'm delighted to know he hasn't believed a word that witch is spouting about me. Moonshiner digs into his pocket and pulls out a tiny carved wooden bat. It sits up in the middle of his palm, the wings spread wide with a pattern carved through them.

"What's that?"

He smiles and looks to Rocks. I can tell he fights his shyness by relying on his big brother for support.

"Go on. You worked so hard," Rocks says.

"For you, Miss. Connie."

I take the offered carving, studying the details. It's magnificent—incredibly intricate and unbelievably beautiful. "Where on earth did you get this?"

If he was pink before, he's now a violent red, bordering on purple. "I made it," he whispers to his shoes.

Nothing could prepare me for the talent, which hides in this colony. Every member has a trade or craft to help the colony make money, but Moonshiner is just a kid—a pup.

"Seriously?"

He nods. I ask Rocks how this is possible, and he explains that Moonshiner is a talent beyond anything they have ever seen. From the age of eight, he started woodcarving, and six months ago, the tanner gave him old strips of leather to see if he could emboss them. He can.

He's been working on whatever pattern and design takes his fancy ever since. None of the adults force him to work, but they can't keep him away. He's drawn to it like a moth to a flame. As a pup, he's supposed to cherish his freedom and learn math and English. The Fledgers are required to start a trade at fourteen, but since Moonshiner has a natural gift, they sell whatever carvings he gives them and let him do occasional work for the tanner.

"This is going to sit on my desk and watch over me when I study." His smile is cuter than Rocks' if that's possible. "You are very talented for a nine-year-old."

"I'm ten now." His chest puffs up. "I gotta go. Macaulay has another special order for harnesses, and I engraved the last ones so he wants me to do these ones too. They're being picked up tonight."

Rocks frowns. "Who ordered them?"

The boy shrugs. "I don't know, but they're the same as last year. I embossed some words I didn't know."

"Spanish." Rocks tells Moonshiner to go finish his work, but after the boy leaves, Rocks sits frowning.

"What?"

"Last year, Vuelo de la Muerte told me they were moving roost. *Now* they're ordering more harnesses? Strange that they haven't moved."

"Maybe this cull business is making them do it now?"

"I guess. It's a massive undertaking to move so ordering those first harnesses to hold the bats who can't fly the distance must have been preemptive. Hmmm ..." He taps his lips. "Speaking of harnesses, should I give this a test flight?"

I help Camazotz Rocks back into the harness and turn on the camera. He jumps off his bed and flies out the door with amazing precision. Leaning out of the wagon, I try to follow him, but he's fast. He flies up into the nearby trees, and I lose sight of the black blur. I step further out, scanning every direction. My ponytail swooshes out, and I can't help jumping when he screeches in my ear as he zooms past. Cheeky bat.

Gonna spy.

I sit on the top step and examine Moonshiner's handiwork. It's hard to believe that shy kid is capable of making something so incredible. I wonder if his father carves too? Maybe because he's the only member of the Moon wing at the Shadows he spends his time alone and entertaining himself.

Rocks returns a while later, zooming in over my head and into the wagon. By the time I turn around, he's flipped and the harness and camera are in his hands. Without his blood on them, they fall off his Camazotz self when he changes.

"It does sound too, right?"

Handing over the camera, I hit playback and we lean in close to listen. On the screen, it only takes a second to see the meeting of the Fold and Clips still hasn't finished. Strickland's voice booms over the others that are still arguing and silence immediately follows. He informs the group their shaman will be consulted before a decision is made.

I look to Rocks. It's my turn to frown. What on earth could that stupid hag have to say about this, I wonder? Rocks explains she will throw the bones and read the future of the Shadows in connection with this event. I can't contain my eye roll, and Rocks shakes his head at the disbelieving aeronaught. I've wanted to mention that the blood blessing didn't "protect" him from his wing being broken, but that can wait for another time. If he believes in the power of blood, then who am I to say otherwise. He'll probably argue it saved him from death.

"How do you know they haven't found the Shadows? That it's the Duskwing the cull are going for?"

"The Sire knows."

"But how? Does he have super sonic Sire senses? If that's the case, he shouldn't have been so shocked when Dad and I 'breached' his sanctuary." I raise one eyebrow.

Rocks frowns for a second, and I sense there's a shred of doubt in his mind. I want to make sure he's taking every precaution while there's talk of a bat cull.

"Don't worry. I'll make sure there are extra sentinels on duty. I'll be extra careful tonight. I promise."

Rocks is keeping the camera because he's paying Enzo's warehouse a visit later to start filming. He wants the place empty so he can get into each room undisturbed. I explain the concept of alarm systems and sensors. With the help of Google, I show him what to look out for. His face turns deadly serious when I mention the frequency of an alarm siren will most definitely knock him out cold.

So far I haven't seen any sensors in the rooms at the warehouse. Each door is locked from the outside, and Enzo obviously assumes nobody will breach his inner sanctum. His men guard the warehouse section day and night, but what he hasn't accounted for is an airborne guest.

Walking back to my car, the meeting has come to an end. Several groups of leaders stand outside still discussing the bat cull. The thought of that happening turns the blood in my veins to ice. Culling innocents like Bailey? I shiver. I have to believe Strickland when he assured me my dad and I are the only aeronaughts who know the location of the Shadows roost. These aren't the Camazotz they're looking for, I chant.

I notice some of the stares, as I pass through the groups, aren't so deadly. My sunshine yellow self isn't as hated by some members as I had believed Sylvana wants. There are still murderous glares from any member of the Plant or Mac wings—because they're acting as though I'm personally responsible for the cull—but I get half a smile from a young woman. It gives me hope for my future with Rocks. Maybe she believes I'm part shaman.

Judge steps away from his followers when I stop nearby. Before he has a chance to speak, I hug him tight around the waist. The thought of Decker not being here—of never seeing the joy of life on his handsome face again—sends my heart into a downward spiral. It's wrong—but it's reality. Judge's thick, muscled arms hug me back. He doesn't even hesitate to touch the aeronaught.

"I'm so sorry for your loss," I manage to say around the lump in my throat. Stepping back, I look up into his kind face. "Decker was such a good friend. He never judged me, and he got that from you. Thank you. And I'm so sorry the colony lost such an incredible member."

Judge's face scrunches up, and it reminds me of Dad when he's trying to do that man thing where they won't allow themselves to cry. "You honor his memory with your kind words. I shouldn't be surprised you noticed he was a Camazotz of worth, but I am."

"Of course, I noticed. He would have made a great leader. He was fair. And funny. Amazing really. I miss him." Judge swallows the pain my words have ignited. It's a good kind of pain, but it hurts nonetheless.

"Thank you for making those photographs Rockland gave me. It is such a gift to know I can look at my son's face a decade from now and not forget."

Now it's my turn to try not to cry. Four little clicks on my phone have given so many here so much. Technology isn't their enemy, and maybe this is a perfect way to prove that to the haters.

"You're welcome."

The surrounding murmurs don't faze me. I'm not sure if they approve or not, and I don't care. Decker's dad has a memory of his son that will not fade over time. If I'd only known, I'd have taken more photos that night in my room.

Judge heads back to the group, and I notice a Camazotz flip to join him. It's Zada. Her flowing hair has black ribbons braided though it which hang halfway down her back. I go to approach but stop when

Judge wraps her in his tight embrace and rubs her back. I can't see her face, but am pretty sure she's crying from the shake of her shoulders. He murmurs to her, and the moment feels so intimate I return to Rocks waiting in the distance.

At my car, I ask him about my suspicion. "Are those ribbons Zada's wearing a sign of mourning?"

Rocks nods, kicking a stone into the underbrush. "Too many are wearing them these days."

"I noticed Rebekkah has them in her hair." As much as I hate mentioning the little bitchy bat, I do feel for her if she lost someone too.

"Yes, her little brother, Isaiah. You saw her the day he died. Don't you remember?"

I shake my head, scanning all my interactions with her before it hits me. "That day in your shop. She was crying …" Rocks nods and pulls me against his chest, wrapping his arm tightly around me and resting his chin on my head.

"Yes. He was her only sibling."

All this time I thought I had interrupted some intimate moment between them, but he was comforting her while she grieved the loss of her brother.

I DON'T SLEEP until his text confirms he's back at the roost. Rocks went out alone because he wasn't sure how long he would be at the warehouse and didn't want to owe any more favors. Jeremiah's Fold member, Levi, isn't exactly Team Aeronaught, but he's not as prejudiced as the others either, so we don't want to give him any reason to side against us. Asking both his sons to risk their necks for me after what happened to Rocks' wing the last time is something Rocks preferred not to do.

Camazotz-aeronaught relations are tense at best due to the cull. No other members can come to any harm because of me, or they really will try to blame me for the cull.

My phones beeps with message after message.

Filmed till battery ended.

Lots of connections.

Joey was there! He got away because I couldn't leave.

I'm safe so get some sleep.

What the—
The text messages beeping one after another have me sitting up in bed. *Get some sleep?* Not likely. I type out three different replies, but delete them all. We decided we wouldn't talk about this over the phone. Joey was there? My mind buzzes with questions. We knew he was involved with the Vipers, but now he's involved with Enzo's ring too?

Holy crap.

I want details, but will wait till tomorrow. It's going to be a long night.

Glad you're safe.

Rocks replies …

So much to tell you.

See you tomorrow after your shift.

I toss and turn, rolling from one side to the other. I can't get comfortable. The urge to call Rocks has my fingers twitching. I have to remember whom I'm dealing with. I get out of bed and put my phone in my backpack and my backpack in my closet. Maybe I'm believing Hollywood and being paranoid for nothing, but maybe I'm not. There are spy cameras the size of beetles these days.

Enzo knew my grades from school, my best friend's name and address, and where Kelly was going to be with Mini. He has ways of spying, and until I'm sure Mini is safe, I can't risk talking over the phone or texting any details.

Johnson and a new dude are waiting for me at our meeting point. When I ask where Brick is, Johnson shrugs. My whole body feels like it's vibrating at some higher frequency than normal. My leg bounces up and down until I notice Johnson look, and I force my foot to glue itself to the floor. I'm not sure if something is going down, or whether it's just because we're so close to getting Mini back. Rocks told me he has everything filmed and won't need to return to the warehouse this morning. It's a relief he won't be out flying around the city during the day, but him not watching over me has me fidgety. I know I was here for weeks without him, but something feels off—my gut is churning.

When I'm done with the count, Enzo requires me in his office. My feet want to turn and head for the hills. Act normal, act normal, I chant with each step toward his office. My crazy imagination keeps picturing a Rocks-shaped hole in the ceiling, and Enzo asking me to explain.

Entering his office, all is well.

"I want to tell you how pleased I am with your work, Contessa. You have the Ascari knack for business."

"Thanks, Papa." I am not an Ascari. I am not. Chad said I was a Phillips, and I know which father deserves my faith.

"I want to talk about increasing your hours. Last night, I had a meeting with my local distributors and I wished I could've introduced you. It's another facet of the operation you'll need to learn."

Holy shit!

Rocks mentioned "connections" but what he was trying to tell me is that he's filmed Enzo's network. The cops are gonna fangirl like One Direction is coming to town when they see this footage.

Enzo is staring at me, and I realize I'm smiling, but not for the reason he thinks. How the hell am I supposed to answer that?

"Um, ah, yeah. Could be tricky but sure." I smile, hoping for added authenticity. Then my smile does become real. This could be my last shift. This could be the last time I'm alone with Enzo. Like with Josie, I can't help but take note of his features and mannerisms. He is my blood after all, but it's blood that I never want to see again for as long as I live.

Then my blood runs cold. I'm about to cross Enzo, and people that cross Enzo Ascari do not live to tell the tale. Enzo would put an end to Mini in a heartbeat. I have to betray him to rescue my sister—he has given me no choice. She might not be my blood, but I'm more a Phillips than I will ever be an Ascari. I swallow the bile that threatens.

Josie and Rocks will not let anything happen to me. I need to stay calm just a little longer. I agree to talk with Chad and Kelly about extending my hours so I can take the next step in learning his business. Enzo is focused on the papers on his desk as I stand soaking up the last details of this man before me.

"Goodbye, Papa." And I turn my back on the father I wish I'd never found.

JOSIE, ROCKS, MOM, and Dad are all waiting around the kitchen island when I get home. They've downloaded the footage onto Josie's ancient laptop to prevent the Feds from being able to trace the file back to Chad. Josie's got street smarts like I never knew. They've kindly waited for me so we can watch it all together.

The first half of the video is upside down. Dad makes a passing comment, and Rocks looks to me. We know why. The footage shows around thirty-five of Enzo's distributors coming to the warehouse, collecting their carton of 'tissues' or 'lip balm' in exchange for a duffle bag. Rocks found a prime position because not only are all their faces clear, you can hear the conversations.

For some reason, this buy isn't the norm—Enzo is present. You can see the look of surprise and shock on many of his distributors' faces when he comes forward to greet them. He says repeatedly that it's good to have some face-to-face time occasionally, and asks them all if there are any complaints, or ways he can make the process smoother and safer. The universe really has smiled on me big time, and I won't be forgetting that any time soon.

After the last buyer leaves, the footage is crazy. Rocks is flying across to the air vent. I try to stay calm when Dad comments again that he's so surprised Rocks wasn't seen or heard swinging around in the rafters. Good Lord.

My heart nearly jumps right out of my chest when a black material covers the lens before the video stops. It's his wing membrane, and I pray silently nobody will guess. Rocks rests a reassuring hand on my shoulder from behind. When the video starts again, he's filming from inside the air vent. The grill partially obscures the view, but what we witness is horrible to say the least. Enzo, Johnson, and two other beefcakes beat the living crap out of Brick. Enzo is recorded saying he knows and has evidence that Brick has been approached by the Feds.

Brick—the spitting image of Rambo—actually turns sheet-white. I never would have believed that hulking man was capable of feeling fear. Enzo yells and screams more accusations. Brick denies everything, but his face isn't calm. Enzo effing *knows*. He walks out of camera shot, and when he returns, he's holding a tire iron.

"Boss, I didn't tell 'em anything."

They argue back and forth about Sophia. It takes a second for Kelly to join the dots and realize I have a sister, and it's not Mini. Her quick glance at me over her shoulder speaks volumes.

"If you told the Feds she didn't witness those cops get murdered, I'll tear you to pieces," Enzo screams. "What I want to know is how you found out she was with me that night? There must be another rat in my walls."

"Christ," Dad exclaims. He takes hold of Mom's hand and gives her a who-the-hell-are-we-dealing-with look.

Josie is as calm as a lake on a windless day. She suggests we fast-forward this section, and nobody protests. No wonder Brick didn't show up this morning. If he's still breathing, it will be a small miracle because the beating he took looked lethal.

The video cuts out again. Rocks explains he had to wait for two and half hours before everyone left the warehouse—except the two armed thugs on nightshift. He watched Johnson arm the alarm panel, and discovered there are no sensors between the rafters and the office. The only area with motion sensors is the coffee distribution area.

"The next part shows copies of all the journals," Rocks explains. He said he was sweating so hard removing the vent grill without making a noise.

"These books have every transaction in them that Enzo makes," I explain. "It's the money coming in and going out. If the Feds can connect the faces from earlier to the code names, then they've got his whole operation in the bag."

Josie's smile is nothing short of beautiful. It occurs to me I've never seen her smile before. Last year during both my visits, she was majorly pissed. And here, she's been the epitome of stern control. She really is pretty when she relaxes those hard facial muscles and smiles. I guess her life hasn't given her a hell of a lot to be happy about. A shiver runs down my spine imagining her telling Enzo she was leaving him, secretly pregnant with me.

Brave woman.

Rocks has videoed the bagging room with the stack of waiting, uncut bricks wrapped in plastic. He gets all the materials showing the Feds the clever ways Enzo moves his product. When the screen goes black, Dad wraps a protective arm around Mom. I view their relationship with new eyes after hearing how they met and fell in love. Even though I'm sure it will be hard for him to see his daughter trapped, my father stays strong and supports the love of his life.

The video starts, and Mini's sleeping body fills the screen. Rocks must be still up in the air vent from the angle.

"I couldn't risk going in there," he says, almost reading my mind. "If she woke up ..." What he doesn't say is "and screamed," then an unconscious bat on the floor would have raised the alarm.

Mom turns in her chair and grips his hand. "Thank you."

"I also don't think I could have left her there, if I got any closer."

That cracks Mom's control and she burst into tears. Mom watches the forty-two seconds of Mini sleeping soundly four times before Dad intervenes. Josie powers down her machine, sliding it into her bag.

As Josie moves to leave, my chest constricts. This could be the last time I ever see her. I adore my folks, but Josie has shown me a side of herself that I'm actually proud of. It's the part of who I am that will allow me to hold my head up high. My blood isn't totally tainted. Half of me isn't so bad when push comes to shove.

I tune out Mom's gushing words of thanks, while I focus on Josie. She meets my eyes and smiles.

"Stay by the phone. The Feds will move quickly when they know a child is at risk."

23

The Cull

"**T**ELL me about Joey," I whisper. Mom and Dad are camped at the kitchen island with a pot of coffee and the cordless. I know they won't come up, but I still can't seem to relax.

Rocks' body language is off-kilter. His muscles are tense, but his shoulders sag. "Strickland would nail my wings to the wall if he ever found out."

"What?" He isn't making any sense.

An emotion I only see on Rocks when Strickland is present is guilt. When he's alone with me in my world, it fades. He relaxes and doesn't feel the pressure to be one thing or another—a bat or a guy—but right now, he's oozing guilt in quantities that would rival mine over the past month.

"Rocks, what? You're freaking me out."

"I chose your family … over mine."

Oh, fucking hell.

When my brain works out what he's talking about, I suck in a breath.

He stayed to film Enzo to free Mini, instead of following the Camazotz who tried to kill him.

"Thank you." I rub his knee. No words can convey how much this means to me. Nothing is enough. "Thank you." I repeat. He smiles, but there's doubt in his midnight blue eyes. "This doesn't mean you're a bad Shadows' member. You made a hard choice, but this shouldn't make you doubt yourself."

I might not know much, but I know this boy takes responsibility for things that are not his concern, and maybe that's what it takes to be a good leader.

"But the betrayal … " His head falls into his hands.

"You're not alone. I get it. I betrayed Enzo."

"Not the same." He frowns.

"It's not the same, but Enzo will see it as pure betrayal. You chose your adopted family over blood." He nods and a small smile appears because I acknowledged his love for my family. "Well, so did I."

Rocks frowns again, thinking on my words. "It's hardly the same."

"Why? Mini's life was at stake, and Enzo was asking me to be someone I'm not. You didn't have a choice either. You saved Mini and me and my whole family by getting that footage. And your blood has been forcing you to be something you don't want to be your whole life. It's not that different really. I don't want you feeling guilty for something you had no choice about. Should I feel guilty about Enzo?"

"No, he's a criminal."

"But he's still my blood. Life is full of hard decisions. That's what Enzo taught me, but once you make a decision, you can't torture yourself over it." I squeeze his hand.

"I know it was the right thing to do, but the Sire … he'd …" Rocks flicks his hair back. "He can never find out."

"He won't." Rocks kisses my hand.

"I feel more at home here than I do at the colony, but … then the guilt sets in. I can't win."

"Guilt for being here?"

He nods. "If they knew … If *your parents knew* what I am, I'd probably never be left alone with Mini ever again." Sadness flickers in his eyes for only a brief second. "They thought I could kidnap her, imagine what they'd think if they knew I was a vampire bat, too."

My heart aches for the gorgeous soul beside me. I shudder at the thought of how Chad and Kelly would react if they really knew Rocks. Yet again, he's left with only more confusion about who he should be.

Promising to keep Rocks safe from his father's wrath is easy. Last night when Rocks arrived at the warehouse, just before he started filming, there was already a group handing over a duffle to Enzo. Rocks was too busy trying to use his claw to switch on the GoPro that it took him a moment to recognize Joey talking with Enzo.

Joey—the mystery, killer Camazotz—is in business with Enzo Ascari.

My lungs begin to wheeze as I reach for my inhaler on the bedside table. What about the Vipers? Is Joey working for Enzo to get inside information on his rival distributors? How did this bat get into not one, but two drug rings? And where does the Camazotz cull fit into all of it?

"I have no idea," Rocks says softly. Blinking, I realize I asked those questions out loud. "It doesn't make any sense. I won't ever regret that I stayed to record the meetings—that was too important to miss—but I, I can't help wonder—"

"What if," I finish for him. He nods. What would we know about Joey if Rocks was able to follow him last night and find out where he's from? "Do you think he's not part of a colony? Maybe he's the rogue?" I ask.

"How could he have time to attack all those humans, get into the inner circle of two drug organizations, and work with the government on the cull if he didn't have support? It's very rare for Camazotz to leave their colony and not join another."

"Either Duskwing are lying to protect him, or he's part of Muerte. Right?"

"All I know is someone is lying, and it's not the Shadows. Cypress cleared the Muerte. I was sent with him when that happened, so it all points to Duskwing. What I don't get is that Moondust is a good man. He would never let this happen if he knew about it."

AT EIGHT P.M., DAD answers *the* call.

Mom is out the door and waiting by the car before he's disconnected. The Feds have Mini in custody and need the folks to head downtown to collect her. When I hear she's safe, my stomach growls in celebration. I can't remember the last time I ate a meal because I was hungry, or one that was less than 70 percent sugar.

Since we are staying put while they go to collect Mini, we might as well eat. I hand over our take-out menu folder and study Rocks as he methodically sifts though each and every dish available. I devour half a packet of cheese puffs, so I don't pass out waiting for him to decide. Rocks asks for pretzels after sampling my snack and continues his methodical dinner research, since in his opinion, he's missed too many aeronaught meals.

I let him dial and order, which is another first we share, and at the mention of a first, we end up a tangle of arms and legs on the couch making out until the doorbell ringing separates us.

It's the first time my stress levels have returned to the less shitty zone. I'm betting they won't return to hormonal-teenager level until I'm sure my boyfriend won't be exterminated by the local county pest control, and Mini is back in this house.

When the folks return with Mini around midnight, Mom insists it's too late for Rocks to head up to the mountains. Paperwork and more police interviews, followed by a hospital check-up was what kept them so long.

Mom is glowing. Dad is a proud papa bear. And Mini isn't left alone for a single second.

"Rocks," she exclaims when her excited eyes land on the dark, midnight boy.

She throws her arms out, almost propelling herself out of my arms in his direction. Little does she know that Rocks is the reason she's home. He saved her. It was a team event, but without his Camazotz side, none of us could have recorded what he had access to last night.

"You brought her home, you know?" Mom and Dad both look his way when I speak. Mini is trying to grab the red bar above his eyebrow.

"No, I didn't."

"Uh-huh, did so." I give him the look, and silently tell him it was the side of him that confuses him the most that saved my sister.

"We did it together."

He's so gracious he has difficulty accepting praise when it's due. I guess he's never had much practice with how Strickland treats him. His whole life he's been on the receiving end of looks of disappointment, disapproval, and rejection.

"All go well?" I ask Dad.

He nods. "They wouldn't tell me who their tip off was from, but they said they have enough evidence on Enzo and his colleagues to put them away for a very long time."

"No mention of me?" I wipe my palms on my jeans.

"None. Josie delivered as promised. I guess only time will tell if Enzo wants to incriminate you. Apart from him, there's no link between the two of you. Nothing official or on record." He smiles and I notice the new lines across his brow. The last four weeks have taken their toll, but Mini is safe, and it's time to celebrate.

"Hey, Happy Easter!" I say looking from one shocked face to the next.

"Oh my goodness, no, it can't be!" Mom exclaims in a fit of panic.

"Yep, the bunny comes tonight, Mini." Her eyes light up with joy while Rocks' fill with confusion.

"I'm off to Walmart," Mom announces, patting down Dad's pockets for the keys. He tries to convince her it doesn't matter, but she insists that two Easter baskets will not be empty in the morning, and that the Phillips will celebrate Mini's return in home-cooked heaven.

"Can you tell Bunny we have three baskets this year?"

Mom grins at my request as her eyes dart to Rocks.

"Three," Mini says, holding up five fingers.

Rocks needs to experience Easter first hand. The fact my parents still lay out eggs for me during the night is to keep the myth alive for Mini, and so long as I'm getting free chocolate, I'm happy to play along until she's my age. Rocks will definitely be on board.

EASTER SUNDAY, LONG before the sun's rays break the stark darkness, I sneak down the corridor. My heart can't keep me away a moment longer. Our separation has taken its toll, and I need some time without the folks hovering.

In Mini's room, I stand guard over her sleeping form. I can't help myself. My sister is home and I need reassurance that she isn't damaged by her ordeal. The rocking chair is too far away, so I crouch beside her crib and memorize the details of her precious little face. When the birds begin to chirp and my toes have lost all feeling, she stirs. Her tiny eyelids flutter once, then twice before her open eyes land on mine.

Her megawatt smile is enough to tear my heart in two and mend it with the very next beat.

"Nee," she coos, sleepy eyed, before getting to her feet and holding up her arms.

The smile never falters and relief floods my system. Emotions I didn't know needed to be released burst free as I grab her, wrapping her in my embrace and start to sob. My sister is safe and her innocent youth prevents her from holding me responsible for her ordeal. Somewhere deep down inside, I thought she was going to recognize I'm not her sister, but a stand-in that causes trouble by the truck load.

"Hello, gorgeous girl," I whisper against her temple. I jig her up and down and slowly make a circle of the room. "I love you, little one. I love you so much I swear on the blood in my veins and in yours that I will never let anything happen to you as long I live. I swear it, Jasmine. You are mine, and I will protect you from any evil that ever comes near you. You're the only sister that matters to me."

Mini sits back and her tiny finger presses into my chest. "Sister," she repeats with her toothy grin. "Nee, my sister."

"Yes, darling girl, I'm your big sister and that's the way it's going to stay."

"Ma-ma," she announces. Turning around I see Mom wiping her eyes from the doorway.

"I'm so proud of you, Connie. I never got a chance to tell you, but you went up against that evil man to keep her safe and then brought her home. Your father and I still can't believe it. You held it all together while we fell apart. I love you so much. Thank you for being you."

My sobs from earlier make another appearance. She loves me just the way I am. She's not embarrassed or ashamed at the identity of my parents.

"Thanks, Mom. I love you too."

My Easter morning only gets better. Next, I witness a phenomenon that absolutely must be added to our growing list of firsts.

Rocks is wearing blue.

I didn't realize how accustomed I was to seeing him in black, red, or grey. The royal blue, long-sleeved Henley looks al-mazing, but so out of place at the same time. Rocks, the aeronaught. If I grow up to be half as organized as Kelly, then I'll be a force to be reckoned with. She remembered Rocks wouldn't have a change of clothes for lunch today and got him a shirt during her Easter raid at the store. It was folded up at the bottom of his basket.

Part of me loves seeing Rocks in a color so vibrant, but it's like he's lost part of himself. It's odd how much our species identify with our clothing and what it announces to the world. The mystery has lessened around him, but those shadows go way deeper.

"What do you think?" Rocks says outside my bedroom. I scan him from head-to-toe.

"You look good but different."

"Good, huh? Better than the vest?" He wiggles his eyebrows.

"Never." I grab a handful of cotton and pull him down for a quick kiss while we're alone.

The Phillips Easter ritual starts with an egg hunt in the backyard. Rocks chases Mini from shiny egg to shiny egg, allowing her to swoop in on the prize just before him each time. Her basket is overflowing, while ours are pathetically lacking. Nobody is gonna deny that kid after what she's survived.

"Bailey would be in heaven with this," he whispers when he gets close. "A magic rabbit that brings chocolate? Her dragon might go down a notch or two." He winks.

Despite the fact that my aeronaught gifts are contraband, I pack up an Easter basket for Bailey, and one for Moonshiner too. Rocks is laying on my bed rubbing his sore belly, watching me load my backpack. Easter lunch was up there with Thanksgiving this year. How Mom managed to produce so many dishes in the last twelve hours is a modern mystery of the universe.

"Come on, we should get up there and see what they've discovered about the cull."

He groans sitting up. "They won't be back yet."

"Who?"

"The Camazotz sent to Duskwing and Muerte. Sylvana's bones foretold death, but she couldn't see who was going to die," he says.

"Wow, her abilities astound me. Here, let me try." I rub my temples with my eyes closed and start humming. "The Duskwing are in *grave* danger if we do not give them aid," I announce in the deepest voice I can do without choking.

"It's not funny."

"I know, but her visions don't exactly predict much. We know bats are going to die. It was in the freaking newspaper! Those Camazotz need help, and I can't understand why Strickland isn't doing something." Camazotz numbers are down enough as it is. Why on earth would he allow his kin to be slaughtered?

"Strickland sent three members to each colony to warn them. He said he couldn't have Camazotz blood on his hands even if they were breaking our laws."

Finally, he's doing something sensible.

I dig though my closet for something dark. My laundry basket is overflowing, and I've worn all Camazotz-camo gear.

"Ah-huh, don't you dare," he says, watching my every move.

"What?"

"Change. I like your shirt and so will Bailey." The shirt he's referring to is my Easter special. It's a brilliant blue that almost matches Rocks' new shirt, but the front is covered in crazy, colored eggs. Mini can spend endless attempts trying to count them.

"I don't want trouble."

"What you wear will not cause trouble, and I don't want you trying to be something you're not because of my issues. Let's leave the identity crisis to me, shall we?" He grins.

When we reach the quirky mountain town of Helen, it's almost dark. Mom wouldn't let Rocks and I leave because she was so happy to have the family together again. The GoPro got a serious workout. I have a feeling the folks are going to make up for the month they missed with Mini by recording her every step.

The speed limit through this Alpine replica town is probably the same as it was back in the 1800s. Slow doesn't even begin to describe it.

I still smile passing through Helen because it's like no other place in the U.S.

I brake at one of the many pedestrian crossings, just near the bridge over the river. A young girl dressed in dark clothing, stumbles across the road. She's looking from left to right and all around at the shops ahead of her. With her attention on everything else, her journey across the two-lane road takes forever. It's probably her first visit. I know my jaw didn't close the first time I saw the colorful architecture.

Rocks leans forward in his seat. I follow his eyes back to the thin teen.

"Let me out." His hand is pulling on the door latch.

"What?" I glance in my rearview mirror; thankfully there isn't anyone behind me.

Rocks is out of the car and striding toward her a second later. In my headlights, I see her eyes widen in shock, before she collapses on the sidewalk and starts to cry. That's when I notice her dress is dark and lacey.

A little Goth princess in the making.

Rocks looks up and down the street before scooping the girl into his arms. He points to the side street ahead, so I pull off the main road and park illegally, before going to him.

Moving away from the streetlight, Rocks sets her back on her feet. She's deathly pale, and her hair is stuck to the side of her face. She wipes her eyes with the back of each hand. The poor poppet looks exhausted.

"Moonshadow, what are you doing here?" The bat in Rocks emerges as his senses take over. He's listening and sniffing the air, trying to sense danger. "Are you alone?"

She nods. "I escaped the bad men. I've been flying ever since, but I couldn't remember where your market is."

"What bad men?" I ask, unable to hold back. I silently pray this isn't the cull.

Her eyes pop as though she hadn't noticed my presence. I watch as they move to my blond hair and then over my aeronaught Easter egg t-shirt.

"This is Connie. She came to Duskwing one day. It's all right," he says in a gentle voice. It reminds me of the night I was lost in the forest. He was so calm despite the fact he knew the Camazotz were angry at the lost gatecrasher. Moonshadow is little Moonshiner's half sister.

"The men who took my family," she says, her eyes glassy as though she's still witnessing the horror.

Rocks reads the worry written clearly over my face. He tells her he'll take her to the market where she'll be safe. I offer a ride in the old Honda, but she steps back in fear at that craziness.

"Head for my wagon," he says to me, putting a hand on her shoulder.

The pair disappears down the side of the nearest building, and a moment later, two bats flap their wings hard to gain height fast. I'm behind the wheel and completely ignoring the speed limit in hot pursuit.

I pull my Honda up at the market, taking up two parking spaces. It's not like any one else will be visiting after hours. Rocks had said to meet at his wagon so I race up the path, turning left.

"Shit!"

My nose collides with a wall of hard muscle. One second the path was empty, the next I barrel into a hard chest face first. Stepping back, I rub my nose and watch as the Camazotz before me rubs the center of his bare chest. He's only wearing a vest, and even in the fading light, I can see the dark tattoo across his breast. It's a large old script M with a shape that reminds me of angel wings hovering above it. He glares.

"Sorry, I didn't see you flip." I go to step around, but he moves with me, blocking the path. "Hey?"

"You're not allowed, naught. You're *banned*, remember?"

"Not this shit again—are you kidding?" I study his face. I know this bat. I've seen him at the hotdog stand with his constant frown. "You're Mackie, right?"

The narrowing of his eyes is my only answer. "Leave!"

"Look, I'm here trying to help you. Trying to save your sorry techno-phobic butts. Let me through."

"The only way you're getting through is if you go through me."

"Oh, I'll be getting through you." I pull out my phone and dial Rocks. "Tell Mackie the misguided guard *dog* that I'm allowed in."

Mackie reacts exactly how I predicted at being called a dog. He's never going to be my friend, and if he thinks he can call me nothing and get away with it, then he's got a bit to learn. "Ah-ha. Right." I hold out my glowing phone. "Rockland would like to talk to you."

Mackie jumps back a good foot as though the evil, aeronaught device is going to make his wings shrivel up and his fangs fall off.

"Hey!"

"It's for you." He shakes his head. I put the phone back to my ear. "He's too scared of the wittle tewaphone. Can you yell really loudly because I know his batty ears will hear it?" I ask Rocks.

Before I realize he's not on the line, Rocks flips in the space between Mackie and I.

"The Sire wants to see you. Connie has been providing information on the cull so you better have a good reason for stopping her," he snarls at the much shorter boy inches from his face. "And if you called her naught, you better apologize. Right. Now."

I'm not sure how sincere apologies can be when they're littered with four-letter words, but I'll take it. Just the look on his face alone was worth the hassle.

"You okay?" Rocks asks, running the back of his finger down my cheek.

He leads me up the path to find the girl sitting on Zada's lap on the wooden bench seat outside the candle shop. She's almost too big for a lap, but her fear needs the comfort of touch Rocks, Zander, Phoenix, and two other Camazotz women I don't know are crowded around them.

"Pegasus has gone to get Strickland from the roost," Rocks explains.

Phoenix gives me a shy head nod, which I return. When Zander greets me by name, the other Camazotz follow his example and offer a polite hello too.

Bailey and several of her pup friends are running around in the dark shadows behind the picnic table. Each of the kids has a Beanie baby tucked under their arms. I guess even powerful Strickland couldn't pry them out of their clutches.

We all wait in silence. Being familiar with telling scary, unbelievable tales, I'm glad they don't make the girl tell us what she witnessed twice.

I can't help but notice all eyes checking out my colorful, egg-covered chest, before they dart to Rocks wearing blue.

Crap.

Zander looks up. Doing the same, I spy the stars starting to peep out for the night, and once my vision adjusts to the darkness, a dozen bats take shape in the distance. The arrowhead formation gets bigger and bigger and slowly lowers over the building. A foot away, in unison, they flip. Their heavy boots hit the ground in one low thump.

All the members of the Fold are here, along with Jeremiah, Ash, Mazal, Malachite, and little Moonshiner. Glancing at the young males, I sense it's a gathering of each Fold member and the son that will take over the autocratic position in time. They slowly pair up, proving my theory as Mackie stalks up the path and takes his place beside his father.

"Where is she?" chirps the usually near-silent Moonshiner, pushing through the sea of adult legs to get to the front of the group. He stops before her.

Rocks explains to his father where we found Moonshadow, while Zada performs the introductions. This is the first time Moonshiner has meet another Camazotz from the Moon wing, let alone one of his siblings.

"How old are you?" he asks.

"Twelve. You?"

"Ten and a bit—"

"Not now, Moonshiner. Go play with Bailey," Zada scolds.

Moonshiner's nose wrinkles at the idea of playing with little girls. Some things are the same whether you're a Camazotz or not. I understand the dozens of questions that must be burning his tongue. Finding a family member for the first time is huge. Strickland kneels before the young girl on Zada's lap.

"Tell me everything from the beginning. We want to help you, but we need to understand what has happened to your colony."

The girl's voice is a half-whisper as she starts her tale, but she soon finds her courage. Just before dawn, two men crept into their roost. She hesitates and stutters when she reveals that the Duskwing colony is high on mountain crag, impossible for aeronaughts to enter. Strickland assures her she hasn't broken her blood oath, and she continues talking.

She describes strange ropes around the waists of the two invaders, and I know all the bats present have a clear memory of Dad and I decked out in our rappelling harness. These Camazotz know what the shock of two aeronaughts entering their sacred nest feels like.

Moonshadow explains that since her mother is a Fold member and her father is the Sire, she doesn't *exactly* have to follow orders like the rest of her colony. I notice Strickland's eye flick to his son at her admission. The girl says being in her human form is what saved her from the bad men. Strickland asks her if any other Camazotz were human with her.

"Just me. I should have been up with my wing on the cave ceiling. We don't have enough room for everybody to be in human form."

She describes the tightly packed scene and explains that the whole colony only gathers in their roost for emergency protection.

The previous day, her Sire had ordered every member to the roost. Only about a third of the Duskwing usually sleep in the roost because they prefer to stay at the farm. All members had been ordered to hide in the roost until further notice because of a deadly threat.

"The cull?" Strickland asks.

She shrugs. "What does that mean?"

"Never mind. What did the bad men do?" Zada asks.

Moments after the men entered their cave, an ear-splitting alarm sounded. Moonshadow recalls it being so loud, that even in her human form, it made her cover her ears and double over in agony. Every member of her colony dropped from the ceiling and nesting nooks to the cave floor.

Unconscious.

Strickland swears and is on the receiving end of a Kelly-worthy glare from Zada. All moms must learn evil eye techniques.

The bad men leaned out of the narrow cave mouth and pulled up a package from below. Inside it were four special harnesses designed to carry lots of bats.

This information causes Rocks, Strickland, and Cypress to swear in unison.

"Am I in trouble?" she asks, looking up at Zada.

"No, little pup. Tell us what happened next."

"When the harnesses were open on the ground, one man with strange glasses on top of his head, grabbed the other aeronaught and pushed him out of the cave entrance. The falling man screamed and screamed."

She describes how the first man then cut the ropes attached to the man he pushed.

Holy shitballs!

But the murder of the man—no doubt a county employee—isn't the surprising part. Moonshadow tells us that more Camazotz than she could count came flying into her home and flipped. The men and women started to load all her unconscious colony members into the harnesses. They worked fast, and Moonshadow was so scared she stayed deep in the darkness at the back of the cave watching.

"Before the sun could even get up, half the Camazotz flipped back," she says. "The bad man and others helped attached them to the harnesses and then one group at a time, they took my family away."

Strickland's chin rests on his hard chest. Nobody says a word. My brain is fuzzy from the huge two days I've just survived, but then it clicks.

The Camazotz weren't culled—they were bat-napped.

Taken.

"Holy—" Several sets of eyes dart to me and I shut my mouth.

Rockland bends down to her eye level. "Did they say anything? Use any names?"

She nods. "I couldn't understand most of it, but one man's name was Tronido."

Cypress lets lose in English followed by Spanish, and Zada covers Moonshadow's ears. The things he spits out even make my ears burn. The other Fold members all turn on him.

"She swore a blood promise to me that the Muerte were *not* involved with the human attacks." It's the first time I've ever seen the man flustered. "She swore," he pleads from one pissed off member to the next. "On my honor, I did not know of this."

Seeing Cypress in a jam makes me want to dance like I'm on MTV, but the reason behind it is too serious. The Vuelo de la Muerte has taken over the Duskwing colony—without their consent. Judge and

Zander start grilling Cypress about the fact he has a pup with one of the Vuelo de la Muerte Fold members, and apparently doesn't know of their plan. He was sent to find out if they were involved since he has blood ties, and his word cleared their colony of all involvement when he returned.

"But why would they do this?" I ask, totally confused by the events that have taken place.

"That's a question I'd like answered," replies Strickland. "Now we know the Muerte are to blame, we must be vigilant. We could be next."

"It's punishment for their love of being human," Macallister states.

I don't even try to hide my eye roll. *What-ever, McDick!*

"It is the presence of a sanguine moon," shrieks Sylvana, stepping out of the darkness. "Two nights ago was a blood moon." She shakes her ringed fist at the stars twinkling above, and I can't help but look up. "A sanguine moon is the marker of doom. A dark omen not to be ignored. Our kin have paid a heavy price this cycle." She spins around in the center of the group, before howling at the top of her lungs, and little Moonshadow jerks in surprise.

Funny how Mrs. Witchy-bitchy never mentioned this evil omen earlier. I watch as she moves to Strickland's side and whispers in his ear. If she tries to blame a lunar eclipse on me, I'll shove those little bones she likes to scatter up somewhere she would rather I didn't. She's a constant thorn in my side, so I'll happily be a pain in her butt if she dares involve me.

Strickland gestures to Pegasus, Jeremiah, Malachite, and a guy with a mean crew-cut. "Inform the Clips and set up night guards. Tell those at the roost it wouldn't hurt to be" —his eyes narrow and he swallows hard— "to be human for safety."

My dancing urge morphs into the need to do cartwheels and howl at the moon—regardless of whether it's red, blue or purple—as well. The Sire issued a directive stating it's safer to be human. I shove my hands in my pockets so I'm not tempted to offer Rocks a high-five. I must celebrate an aeronaught win with dignity. Who knew it would be this hard to control my glee?

Ash gives me a death stare, and checking the Sire is still busy, I poke my tongue out at him. Dignity be damned.

"Do you still have the picture of Joey?" Rocks asks. Pulling off my bulging backpack, I pray it doesn't erupt with a spray of shiny, foil-covered eggs when I unzip the sucker. With his help, I rummage to the bottom and hand over the crushed printout.

"Do you recognize him?" Rocks holds up the color screenshot to the nervous little pup.

Moonshadow jumps free of Zada's arms and stumbles backward away from the photo. Fear and horror cloud the sweet delicate features she shares with her half brother.

"You know him? He's your friend?" she asks, her eyes bigger than the last blood moon.

Zander's tattooed arm grabs the girl. "Easy, pup," he says, pulling her back into the circle of adults.

Rocks talks fast telling her this man tried to kill him and asks again if he was at her roost. The tension drains from her body, and she moves back to Zada's open arms.

"That's Tronido. The bad man."

Everybody—including me—swears.

ROCKS AND I are sitting on the top step of his wagon keeping an eye on the group of pups. Five-year-old-mother-hen Bailey has adopted Moonshadow and handed over her precious pink seahorse. The older girl acts disinterested in the bedraggled oddity, but when I look back later, it's resting on her lap.

The Fold and other adults were all given instructions from Strickland to secure the market and roost. Without knowing why the Muerte have taken the Duskwing members, it's impossible to guess their next move, and whether they will be bold enough to come for the Shadows.

Rocks whispers his father will be fearful of a takeover. The Muerte with the Duskwing in their ranks will now outnumber the Shadows, and he could lose command of his colony.

Bailey leaves the makeshift circle of children and joins us. Looking up from ground level, she informs her brother she's going to get her dragon book to read to Moonshadow.

"No, stay here."

"But I'm human, I'll be safe from owls," she says, looking up into the darkness around the wagon.

Rocks huffs. I know he doesn't want to scare the pups any more than they have been already.

"I'll go. Where is it?"

Bailey explains and Rocks lifts her under the arms and sits her next to me. As Rocks stalks off, she smooths out the folds of her dress.

"The adults were talking about Elm and Oak. They didn't know I was listening," she admits to her dragon. She flicks her head sideways to see if I'm paying attention. "They said they wanted to be aeronaughts." Bailey bites her lower lip. The eye patch lessens her frown, but she's clearly got a lot on her mind. "Are you gonna fix my brother too?"

I rest my elbows on my knees and face her as much as I can. It still makes my blood boil knowing that with modern medicine, she would probably still have perfect sight.

"Rockland is all better. I can't say I fixed him, but I helped. He flies perfectly. Haven't you seen him?"

"No, I mean like Celand."

"What about Celand?"

"You know," she says.

Rocks steps out of the darkness and stands in front of her. With his crazy hearing, he probably heard the whole confession.

"Bailey," he admonishes. I look back and forth between the two of them, taking note of the similarities only siblings share. She looks down at her scuffed, brown boots.

"Sorry." She sniffs like she's trying to hold back tears.

What is going on? If they weren't both in human form, I'd swear they were having a telepathic conversation. Bailey won't take her eyes off her feet, and I'm shocked when she swipes at her cheeks.

Finally, she looks up from under her little lashes and whispers. "I know what Celand did."

Rocks opens his arms, and she flies into them from the top step. He hugs her tight to his chest, but even if he let go, I know she wouldn't fall because she's clinging to him with a desperation no five-year-old should know.

"It's all right, little one," he murmurs. "I didn't know you knew about that."

She lifts her head off his chest and peers into his eyes. Hers glistening with unshed tears. "It's why Celand never visits us. She got fixed."

Rocks hisses out a breath. The mention of details about his missing sister has me on high alert. This topic is rarely up for discussion, and since the day he promised to not keep secrets from me, it hasn't come up.

She rests her head on his shoulder and Rocks spends a moment whispering in her ear. He walks in slow circles calming her down. I bet he could have Mini asleep in her crib in ten minutes tops with that technique.

Eventually, he puts her down in the circle of pups and hands over her precious dragon book. She smiles up at her hero when he captures her cute button nose between his fingers.

"What did all that mean?" I ask as soon as his warm body sits down close. I snuggle in not realizing how cold I was without him.

"Just ignore what Bailey said. Celand is gone, and she just misses her."

"What does fixed mean? At Duskwing, that Fold member said lots of their young were fixed. I thought ... well, I thought they'd been ... you know, like what you do to your dog?" I cringe the second the words leave my mouth.

Rocks frowns, and for the millionth time, I pray he doesn't know what I'm talking about. "Dogs? I don't know what dogs have to do with it, but it's—"

"Bat business?" My arched brow says he's got to be kidding if he thinks he's going to get away with that answer.

He rolls his eyes and shoves me with his elbow. "I was *going* to say that, but I promised you the truth. The fix is a fantasy is what it is.

Some Camazotz believe they can be fixed in one state. I believe it's what happened to Celand."

"Wait …" I can't risk jumping to the wrong conclusion.

Rocks had said the only way he could be free from being a Camazotz was if a witch or shaman undid the spell that turned them all. "Fixed in one state?" I ask.

"Yes, it's a way of making me human without reversing the original curse."

The Fold History

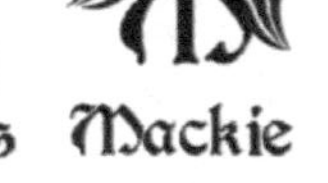

Ash (Plant Wing) — m. Son of Cypress and Hannah. Older brother of Cedar and half-brother of Elm and Oak. Aeronaught hater like his father. Tattoos: fangs on his lips and chin. Potential heir of the Plant Wing.

Asteroide (Vuelo de la Muerte - Planetary Wing) — m. Son of Saturno and future heir. His name means asteroid.

AuburnSky (ColorNature Wing) — f. A young female chosen by the Sire to bond with Rockland. Appearance: short, bob length hair. Tattoos: both hands are tattooed with a design that can only be seen when she's a bat.

Bailey (Trade Wing) — f. Daughter of Zada & Judge. Sister of Decker & Baxter. Half-sister of Celand, Rockland, Graceland, and Moonshiner. Only has one eye after surviving an owl attack. Loves dragons and seahorses.

Baxter (Trade Wing) — m. Son of Judge & Zada. Brother of Decker & Bailey. Half-brother of Celand, Rockland, Graceland & Moonshiner.

Carnelian (Gem Wing) — m. Fold member. Father of Jet and Malachite. Uncle of little Sapphire. Appearance: thick dark hair. Only one visible tattoo high on his shoulder of the Gem Wing symbol. Wears leather cuffs on his wrists. No visible scars.

Cedar (Plant Wing) — **m.** Second son of Cypress and Hannah. Brother of Ash and half-brother of Elm and Oak.

Celand (Land Wing) — **f.** Daughter of Strickland & Zada. Rockland's mysterious older sister. Half sister of Decker, Baxter, Bailey & Moonshiner. Dated aeronaught Alex Green.

Concha (Vuelo de la Muerte - Ocean Wing) — **f.** Daughter of Fold member Océano. Her name means seashell. Sister of Mantarraya. Tattoos: Both forearms have crashing waves from elbow to wrist.

Cypress (Plant Wing) — **m.** Fold member. Father of Ash, Cedar, Elm and Oak. Also fathered Willow from the Vuelo de la Muerte colony. His Grandfather, Spruce, was the Sire in his day. Aeronaught hater. Tattoos: humans and animals all over his body gushing blood from neck wounds.

Decker (Trade Wing) — **m.** Son of Judge & Zada along with Baxter & Bailey. Half-brother and best friend of Rockland. Cousin of Jet & Harper. Potential heir of the Trade Wing.

Elm (Plant Wing) — **m.** Human born twin of Oak. Son of Cypress and PurpleSky. Half-brother of Ash and Cedar. Appearance: shoulder length, dark hair. Almost delicate facial features. Has three puckered, red scars down his neck from an owl attack.

Ezra (Hebrew Wing) — **m** Second son of Levi and Sunshine. Younger brother of Mazal. Half-brother of Jeremiah and Odelia. Tattoos: the Hebrew Wing symbol on his left forearm. Very deep voice and looks similar to Jeremiah.

Foxfire (Fox Wing) — **m.** Son of Foxhunt. Third cousin of Rockland through Rockland's Great Grandmother Foxtail. Is waiting for his chance to be groomed for leadership. Appearance: shaggy hair. Tattoos: fox head on the side of his neck.

Foxhunt (Fox Wing) — **m.** Father of Foxfire. Clip of the Fox Wing. Trying to position his son Foxfire for a future Fold position. Has a loud, booming voice.

Ganymede (Duskwing — Planetary Moon Wing) — **m.** Is named after the largest moon of Jupiter. Fold member for his wing. Tattoos: a blazing sun inside his forearm.

Graceland (Land Wing) — **f.** Daughter of Strickland & Zada. Sister of Celand and Rockland. Half-sister of Decker, Baxter, Bailey, Moonshiner and Ireland. Not a fan of aeronaught interaction.

Harland (Land Wing) — **m.** Rockland's hard-edged cousin. Son of Kirkland & Snowflake. Appearance: shoulder length jet-black hair, viper bites on his lower lip. Likes grape soda a lot.

Harper (Trade Wing) — **f.** Daughter of Shepard and Lotus. First cousin of Decker, Baxter, Bailey, Sapphire, and Jet. Was rescued by Decker in the owl attack, but bled to death.

Ireland (Land Wing) — **f.** Only daughter of Strickland & ScarletFall. Half-sister of Celand, Rockland, Graceland, Decker, Baxter, Bailey & Moonshiner.

Jeremiah (Hebrew Wing) — **m.** Son of Levi and Neon. Older brother of Odelia. Half-brother of Mazal and Ezra. First cousin of Ash and Cedar. Appearance: missing half his ear. Tattoos: the Hebrew wing symbol on his right bicep and the Elemental wings symbol on his left bicep. Mr. McChatty.

Jet (Gem Wing) — **m.** Son of Carnelian and Sawyer. Half-brother of Malachite. First cousin of Decker, Baxter, Bailey, Harper and Sapphire. Appearance: thin and wiry build.

Judge (Trade Wing) — m. Fold member. Father of Decker, Baxter, & Bailey. Brother of Shepard & Sawyer. Uncle of Jet. Step-father of Rockland. Appearance: has a massive, puckered scar that runs down his face from temple to chin. Very muscled with a thickset chest. Likes sweet potato fries.

Kyanite (Gem Wing) — m. Father of Sapphire. Brother of Carnelian. Uncle of Jet and Malachite. Was killed in the first owl attack on the colony.

Lavender (Plant Wing) — f. A young girl who was chosen by the Sire to feed Rockland and form a blood bond. Tattoos: sprigs of lavender all over both arms.

Levi (Hebrew Wing) — m. Fold member. Father of Mazal and Ezra with Sunshine, and father of Jeremiah and Odelia with Neon. Brother-in-law of Cyprus through his sister Hannah, and second cousin once removed of Carnelian. At age 50, he is the oldest living fold member. Isn't team aeronaught but accepts Connie's offer to try a cheeseburger.

LittleSong (Little Wing) — f. Mate of Zander and mother of Zulu and Zara. Her father, LittleStorm, was a fold member, but the Hebrew wing took over from the Little wing because LittleStorm only had female offspring. Her sister LittleBee is mated to Carnelian. Aunt of Malachite and Jet.

LittleStar (Little Wing) — f. Potential mate for Decker. The Little wing is trying to position themselves to return to power in the fold with future offspring and the support of powerful wings. Tattoos: single star on her chin.

Macallister (Mac Wing) — m. Fold member. Father of Mackie with MagentaSpring. First cousin of Cyprus. Hates aeronaughts with a passion. Appearance: hard, solid man with dozens of faint, thin scars down his left arm.

Macantia (Mac Wing) — **f.** A young female chosen by the Sire to feed Rockland and form a blood bond. Appearance: short and overweight. Tattoos: has the Mac symbol tattooed on both shoulders.

Macaulay (Mac Wing) — **m.** Macallister's half-brother. Works at the tannery. Appearance: has three fingers missing on his right hand.

Mackie (Mac Wing) — **m.** Only son of Macallister and MagentaSpring. First cousin of Elm and Oak. Second cousin of Rockland, Decker and Jet. Frowns a lot. Tattoos: a large Mac wing crest in the center of his chest. Potential heir of the Mac Wing.

Madison (Son Wing) — **f.** A young female chosen by the Sire to feed Rockland and form a blood bond. Appearance: high undercut half way up her head. The remaining hair is long and hangs forward almost covering her eyes. Tattoos: lace collar that covers her neck from collarbone to chin.

Malachite (Gem Wing) — **m.** Son of Carnelian and LittleBee. Half-brother of Jet. First cousin of Sapphire, and third cousin of Jeremiah, Ash and Rebekkah. Appearance: large, predominant nose. Was the Camazotz that tried to scare Connie away and is Graceland's boyfriend. Potential heir of the Gem Wing.

Mantarraya (Vuelo de la Muerte - Ocean wing) — **m.** His mother is the Fold member Océano. Younger brother of Concha. His name means stingray. Tattoos: has a dozen stingrays swimming up his right arm.

Mazal (Hebrew Wing) — **m.** Son of Levi and Sunshine. Brother of Ezra. Half-brother of Jeremiah and Odelia. Mazal has one pup called Joaquim II with mate Foxpaw. Appearance: deep age lines from a hard life. Looks older than his 28 years. Has a buzz cut to show off his skull tattoo. Tattoos: a gothic bat that wraps around the back of his skull and the wing tips end on his temple almost touching his eyes. Potential heir of the Hebrew Wing.

Moondust (Duskwing - Moon Wing) — m. Sire of the Duskwing colony. Father of little Moonshiner from the Shadows colony with Zada. Father of Moonshadow with Fold member Starjewel. Appearance: spiky, black hair and very muscular chest and arms. Tattoos: full arm sleeve depicting the planets and solar system.

Moonlight (Duskwing - Moon Wing) — f. A young female at the Duskwing colony. She is Moonshiner's first cousin. Appearance: slender with fine hair and a pretty smile.

Moonshadow (Duskwing - Moon Wing) — f. Daughter of Moondust and Starjewel. Half sister of Moonshiner. Appearance: wears her hair in two braids.

Moonshiner (Shadows - Moon Wing) — m. Son of Zada and Moondust—from the Duskwing colony. Is the sole member of the Moon Wing at the Shadows. Half brother of Celand, Rockland, Graceland, Decker, Baxter, & Bailey. Has a half-sister called Moonshadow at the Duskwing colony that he has never met.

Nighthawk (Duskwing - Night Wing) — m. Oldest Fold member at the Duskwing. Appearance: could be mistaken for an aeronaught farmer.

Oak (Plant Wing) — m. Human born twin of Oak. Son of Cypress and PurpleSky. Half-brother of Ash and Cedar. Appearance: shoulder length, dark hair. Almost delicate facial features. Has three puckered, red scars from his elbow to his wrist from an owl attack.

Océano (Vuelo de la Muerte – Ocean Wing) — f. Fold member of the Ocean Wing. She has two children—Concha and Mantarraya. Her name means ocean. Appearance: Looks sad with deep age lines around her eyes. Dresses from head-to-toe in black at all times.

Odelia (Hebrew Wing) — **f.** Daughter of Levi and Neon. Little sister of Jeremiah. Half-sister of Mazal and Ezra. Bailey's best friend who didn't have a beanie baby to love.

Pegasus (Mythical Creatures Wing) — **m.** Eldest son of Peryton. Older brother of Phoenix. Appearance: looks like a body builder. Has shark bite piercings on his lower lip. Tattoos: three crescent moons with a set of huge wings high on his shoulder. Is being groomed as the potential heir of the Z Wing.

Peryton (Mythical Creatures Wing) — **m.** Clip for the Mythical Creatures Wing. Father of Pegasus and Phoenix. Has worked his whole life supporting the Z wing in the hopes that his only son may be voted in as a Fold member with the Z wing's support.

Phoenix (Mythical Creatures Wing) — **f.** A young female chosen by the Sire to feed Rockland and form a blood bond. She is a good friend of Rebekkah and Zabreena. Is madly in love with Rockland. Appearance: slim, pretty, young Camazotz. Tattoos: stars around her eyes.

Rebekkah (Hebrew Wing) — **f.** Daughter of Gavriel and Helium. Older sister of Isaiah, who was killed in one of the first bat attacks. Second cousin of Jeremiah, Odelia, Mazal, Ezra, Ash and Cedar. Has been groomed to be Rockland's future mate by her wing, and was chosen to create a blood bond with him while he was recovering. Appearance: elf-like features and fine waist-length hair braided with black satin ribbons.

Rockland (Land Wing) — **m.** Son of Strickland & Zada. First born male in Strickland's bloodline & potential heir. Has seven siblings. Appearance: over 6'4", lean, muscled and toned, ridiculously good-looking. Has long raven-black hair at the front that hangs over his eyes when he wants to hide from the world. Tattoos: full black and grey sleeves on both arms. The design is the Shadows bat but can only be seen when he's a Camazotz.

RedFaith (Red Wing) — A young female chosen by the Sire to feed Rockland and form a blood bond. Appearance: extremely tall with one brown eye and one blue. Has butterfly kiss piercings under each eye and studs implanted along her collarbones. Tattoos: vivid colored butterflies covering both arms.

Sandía (Vuelo de la Muerte – Fruit Wing) — **m.** Fold member of the Fruit Wing at the Vuelo de la Muerte colony. His name means watermelon. Appearance: Dresses in black from head-to-toe. Has a scar across his left temple and small beady eyes. Tattoos: vines wrapped around his wrists that twist up his forearms.

Sapphire (Gem Wing) — **f.** Daughter of Kyanite and Snowflake. Niece of Carnelian and first cousin of Malachite, Jet, Decker, Baxter, Bailey, and Harper. Decker rescued her in the owl attack.

Saturno (Vuelo de la Muerte) — **m.** Sire of the Vuelo de la Muerte colony. Walks with a cane and is hunched over from deep internal wounds in a recent owl attack. Father of Asteroide.

Sawyer (Trader Wing) — **f.** Mother of Jet with Carnelian. Sister of Judge and Sheppard. She was killed in the first owl attack protecting a group of pups.

ScarletFall (Color+Nature Wing) — **f.** Mother of Ireland with Strickland. Her father, IndigoRiver, was a previous Fold member, but was only blessed with female heirs, and their wing lost power. Half-sister of MagentaSpring and PurpleSky. Aunt of Mackie, Elm and Oak.

Shepard (Trade Wing) — **m.** Deceased brother of Judge and Sawyer. Father of Harper with Lotus.

Snowflake (Snow Wing) — **f.** Mother of little Sapphire with Kyanite.

Aunt of Malachite and Jet. Appearance: short, bob hair with black satin ribbons braided through it.

Starjewel (Duskwing – Star Wing) — f. Fold member for the Star Wing at the Duskwing colony. Mother of Moonshadow with Moondust. Appearance: bright, blue eyes. A kind, peaceful face. Tattoos: has stars tattooed on the palms of her hands.

Strickland (Land Wing) — m. The Sire. Has children with Zada and ScarletFall. Is responsible for the entire Shadows colony. Appearance: shorter than his son Rockland. Hard, muscled, and strong. Highly judgmental. Usually scowling and/or frowning. Tattoos: three thick bands of black ink circle his forearms.

Sylvana (No Wing) — f. The medicine woman & shaman of the Shadows colony. Traditionally the medicine man or woman should not belong to a wing so that they don't favor any one wing. They need to be concerned and focused on the colony as one. Appearance: long, wild, grey hair. Full skirts and flowing clothing that smells of incense and healing herbs. Tattoos: pagan signs and symbols inside her wrists.

Temblor (Vuelo de la Muerte – Mother Nature Wing) — m. Guard at the Muerte compound. Appearance: has a barely healed, ragged scar that runs from the middle of his forehead across his left eye to his ear. Scruffy, dirty hair. Tattoos: anatomically correct bones tattooed on the back of his fingers and hands. His name means earthquake tremor.

Tromba (Vuelo de la Muerte – Mother Nature Wing) — f. Guard at the Muerte compound. Appearance: extremely thin with dead straight should length hair. Wears gold hoop earrings and dozens of gold bangles and chains on both wrists. Black leather pants and vest. Her name means whirlwind.

Tronido (Vuelo de la Muerte – Mother Nature Wing) — m. His name means thunderclap.

Venus (Vuelo de la Muerte – Planetary Wing) — f. Sister of the Vuelo de la Muerte's Sire. Mother of Willow with Cypress from the Shadow's colony. Appearance: middle aged, yet super model gorgeous with thick, long hair worn in two braids over her chest. Her name means Venus.

Violet (Plant Wing) — f. A young female chosen by the Sire to feed Rockland and form a blood bond. She is a good friend of Rebekkah and Zabreena. Has had a huge crush on Rockland since she was a pup. Appearance: tiny, petite girl with scars from the early bat attacks across her forehead and down her arms.

Willow (Vuelo de la Muerte – Plant Wing) — m. Son of Cypress. He lives at the Vuelo de la Muerte colony, and at twenty, is the oldest member of the newly formed Plant wing. Appearance: is a very handsome young guy that takes after his gorgeous mother. Tattoos: the Plant wing crest on the inside of his right forearm. A matching swirl on the inside of his left forearm that shows the Plant wing crest when he's a bat.

Zabreena (Z Wing) — f. Daughter of Zambia. Second cousin of Celand, Rockland, and Graceland, and Decker, Baxter, and Bailey. Best friends with Rebekkah. Appearance: angular, hard facial features. Wavy, wild hair. She wears very low cut and revealing clothing that shows off her assets. A large scar runs from the corner of her lip down under her chin. Tattoos: half-inch wide bands across her eyes creating the look of heavy eyeliner.

Zada (Z Wing) — f. Mother of Celand, Rockland, Decker, Graceland, Baxter, Moonshiner, & Bailey. Sister of Zander. Appearance: long, dark brown messy hair. Tattoos: colored flowers on her neck, chest, and back.

Zander (Z Wing) — m. Fold member for the Z Wing. Father of Zulu and Zara with LitteSong. Younger brother of Zada. His father, Zeth, was a fold member, and his Grandfather, Zan, was a fold member. Uncle of Celand, Rockland, Graceland, Decker, Baxter, and Bailey. Uncle by marriage of Malachite. Appearance: shoulder length, straight black hair. He has the same high cheekbones as Rockland and is very good-looking for a thirty-five-year-old. Has a nice, kind smile. Tattoos: like Rockland has swirls and patterns covering his arms which only create a tattoo when he's a bat.

Zola (Z Wing) — **f.** Zada's cousin and Rockland's first cousin once removed. She runs the dairy and makes cheese to sell at the market. Rocks swapped her some goat's milk if she would charge his phone since she has an industrial refrigerator in the dairy.

Glossary

Aeronaught: an ordinary human that cannot fly.

Camazotz: a human with the ability to shape-shift into a vampire bat. Any offspring born of a Camazotz will also have the ability to shape-shift.

Clip: the leaders of the other smaller wings not represented in the Fold. Each wing votes for a leader. From these leaders the seven Fold are chosen. When the colony faces grave danger, the Clip are invited to help the Fold and Sire make a decision.

Fledgers: name given to Camazotz aged fourteen to eighteen years of age.

Flip: the involuntary shape-shift from human to vampire bat that occurs thirty-six hours after their last shift. This prevents the Camazotz from choosing to stay in their human form forever. However, Camazotz and can choose to flip at any point in time as well.

Naught: a derogatory term for a human.

Pups: name given to young Camazotz from birth until thirteen years of age.

Roost: the top secret location where the Camazotz live as bats.

Shaman: someone who can cast spells or curses of great power. They can summon good or evil spirits and were labeled witches throughout history. The Camazotz rely on the shaman for healing.

The Fold: the members of the ruling council that create the laws and decide the fate of the whole colony. There are seven members in the Fold. They are usually the heads of the most powerful wings, but are voted onto the ruling council by all adult and fledger colony members.

The Sire: the leader of the colony voted into power by the Fold members. The Sire will rule indefinitely until he decides to step down or is challenged by another Fold member. This usually consists of a fight to the death.

Wings: family bloodlines within the colony. Each member sees themselves as part of a wing rather than part of this family or that. Members born into each wing are named for that wing to identify their father's bloodline.

About The Author

Sanguine Mountain—Book One in the Camazotz Trilogy—was the debut novel of Jennifer Foxcroft. The story of Connie and Rocks continues in Sanguine Moon.

Jennifer was born and raised in Australia. She spent her youth dreaming of far away lands and the crazy critters that inhabit them. When she wasn't swimming in the backyard pool or training the family pet to ride a bicycle, she would visit those magical lands and accompany her characters on their exciting adventures. Even as an adult, her daydreaming of fanciful lands never ceased. To this day, she regards herself as a teenager trapped in an adult body. This series is a glimpse of the characters and places she often visits.

For more information about the author and her series, please go to

www.jenniferfoxcroft.com

Sign up for the newsletter when you visit.

Twitter: @MsJenFoxcroft

Facebook: facebook.com/jenniferfoxcroft.author

Help An Indie...

Indie authors need you!

Yes, we need your amazing book reviewing skills. If you enjoyed reading Sanguine Moon, Jennifer would greatly appreciate a review. And you know how obsessed with technology Rocks is. Imagine his smile when he checks the review count on his phone and sees one written by you. You'll make his day.

Reviews are welcome on Amazon, GoodReads, iTunes, and Barnes & Noble.

Thank you so much. You helped an indie author today.

www.ingramcontent.com/pod-product-compliance
Lightning Source LLC
Chambersburg PA
CBHW031129120726
47905CB00006B/1621